Praise for
winner of the 2004
and 2003 Roman
RITA

"Nobody writes military romance like Catherine Mann!"
—*New York Times* bestselling author
Suzanne Brockmann

"As we say in the air force, get ready to roll in hot!
From page one, Catherine Mann's military romances
launch you into a world chock-full of simmering passion
and heart-pounding action. Don't miss 'em!"
—*USA TODAY* bestselling author Merline Lovelace

"Catherine Mann is one of the hottest
rising stars around!"
—*New York Times* bestselling author Lori Foster

"Hold out for a Catherine Mann hero! Her air force
flyboys will wing their way straight to your heart."
—bestselling author Joanne Rock

"Talk about more bang for your buck!
Ms. Mann weaves…just the right amount of action
and romantic intrigue and comes up with a winner.
An excellent read!"
—*Old Book Barn Gazette* on
ANYTHING, ANYWHERE, ANYTIME

Dear Reader,

What constitutes a steal-your-heart hero? Certainly they strut onto the scene in many forms. But for me, the ultimate, spine-tingling hero wears a military flight suit—no surprise to those who know me, since I'm married to my very own flyboy. Through my Air Force romance novels I strive to showcase the inherent honor of a man in uniform, the altruism of his willingness to offer his life for his country and, yes, the mystique of that zippcr-suitcd sky god who touches the clouds in the air and swaggers on the ground.

However, I've chosen to focus on the Air Force for reasons beyond my loving a man who's called to fly. We hear much in the news about Army and Navy Special Operations forces, but not as much about the equally active and deployed Air Force Special Ops aviators who soar into the heat of battle to deliver, retrieve and rescue them. While my "Wingmen Warriors" cargo plane stories will continue in Silhouette Intimate Moments, *Code of Honor* launches my new Air Force Special Ops series for HQN. I couldn't have chosen a better aircraft to showcase their hair-raising missions than the cutting-edge CV-22 tilt rotor, soon to be based out of Hurlburt Field near Fort Walton Beach, Florida.

I hope you enjoy Joe and Brigid's story. And keep an eye out for Postal's book coming up next! Welcome to my new squadron of flyboys….

Aim High!
Catherine Mann
www.catherinemann.com

CATHERINE MANN

CODE OF HONOR

If you purchased this book without a cover you should be aware that this book is stolen property. It was reported as "unsold and destroyed" to the publisher, and neither the author nor the publisher has received any payment for this "stripped book."

ISBN 0-373-77049-9

CODE OF HONOR

Copyright © 2005 by Catherine Mann

All rights reserved. Except for use in any review, the reproduction or utilization of this work in whole or in part in any form by any electronic, mechanical or other means, now known or hereafter invented, including xerography, photocopying and recording, or in any information storage or retrieval system, is forbidden without the written permission of the publisher, Harlequin Enterprises Limited, 225 Duncan Mill Road, Don Mills, Ontario M3B 3K9, Canada.

All characters in this book have no existence outside the imagination of the author and have no relation whatsoever to anyone bearing the same name or names. They are not even distantly inspired by any individual known or unknown to the author, and all incidents are pure invention.

This edition published by arrangement with Harlequin Books S.A.

® and TM are trademarks of the publisher. Trademarks indicated with ® are registered in the United States Patent and Trademark Office, the Canadian Trade Marks Office and in other countries.

www.HQNBooks.com

Printed in U.S.A.

To our wounded military veterans
who have faced a recovery battle
as fierce as any fight in the field, sea or air.

ACKNOWLEDGMENTS

Story ideas come to me begging to be told, and some of those dictate an extra dose of research. This happened to be one of those books. Luckily, through the generosity of experts, I managed to gather the information needed to tell Joe, Brigid and Cooper's story. Any errors, liberties or stretches in regard to the information are totally of my own making.

For offering real-life insights on Brigid's career, I owe a huge thanks to Karen Ballard, freelance photographer, whose amazing political and military photos have appeared in *Time, Newsweek, U.S. News & World Report* and other major publications. Thank you, Karen, for sharing your expertise and experiences in Iraq. A special thanks also to Patricia McLinn, an editor at the *Washington Post,* a Silhouette Special Edition author extraordinaire and a great writing friend. I appreciate your help in locating information on photojournalism.

For details and insights into Cooper's injuries, many thanks to my dear friend Karen Tucker, R.N. and my brilliant sister Beth Reaves, MSW, LISW. Also, my heartfelt gratitude to Paul Sanchez for generously sharing details about his recovery journey after the Vietnam War. You are a true hero.

As always, tons of thanks to my tremendously talented critique partner, Joanne Rock, for tireless brainstorming and for reading over this book—twice. You're a gem!

And of course, I owe boundless thanks to Lieutenant Colonel Robert Mann, my own flyboy, for his help with military details and for the mountains of research on the CV-22. Most of all, thank you for being a man of honor. I love you!

PROLOGUE

Iraq: Two Years Ago

"MAYDAY! MAYDAY! MAYDAY! Calling any Coalition aircraft."

The SOS crackled through Captain Joe "Face" Greco's helmet, all other chatter dissipating faster than the clouds outside his windscreen. Adrenaline snapped through him, narrowing his focus. The two-hour flight in his Pave Low helicopter to ferry around a photojournalist should have offered a break from months of knife-edge missions.

Keeping the peace was a deadly endeavor.

Hands steady on the stick, Joe scanned the cracked desert rolling below and listened for the rest of the call, ready to launch if the threat fell into his range.

"This is Alpha one-six-three, seven miles west of Fallujah." Gunfire popped in the background with the panting voice. "Requesting air support and evac."

Alpha one-six-three? Dread kicked into high gear. Distinguishing voices over the radio might be tough, but Joe also remembered the number designation. The staticky shout for help blended with the *chop, chop,*

chop of his helicopter blades, stirring hellish recognition. He'd dropped off that Special Forces team yesterday to track insurgents. He knew these Green Berets.

He knew their leader—Cooper Scott.

Shit.

Muscles tensed for action, Joe barked to the copilot beside him. "Postal, get me a heading to Fallujah."

"Jesus Christ, Face, shouldn't we radio command post for authentication?" First Lieutenant Bobby "Postal" Ruznick clicked keys on the navigational computer even as he argued. "I'm up for a gun battle as much as the next guy, more so probably. But if I'm going to get my ass shot off, I'd rather not go down in some set up ambush."

"I've got voice confirmation on this one."

"Roger that, then. Spinning up directions for Fallujah as we speak, boss."

Joe resisted the urge to twist the cyclic, dip the rotors forward and plow ahead, follow his nose and to hell with directions. Those dudes should have been safe. He'd landed his Air Force Special Ops helicopter randomly twenty times yesterday to disguise placement of the twelve Green Berets tasked to track Al Qaeda foreign fighters, terrorist insurgents on suicide missions with no respect for rules of war. How the hell had the team been uncovered?

He'd figure that out later. After he pulled their bacon out of the fire. First he needed to call the air operations center while Postal plotted a flight path.

Joe thumbed the radio button. "Bear Cave, this is Yogi two-three. I'm in receipt of a mayday transmission."

Flight name themes changed by the day. Yesterday they'd all flown with Superman IDs. Today some guy with a sense of humor had opted for a cartoon. Humor in hell—sometimes all that kept them sane. Too bad a literal guy like him sucked at humor. "Proceeding seven miles west of Fallujah to aid Alpha one-six-three. How copy?"

"Bear Cave copies all," the control center responded.

"Heads up in the rear," Joe radioed his gunners, two in the side windows and one at the helicopter's back deck. "We've got a mayday call. Make sure your guns are charged, and buckle down our guest."

Damn, damn, damn it, why did they have to be carting a civilian today? An innocent *female* civilian who expected to change the world with her camera. A female who meant too much to Cooper.

Joe refused to think about what she could have meant to him.

His headset cranked up again. "Yogi two-three, this is Bear Cave, confirming that your mayday is valid. We're scrambling two A-10s for support in ten mikes."

Ten minutes. An eternity for Cooper and his men.

Postal straightened in his seat. "Pick up a heading of three-three-zero while I get something in the nav system. I'll give you a heading marker in a second."

Joe twisted the cyclic, tilting the rotor blades on top

of the helicopter forward, dropping the nose to bite into the air and propel. The *chop, chop* sped to a roar. His other hand steered the stick, while his feet worked the rudder pedals to maneuver the tail. Hands and feet synched to dance the craft through the sky.

Too many valuable seconds were ticking by. He keyed up the radio. "Alpha one-six-three, responding to your mayday. We're on our way, a single Mike Hotel five-three—" MH-53, Pave Low "—what's your situation?"

Would Cooper recognize his voice, as well?

"Our hide site got blown. We're on the run." Gunshots sputtered between his words, fire, return fire, explosions. A scream. "We've got about fifty guys on our ass. Several vehicles, too, with mounted weapons."

Now the scratchy voice over the airwaves spurred images from the past in a macabre parallel—his elementary school pal on the other end of a walkie-talkie, playing war games in Joe's backyard, practicing for the day they would grow up and live them out for real.

This was too damn real with no chance for do-overs.

The headset blasted with another explosion. Closer to Cooper's radio. Louder again. "Crap. We're getting nailed. How fast can you get here, Face?"

No question. They both knew who they were talking to, and he and his crew weren't the only ones listening. Their passenger heard, as well. Photojournalist Brigid Wheeler would document much more than she'd bargained for when they'd left their Kuwaiti base this morning.

At least Cooper didn't know she was onboard, and her headset wasn't wired for responding. Only listening. Joe could almost hear his pal chewing him out for not flying her back ASAP. Not an option. She'd signed her liability waiver when she'd taken the press tour in a war zone. But then, Cooper wasn't much for rules.

She might not recognize Cooper's voice garbled through static, since she'd experienced far less time on military headsets.

"We're ten miles out. Five mikes. Just hold on. We've also got two A-10s taking off from Baghdad International in eight mikes."

Flat desert rolled past below him. Empty. Sun broiled through the windscreen, reflecting off the sand for a double dose of hellish heat. Light revealed too much. After-sunset flights offered the advantage of state-of-the-art night vision goggles and an infrared camera.

Forget bitching about the hand that fate dealt. Work with it and win.

"Hey, bud…" Joe stopped himself short from using Coop's name, which would alert Brigid if she didn't already know. "Give me a better fix on your position. You got any coordinates to share?"

"Negative on coordinates. Little too busy running and shooting to check my GPS," he said between gasping breaths. "Once we snag a defensive position, I'll get a read. Best I can tell now we're seven miles west of the edge of town. We're running west in a wadi—" a gully trench in the sand that wouldn't offer much protection "—and we're trying for an abandoned village a mile west of here for cover."

"Roger that. Will continue inbound." Sweat stung his eyes, soaked his flight gloves, the stench of body odor and hydraulic fluid swelling.

Hopefully Cooper's Special Forces team's return fire would be enough to hold off the insurgents. Rugged terrain would slow the vehicles. There was a chance.

God, what he wouldn't give for a joke to connect with his bud right now. Too bad his hands and brain were too busy to reach for his PalmPilot and look one up.

Instead, he settled for one of their childhood sayings. "You're still the baddest dude in the jungle."

A choked-off laugh huffed through. "Hell, if I was in a jungle I could take a GPS reading from behind a banana tree."

Not even a palm in sight.

The copilot tossed aside a map and started logging fresh data into the navigational system. "I think I've got a lock on their location from the wadi. Follow the heading marker."

"Copy." Centering up on the heading marker, Joe shoved aside relief, which would only waste seconds.

He tipped the rudders and squeezed another couple of miles per hour out of the Pave Low, 145, 150, until she strained and rattled, giving all she had and more. She was a good old war hound. But just that—old, penetrating deep into enemy territory with only so much speed to haul in and haul out.

Scrap negative thoughts. Concentrate on flying and the beer at the end of this rotation when they got back to the States. Cooper stationed in Georgia, with Joe a short jog down at Hurlburt Field in the Florida panhandle.

Finally, dots appeared on the horizon, a city stretching ahead of the racing men. Fallujah.

Twelve Army soldiers—one officer and his team of eleven—were losing ground. In hand-to-hand combat, the Green Berets could take the insurgents gaining on them. But they were outgunned and on foot, chased down by crappy trucks and jeeps. Urgency pounded harder than his blades overhead. Sand churned below from the chopping rotor.

"Come on, come on, baby," he coaxed. "Almost there. All right in back. Target area approaching. Gunners engage trucks coming up on the right-hand side."

He swept over trailing trucks in the convoy as the ground neared, gunfire sputtering down. One, two, three vehicles exploded. Five more ahead were almost on top of the team. Almost there. Almost…

Out of time.

Sweat seared his eyes, friend and enemy mixing as the insurgents overtook the Special Forces team. Whispers of defeat buzzed in tune with the howl of the engines. He couldn't keep spraying their attackers with fire and risk killing whatever remained of their own. Not to mention further pissing off the bad guys, who were now seconds away from having American POWs in their hands.

If he landed, his crew would be taken. He couldn't even let himself think what those bastards would do to a woman. There had to be a way to keep things together until the A-10s arrived. His mind clicked through options. He counted vehicles again, five… One lagging behind so close he could almost see the face of the man in back as he…

Pivoted.

Hefted a rocket launcher onto his shoulder.

"Fucking A!" Joe jerked left. "Hold on to your ass in back."

Whoomp. Hiss.

The RPG—rocket propelled grenade—hurtled toward them. The Pave Low tipped to the side, strained to avoid.

His windscreen imploded.

The force slammed through him, numbed his brain. Glass sprayed inward as the helicopter jolted. A shout shot through the crew compartment, bouncing off the walls in a hideous echo.

Joe jerked to check his copilot. Postal slumped in his seat. Dead or alive? There wasn't time to confirm either way if he wanted to keep everyone else breathing. His crew. Cooper.

Brigid.

Who'd screamed? A body swayed forward. The flight engineer, hands clamped over his face. Blood streamed between Sergeant Chen's fingers.

His flight engineer groaned over the airwaves. "I can't fucking see!"

"Roger, Chen. Hold on for help." Joe worked for calm command in his voice while swallowing down bile and dizziness. "Crew, we've taken a direct hit in front. Report in! Can somebody come up and help Chen?"

"No injuries in the back," said the senior gunner. "Our passenger's a-okay. On my way up front."

The senior gunner's calls swirled with the whine of ailing engines. Joe combated the stick and rudders as the tail fought him, hungry to swing the helicopter into a death spiral. Wind whistled through the shattered windscreen, the howl of fate ready to bite them all on the butt if he didn't regain control.

Joe moved his hands to fly and— What the hell? His arm wouldn't obey. He tried to will it forward. Nothing—except pain.

Heat seared from his shoulder down to his fingers. Slowly his brain caught up to read the signs that adrenaline had numbed. Dislocated shoulder. Agony fired through his veins. His arm hung limp.

Another explosion split the ground, the force rocking the Pave Low. Sand blasted upward, mixed with dirt, weapons. Body parts. Blood sprayed the jagged edge of the windscreen. Spewed inside on the controls.

Noise, so much damn noise. And screams. Inside or out? Past? Or a premonition of ones to come? But nothing he recognized as Cooper.

Everything grew closer, ground and air, then and now, he couldn't tell as consciousness fuzzed in and out in white sparks. The war zone where he'd grown up as a kid in Macedonia merged with the battle below. American soldiers rescuing him then, now he had to save them.

Shaking his head, he cleared his vision, wiggled his fingers. Needle pricks stung, but he could make a fist. Except his useless arm wouldn't move his hand to the cyclic. He couldn't put his shoulder back in joint without releasing the stick.

The craft careened out of control. Faster. No time to coddle himself. His feet battled the force of the tail begging to gyrate free. Soon they would stall, plummet.

He twisted at the waist toward the control panel, flinging his useless arm forward. Fiery pain ripped a growl from him. His hand slapped the cyclic. The helicopter lurched. He closed his fingers around...

Air.

The desert rushed toward him in a canvas of gunfire and exploding sand. With a hoarse shout, he wrenched, leaned, guided his groping hand with the force of his body... To the cyclic.

Yes. His fingers gripped tight. Pain sliced the mist threatening to swallow him. He fought unconsciousness.

He could barely hear over the headset through the shriek of engines, pain and loss. No way could he hear people not on radio. Still, screams ricocheted in his brain, one a different tenor mixed in with deeper male shouts.

Brigid's cry clawed down him, erasing any doubts.

She knew, just as he did, who'd been on the other end of that radio transmission.

"Cooper? You out there, bud?" he called, no longer concerned with hiding his friend's identity from Brigid when they could all be dead in seconds.

Nothing but gunfire, grunts and screams answered.

The weight of failure clung to him, thicker than the blood on his flight suit. Somebody's guts on his bashed windscreen.

His teeth chattered with impending shock. He couldn't fly much longer before he passed out. Panel instruments fluctuated with wild readings, a full hydraulic system crash seconds away. He couldn't shoot. He couldn't land.

Nothing left for him but to save his crew. Save Brigid. And as long as Cooper survived, there was hope.

Joe twisted the stick, cranked the cyclic with a twitch of his battered arm—and welcomed the penance of pain keeping him conscious as he turned his crippled craft for an emergency landing at Baghdad International.

CHAPTER ONE

Ft. Walton Beach, Florida: Present Day

"WAIT… WAIT FOR IT, BABY," BRIGID chanted to herself. Patience almost always brought the perfect camera shot.

Belly flattened on the beach, she aimed, focused, *click, click, clicked* images of tiny ghost crabs scuttling along the Gulf Coast shoreline. Moonbeams illuminated their translucent bodies in a marvel of nature at its most elemental and beautiful.

She preferred beauty and peace these days to the savage roar of her previous job as a photojournalist for *World Weekly*. She'd thought to change the world with her trusty Canon and wide-eyed ideals. Instead, the world had changed her—and not for the better.

Now, she savored salty breezes cooling the sweat pooling in the small of her back where her T-shirt rode up, the gentle abrasion of damp sand against her legs. So what if her favorite silk skirt got dirty? At least she wasn't wiping blood off her wide-angle lens anymore.

Some of her print media comrades called her a coward for retreating. She didn't care what others thought anymore.

Well, except for Joe Greco.

She cared about her dear friend very much. Without him, she wouldn't have survived Cooper's death two years ago. Cooper Scott had been her first real love.

And he'd been Joe's best friend. Joe, who'd held her while she'd cried. Eventually she'd held him while he cried, tears coming slower for a man and tearing a fresh hole in her heart with their raw pain.

They shared a bond in their grief. Tonight she hoped they would forge a bond that went beyond the pain, beyond Cooper.

If Joe ever arrived.

Not that she was worried. Joe was always late. Could be anything from helping a bud change a tire to assisting some new pilot mission planning. Joe was always there for anybody in a pinch.

Still peering through the viewfinder, she reached to adjust her light. She kept her ears perked for the growl of Joe's truck. She'd left him a message to meet her at the beach by her photography studio, a far more interesting place to wait than her empty apartment. Where was he?

Only the crash of waves answered, the laughter of a couple strolling and a father with his kids making their way back to a holiday condo, empty businesses and packed restaurant decks in the distance. *Rat, tat, tat* stuttered overhead from an AC-130 gunship from nearby Hurlburt Field shooting their cannons in practice maneuvers—planes from Joe's base, the home of Air Force Special Ops.

She'd settled in the Florida panhandle near him

after Cooper died, since she'd quit her magazine job, her only tie to Washington, D.C., anyway. She'd never had much of a family life growing up, so what did it matter to her where she parked her camera? Life was about the people, not the place. Now she lived close to Joe and earned a living by snapping studio portraits of precious children she would never have.

She was definitely a coward. But she couldn't open her heart to love again through marriage or a child, a decision she'd made two years ago and still found solid.

However, as time passed, she discovered a flaw in her plan. Celibacy. Beyond the sex, she also missed simply being touched, the warmth of masculine arms around her when she watched a technicolor sunset.

Except, she wasn't the casual-sex type. Which brought her back to thoughts of Cooper when she really didn't want to think about him tonight, on her thirtieth birthday, a landmark date perfect for new direction.

Somewhere between the cake at work from a bunch of acquaintances and no cake waiting for her at home, she'd realized something needed to change. Who better to trust on her new path than her oh-so-hot best bud? Joe wasn't seeing anyone right now. Gossip and his dating history proved him to be definitely straight. Instinct told her he found her attractive. Perfect for her plan.

If he would ever show up.

Stretching along the sand, she tracked two ghost crabs tackling each other in a sideways game of crustacean football. Funny ghosts beat the hell out of her real ones any day of the week. She angled her camera left, rolling to her side.

And found battered deck shoes beside her, no socks, strong ankles and luscious sworls of dark hair dusted with sand.

Joe.

She hadn't even heard him arrive. Her belly clenched with nerves and desire. She flipped to her back, damp skirt sticking to her legs, camera angled up. The width of his chest in a navy polo filled her lens, eyes and senses.

Brigid narrowed the focus past broad shoulders up to his face. Bold cheekbones and stark angles spoke of his Eastern European heritage, adding an elusive air to an otherwise all-American guy. Close-cropped hair glistened in the humidity, dark, the total picture so very different from her sunny and auburn-haired Cooper, which somehow made Joe all the more appealing.

She reassessed him as a potential lover, rather than just a friend. Long legs in khaki shorts. A little blah in the wardrobe department, but who cared since he had a great body inside the clothes?

Deep-brown eyes peered back down at her, so dark and impenetrable she ached to stroke away his tension.

Whoops. Far too intense for what she had in mind tonight.

She slid her camera from her eyes and hugged it to her stomach. How would he react if she reached up to topple him onto her? Fun, impulsive, and very likely to surprise the crap out of serious Joe. Better to wait for the right opening.

Meanwhile, she could indulge in a moment to stare back up at him and fantasize about all the ways they could celebrate her birthday. Without their clothes.

CHRIST ALMIGHTY, what he wouldn't give for the chance to peel Brigid's ocean-damp clothes off and taste her naked skin in the moonlight. Joe clenched his fingers around the birthday gift at his side while lust slammed through him like a tidal wave.

Unwelcome, dangerous and fiercely elemental.

He grappled for self-control. A man didn't screw his best friend's woman even when the dude was dead. *Especially* when the dude was dead, two years buried in Arlington National Cemetery on a sunny day that still seared Joe's mind.

He would honor his friend's memory as well his current friendship with Brigid. Without his honor, Joe figured he might as well dig himself a hole right alongside Cooper.

Honor. Code. The measure of a man.

He and Cooper had kept their rules simple. Rule number one: Never pull punches in a fight since a cheap win led to weakness. Rule number two: No girlfriend poaching, because friendship was all about trust.

Joe sucked in a drag of humid night air. Tone it down a notch.

Easier said than done when Brigid filled his eyes and senses. Her red curls splayed over the sand, so much like locks over a pillow that his groin tightened. Palm trees shifted in the muggy summer breeze, bringing to mind rustling sheets and sweaty sex. She stared back up at him with what looked mighty close to reciprocal lust.

Yeah, he was tempted. But he couldn't act on it, not on a public beach. And especially not while she cradled her camera to her stomach like a child she should have been carrying by now if Cooper had lived.

Joe crouched beside her, closer, but at least his reaction to her would be hidden. Maybe one of those waves could roll higher and douse him.

"Happy birthday, Red." He held her gift in front of him with both hands, a new 35 mm zoom lens wrapped in an overlarge lens cloth. "Sorry I'm late. Something came up at the squadron and I couldn't get away. Thanks for leaving a message where I could find you."

"You're a good guy to stick around and help out. What kept you this time? Postal didn't have another flat tire on that junk heap of his, did he?"

"Nope. His girlfriend told him if he didn't get the car completely serviced she wouldn't risk her heels on another hike back into town after it broke down." Joe held up a hand. "And don't even ask why the cheapskate doesn't call triple A."

He wished it had been as simple as helping Postal with a car crisis. Instead, a tasking order had come through late in the day for a mission. Details on that upcoming assignment brought thoughts of Cooper to mind at a time when Joe had been about ready to strike rule number two. He'd let his old friend fade.

Guilt sucked. "I'll make it up to you."

"No worries."

She brushed aside being left waiting for three hours as if it didn't matter, when most women would have had his ass for lunch. But then, this free-spirited woman never did what he expected, and damned if he didn't like that most about her.

Brigid toyed with the big knot he'd made from the four ends of the gray lens cloth. "The ghost crabs and I had a blast. You and I can always celebrate later. Frankly, I'd as soon let this day pass. You're the one who wanted to make a fuss over me hitting the big three-oh."

"Paybacks are a bitch, Red."

"Still haven't gotten over the black balloons and singing clown I sent to serenade you at the squadron in front of your crew on your thirtieth, have you? Okay, so Postal took a few pictures of you in the birthday-boy hat—"

"And slipped them into the Friday-morning crew brief for everyone else to see."

Her hand slid from the bow, up, until her arm draped over his shoulder. "What a heartless man you are to carry a grudge for seven months."

Her willowy arm suddenly seemed heavy, urging him down with only a simple stroke against the back of his neck. The starry sky and opaque ocean brought an intimacy in spite of the couple walking a puppy in the distance.

He swallowed down a sandy breath. "So what should two mature thirty-year-olds with no reservations on a Friday night do with the rest of the evening?"

"Hmm." Cupping the nape of his neck, Brigid arched from the beach. The glide of her back and breasts upward looked too much like a woman urging a man down to join her. "I was thinking since it's my thirtieth birthday, we should do something we've never done together."

She finished her arch upward, her face inches from his as she tucked her legs to the side and leaned on one arm. She couldn't mean that the way it sounded.

He thrust the package forward. "Can't forget the gift first. Hope you like it, but I've got the receipt if you want to exchange it."

"I'm sure it's perfect." She lifted the package from his hands and clutched it to her chest. "Do you mind if I unwrap it later tonight? I enjoy thinking about the surprise almost as much as the surprise itself. Anticipation makes it all the sweeter."

Anticipation heightening the pleasure of the payoff? Yep, he agreed on that one hundred percent. "It's your present. Open it whenever you want."

"Thanks. You really are too good to me, you know." She tucked the gift into her bag along with the camera and light, before slinging the sack over her shoulder. Rising, she wriggled her feet into her flip-flops. "Let's walk back in the water."

He felt like shit. She thought he was some altruistic saint because occasionally he passed a guy a tire iron and remembered birthdays.

The uniform and its code of honor was everything to him. Without it, he would have died as a kid in a war zone overseas. He'd lived for the day he could be like the uniformed men who'd rescued him.

He needed that structure and regimen—control—now more than ever.

Dodging the couple walking a beagle puppy, Joe trekked closer to the breakers, closer to Brigid. "You're not really freaking over turning thirty, are you?"

He forced himself not to think of his friend who hadn't seen twenty-nine.

She shrugged, gathering her tangle of auburn hair up behind her head. "Not freaking, per se. Just doing a life reassessment as I hit one of those landmark dates. Thinking about the future and changes I need to make."

"Thirty's cool."

"How so?"

He opted for honest. "You're wiser, richer, and you still look hot."

"You think I'm hot?"

Dangerous territory, pal. Keep it light. Get back to the friendship footing. Except none of his other friends wore a thong, the T-back visible just above the lowriding waist of her skirt.

He shoved his hands in his pockets and stopped. "Is that one of those trick questions like 'does my butt look big in this dress'?"

Way to go, dumb-ass, steering the conversation toward her sweet butt with perfect curves for cupping.

She slowed, glancing back over her shoulder at him. "So you don't think I'm hot?"

"I think this isn't a friend question and I'm sure

there are plenty of guys who'd give their right nut to answer this for you."

"Right nut, huh? Charming." A speedboat raced in the distance, lights blinking like the mischievous twinkle in her eyes.

"Friends don't have to be charming."

"Good point. And a friend would tell me honestly if an outfit made my butt look big." She twirled on the beach before facing him again. Water soaked the bottom half of her skirt, molding it to her legs.

He advanced with slow steps to pace his heart rate back to normal, sand shifting away under his feet. "Well then, speaking as a friend, I can assure you that your butt looks damn fine."

"Thank you, *friend*."

She stared at him with that assessing stare, a bar-pick-up stare he'd seen and used many times. Definitely not a pal-like look. A reaching wave slapped his ankles, filling his shoes, spray misting before it stole away again.

Tension stretched, snapped, heated until she eased back with a laugh and jab to his side. "Lighten up. I'm just teasing you."

Brigid launched ahead, kicking through the surf and seaweed while he sorted through her words. He'd left Macedonia twenty-four years ago when the Grecos had taken him in an overseas adoption. He'd even started thinking in English after a couple of years in the States, but still language nuances tripped him up sometimes. Was she really just joking?

Or flirting?

He called after her, "If you're looking for a friend with a gut-buster sense of humor, you're hanging with the wrong guy. Hell, I even have to store jokes on my PalmPilot because I can never remember exactly how the punch line goes."

Cooper had always taken center stage from the time they'd first met in elementary school, and damn but the world was a darker place without him.

"You're funny." Spinning around, she walked backward through the foaming waves to face him. "You're one of those one-liner kinda guys. Somebody may have the stand-up-comic kind of humor for an hour and then, zing. That dry humor of yours slips in, even funnier because nobody saw it coming. You have a way of sneaking up on people like that."

Cooper had always said the same thing. Shit, but it hurt even thinking about him tonight, with everything at the squadron bringing up that god-awful flight.

He wasn't idiotic enough to blame himself for Cooper's death. Facts proved he and his crew had done everything humanly possible to make it there in time. The Pave Low just wasn't fast enough. In a fluke of fate, the cutting edge Special Ops craft he flew now— the CV-22—would have made all the difference.

Too late on so many counts.

Searching for ways to make sure no one else died from lost seconds in an aging aircraft, he had landed the plum assignment as the first Hurlburt CV-22 pilot, with Postal as his copilot. They'd been trained as part of the original multiservice operational test team—MOTT—at Pax River in Maryland, then come back to Hurlburt and the 18th Flight Test Squadron to prep the aircraft for follow-on operation test and evaluation. Before long, full squadrons would stand up.

Hell, yeah, he'd forged ahead and looked out for Brigid as Cooper would have wanted him to, until somehow over the past couple of years she'd become his friend, too. He could almost forget that the first time he'd seen her, he'd wanted her. Almost enough to take her away from Cooper.

Almost.

Thank God, her Jeep finally came into sight, a beacon of yellow parked outside the thatched hut photography studio owned by a local artist looking to support his craft by also selling beachside portraits. Joe continued in silence up the dune, past swaying sea oats to wooden steps.

Stopping at her bumper, she gripped his arm. "Are you okay? You seem distracted."

"I'm fine. Just a long day, and I'm pissed over being so late we missed the concert."

"There'll be other concerts." She gripped the roll bar, toying with a red, white and blue flag streamer left over from last month's Fourth of July party on base. "We have years of birthdays to celebrate."

Years? Probably not after he told her about the meeting he'd just left, and what she would have to do. But then, friends didn't pull punches and let the other be weak. Brigid was stronger than she knew. He just hated that she would have to be tested.

Maybe he could delay telling her for a few more hours. Let her have her birthday before he blew everything out of the water with what he had to explain.

Where he had to take her.

"Since I screwed up the concert plans, the least I can do is make it up to you. What would you like? We could probably find seafood in Destin without waiting too long if I tip big. Or how about driving over to Pensacola and eat at Flounders? Whatever you want."

"Whatever I want?" She lounged back against the bumper, so lush and sexy he almost dropped to his knees.

Hang tough. She deserved a birthday to remember before the roof caved in on her peace. "You name it. I'll make it happen for the birthday girl."

She arched away from her Jeep and melted against him. No hiding his hard-on this time, and no mistaking her deliberate intent. What was going on here? And when had he reached to span her waist with his hands?

A slow smile slid across her face, her eyes turning sleepy-lidded with pure sexual power.

Shit. He was so busted.

"Anything? Anything at all for my birthday?" She looped her arms around his neck, fingers toying with his hair and dwindling willpower. "I want us to be sex buddies."

CHAPTER TWO

COULD JOE LOOK any more horrified? Not likely.

Brigid stifled a wince, the ocean rush overloud in her ears. The moon and streetlights illuminated his shock all too well. At least no one could see them in the deserted parking lot. If she didn't have his rock-solid erection branding her stomach, she might feel unwanted and even insulted.

Instead she put her stung feelings on hold and reminded herself she *had* blindsided her ever-logical friend. Which overall wasn't a bad thing, because if she let him—or herself—think about this, one of them might come up with a valid reason to shelve her idea.

She needed to speak fast and first. Joe, the ultimate thinker, brooder, leader, would take charge before she could blink, and she wanted to point this charge in a specific direction.

Brigid slid a hand over his mouth, and holy cow why had she never noticed his sensual lips? "Just hear me out. You haven't been dating anyone since you broke up with what's-her-name about five months ago."

"Phoebe," he answered against her palm.

"Right. Phoebe." A big-haired, snobby bitch who wasn't good enough for him, anyway. "So you're free. Unless Miss America picked you up on your way over here tonight?"

He gripped her wrist, lowering her hand. "I must have missed her when I stopped for gas and a cherry slurpee."

God she loved his dry wit he didn't even seem to realize he had. "And you know I'm not seeing anyone. Honestly, I don't want a serious relationship, but I'm…" Horny? Ugh, that sounded rather crass. She settled for a softer and no-less-true word. "Lonely."

His thumb twitched, stroked against her wrist. Promising move.

She dropped her hands to his shoulders, picking at the seam on his polo shirt. "I'm attracted to you, okay? And could you please say something soon? You may be my best friend, but this is still embarrassing since I was hoping you would let out a war whoop of gratitude over having a willing woman hit on you. Especially one you think has a nice butt."

He slid his hands up—was that her purring?—and gripped her arms. "We need to talk."

Talk? More like make a list of pros and cons on his PalmPilot, with the cons certain to win. Nuh-uh, buddy. "If you're going to revise your opinion on the butt issue, now probably isn't the best time to fess up."

Come on, Joe, smile with me, laugh and make this okay, because she would absolutely curl up inside if she'd ruined their friendship. Her eyes stung. Looking away, she blinked fast, the image of their footprints side by side in the sand blurring.

"Brigid…" He bit out through gritted teeth, dropping his hands back to cup her hips and still her.

She hadn't even realized she'd swayed closer for comfort—ah, crap. Or had he drawn her closer? On purpose or subconsciously? Hmmm…both exciting options.

Liquid heat flowed through her veins, hungry for an outlet. Hungry for him.

His eyes slid closed as if in deep concentration mode. Her hands trailed from his shoulders to his chest. His heart kicked up against her fingers.

Time to take a chance. "I do have a condom in my camera bag, in case that's what you wanted to talk about."

His eyes snapped open.

He wanted her. She couldn't miss the interest sparking from his gaze, just as telling as any erection in his conservative khaki shorts. Her grin spread along with hope that maybe she wasn't crazy to pursue this after all. "I realize what I've said probably catches you by surprise. I've had time to think about how much I want this, how much I want you."

A growl rumbled low in his chest. *Yes*.

"I'll try to be complimented by the fact that our friendship is so important that you don't want to rush into anything, but honestly, the trust and friendship we have is a big part of why I think we could be really good together—"

He cupped a hand over her mouth as she'd done to him minutes prior. "Hey, Red, listen."

She waited, resisting the urge to lick his fingers and put an end to discussion so they could move past this awkwardness. Her senses went on high alert from taut nerves. Cars passed on the nearby street, headlights swooping brighter, radios reverberating. Suddenly she could even hear live music carrying along the breeze from a nearby restaurant. She felt more alive than she could remember in almost two years.

Finally his hand slid away. "Are you finished?"

"Babbling? Right." She hadn't realized until this moment how much having him say yes meant to her. "This would be a good time to pull a joke off your PalmPilot and make us both laugh."

"No laughs. Sorry." His callused fingers caressed her waist again until she fought to keep her eyes open. "Most of all I'm sorry for not saying the right thing the second you made that incredible offer. I don't have any excuse for my dumb-ass response other than all my blood rushed south so fast there wasn't much left to fuel my brain."

Oh, God, it was good to see him smile again. "You came through with the laugh after all and you didn't even have to check your PalmPilot."

"Well, imagine that." His fingers continued their gentle rasp against her skin. "Damn straight I'm not immune. I'm tempted and complimented. *And* scared as shit I'll say something to hurt you."

"There's only one way you could hurt me—"

If he said no.

Ouch. Big-time ouch, and oh, man, she had to salvage the friendship. Brigid dropped her forehead to his chest. "I've totally embarrassed both of us."

Thank goodness he didn't make her look up, but smelling his bay-rum soap mixed with a hint of sweat… Holy guacamole, her mouth watered.

He palmed her back with both hands. "I was going to wait until after supper to tell you this, but I think we need to go ahead and talk now."

"About?"

"Why I didn't show up earlier."

Her mind sprinted back to what he'd said right after he arrived, something about being late because of work. A fresh heat prickled over her with dizzying heat, and not the good kind. "You're heading out."

"Yeah." His answer rumbled in his chest. "I'm leaving first thing Monday."

Heightened nerves stung, as if sand ground against sunburned skin. Like desert sand of the Middle East that seemed to find its way into everything and never left, no matter how many times she'd blasted her camera with an air can.

If only the gritty parts of life could be blown away. She tried not to think about the dark places Special Ops flyers went. Why couldn't she have chosen a bean counter for a best bud?

Instead she had to hook her feelings onto this guy. Given her old job, she knew too much about his work in the Air Force. She'd captured images of SEALS,

Pararescuemen, Delta and Special Forces who carried out the hairiest missions on the ground. And every time, someone like Joe flew into the fire to get them there and haul them out again.

"Somewhere bad?" It must be, for him to make such a big deal about telling her. He usually tried to downplay his deployments because of how they'd lost Cooper.

She knew what those missions held, had snapped thousands of photographs, studied and edited every graphic detail. But nothing compared to the horror of hearing the man you loved die.

"Wait." She stepped back and plastered on a fakey smile at best. "Forget I asked about the mission. I don't need to know." Just thinking about it made her stomach pitch worse than after a college keg party.

"Actually, it's not a dangerous mission, not even a deployment. Just a TDY."

Only a temporary duty assignment.

Relief stole the ground out from under her faster than the tide sneaking sand out to sea. A TDY was just like a regular business trip, she reassured herself. She could almost delude herself into imagining him at a conference table, rather than flying a combat aircraft. She squelched the old newshound voice inside her that insisted there was more to his TDY. "Where are you going?"

"It's a simple goodwill mission to South America."

"South America?"

"A little coastal country called Cartina. The U.S. Government is giving their government some of our

Pave Low helicopters. We're flying the first down next week, when we'll also take a CV-22 to show them the newest aircraft coming into our fleet. This trip's a great deal for us test guys."

"Wait. We're *giving* Cartina multimillion-dollar aircraft?"

"Ones that are being replaced by the CV-22. The helicopters would have gone to the boneyard anyway. But yeah, it's still a high-priced gift to a new democracy to help them with drug interdiction patrols. Hopefully, if they take care of their own problems, their problems won't make it up here."

"Sound logic." She could almost breathe easy again.

Still, the photojournalist, not quite totally buried inside her, niggled. *Story alert.* She smelled it, stronger than the dank marsh of rotting seaweed.

If she didn't haul butt soon, she wouldn't be able to resist following that scent to the source. She'd have her Macintosh laptop out and ready to beam up photos before you could say, "Inmarsat Began portable satellite."

Did running make her a coward? Hell, no. It made her wise. She wouldn't get sucked back in. She'd learned she was too emotional for that job. If she ever mastered the art of cool composure like Joe, then maybe. She admired that about him, but couldn't emulate.

She unzipped her bag and dug for her keys. "Should we take my Jeep or your truck to supper? I think I prefer Destin, if it's okay with you."

Destin was closer to Ft. Walton, which would end this derailed evening all the sooner.

"Don't you want to hear the catch?"

"No."

"Sure you do." He plucked her keys from her hand. "You can hardly stand not asking. I know things right now that will make headline news shortly. Some of it I'm even able to tell you."

"Restrain yourself."

"How long do you think you'll last?"

He wanted to play hard-ass? She might be more emotional, but she was still tougher than she looked these days.

"I'd rather talk about how long *you* can last." Now didn't that shut him up? "Which brings us back to the fact that you never answered my question."

Joe blinked, twice, then recovered. "You're right. I haven't." He shoved her keys into his pocket as if he expected her to bolt. Smart man. He knew her well. "Our group commander wants good press on the mission from a reporter we can trust to get this story out there. We've worked with you. We trust you."

Self-preservation blasted a great big *no* through her, echoed by a *hell, no*. "I'm not an embedded reporter. Never was. I'm a photographer."

"Photojournalist. Embedded. Semantics. Besides, we have a reporter. Sonny Fielding from *World Weekly*."

"He's good and fair." They'd worked together before she quit. "You'll get your fair shake with him."

"We still need a photographer, and Sonny wants you back onboard with him as much as we do. *World*

Weekly is willing to offer you a helluva freelance fee to keep him happy."

Professional ego strokes. God, they were seductive.

"No. But please pass along my thanks. I'll make a list of other photographers I would recommend—"

"Come on," he urged, as if he could sense her weakening. Of course he could. He really did know her too well. "It's just a few pictures in a tropical paradise, on an all-expenses-paid vacation."

"You want to take me to a tropical beach?"

He leaned against her Jeep, take-charge Joe at full persuasive power. "We'll be giving demos of the CV-22, showing off a little for another country. Exciting as hell, cutting-edge stuff since the CV-22 program is still a year or so from completing the testing phase, after which, we'll stand up official squadrons."

"Wait." She flattened a hand to his chest, hard muscles rippling under her fingers until she resisted the urge to yank back defensively. "What does all of this have to do with my question? You're really starting to piss me off, Greco. I know you want me."

"I do." His simple begrudging statement carried a wealth of sincerity.

Finally. Real reassurance.

She braced her other hand against his chest, allowing herself the pleasure of tracing her fingers along the cut of honed pecs. "Then why can't we become lovers? We're friends. We have affection and attraction. This should be a beautifully simple step for us. Why do you have to make such a big deal?"

"Because I don't think you're over Cooper."

His words stunned her with the near-blinding impact of her 550 Canon flash.

Her fingers fisted against his chest. "That's a low blow."

"It's the truth."

She'd had enough. Enough of him jerking her around tonight when she'd put her feelings and their friendship on the line. Enough of his judgmental attitude.

It hurt. And that really made her mad. "So, hotshot, are you over his death?"

"I wasn't sleeping with him."

Joe and his one-liners. Except she wasn't in the mood to laugh anymore. "Well I'm certainly relieved to hear that, given I just propositioned you. But I think you get the point I'm trying to make. Real caring doesn't end even after someone..."

Died. She couldn't even say the word, which lent too much power to the notion she still needed to heal. "But it doesn't mean we can't care for other people. Even when that other person is being a first-class asshole."

She reached into his pocket—startling him quiet for a second time in one night—and fished out her keys. "Thanks for a memorable birthday."

Tears blurred her vision again, and damned if she would let him see them. Spinning away before he could offer sympathy she totally didn't want, Brigid yanked open the door.

"Brigid, I said there were things about this mission

I couldn't tell you. And some I can. One of those involves how Cooper died."

His words stopped her half in the Jeep. She sank to the seat, her legs still out, feet rooting on the running board.

Joe propped a hand on the roll bar. "I mentioned drug patrols and I can't give you specifics. But suffice it to say, if you spend thirty seconds searching Internet news you'll find dozens of reports of terrorist cells around the world. Including South America."

"What does any of this have to do with Cooper?" Even the name sliced inside her. And it would for Joe, as well. She grounded herself in that thought to keep from running.

"We think the group that infiltrated intel to ambush Cooper's team is linked to a cell in Cartina. We're hoping to find out more about that. We need to be sure we have press along that we can trust not to leak the wrong things."

Cold seeped through her in spite of the ninety-five-degree summer evening.

He looked away for the first time, over to a band of sea oats. "I have to do this because, hell, no, I'm not over losing the best friend I ever had."

The best friend.

Crashing waves thundered in time with lightning realizations. Strange how she'd known intellectually. Joe and Cooper grew up together, after all. But somehow she'd thought of herself as one of Joe's best friends, as well. She was wrong.

Brigid clutched her keys until they cut into her fingers, pain grounding her in the moment so she could listen to him.

"And I don't expect you to be over him, either. I was with you afterward. I saw what his…death did to you." His head dropped for three labored breaths before he met her gaze again, his hand clenching on the roll bar. "You saw what it did to me when my friend, a man as much my brother as any blood, came home in a fucking box."

His fist slammed the roll bar over her head. She winced, the air thick with his pain, until she struggled to breathe, definitely couldn't talk.

Now she couldn't even touch him, comfort him.

Joe's fingers unfurled in time with his exhale, his jaw still tight. "I need to find out how he got there. I thought you needed to know, too. He wouldn't want you to spend the rest of your life taking pictures of rotting jellyfish because of him."

The rest of the realization flashed clear. Sure, she was his friend, but she saw now how that friendship was born of responsibility. Joe was looking after her for Cooper. No wonder he'd been horrified at her question and frustrated by his own reaction. Part of her wanted to tell him he could go to South America alone—and then go to hell. The other part of her knew he'd won. She would pack up her camera gear for Cartina.

As much as she'd hoped to slice away the past, the old Brigid still breathed deep inside. If there were answers to how Cooper died, insights into those horrible last minutes of his life, then she couldn't leave a minute of them unrecorded. She owed him every second of life—even after death. His sacrifice needed to be documented to the fullest.

Brigid jammed her keys into the ignition.

"Fine." Liar. She'd just lost more tonight than a potential lover. She'd lost her best friend. "I'll call Sonny Fielding in the morning and tell him I'm onboard."

Cartina, South America

LENA BANUELOS CALCULATED her chances at fifty-fifty for keeping her clothes while onboard Alessandro Aragon's yacht.

Even odds, by midnight Alessandro would be too coked up to maintain an erection, much less strip her naked. He was already on his second line, enjoying his drug-induced haze while laughing with the new minister of defense. Not that anyone else here could tell, since they were either high, as well, or ignorant. But she had become an expert at reading Alessandro.

Her survival depended on it

Smiling, she angled through the crowded deck, skirting small tables and uniformed waiters as she made her way toward the luxury ship's railing. All treated her with deference because of Alessandro's power—and with an underlying disdain for her that he would never be sensitive enough to perceive.

She'd never expected to be a drug lord's mistress—

or rather his "personal assistant" at Aragon Textiles, as he always introduced her. But then she'd also never expected to be alone in this country where women disappeared into the black market daily. He'd known she was only a peso away from poverty when she'd applied for the janitorial job ten months ago. She'd been so grateful when he'd strolled past the interview cubicle and offered her a receptionist's position instead.

Dios Mio, she'd been a fool but still didn't know what she could have done differently. Gripping her glass in one hand and the rail in the other, she drained her seltzer. Not that it helped the near-smothering sensation she'd lived with since stepping into Alessandro's world.

Lena stared down at the indigo bay, stars sparkling along the gentle crests, and she longed to escape under that watery blanket. But she wouldn't. She focused on Cartina's distant city lights as a beacon reminder for why she had to live. She wouldn't crumble like the ancient Inca ruins sprawled on the shore.

Although she felt nearly as old.

In the early days, she'd considered sacrificing her immortal soul to suicide preferable to sacrificing her body daily to Alessandro. However, her reasons to survive overcame her disgust, and slowly she'd numbed from the inside out.

Then a blessing in disguise emerged. His cocaine habit increased, draining him. At most, she went through the motions of "enjoying" his touch no more than once every few weeks now.

She'd last been with him seventeen days ago. Her time was running out. Fifty-fifty odds tonight.

Behind her she heard the gurgle of champagne flowing from a fountain in understated elegance and tried to let the sound soothe her jangled nerves. Even after she'd begun sleeping with Alessandro, she'd still been fooled for months about his textiles business. Didn't criminals wear flashy suits? Or diamond-studded pinky rings and have a big-breasted bimbo half his age hanging off each arm while another waited in the wings?

Her A cups only achieved cleavage thanks to the import of Wonderbras to South America, not that she needed support tonight under her yellow satin evening gown, high to her neck and swooped low in the back. Sexy but simple. She might not be a genius, but she was a long way from a bimbo.

Rather than being half his age, she was three years older than her thirty-two-year-old lover. The man wore understated tailor-made suits and no jewelry, but his parties included politicians, royalty, well-known crime lords. And bodyguards. Men stationed on every level of the yacht, wearing loose fitting jackets that covered a shoulder harness. Others, more overt in their task, stayed outside along the deck with machine guns. Their newly elected president didn't have security this good.

Guests enjoyed their safety in the middle of a pit of snakes. Well-dressed snakes, who draped their women in enough jewelry to buy her way out of Cartina many times over. Probably why Alessandro only gifted her with jewelry like her yellow diamond bracelet for the duration of his parties, securing it in his safe before she returned home to her small flat in downtown Cartina.

Her spine tingled with the awareness of being watched, an important sense to hone, given the quantity of spies Alessandro employed. She pivoted on her gold heels, satin gliding along her skin as she turned.

The man did not even attempt to hide his attention—or interest. Her eyes locked on Aragon Textile's director of international sales, recently promoted as a sign of Alessandro's deepening trust.

All the more reason for her to stay clear of this particular snake, a blond god wearing a tuxedo but no tie, his top button undone in defiance of Alessandro's rules.

A reason to perhaps like this man after all.

So many people and no one to trust, no way to tell who might be a spy. For Alessandro or his enemies. For the government—Cartina's or the United States. She could trust no one, most especially not this blond-haired god who had trailed her far too frequently the past six months, especially the past three weeks. Whether he was a spy or simply interested in her, he put both their lives at risk.

Or could Alessandro be testing *her* loyalty?

If so, he'd certainly chosen tempting bait. The man's burnished gold hair blazed in the cluster of her countrymen, where only a smattering of blonds shone through like stars in an inky sky. Even his slight limp added a strange appeal, that of a wounded god still facing the world on his own terms.

This wasn't a man she could control, and that scared her.

Mierda. She could not afford fear. The snakes in this world smelled the scent of panic and devoured.

She tipped her chin and resurrected her best haughty stare. Daring him. He lifted his glass in salute and ambled toward her. Her stomach clenched in a panic—and an anticipation she hadn't felt in so long she almost did not recognize the sensation.

"How about a refill?" The blond god stood beside her, speaking in English.

Yes. She wanted one, two, three refills of something stronger to numb her for what would happen later with Alessandro if he bypassed another line. But she needed to stay sober and watch herself. Watch others. She could not risk the self-indulgence of drunken oblivion any more than she could allow herself fear.

Still she had a role to play.

Lena rattled her ice and answered in Spanish, although they both knew she spoke English fluently. "As a matter of fact, I would like another." But she couldn't ask for seltzer water, which would seem out of character. "What about a drink to honor your United States? I believe I will have a—what do you call it?—that New York City drink."

"A Manhattan?"

"*Sí,* one of those." With any luck, the bartender would have to look up the ingredients, which would give her more time to slip away.

She expected him to leave, then she could disappear

into the crowd. Instead he cupped the small of her back, hot skin to skin as he guided her to the bar, her loose hair skimming just above his touch. His pointer finger stroked her spine, one sensitive vertebra at a time until her breasts beaded, suddenly oversensitive to the gentle slide of satin against her bare skin.

This man wasn't just an idiot. He was suicidal.

A suicidal idiot who was seconds away from ordering a drink for her that she didn't want and would now have to take. Time to invent another excuse.

"Oh, no, wait." She snapped her fingers, sidestepping away from his hand. "Alcohol does not mix well with Valium, does it?"

"That's what I hear."

How dare he condemn her with his judgmental eyes flecking blue ice over her with each assessing gaze? What in the hell did he know about her? Or her past?

With all his American privilege, money and choices to protect him, he judged her. Well, damn him. She judged him too, this man who had choices and *decided* on corruption and greed. "It has been a two-Valium day." Not a lie. She certainly *could* have used two. "I should have water so I do not fall asleep. And do not forget the lemon slice."

"I won't if you're here to remind me."

He palmed her back again, his touch so firm she couldn't step away without creating a scene. The man might be suicidal, but she didn't want to sign his death warrant by drawing attention to him.

By her side, he guided her through the press of bodies, scents mingling—cologne, alcohol, sweat. Lust. Their legs brushed with each stride, his limp bringing them closer, each dip to the side skimming his jacket against her, the satin of her dress so whisper thin she felt each caress. Her life hadn't included gentleness in a long time.

A foreign swell started in her chest. She swallowed hard and embraced anger instead.

"You're limping more than usual." Perhaps bad manners would send him running off. Or limping off.

"Jogging accident. Really screwed up my ankle." He stopped at the bar to place her order without releasing her.

"You should rest it, then." And quit chasing reluctant women around the deck.

"You're right. I should. There are a lot of things I *should* do, and still, here I am." He passed her the drink.

She expected him to touch her during the exchange in some transparently seductive insinuation. They all did. Sly little moves with a knowing smile hinting where she should look when Alessandro finished with her. So many demeaning little touches.

But he didn't. Why? "What do you want?"

His smile creased dimples into his cheeks. A dimpled god. What a tempting dichotomy.

"Are you this rude to everybody or do I need to change my deodorant?" He shifted his weight to one foot, favoring his other. "I want to talk to you. I'm a part of Aragon Textiles. So are you. Any crime in that?"

Plenty of crime. She stared silently. Waited.

"What?" His clear-blue eyes glinted like the ice in his glass. "Do I have eggplant stuck between my teeth?"

She fought a grin. "Eggplant?"

"Got ya to smile. Comedy's all about the unexpected."

She refused to be charmed. "No eggplant. Your deodorant is holding up as best I can tell from here, and I am truly not interested in a closer check. Thank you for the drink."

Lena turned away—and came face-to-face with Alessandro. Her stomach lurched and she thanked heaven she had not eaten during breakfast with her son many hours past. She needed to remember her child now, her only reason for surviving.

Alessandro placed his empty glass on the bar. "How good to see my director of international sales is keeping you entertained. Your smile suits you better than any jewels." He stroked along her diamond bracelet—*his* bracelet—before hooking a lean arm around her shoulder to face the blond god. "I trust you are becoming acquainted with everyone, no?"

"I'm working on it, Señor Aragon." The young god nodded politely without kissing Alessandro's ass as did everyone else on this deck.

What an odd contrast they made, two sides of a coin, one so fair and the other dark-haired. Both blindingly handsome exteriors covering up heaven only knew how much corruption. Her fallen-angel lover and this golden god. Fanciful notions for a woman who yearned for a return to practicality.

She listened to the two men exchange words about his new promotion as director of international sales and did not want to like this man from the United States. While the men talked, Alessandro stroked a possessive hand along her bare back exactly where the other man had touched, as if reclaiming her. She barely registered the sensation of Alessandro's touch. But she felt so heavily the weight of the gaze of the young man in front of her.

He made her feel much. Too much. A feeling she'd scoured away long ago in order to survive, but it swelled to life inside her now. *Shame.*

She hated him for that, hating him even more for making her feel anything at all. She'd mastered numbness without the aid of alcohol or drugs, and damn him for taking away her best defense for surviving this with her soul intact.

Alessandro dismissed her condemning god. Before she could register the shift, her lover steered her toward the edge of the crowd. *Dios Mio.* She already knew the destination. *Not now,* she wanted to scream. She needed a few seconds—hours, weeks—to regain her composure.

The icy heat of blue eyes burned into her back thanks to her resurrected feelings. Alessandro swung open a door, a hall stretching ahead toward the stateroom.

Alessandro's bedroom on board the yacht.

"Let us slip away." He skimmed his mouth over her

neck, raising goose bumps of revulsion. "No one will notice if we're gone for thirty minutes or so."

It was not a question.

Numb. She needed numb. A couple of Valium would be nice, too. Scrounging deep into her sadly shallow emotional reserves, she forced her mind to blank. The stateroom door closed behind them with a cell-block click. Her prison sprawled in spacious wealth of silver and silk, a brocade sofa and chair in the sitting area to her left.

A king-size bed to her right.

Alessandro backed her into the room with sloppy kisses, sliding the loose front of her dress to the side, slipping his hand to her breast. Uncoordinated, rough, pinching her nipple as he ground his hips against her. She struggled not to wince.

Not to think of the blond god and his judgmental eyes.

She had to concentrate on Alessandro and gauge his mood carefully. Not only *her* life, but her child's depended on her surviving a couple more weeks, three at the most.

Alessandro was definitely stoned. How much so? The fifty-fifty odds teetered back and forth in her head. On one side of the scales Alessandro's libido drained by drugs. The other side of the scales Alessandro enraged by his impotence and releasing his frustrated passion by beating her.

Fifty-fifty odds of landing in hell. Or in hades.

He slid his hand from her breast, up, gathering a

fistful of her hair in a painful snarl. He dropped into the chair, guiding her to her knees by twisting the strands. Tighter. "What were you and he talking about?"

Her scalp stung, but not her eyes. She would not cry in front of him. No need even to ask who or what he meant.

She had to be honest in case the young man reported back to him, but work the best spin for Alessandro's ego. "My drink was empty and he brought me a refill. I really do not remember what we discussed."

"Why am I finding it difficult to believe you? I want to trust you, my dear. Help me make that happen."

She knew what he wanted to hear and what needed to be done to pacify him. Lena unbuckled Alessandro's belt. "I did not listen to his words because I was thinking of when we would be alone."

Somewhat true, only not as pleasant a thought as she led him to believe.

"Ah," he sighed, his hand gentling, and she could almost envision her clothes being peeled away soon, her body bared, but never her soul. "That's my Lena, no?"

No.

With an arrogant flick of his head, he cleared his hair from his forehead and angled down to kiss her, his fist loosening while she unzipped his tuxedo pants. Blanking her mind, she reached inside…

Flaccid. She forced herself not to tense. The slaps hurt less if she went as limp as his penis. His fist clenched against her head again, tugging until her scalp burned an advance warning.

She would most certainly be keeping her clothes on tonight.

CHAPTER THREE

JOE FELT like a deodorant commercial gone bad, runway heat and woman-induced tension working overtime to do in his sports-level layer of protection.

Brigid, on the other hand, seemed to be keeping her cool just fine while snapping photos of the CV-22's guns perched in the side doors. Sure she was pink-cheeked and flushed like the rest of them, but her cold shoulder could freeze a polar bear.

He was definitely in an icy doghouse.

The sun reflected up from the tarmac until his flight suit stuck to his back with sweat. Wind whipping in from the nearby ocean through the pines and palms did little to take down the temp. Of course that could have something to do with Brigid's out of left-field, sex-buddies request hammering through his head until he couldn't peel his eyes off her.

Loose cargo pants swallowed her long legs, while a white cotton button-down shirt with the tails tied at her waist showed a hint of skin every time she raised her arms to snap another photo. A man's shirt. Not his. So whose, and why was he jealous at the thought when he knew she hadn't been with anyone in two years?

And unless he missed his guess, she'd used the lens cloth he'd given her as a hair tie. Only Brigid could make that look sexy, as if she'd rolled out of bed at the very last second from an all-nighter. Such a natural beauty, she didn't need a palette of face paint to greet the world.

Still, even with her scrubbed-fresh look, he couldn't get a read on her. She'd shut him out. After deciding to join him on the mission, she hadn't referred to any part of their conversation again. She'd simply said she wasn't hungry after all, and she should start packing.

The wind picked up force and sand, drifting the fragrance of her shampoo—kiwi scented maybe—right under his nose. Brigid's, no doubt, since he was fairly certain his copilot ambling beside him didn't use fruity blends.

Joe kicked the oversize plane tire. Shit, he needed to finish the preflight walk around, not drool over a woman like a horny adolescent.

He half heard his copilot talking to him, but then Bobby "Postal" Ruznick was always flapping his jaws. Probably part of why they worked so well together for so long. Bobby got carte blanche to keep on yakking and Joe didn't mind listening.

Or at least pretending to listen today.

They'd flown a lot of miles together, most good. Some not so much so.

Once they'd returned from Iraq—after the terrorist dickhead blew out their windscreen and blinded their flight engineer—Joe and Postal had both been chosen to transition to the CV-22 tilt rotor as part of the initial operational test team. Postal was a crazy son of a bitch, no question, but they balanced each other in the air. Reason and risk.

Time to quit thinking about Brigid and hold up his end of the work. Joe strode across the cement to the refueling probe—a long boom sticking off the nose—to check for damage and leaks.

Postal patted the probe. "Glad to see it still has a hard-on."

Normally he'd laugh. Not today. "Are you sure you're not still in high school?"

"A bad case of arrested development. What can I say? The women don't seem to mind my charming way with words."

"Go figure."

"As long as they accept I'm a head case with no intentions of changing, we rock along just fine. And speaking of rocking along…" Postal jabbed a thumb toward the milling reporters and gunners behind them. "When are you *finally* gonna tap that?"

Another conversation he preferred to ignore. "I'm *finally* going to finish this walk around."

"Uh-huh. But what about the photographer chick?"

"What about her?"

"Are you and Brigid finally going to, you know…" Postal rocked from foot to foot, punching the air, making a squeaking sound that couldn't be ignored anymore than this crazy-ass copilot.

"Is that supposed to be a squeaky mattress?" He so

didn't want to talk about Brigid and sex while her proposition rattled around in his head.

"Pretty much, but hey, I'm a pilot, not a mime. Wonder how you spell that sound so I can get it just right when I pencil this day into my diary tonight," Postal rambled while Joe moved on to the nose radome, inspecting the nose and camera sensors for cracks or other signs of damage.

Joe glanced back over his shoulder. "Remind me again why I choose to fly with you?"

"For comedy value, of course."

"Uh-huh." Joe strode down the left side of the plane, checking the antennas, pulling covers off the pitot tubes that measured airspeed and temperature, while the three door gunners—Stones, Padre, and Sandman—took care of their own guns.

With Brigid there every step of the way with them. Cool. Pretending all was fine when he knew better.

Images of the Iraq flight bombarded him, explosions, blood splattering through the shattered windscreen onto his clothes. Brigid's scream in his ears...

Joe swallowed down bile. At least this mission wouldn't take her in harm's way. They weren't entering a war zone, and she wouldn't be riding along on the only dangerous flight. Still, the urge to tell her *Never mind, head on home* burned hotter than the Florida sun searing the back of his neck.

Postal's smile faded. "Probably need to shut my pie-hole."

"No worries, dude." Joe walked around the edges

of the wing, scanning for leaks. "We all know you're a crazy bastard. And that's one of the things I like best about you."

"Well, in that case—"

Joe raised a brow.

"Roger."

Voices carried on the salty wind over the plane, Brigid asking questions while the flight engineer, Vegas, explained about the engines and systems in an aircraft unlike any other in the inventory. The boxy gray craft carried oversize rotors on the wings, tilted up for takeoff like a helicopter.

Once airborne, the pilot could rotate the blades forward so the craft flew like a plane, able to reach speeds nearly twice as fast as the Air Force's Pave Low or the Army's Apache. With the extra speed, crews could penetrate deeper into enemy territory with less danger of being popped by the first terrorist toting a rocket launcher on his shoulder.

He and Postal would be putting it to the test soon when they assisted in stopping an illegal cocaine shipment into the United States. Not that Brigid would know about the potentially dangerous airdrops of troops around the drug lord's compound.

Authorities couldn't stop every drug transfer over the border. But a CIA plant in a small family run company called Aragon Textiles sensed something squirrelly in the works with an upcoming shipment. Something linked to a recent increase in terrorist chatter from the network of radical cleric el Jedr. But there were so many shipments from Aragon's factory, raiding the wrong one would blow an undercover op months in the making.

Since the goodwill mission to Cartina was already slated, they'd simply moved up the date of the CV-22 demo, using the ceremony as a cover for recon missions. A Special Forces team and Delta boys would ride over in the Pave Low. Before the week's end, he and his crew would drop the team into the jungle around Aragon's lab to do strategic reconnaissance of the bad guys' schedule. The D-boys would launch the raid when the shipment was being loaded. Brigid and other nonessential personnel would be told the extra military passengers were maintenance crews to teach the South American government about the craft.

Joe swept around the tail and back up the copilot's side where Brigid finished her tour with Vegas. Damn, kiwi shampoo smelled good, even laced with a hint of hydraulic fluid.

Postal glanced from Brigid to Joe and back again, then thumped Staff Sergeant Shane "Vegas" O'Riley on the back. "Hey, Sarge, the sonic transducer sounded like it was acting up, making this crazy noise. Let's go check it out."

Sonic transducer?

Joe resisted the urge to snort. At least Brigid wouldn't know Postal invented a plane part that sounded more like a spaceship component.

Following, Vegas just rolled his eyes and muttered to the senior gunner, Stones, "Officers."

Joe swiped his wrist over his forehead. And then he was alone with Brigid, thanks to Postal, crazy as a loon and sometimes oddly intuitive. "How are you?"

"Sweating. But that's Florida for you."

She tipped back a water bottle, giving him that lame-ass innocent stare that defied him to talk. She managed the blank-wall shift so effortlessly, he wondered for the first time how much more she'd kept from him in the past.

"Brigid—"

"Where did your new flight engineer come by the call sign Vegas? When his real name is…what?"

"Shane O'Riley."

"Right. Shane. Since Vegas isn't a play off his name, then there must be a story somewhere."

Okay, so she was pissed at him for insisting she return to her old job and for bringing up Cooper when she made a point of never discussing him anymore. Still, she'd come along. He'd gotten his way. Let her have this small victory.

"Back when he used to run the guns on an AC-130 gunship, Shane went TDY to Vegas once. Got totally shit-face drunk and woke up the next morning wearing nothing but his Halloween boxers and a pair of pasties."

"That would have made a picture sure to capture a reader's attention in *World Weekly.*"

"Oh, there were definitely some pictures taken. A helluva bar fight broke out over them. Lucky for Vegas, one of the gunners—Padre—stepped in. Padre defused the whole thing by bumping a couple of thugs' heads together in his traditional come-to-Jesus meeting style that earned him his name."

She rolled the water bottle over her forehead. "So Vegas is a party guy, huh?"

"Actually not. His wife had just left him, dumped him on the phone, and he drowned his sorrows. They got back together, but the name stuck."

She laughed, low and not nearly long enough.

His fault. "I'm sorry."

She met his eyes dead-on for the first time. "But not enough to change where we are right now."

Busted. "No. I guess I'm sorry for that, too."

He wished to hell he could have avoided this. But now more than ever he believed she needed to stop hiding from the past and start living again. Otherwise she wouldn't have suggested they start a no-risk relationship. She needed his help in moving forward, and he'd never been able to walk away from a person needing help.

And Brigid was more than just any person.

Wisps of her loose red hair curled in the humidity. Sun-bleached streaks glinted through the auburn in the unfiltered Florida rays. Last week he would have hooked the strands behind her ear.

Easygoing Brigid let most things slide off as quickly as the bead of sweat trickling down her temple, but he also knew she carried grudges. Tearing down the wall she'd put between them wouldn't be simple.

He waited for her to accept his apology. And waited,

until her answer became so important, for the first time he considered that his reasons for pushing her forward might be selfish.

A low squeak echoed from over by the wing. Joe jerked his gaze and attention free to find...Postal grinning as he finished up a second round of his mattress mimic.

Shit. Intuitive—and a pain in the ass.

Joe angled around and past Brigid, working like hell to ignore the scent of kiwi on the breeze. "Guess they're still having trouble with that sonic transducer."

How SURREAL to fly with Joe again.

Riding up front in the new CV-22 cockpit, Brigid leaned to snap photos of the older Pave Low helicopter taking on gas behind an HC-130—a modified 130 with refueling capabilities. The two craft flew in tandem. A huge hose swooped off the wing of the 130 with a cone basket on the end, the helicopter's nose probe inserted.

Watching the Pave Low fly stirred a funky déjà vu feeling of seeing her past replay through the camera. The new car sort of scent in the CV-22 brought the sensory contrast of the musty smell of her prior flights in the helicopter. She even had pictures of that last flight with Joe, images that stopped seconds before the world blew out of focus, when she had to hold on to her ass and sanity with both hands.

Now here she sat in a military aircraft, a place she'd vowed never to be again. She'd spent two years refocusing her life. Then everything had blurred again on

Friday night until she could only stumble along, hoping she didn't walk off a cliff.

Problem was, she still wanted Joe, in spite of the hurt. So what did she intend to do about it? Not one thing. She would keep her distance from him, because if she didn't move, she wouldn't fall off that mountain.

Brigid peered through her zoom lens, a much safer way of viewing the world when she could control and narrow the image to one frame at a time. She adjusted the aperture to account for the brightness as they flew above the filters of pollution. The helicopter in the distance slowed, broke away, the basket swinging free. A spray of gas dissipated in the air.

Her finger twitched repeatedly, snapping images while Joe and Postal ran their pre air-refueling checklist before their turn, Vegas calling in engine-health updates. She shifted her lens to Joe's hand gripping the stick, maneuvering the plane to turn behind the HC-130. A strong, broad hand she'd hoped would one day touch her skin without the flight glove.

She swooped her Canon up to the windshield again and—

"Ohmigod!" She dropped the camera in her lap and stared at the rear end of the HC-130 filling the view. "Uh, I didn't realize how close this would be."

She'd never ridden upfront during refueling before.

Joe didn't even break a sweat. "Hold on." His voice rumbled over her headset. "It gets better. This is just where we stabilize before we begin to close on the basket."

Closer? "How near?"

"We're at three hundred feet now. We'll connect at fifty feet."

She grappled for her seat harness, cinching tighter. Then checked her helmet for good measure. On her head. Buckled tight.

Chuckles swelled, Bobby Ruznick's uninhibited laugh mixing with Joe's low, quick bass. Their laughs faded as they went back to work, their voices rapid-firing back and forth with the refueling checklist.

Joe called to the refueler, his voice reverberating in her headset, just as Cooper's had during that last mission. "Ready for contact."

"Roger," the HC-130 responded. "Clear to contact."

His gloved hand closed around the stick between his knees, finessing forward. Mesmerized, she watched the micro movements, almost forgetting to snap photos.

She raised her camera from her lap, pointing through the windscreen. Outside, the refueling basket danced, seeming to come right at the windshield. The basket dipped lower, toward the probe she'd seen on the front of the plane before she'd boarded earlier. Eased back, then up, up, until the probe hit the edge of the basket and was guided inside.

Clunk.

Nobody hollered so she figured the clanking noise must be a good thing.

A green light flashed on the control panel.

"Contact," Postal announced.

Joe nodded. "We'll take our scheduled onload."

Brigid settled in for the ten-minute slow dance of planes. She switched to the second camera around her neck, rather than swapping lenses, and aimed at the flight engineer's Irish-boy face. The big earnest lug smiled politely, all manners as usual, and she couldn't help but think about Shane O'Riley grieving drunk in Vegas with pasties on his chest.

Guess she didn't have the market on stupidity lately.

She swung toward Postal, a man with constantly darting eyes and flames painted on the front of his helmet.

He winked through her 35 mm lens. "What are you doing hanging out with a guy like him when you could have a wild ride like me?"

What a flirt. Fun, uncomplicated, the perfect sort for a sex-buddy relationship. And totally not attractive to her in spite of his edgy good looks.

"Joe's a close friend." Or he was.

"Ah, cool." Postal's head bobbed. "Then you won't mind about those two hookers in Cantou."

"Postal," Joe growled.

Hookers? Joe? Not hardly. She laughed more at Joe's pissed-off scowl now filling her lens than at Postal's ribbing.

"No worries, Face," Postal said. "She knows you're a Boy Scout, so she also knows I'm pulling her leg. Shit, you're even polite to your right hand."

"Nice talk around a lady."

"Boy Scout, just like I said. Maybe we should change your call sign. You used to be Gecko after all, then Face. What's another change for our mercurial mood pilot?" Postal tossed a knowing wink Brigid's way. "So, you've never seen him naked?"

"Afraid not." But thanks for bringing it up so her imagination worked overtime.

"Ah, you haven't seen *it* then." Postal swayed in his seat even as he faced front. Did this guy ever sit still? "It's a piece of art. Museum quality. If only Michelangelo had thought to give David one of these. Not that I've been gazing, but men shower together and well, we all can't help but stare. I mean, Jesus, it's so…out there."

Sheesh, this guy was a nut, funny, but a nut. "Do you all speak this openly about things like showering with each other?"

Joe pulled a tight smile. "No, just Postal. You'll notice they don't call him Lucid."

Postal gasped in mock outrage. "I'm crushed. And what's so bad about a Notre Dame Shamrock tattoo on a guy's ass?"

"Tattoo? On Joe?" Now that did surprise her—and excited her thinking about something so unconventional under his uniform and straitlaced civilian clothes.

"What did you think I was talking about?" Postal clapped a hand over his heart. "Oh. My. God. You thought I meant his— Well, I can't say the word around a lady, but get your mind out of the gutter, my friend."

Joe shook his head. "Sorry for his behavior, Brigid. I wouldn't even let this man on the plane, but he gives the most wonderful backrubs." He mimicked Postal's mock gasp of surprise. "Oh, did I say that out loud?"

Postal conceded with a nod. "Well played, Face.

Good golf shot. You don't putt often, but when you do, you're the master."

How could she resist Joe and the way he had of making everyone around him smile without turning verbal gymnastics in some stand-up-comic routine like Postal? Only a few hours into the flight, and already keeping her distance from Joe was all but impossible. His one-liners were only further testament to how he didn't have to be the constant center of attention. Another admirable trait in a guy who was already so close to perfect she struggled not to check her lopsided halo for tarnish.

Was Captain Almost Perfect right about her need to move on, when more than anything she wanted to take life a day at a time? She didn't know anything for sure except that she really, really wanted to see that clover tattoo under his undoubtedly plain boxer shorts. Or was he a briefs kind of guy?

And now she itched to discover that, too. No question, even when he pissed her off, she wanted more snapshot moments with him, which set her up for another Friday-night disappointment, since friendship didn't seem like enough anymore.

She had a week to settle things either way. A week of snapshot moments, in a peaceful region this time. Seven days to find answers about Cooper's final hours. Seven days to decide if she would have more hours with Joe.

At least if her heart broke again, there wouldn't be any bloodshed.

ALESSANDRO ARAGON braced his forehead against the bathroom mirror while blood dripped from his nose into the sink. *Fuck.*

He had a meeting in ten minutes to walk around the factory, and he could not afford to meet a customs official with toilet paper packed up his nostrils. Once the embassy attaché smoothed the way with the New York Port Authority, Aragon Textiles' crates of llama wool sweaters would slip into the United States… Along with all those beanbag-size silica packages, half of which contained cocaine.

Laced with a hybrid form of the anthrax bacterium.

Of the three forms of the anthrax disease—cutaneous, gastrointestinal and inhalation—inhalation was by far the most severe. What more effective way could there be, then, than snorting it straight up the nose in a line of coke?

He would not think of how many would die, only how many he would save *here,* all those threatened if he did not cooperate. For years, terrorists had targeted multinational corporations in neighboring Colombia, even going so far as to kidnap corporate heads off the streets. Somehow he had not foreseen the possibility they would spider their reach over into tiny Cartina.

He would rather not do business with such a high-profile group and risk bringing increased scrutiny to his drug trafficking. But he'd been left with no choice. Do or die, along with his entire family.

Of course, those who'd hired him had already paid big and would pay even more for success. And he would succeed. The packages would spread around the U.S. with no traceable path or seeming logic. He only needed to maintain his calm until after the coming weekend. While the capital city was distracted with their extravagant ceremony showing off their air force's latest acquisition from the States, he would send his shipment out of the country. Officials would be preoccupied searching for disruptive trouble coming *into* Cartina.

In the past he'd relaxed with a workout in the gym or a game of racquetball. But he didn't have time for recreation, much less relaxation.

Alessandro twisted on the silver faucet and watched the water swirl, pinken with his blood before whirlpooling down the drain. Keeping his head over the porcelain basin, he reached for a hand towel, dampened it and flattened the monogrammed cotton to his face.

He should lay off trips to his private basement room for a line of coke to get him through the day. And he would, after this week. Then he could take a weekend to catch up on the pleasure of having Lena naked under him for hours on end. Lena, with her dusky skin and darker eyes that pleaded *help me,* when no one, but no one had ever looked to him to be the strong one, the rescuer.

Already he could imagine his father laughing if he could see inside his son's thoughts. Well, screw off, old man. His father might be long dead, but Alessandro took care of his mother and sisters now, better than anyone before and during tougher times.

Soon he would give them even more. Lena, as well. At least in the meantime he could trust her not to spread her legs for some other man—such as his new director of international marketing.

Alessandro buried his face deeper in the fluffy folds, trying to press the image of the two of them together out of his mind. He wasn't fool enough to believe Lena actually enjoyed sex, and ironically that made him feel safer. He would not lose her to another man, and their relationship must be about something more for her to stay. She needed his protection.

She needed *him*.

Hands shaking, he lowered the towel, his body craving a hit as much as sex. He definitely needed to chill for the next week, just until the shipment left for the United States. Then he would have so much money and power, no one would risk crossing him. Looking over his shoulder became tiresome.

He wanted to trust his new director. Certainly the man had proven himself over the past months, earning a transfer to the main offices by almost doubling sales to the United States, even setting up this meeting today with a high-level customs employee.

So why was the man sniffing after Lena when he knew damn well she belonged to someone else? A cock blocker like his father couldn't be trusted.

He braced his hands on the sink, cool porcelain against sweaty palms. Yes, she called to primal urges, the drive to protect and possess. That did not mean all men would be fool enough to act on those impulses. He couldn't kill everyone who spoke to her—or filled her water glass.

Perhaps there was his answer, the perfect way to test his new director before entrusting him with details about the upcoming shipment. Once he returned to the main offices in the city where Lena waited, he would throw her in Mr. Cooper's path to see if he was a man who honored his employer.

And if not? Alessandro twisted the golden faucet until the water trickled to a stop. His new terrorist contacts offered endless— painful—options for disposing of Mr. Cooper.

Along with anyone who helped him.

CHAPTER FOUR

JOE WONDERED if Brigid intended to disappear behind her camera for the entire week so he couldn't read her mood.

He wedged his green duffel into the corner of the mirrored elevator before turning to heft Brigid's suitcase since her hands were full with photography gear and her laptop. The Cartina Royal's concierge would have taken everything up to their rooms, but Joe had politely declined.

This crime-riddled country gave him the hives. He'd even made a quick change out of his uniform into civilian clothes and clipped his M9 handgun to his belt while still on base before heading downtown. Military personnel were too often targets in foreign countries these days.

Even in a five-star hotel.

Joe jabbed the button marked eight. Brass cage doors rattled shut, elegant if not particularly up-to-date. The plush box jolted upward.

The air base in Cartina's capital had insisted that a last-minute glitch left them without enough space in their military billeting. And hey, no worries, the crews and journalists would receive ample protection in their more luxurious accommodations downtown. Logical explanations that had happened to him on numerous other TDYs and deployments.

But he hadn't been worried about Brigid's safety then. He intended to stick to her side as much as possible here.

Ding. He glanced up at the numbers to find they'd only reached the second floor and Brigid was still polishing a pristine lens rather than looking at him. Christ Almighty. At this rate, they would spend the whole week here in awkward elevator hell.

He unclipped his PalmPilot from his khaki shorts and scrolled until he found— "So a horse walks into an Irish pub—"

Brigid sighed, shifting her attention from her camera to the top of her flip flops. "Joe—"

"And the bartender says, 'Why the long face?'"

Groaning, she sagged against the brass railing behind her, camera thudding back to her side on its Aztec patterned strap. "You didn't really record that, did you?"

"Ooh-kay. Delete the horse one." He thumbed through keys. "Are you up for some blonde jokes?"

"God, Joe, why can't you let me stay mad at you?" She sounded fairly pissed anyhow. At him or herself?

"Because I'm a good guy and tell a helluva corny joke?"

She stared back, green eyes full of honesty and a wariness he hated having put there. "Because you're you."

He leaned against the elevator wall beside her, close without touching. Playing it safe. Recovering lost ground was too important. "So you're not holding a grudge?"

"Like you'd let me." Her hands fell to her side, fingers twisting her camera strap. "Are you okay with me and what I shouldn't have said?"

Whoa. Back things up. "You were worried about upsetting *me?*"

"Duh."

"There's no way you could run me off." The elevator doors creaked open with a rattle of metal webbing, not that he could tear his eyes off Brigid. "How could you not know?"

"Might have had something to do with the way you almost leaped into the ocean when I offered to jump your bones." Some Brigid spunk slid over that wariness.

Unable to resist—no big surprise around Brigid—Joe slid a hand up to cup her head, his thumb grazing her cheekbone. "You do make it tough for a guy to be honorable."

A gasp jerked his eyes off Brigid and onto the shocked granny frozen in the open portal. Apparently this elderly *abuela* spoke English.

He slid his hand from Brigid's face. "Pardon us, ma'am."

The old lady sniffed and started a litany of mumblings in her mother tongue.

He clipped his PalmPilot back to his belt and hefted bags out of the elevator into the hall before holding the door open while granny shuffled inside in a swirl of black fabric and indignation. The elevator rattled shut, leaving them alone in a hall with guards from this country and theirs.

Brigid clapped a hand over her mouth, a laugh-snort slipping free, anyway. Joe let his own laughter join hers and tried not to notice how good it felt to have her smile back. He hooked an arm around her shoulders as she collapsed against his side.

So soft.

Her laughter faded along with his, the memory of that one simple touch in the elevator springing back to life. Only an arm around her shoulders now, but he turned harder than if some other woman had performed an all-out striptease. His traitorous hand rubbed along her arm, while he breathed in her kiwi scent mixed with a hint of sweat.

The smell of sex. He was toast if he didn't get to his own room fast.

He stepped away. Farther. When did this hall get so small? "What's your room number?"

"Eight-eleven."

Ah, hell. He followed her past 809. His room. Apparently God didn't have to check his heavenly Palm-Pilot for humorous ideas. No doubt they would find connecting doors while the Big Guy upstairs clutched his sides guffawing.

She opened the door, gesturing for Joe to follow. He dropped her suitcase inside with a thud, easing her work gear down with more care. The satellite phone and portable dish had seemed like overkill to him, but she'd said not to trust the dependability of another country's telephone services when on deadline.

Watching her slip so easily back into her old career reassured himself he'd been right to insist she take this assignment. Although watching her might not be the wisest idea right now.

Joe yanked his gaze off Brigid digging through a camera bag with her ponytail swinging a lazy pendulum invitation and checked out their accommodations instead. His senses went on overload from all the reds and golds decorating the room in some kind of nouveau-chic bordello. He couldn't have set the scene for seduction better if he'd placed an...

Ice bucket with champagne right by the queen-size bed with one of those poofy comforters made for rolling around with a woman.

Score another rim shot for the Upstairs Comic.

Brigid plunked her camera bags on the wingback chair, along with a laptop and travel-size color printer. "Quite a bit swankier than the tents where they bunked us in Iraq. But then, this isn't a war assignment."

Small talk. Pronto. He strode to the balcony doors and swept wide the thick carpetlike curtains to scope the outside security, while turning his back on that ice bucket now only two feet away. "Even some peacetime assignments come with tent facilities. Just depends on who's already taking up space."

"Could be more of the Cartinian government showing goodwill."

"Or keeping us off their base as much as possible. Even in the military bases of our allies, they don't like us walking around too freely."

He flung open the double glass doors to the balcony overlooking the city skyline and nearby shore. Muffled honking grew louder while gusts of exhaust and steamy cooking smells wafted in. He scoped farther over the newer industry structures and historic stone buildings, adobe churches, even a crumbling Inca ruin in the distance.

He wasn't thrilled about the entrance from the outside, but they were eight floors up and there wasn't another of these wrought-iron balconies above or below.

Brigid stood in the middle of the room, fidgeting with her lens-cloth hair tie, eyeing the chair full of gear, the empty bed. Back to him. He should just go, except he wasn't tired and he didn't want to leave her alone.

Ever?

He exhaled long and hard. He couldn't ignore the obvious. "This shooting the breeze working for you?"

She shook her head. "Uh-uh."

"Awkward doesn't come close to covering it." And he'd done this to them by allowing his attraction to show. She never would have made the proposition otherwise.

Shit. He deserved a good ass kicking, and Cooper was the only one who'd ever been able to give him one. Talk about a face-full-of-cold-water moment. "I should go and let you sleep."

At least he was next door for safety—a double-edged sword of security and torment.

"Uh, Joe?" Her voice tugged him back around to face her. "I'm too keyed up and we've got a couple more hours before dark. If I go to sleep now, I'll wake up in the middle of the night."

Christ Almighty, she was out to torture him with images of how to fill those night hours. "Damn long day, and I can't even attribute it to jet lag since we just went south rather than crossing a bunch of time zones."

"Let's find something to eat to kill time. Whatever it is those street vendors are cooking down in the market sure smells good."

And take her outside again? "Maybe we should just order room service."

Her eyes skated to the bed before she exhaled hard and tossed her auburn ponytail over her shoulder. "Listen, Joe, I'm trying hard here to pretend last Friday didn't change anything. But it did." A wry smile kicked at full lips devoid of lipstick as if someone had already kissed it off. "I know that's my fault, but I'd appreciate a little help from you."

No room service. No more comfortable hanging out together like they'd done for the past two years. Not that he could remember a time at the moment when he'd ever been unaware of how hot she looked.

He weighed the risk of outside. She'd been in worse places, but he still couldn't shake the need to keep her locked up for the rest of the week. Bottom line, though, he couldn't make Brigid do anything she didn't want to, and right now she wanted to go outside.

She would be safer with him and he would keep them close to the hotel and all their supposed "security" supplied by the Cartinian government. He could stow his gear here for now rather than risk a trip to his room with another inviting bed. And his 9 mm clipped to his belt under his loose shirt would add some extra insurance.

Done deal. "I believe I still owe you a birthday meal."

Thank God she smiled. "Race you to the elevator."

AFTER A BLESSEDLY SHORT elevator ride down this time— apparently God was either snoozing or being benevolent—Joe guided her out of the lobby onto the street.

He didn't need to ask where she would want to eat. They both enjoyed street vendors and experiencing different foods. Good thing, since he planned to avoid like the plague the romantic setting of a seaside café.

He started forward only to stop short when Brigid didn't move, too. He turned back to check on her, and found her...

Inhaling. Looking. Taking in the world around her with an alertness he hadn't seen in a long time.

Only a few hours in South America and already there was lightness to her again. The way she stroked along her camera strap, eyed the world around her. She had a new edge, excitement, anticipation oozing from her.

Enticing as hell. But all the more reason for him to stay his course. Watching her come back to life only reminded him that he'd been right to keep his distance.

Even if his head was about to explode from deadly testosterone overload.

Food. Focus on feeding at least one of his appetites.

Late-day muggy heat blasted over him, scented with decaying buildings—and grilling meat. He followed his nose down the walkway, past Vegas parked on an iron bench, cell phone to his ear—outside for better reception?—listening and nodding, not speaking much except for the occasional, "That really sucks, babe…. Sorry you have to deal with that alone…. I'm going to be home as soon as I can…."

They exchanged nods as Joe strode past, his hand firmly around Brigid's soft upper arm. A block later, they hit the market section with a string of *Los Bovedas*—old military dungeons and towering cells converted into shops—some of which would be open for at least another hour or so for the after-work crowd. Joe scanned the different vendors for one that grilled food fresh, rather than pawning off precooked wares that could have been sitting around all day in the heat.

Brigid bypassed the hot dog stand—*panchos*—and pointed to the vendor grilling what appeared to be steak sandwiches.

"Ah, my birthday dinner." She sighed with an anticipation he would have killed to hear her whisper during sex.

"Lady, anybody ever tell you you're a cheap date? I was willing to spring for a lot more."

"Beats the MREs and honey-yogurt power bars I ate last time I went on assignment with the military." She only hesitated for a second at the mention of that last assignment before she plowed ahead. A good sign. "Remember all the times you wanted to swap your Thai chicken for my bean burrito meal?"

She was trying so hard to keep things light and prove she was okay; he wanted to gather her up close and say to hell with it. But he knew better. This was right. "I remember."

"Then you'll also remember how hungry I get on the road. Wait until you see how much I intend to eat. I'm absolutely starving today."

He so didn't want to talk about appetites right now.

Joe stopped in front of the teenage vendor wearing a grease-splattered apron with a rolled-up newspaper sticking out of the pocket. *"Churrascos, por favor. Dos."*

He added two sweet *arepas,* corn cakes filled with cheese, before turning back to Brigid.

While they waited for their order, Brigid glanced over her shoulder. "Is Vegas okay?"

The new dude on their crew might be tight-lipped, but his wife wasn't. Everyone knew she was having trouble with her husband's job in Special Ops.

"His wife's stressed over the TDYs and long deployments." And the inherent dangers. Not that he wanted to showcase that part for Brigid, who'd already felt the worst from loving a military man. "They have kids and he's gone all the time. It's tough for anyone who hasn't had enough experience with military life to understand what they're getting into. A lot of marriages don't survive." Part of the reason he planned to wait.

"Stress from an absent spouse and long hours aren't exclusive to the military." Brigid snagged a couple of water bottles and made tracks for a bench.

He paid the vendor, gathered up their food and caught her in two long strides. "Your parents?"

She settled onto a stone bench against the stucco wall. "They divorced years before my mom died. My dad did the corporate America gig, high finance accountant and troubleshooter. He was on the road all the time."

Brigid unwrapped her lunch with studied concentration. "When I was twelve, he announced another four-month trip overseas, and Mom pressured him to work some sort of job transfer that would keep him home more." She paused, shrugged and lifted the steak sandwich to her mouth. "He balked, and we never saw him again."

"Shit. That really sucks."

She filled her mouth with food instead of answering.

He didn't remember much about his biological parents, and there weren't any photos. Just hazy memories of a dark-haired man and woman who'd seemed tall and old to him at six. Most records in the local courthouse and his home had been blown up in the civil war crossfire. He only knew his parents had owned a small restaurant.

Did that knowledge create memories of standing in a kitchen on a metal stool between a man at the stove and a woman at the sink? He wasn't sure but could have sworn he smelled yeasty dough and some kind of stew.

He also remembered a younger brother whose name he couldn't even call back, a kid almost his size trying to climb up, too, a thought that caught in his throat. A brother who'd died in a raid on their town during another battle in the ongoing conflict. A brother Joe had taken his eyes off for only a split second in their sprint to safety after their parents died.

Those hazy memories he damn well didn't want, preferred to let them fade. But when he'd come to the States, there had been a void in his childhood life that Cooper stepped into. Their friendship had saved them both as kids.

Brigid finished chewing—half of her sandwich already savored with a sensualist's delight—and dabbed a drizzle of salsa-stained grease from the side of her mouth. "A couple years later we found out he actually had another family, the reason we never saw him all that often. Dad got eighteen months in a minimum-security prison for bigamy, and I got two new half brothers who wanted nothing to do with us."

Holy crap. Why had she never told him this before? People didn't hold out on him. He was the shoulder guy, the one everybody came to with troubles.

He passed her another napkin in case she needed to cry. "That must have been tough for you."

"The papers had a field day with it, since nothing much else was going on in the world at the time," she continued, not a tear in sight. "Guess that's part of why I decided to join the press corps and make sure anybody on my watch received a fair shake."

"You succeeded."

She downed another quarter of her sandwich while a *chiva* full of passengers honked by, the colorful vehicle more of a Peruvian *Partridge Family* bus than public transportation. "He lost everything to legal fees and seized assets, and still landed in jail."

Joe listened silently, tearing off a quarter of his sandwich.

"I always suspected she knew and just tolerated his lies over the years to keep him. Then the first time she put her foot down, he left and she was devastated. I mean totally crushed, barely able to function. None of us were surprised when she died of a heart attack once I left for college."

"So you really lost both parents at once." He wanted to kick both of their selfish asses for abandoning their daughter.

"I never thought of it that way." She glanced up, shifting the trail of her red hair draped forward over one breast. "You'd think I would realize the image is all about who's looking through the viewfinder."

Damn, he wanted to kiss her. A normal reaction to a hot woman he really liked and admired who was baring her heart to him. So why didn't he just go for it? Any reasonable human being would tell him that his friend being dead nullified the no-poaching code.

But he couldn't shake the sense of Cooper watching, so close, if Joe looked over his shoulder, he would find his old pal grinning as he proclaimed himself "the baddest dude in the jungle." Sure there were times he picked up the phone to call Coop without thinking first. Or turned during a football game to commiserate over a bogus call by the ref—only to find air.

Except this felt different, a presence so thick he kept his breakfast, lunch—whatever meal it was based on time zone—gripped in his hand. Who the hell could swallow right now, anyway?

What the fuck was wrong with him?

When the flight doc deployed to Iraq treated his dislocated shoulder, they'd put him through a battery of psych evals. He'd passed, but the doc had privately suggested Joe look into grief counseling. He'd resisted the urge to tell Doc Clark to shove it, and settled for saying that a good drunken binge would purge him just fine, thanks all the same.

For the first time, he wondered if maybe the doc had been right. Otherwise, why would he still be checking his tail for his dead pal all because he felt guilty as hell over wanting to break an old pact?

He needed to get a grip. He'd watched them lower that coffin into the ground, for God's sake. Heard it thud, before clods of earth pounded against the lid, could even now hear Cooper's mother crying, screaming even in the small gathering—

What the hell?

A woman's shriek. Down the street.

Brigid shot past him toward the action, her camera

already hooked over her shoulder and on its way up to her face.

Joe launched forward and looped an arm around her waist. "Not so fast, Vicky Vale."

On his own, he would rush into the fray in a heart-beat, but not with Brigid along. He needed to get her safe, and then he could help.

Brigid struggled in his arms, leaving him no choice but to tackle her. He twisted to cushion her fall. Shit. His shoulder throbbed.

He rolled to cover her from the sudden street stam-pede, anchoring her to the pavement with the length of his body. His face pressed to her cheek, her hair tick-ling his nose and senses.

Damn. He should be thinking about getting her to safety. Instead his brain went on stun until he could only feel her soft and warm and right the hell under him, her bottom pressed against him, rousing fantasies of how hot it would be to take her just this way.

Adrenaline fueled a guy's sex drive fine all on its own. Adrenaline *and* Brigid had him steel hard and fighting the urge to play out those fantasies for real.

A DULL BLACK KNIFE pressed into Lena's side, deep, painful, cutting her second scream short until she didn't dare move anything but her eyes in her search for help.

"Do not scream again, *puta*." Hot breath behind her wafted cigarette smoke and danger in the middle of the crowded marketplace where everyone suddenly seemed to be rushing on their way faster, as if to ignore danger at twice the speed. "Or I will carve out a kidney before you finish."

She forced herself to think, assess. A man, medium build but strong, wearing dark clothes. Definitely someone from a nearby region, judging by his accent. Not some desperate foreigner in search of extra cash.

"What do you want from me?" She hated the betraying crack in her voice. But her nerves, still not recovered from her night with Alessandro, could only take so much.

Her jaw, arm and side ached with reminders of her lover's disintegrating control. Working beside him all day had destroyed what remained of her frayed calm. No matter how tender and generous Alessandro acted at times, a monster emerged the minute cocaine blasted away his veneer of civility.

And now she was being attacked outside her home. Was there nowhere safe for her?

"Just your money." The man glided the knife's edge up her side an inch, hidden from sight by the loose folds of her silky dress and the brace of his body. "But not here where people can see."

Walk away with him? She struggled not to shudder, certain money could not be his only goal. Hundreds of horrid scenarios scrolled through her head—of rape or even a kidnapping by a rival organization intent on striking back at Alessandro.

He jerked her arm. What could she do? No one would help her here. She had learned that hard lesson months ago, alone, hungry and fast running out of options. For her son she would do anything to survive, something she had proven time and again the past year.

But *Dios Mio,* total submission was so much more difficult than fighting back. She struggled to contain a hysterical laugh over an image of her striking anyone. Even matched with someone her own size, she was an uncoordinated weakling, the quiet scrawny one in school with glasses. She couldn't even claim great grades to go with those owlish spectacles. As with everything else, she'd been merely average.

The last one any would have expected to end up as a high-class whore. More laughter bubbled like overpriced champagne in her nose, the sort that everyone pretended to enjoy because of the price tag even when the grapes soured along the tongue.

Lena scoured the *Los Bovedas* for options, all the while walking as slowly as she dared past the market vendors and bodies rushing home from work. People, so many people passed by, eyes trained forward by a life that taught them it was safer not to question.

She understood the inclination well. How many souls in need had she walked past throughout her life?

Her attacker steered her down an alley. Deserted. She stumbled, her heel catching on a cobblestone.

A small door swung open. A flicker of hope stirred. An older man stepped out with a rubbish can, a gentleman with pale tawny eyes that still held some old world honor.

Por favor, she pleaded with her eyes.

"Señorita?" He eased down a stone step.

The knife bit deeper, hidden. "A lover's spat." He laughed, easy, insulting. "Women!"

"Ah! Of course."

Old-World chivalry tossed his trash bag by the door and turned away, her last hope retreating along with the hobbled stride and low laugh. His chuckle echoed long after him with the huffing breaths of her attacker and the squeaks of swaying potted ferns hanging from wrought-iron balconies.

Fear wasn't cold or icy, but rather searing hot, like a metal brand pressed to her skin. The possibility of a knife wound did not frighten her. She'd faced worse, and weeks ago might have even welcomed the respite an injury would have brought from time spent with Alessandro. But she could not afford to be injured now, not when her chance to leave the country could come at any second.

What to do? Not that she possessed much in the way of skills to protect herself. For all her life, she'd trusted others to take care of her, her father, her brother… And Miguel. For him, for their son, she would find a way. Thoughts of her little boy strengthened her, just the memory of his precious sunshine smell and sticky small hand in hers so trustingly… He had no one else except her.

"Do you want money?" She inched away, backing toward the more populated street. "My…boss will pay much to see me safe and unmarked."

"And there are people who will pay much more to see you cut." He tugged her toward him, her heels catching on the cobblestones and tumbling her against his chest.

So he had been sent specifically for her. Fear didn't come close to describing the choking desperation closing her throat, stealing strength from her legs. She'd thought staying alive would be enough, but now she wondered what fate worse than death could be doled out by Alessandro's enemies. And what if they targeted her precious son?

"Señorita Banuelos?"

Accented Spanish drifted down the alley, a familiar voice, welcome. Her knees went weaker still, until the knife bit deeper into her side, forcing her to straighten.

"Señor Cooper?"

CHAPTER FIVE

LENA SWUNG AROUND to face her surprise savior.

She angled away from the hidden blade and somehow managed to avoid so much as a nick—thank heaven for miracles and heretofore unknown coordination. Señor Cooper stood a few feet away, with his jacket hooked on one finger over his shoulder. The sight of him at the top of the alley filled her grateful eyes and terrified soul. His chest muscles bunched under crisp white cotton. His jacket slithered to the ground an instant before—

He launched forward.

Closing the gap between himself and her attacker.

Before she could finish gasping, Cooper's hand sliced between them, nailing the man's wrist. The knife clattered to the ground as the two men slammed down.

She stumbled out of the way. Both rolled along the cobbled back street. A ceramic planter crashed to the side, shattered, spewing jagged shards and torn rex begonias. The perfume of crushed flowers exploded into the air, mocked by the stench of violence that threatened to overpower the beautiful fragrance of her country.

The pair rolled until she could not tell where the blows landed. Blood spewed up. Her heart lurched. The bodies shifted to reveal…her attacker's nose swelling. Cooper seemed fine.

But the anger on the other man's face did not bode well. "You will pay all the more for that one, *señor.*"

"I wouldn't expect otherwise."

They both vaulted to their feet in a flash so quick she wasn't sure how things changed. The other man held a rake.

Swung wildly.

Cooper staggered back, his knee buckling. "Shit."

She had not given a thought to his limp and how much his previous injury might hinder him. Like a wimp, she'd slid right back into past habits of letting the man protect her—her father, Miguel, even Alessandro.

No more.

She scrambled on her hands and knees into the bushes. Where was the knife? She reached, patting moist earth.

Her hand closed around the steely blade, pricking the inside of her palm. She grasped the handle and ducked back out to find—

Their attacker sprinted away while Cooper gasped for air.

The knife fell from her slack grasp. Too late, as always. She resisted the urge to shove her now nonexistent glasses up the bridge of her nose and throw herself against Señor Cooper's broad chest.

Instead, she closed her fist to hide the ooze of blood. "Are you all right?"

"Sure. Just winded." He slumped back against the brick wall by the old man's trash and hunched to grab his knees. "I haven't had a good street fight in years."

"You enjoyed that?"

"Of course not. Only a crazy man enjoys a knife in his face." He glanced up and grinned clear to his dancing blue eyes with a bruise already swelling one cheekbone. "Okay, maybe I enjoyed it a little."

"You are crazy, then." And so very attractive her mouth watered for more than the *churrascos* scenting the air.

Cooper angled from the stucco wall, halting just short of touching her. His eyes weren't as polite, instead stroking along every inch of her. His roving gaze cruised to a stop on her arm.

She glanced down. The shoulder of her silky wraparound dress had slipped to reveal her upper arm marked with four purple fingerprints. Even the fading light of day couldn't mask them.

His jaw went hard, pulling skin tight along the strong lines of his face. "Are you sure he didn't hurt you?"

"I am certain." Those bruises had come from Alessandro after he released her hair and jerked her to her feet by her arm. She had lost her clothes that night after all, the yellow satin dress a ripped ruin now, even if he had not managed to perform sexually. "You arrived here in time."

He clasped her wrist, his thumb pressing to the swelling drop of blood oozing from her knife prick on the heel of her hand. "And this?"

"It is nothing." She pushed the words, surprised to realize she spoke English rather than her previous persistence in speaking Spanish to give herself a language edge over him.

Except, right now she did not even want to talk at all, only stand silently and absorb the languorous pleasure of his callused hand holding hers. A pleasure that should only seem this enticing for an innocent, when she was anything but. "I was simply clumsy when I tried to pick up his knife."

He continued to apply gentle pressure to the fleshy swell of her palm at the base of her thumb, his steely eyes applying equal pressure for a peek inside her.

She tugged her hand free. "I am fine."

"Good." He gestured her forward and started in the direction of her building.

Good? That was all he had to say?

What did she expect, some sort of overwhelming display of relief from him because he'd held her hand? She was nothing to this man. She was nothing to any man, and she needed to remember that. A woman as weak as she had been in the past could not afford even a moment of softness.

Still she clasped her hands together to capture the comfort of his touch a little longer. "Thank you for coming to my rescue."

"You're most welcome." He guided her around a

corner, back into the crowded market. "I'm glad I was in the right place at the right time."

A whisper of suspicion smoked through her brain. "Why is it that you are here, near my apartment?"

She knew from his personnel file that he did not live in this section of the city. And damn it, she did not want to think of how curiosity had led her to read about him, a dangerous risk if Alessandro had discovered her poring over the information late one evening while supposedly catching up on dictation.

"Are you insinuating I'm some sort of stalker?"

"Of course not. You are simply a man who constantly shows up wherever I am."

He grinned. "Like a stalker."

"You said it, not I." She strode ahead, weaving around sidewalk café tables and the press of people.

"Slow down." He gripped her wrist. "Aragon asked me to escort you home today since you were working late, but the phone rang as I was heading to your desk and then you were gone."

Alessandro sent him? Sent a man he had questioned her about a few short days ago? A fresh fear prickled over her. Her jealous lover had an agenda, no question. She would think later about the fact that Alessandro had also noticed her late hours at the factory.

She continued to walk, letting him guide her rather than jerking away and betraying her anger. Betraying that his touch affected her. "Alessandro is a very thoughtful man."

Cooper snorted.

"Excuse me?"

"What?" Cooper stared back with unrepentant humor, raising his brows—then wincing at the tug to his swelling face. His feet slowed at a corner building, a rug shop with apartments to rent above. "This is your place right?"

"*Sí.*" Here it would come, the request to accompany her into her little courtyard, up the side stairs and come in for a bandage or a drink of water followed by a drink of her. She would almost be relieved to get past the tension of wondering when he would make his move. Then she could threaten to tell Alessandro if he did not leave her alone.

"I'll wait until you're safely inside before I go."

Oh, he was good. "Come inside and I will find some antiseptic and a bandage." A dangerous anticipation snaked through her veins as she gripped the metal railing along the stairs.

"Thank you. But I like my intestines where they are."

Her hand hesitated on the banister and she glanced over her shoulder. "Pardon me?"

"Aragon may have asked me to watch out for you, but I'm mighty damn certain he would gut me if he learned I'd set foot inside your place."

How strange it was to hear someone openly acknowledge her relationship with Alessandro. Most never mentioned it, which cast her all the more in the role of mistress rather than simply a girlfriend. "You will be all right, then?"

"I'm not going to die from a black eye."

"What about your leg?" She regretted the words the second they left her mouth. Damaging a man's pride could be dangerous. Her ribs throbbed an affirmation.

"No worries." His lopsided grin pushed toward the bruise blooming purple and green along his cheekbone. "I'm the baddest dude in the jungle."

"JESUS, JOE, is that a gun or are you just happy to see me?" Brigid gasped out, cheek pressed to concrete. Although she was mighty darn certain there was both an impressive gun *and* an even more impressive erection prodding her spine.

She wriggled until she flipped onto her back and faced him. Wrong move because now, ohmigod, ohmigod, ohmigod, she was all the closer to his six-shooter—both of them. She gasped for breath.

Not exactly the way she'd dreamed of having him pin her to a flat surface for the first time and certainly not wise given the mess she'd started last Friday. But she'd needed to make sure he didn't launch himself into the middle of some fracas in a foreign country. There had already been plenty of other saviors on the way.

She'd seen a vendor stop a cop, and then the back of some man rushing to the scene. *They* could take care of it all just fine, because she didn't want Joe landing in some crap prison here for God only knew how long it took to weed through diplomatic red tape.

Protecting her would be the only thing to stop him,

so she'd lifted her camera and catapulted forward, knowing full well she wouldn't get farther than three steps at the most.

She'd made it all of two before he tackled her.

"Gun," he answered, his face tight and focused on scanning the area.

Her Joe, her laid-back buddy, seemed to disappear, the military man returning in a way no khaki shorts or preppy plaid shirt could disguise. This man, she remembered well from snapping photos moments before he took off for missions in Iraq. Only now did she realize he'd kept this side of himself well hidden from her for the past couple of years.

The setting sun cast shadows along his face that made her itch to capture him with her camera. Dark brows, a thick five-o'clock shadow that would look more like a two-day shadow on others screamed of extra testosterone. Then those heavy-lidded dark eyes that sparked with intensity, danger.

Desire.

Her heart pounded loud enough she wondered if he could hear. She wouldn't be able to say with a straight face that it had anything to do with whatever problem had erupted a few stalls down from them.

At least the altercation had quieted faster than the turmoil in her gut. Vendors returned to hustling their wares while the honk of impatient traffic muffled any last remnants of excitement a block away.

Joe flipped off her and rolled to his feet. She gasped for air while he checked his gun in the waist holster.

He'd been carrying that around all this time? So much for laid-back Joe. What else had he been hiding from her?

His face hardened, anger mingling alongside passion in his eyes, her Joe and the warrior cohabitating for the moment. "What the hell were you thinking?"

She shoved up to stand beside him, hitching her camera along with her. "About getting a Pulitzer Prize winning shot?"

And didn't it scare the spit out of her how quickly she'd fallen into old instincts and routine, even when playacting. Adrenaline still crashed through her veins. How could she have forgotten the head rush? She burned to shove Joe out of the way, sidle around corners and parked cars to capture the moment with her camera. To nab that one-in-a-million photograph that would spark people to mind-blowing thoughts.

This photo op was supposed to have been a one-shot deal, simple "pretty pics" of airplanes and goodwill. No more gunfire. No more heroes running through flames to save the world.

But Joe *flew* through flames all the time. Wasn't that the same?

She preferred the off-duty Joe, when at least he hid the gun. As a friend, she could make that distinction and pick. Right?

Joe stepped closer. "And I was thinking about how I could help that poor woman." He stepped closer still, his voice not rising yet definitely going darker. "But I was too busy keeping you from getting knifed."

He hauled her against him, his hug not gentle, not

even comforting. Somehow arousing in its rib-bruising intensity. Joe's heart slammed against her oversensitive breasts. His cheek pressed hard against her hair, hot breath steaming into her like a sauna that relaxed and stimulated all at once.

They could have been clutching each other in the aftermath of frenzied sex instead of street fights and danger. Until now she hadn't realized how closely the feelings mimicked each other. Every nerve tingled to life during a moment of total risk.

From the street fight. Yeah, that had to be it, because while she wanted Joe, she never again wanted her need for a man to wipe out everything else.

His arms twitched once before he released her so suddenly she almost fell over.

"Be more fucking careful."

Well, damn. Didn't asinine comments like that make it easier to resist the man? "Sorry to have freaked you out. But pulling that camera to my face is as much an instinct as it is for you to haul me behind the bench at the first hollcr."

And as much as the adrenaline in her veins screamed for the photo, it blared even louder for her to grab hold of Joe and take that kiss they'd come so close to sharing.

The only thing stopping her? She'd realized in that scary moment on the beach how much she valued his friendship.

What was he thinking about as he scooped up the remains of their lunch?

Joe pitched the wadded-up sandwich and greasy

paper into the trash bin before hooking an arm around her shoulders to steer her back toward their hotel. "Cooper and I started this pool-cleaning business when we were in high school."

Cooper? She struggled to follow Joe's conversational leap when her adrenaline-saturated body wanted to shout back at him. Or shout with him. Or just savor the hard weight of his arm around her shoulders. Except he was talking about Cooper, which put a third person walking alongside them.

And didn't it always come back to Cooper? For a man who said he wanted to move forward, Joe sure spent a lot of time talking about the past.

Guilt pinched. She was being unfair. This trip had to bring back thoughts of Cooper for Joe. Just because she wanted to cut out the past to get over it didn't mean the same applied for Joe. But how weird was it to be talking about her old lover with the guy she wanted to sleep with?

If she wanted to be with Joe someday—and, whoa baby, did she ever—then she needed to figure out how to let discussions of Cooper be a part of their present. "He never told me that. Sounds like there's a fun story, though."

"He didn't need the cash. His mother was stinking rich, married into money."

She hadn't known that, either. Had the two of them talked about anything important other than how to find a place to be alone together? She'd told Cooper about herself but only now realized how much he'd kept back about himself. "Why was he looking for a summer job?"

"So he wouldn't need her for anything. He figured out pretty fast what a waste of air space his mother was."

"Because?"

"Her looks bought everything she wanted. Thing was, Cooper said he'd already been spoiled enough by the good life not to want to do serious manual labor. And at sixteen he didn't have jack for skills." Joe angled them past a stream of business types piling off a bus, keeping her pinned to his side, his holstered gun reminding her of another steely press against her earlier.

Gulp. "How does this translate into a pool-cleaning business?"

"His mom had a service, but my old man—the judge—made me clean out our pool. He said I didn't pay for the pool, so if I wanted to use it, I needed to work."

"He sounds like a man with solid values."

"The best." His frowning slash of thick eyebrows softened enough to let the old Joe—her Joe—return at least a little. "I learned a lot from him. He expected me to learn the value of sweat equity as well."

"What about Cooper's parents?"

"Parent. Only a mother, since his father was dead. And when it came to values, let's just say she drank, snorted, partied most of hers away long before Cooper hit puberty. He spent as much time as he could at my house." Joe went silent for a few steps around a clothing and jewelry stall just outside the towering stucco hotel. "Back to the opening of our summer business.

I couldn't leave home to go out until I finished the pool."

"So Cooper started helping you so you could go sooner."

"Exactly."

And Joe had given Cooper a way to escape his house in a productive way, offering him a reason to be someplace else. Joe always tried to ease people's load, an undeniably admirable quality that came with a touch of bossiness and the arrogant assumption he knew what people needed better than they did.

He pushed through the door into the hotel lobby. Ceiling fans swooshed overhead, stirring air and towering potted trees.

As much as she'd loved Cooper—and she had loved him, damn it—she felt selfish for how much she'd depended on Joe to help her heal. Sure he'd cried on her shoulder once after a few too many beers on what would have been Cooper's twenty-ninth birthday. But how much had she really been there for Joe?

She'd questioned the level of his friendship for her when she should have been questioning how good a friend she'd been to him. She'd been so caught up in her own pain, her own needs, she hadn't fully seen Joe's. God, she so sucked.

Brigid cupped Joe's cheek, resolute in her intent to be a real friend to him. "You two shared a lot of memories."

He didn't go all soft and sink into the caress of her hand. But throughout the long slow slide of his throat in a hard swallow, he didn't pull away. "He was always the baddest dude in the jungle, you know. I never even thought about the possibility that Cooper could die."

COOPER SCOTT—or Scott Cooper as he was known in Cartina—checked the rearview mirror on his Mercedes sedan. Lost the tail. He didn't even bother to exhale his relief. He didn't have time. Ninety minutes from now he would have to slip back into Aragon's radar.

After touching base at the CIA safe house to check the latest video feed from the pinhole cameras placed in Aragon's textile factory.

Now that he wasn't being watched, Cooper spun the steering wheel into a sharp turn back the way he'd come. He needed to clean up after the fight, but could do that at the safe house as well. Setting up the mugging had been risky, but he was running out of time to win Aragon's trust.

Images of Lena Banuelos's terrified face tickled his conscience. She'd never been in danger, though, he'd made certain of that. If she wasn't guilty, then he was saving her from a larger danger. And if she was a part of Aragon's dealings? Then she deserved the fear—and more. Either way, he refused to let an irrational attraction shake his focus.

Cooper forked his fingers through his tousled hair, rougher, a byproduct of bleach used to lighten his natural red to blond. Longer now, too, another part of his changed appearance. Not that anyone expected to see him, since the world thought he was dead, six feet under in Arlington National Cemetery.

And dead he intended to stay for a while longer.

How long? Until he dismantled that radical cleric bastard el Jedr's network, the underground terrorist faction responsible for the ambush slaughter of his men. And now somehow el Jedr had convinced Aragon to put anthrax in a cocaine shipment. They had to trace Aragon's supplier for the *bacillus anthracis*—bacteria that formed the spores responsible for spreading the anthrax disease. Once he pinpointed that connection, it would lead them straight to el Jedr.

Locating the anthrax bacteria in Aragon's factory hadn't been that difficult, just involved tapping into some Special Forces stealth and ingenuity. Once he'd identified the blind spots in Aragon's security cameras, slipping around the factory at night presented no problem. Using the original factory plans, he'd paced off corridors and rooms until he discovered the missing space—a secret chamber room below the meeting area Aragon used for conferences—accessed through the bathroom. Most drug lords had safe rooms and emergency exits, after all.

He checked the room regularly to ensure the toxic crap hadn't been moved. He *could* steal one of those presealed packets and send it back to the U.S. Since anthrax strains each had a DNA fingerprint, labs could pinpoint the nationality or pedigree as some called it. But handling the lethal garbage was damned dangerous if it went airborne and not just for him.

Hell, he didn't much care about living beyond finding justice. He figured he was riding on borrowed time already anyway. But he wouldn't risk other lives.

His leg throbbed as he worked the clutch through bumper-to-bumper exhaust-filled traffic, the brake and gas pedals offering a constant reminder of his own injuries, his own losses. But he could live with that because he *had* lived. Unlike his men. He couldn't be with Special Forces anymore, but he would still fight to the end however he could to avenge the ambush death of the soldiers under his command.

When he'd woken, alone in that shit hole shack in Iraq and realized the injuries to his leg ended his career as a Green Beret, he'd cracked up little. He stayed alive by focusing on two goals: survival and revenge.

Finally Delta Forces had invaded his prison home deep in the desert. Most of the terrorists had fled the camp by then, leaving him for dead. By the time he regained consciousness who-the-hell-knew-how-long later, a CIA operative was waiting at his hospital bedside at Ramstein AFB in Germany to tell him the world thought he was dead. Would he consider the possibility of letting them continue to think so, even stage a funeral? Then he could launch a new career. On a new battlefield with no rules. Given how screwed up he was, he couldn't see his way clear to any other choice.

Weaving around an overburdened produce truck, Cooper whipped the car into a sharp right off the main thoroughfare, wincing at the quick jar to his knee. Thank God the CIA didn't care about his injuries as long as he was mobile, and even that was optional in the right setting. They needed his brain and other skills he brought from his covert operations training in the Special Forces.

And about the people he'd hurt by playing possum for two years? His whore of a mother had made it clear she'd rather spend her time working on her next hookup than hanging with the son she didn't give a rat's ass about.

But Joe? Cooper cricked his head from side to side to work out the knot of guilt and override it with logic. Sure Joe would be pissed, probably beat the crap out of him someday, but eventually he'd understand because of his own military career and big-ass heart.

Which just left Brigid. That was a tougher one.

Stopping while a farmer guided his cow across the road, Cooper jangled his keychain until the band of braided hemp worked its way around. He rubbed the coarse hair tie between two fingers, a memento he'd carried into that last battle, tied to his bootlace.

Somehow he'd managed to keep it with him throughout his capture. Small fucking miracle. Seeing it, touching it, remembering Brigid tugging it free from her thick red hair before she draped those locks over his chest had kept him alive on some of the darker nights.

Nailing the accelerator as he lunged free of the city limits, he stroked his thumb over tan beads woven through the hemp strands, thinking back to the night before his last mission in Iraq. She'd dared him to call her a sap for presenting her hair ribbon to him like some medieval woman bestowing her favor on a knight going into battle. They'd laughed together, even if hers was a little watery, and she'd kissed him before making sweet goodbye love to him. A helluva woman. A strong woman.

Salty wind breezed over him as he merged onto a seaside road. Intellectually he knew that real love didn't give a shit about injuries and a messed-up head. But he hadn't been able to make himself put either of them to the test. Which he took as a sign he wasn't good enough for her. He knew from checking up on her that she was doing okay with Joe looking out for her.

Cooper massaged the ache in his knee that would never go away. He would make it right for Brigid some-day, once he had all the pieces of himself back together again, when he could think beyond survival and re-venge.

And no way in hell would he let Aragon or his high-class mistress get in the way.

CHAPTER SIX

JOE JABBED the elevator button, his heart still stutter-
ing like the guns on his plane every time he thought
about Brigid sprinting toward a mugging with her camera.

She clutched the rail behind her on the mirrored
wall, neither of them talking through the slow slide up
to their floor. Good thing since he'd had enough of
chitchatting down memory lane for one day. Apparently she had, too, since after their conversation about
Cooper she'd gone all pensive, which he should take
as affirmation he was right in keeping his distance. And
for making her come to Cartina.

The elevator doors swished open to an empty hall,
no censuring granny sniffing at them. But where were
their guards?

His free hand slid to his 9 mm in the harness clipped
to his belt. A step deeper into the hall revealed their
guards, one Cartinian to the side of the elevator and
two U.S. Army, each standing by a stairwell.

He nodded to their uniformed chaperones before
plowing down the corridor with Brigid. "Still not much
of a birthday dinner."

"You sure know how to make a memorable date."

Date. She winced as if already regretting her word choice. Freudian or flat-out unintentional? God, he'd wanted her for longer than he could remember. He'd kept his distance for Cooper, and damned if he could remember at this moment why he should keep on doing that.

She leaned against the wall, red and gold scrolly paper making a flaming backdrop for a fiery woman. She swung her camera around and up into her hands. She clicked through her saved images on the display screen. Neither of them mentioned stepping inside, and that said too much about how easy it would be to tumble into one room.

Propping a shoulder against the wall, Joe looked along with her at photos Brigid had taken from the runway just before boarding to leave Hurlburt Field. "I thought you were using a regular camera, with negatives to be developed."

"I use both, actually, although we've gone mostly to digital now." The open V-neck of her button-down shirt slid to reveal her collarbone, damp with sweat he wouldn't mind licking. "Digital makes for faster reporting since we can e-mail things instantaneously from the field using a portable satellite. But then, sometimes there are nuances that can only be captured with the good old-fashioned method of film."

"Seems like you capture it all either way."

An image came into focus of his face behind the windscreen of his CV-22 when he was preflighting. Intense. Focused. Was that how she saw him? Certainly different from carefree Cooper.

And Postal for that matter. The next photo showed the copilot hooking a garter on the refueling probe. "You capture the person well."

"Thank you. Sometimes my camera's smarter than I am."

"But you're in control of the camera."

"Not really. It's an artist thing, I guess. Like musicians or painters or writers who lose themselves in the creative process. Am I there? Or channeling a muse?"

That was part of why her studio portraits of children were so successful. Even with the same stock setting of dunes, sea oats and ocean, each photograph carried a different tone.

Personality. Brigid couldn't stifle the vibrancy she brought to everything she touched, no matter how much she shut herself away. Even as he worried like hell about her, he also couldn't miss the light coming back to her eyes, an alertness. She was opening her camera lens wider to let the world back in again rather than shutting herself away.

He tapped the edge of a picture of his CV-22 bathed by a sunrise. The stark gray paint of his plane seemed to come to life with the reflected oranges and golds, also flickers of red between the propellers that brought to mind flames or even blood. Majestic but dangerous. So not the sort of thought he would ever have on his own about a hunk of metal, but her artist's view made a person see things differently.

She brought nuances to a regimented military world that showed the individuality many missed.

"Muse or not, your touch is very much there."

"Thank you again." She smiled back up at him, her auburn hair slipping out of the lens-cloth tie, her face exhausted, a grease stain on her white shirt right over the lush curves of her breasts.

Joe jerked his eyes back to the camera. An image of the Pave Low that accompanied them clicked into focus, the craft he used to fly. Déjà vu kicked into afterburners, reminding him he was here for Cooper, to avenge his death and give Brigid a chance at a future clear of ghosts.

He wasn't here to play out fantasies of getting naked with this woman. He had a shot at blowing a serious hole in el Jedr's network, a radical cleric terrorist reputed to be one of the most active around the time of Cooper's ambush. It wouldn't bring back Cooper, but he owed his friend. His brother in arms. Cooper would do the same for him.

The answers had to be here, because he could not accept that it had just been dumb luck on the enemy's part that Cooper's hide spot had been blown.

Brigid continued to click through her photos, while he stared in a half-present daze at the granny, condemning and cranky. Then the young vendor, watching them with the knowing smile of a voyeur.

Next image, please.

A woman's horrified face filled the display screen. Slim, fragile, with sleek dark hair twisted into a clip securing the strands to the back of her hair. Her chic silk dress could have passed for business wear, but her face relayed none of the confidence of a high power executive. Crime sliced away all vestiges of importance for a discerning eye like Brigid's.

Brigid glanced down to the closed door at the end of the hall, Sonny's room. "The cops might be interested in these pictures. And I need to hook up with Sonny to see if he can spin a story out of what happened down there."

"It was just a mugging, a mugging that didn't happen, actually, thanks to whoever stepped in."

"Just a mugging attempt? Depends on the angle of the photos." She clicked to the next picture, the sparse smattering of pedestrians peeling away, heads turned as they abandoned the woman. Sure someone tapped a cop, but so many more didn't.

Joe frowned. "Maybe something along the lines of how the area needs cleaning up?"

"Perhaps. I won't know for sure until we spread out the proofs." Absently she picked at a stray hair stuck to her damp lips. "But a picture is about more than reporting an event. It has to resonate on a personal level." Brigid clicked controls for a close-up, enlarged view of just the woman's face. "See the desperation on her face? There's no anger."

"Anger? She's scared shitless."

"Sort of. Except fear is often mixed with underlying anger at whatever brought on the terror. But for her it's more like she's…resigned. I've seen this sort of hopelessness, usually on the face of someone in abject poverty with no foreseeable way out. The quality of her clothes indicate she has means."

She tapped the woman's image. "Yet, there's complete desperation and submission in her stance, like life has kicked her so hard and often why bother fighting back. A story, a picture, even life—it's all about the layers. Do you see?"

Hell, yeah, he saw, except he was looking beside him at a mesmerizing redheaded lady with more depth than anyone he knew. And, yeah again, he could see her take on the photo.

Hadn't he been somewhat like that as a kid himself? From a loving family, until a rebel blast in a civil war took away his parents, brother, even grandparents. He hadn't starved, but God, what a culture shock going from being a pampered son to just one of a hundred orphans in a crumbling old church. His adoptive mom and dad—the Grecos—told him he'd only been in the orphanage for eight months. An eternity to a kid.

Brigid clicked through the rest of the stored digital photographs, the swoop of the camera upward as Joe tackled her. Then a series of shots from ground level she'd clicked out of some buried instinct even though her camera rested on the cobblestones in front of her. The next shot zoomed closer into the alley at high heels and a pair of ratty athletic shoes.

Click. Another set of feet joined the pair at the head of the alley. Shined dark shoes. Expensive shoes.

Brigid stopped the advance, thumb outlining the small square screen. "Looks like she had a rescuer. I wish I could have captured that in full, as well. I think that's a part of why my old job became so tough for me. I recorded the desperation. I never could hang around to savor the victory."

No wonder she'd cut and run after Cooper died. There sure as hell wasn't a victory shot in that. Although he hoped to give her one now, two years after the fact.

Brigid clicked through once more to a blank screen. No more stored photos. She glanced up from her camera, met his eyes, her own turning a little sad before she tapped his cheek. "A horse walks into a bar and the bartender says—"

"Why the long face?"

She traced the corner of his mouth up into a smile. "That's better."

"So you meant it earlier when you said you couldn't stay mad at me."

"Of course I meant it."

Thank God. He stepped away before he did something dumb-ass like take her up on the sex-buddies offer before thinking it through. "Be sure to leave the connecting door unlocked."

Her startled green eyes widened.

"For safety."

"Right." She backed into her room. "Good night, friend."

The door clicked closed behind her.

Friend.

He'd once heard it said the Greeks had many words

for love. As far as he was concerned, the same should apply for the word *friendship*, as well. And they were both realizing the first layer wasn't enough anymore.

He turned away to find the guards, who reminded him of the photos—the voyeur vendor, the frightened face of someone wearing the clothes of a lifestyle that doesn't fit. And a masculine mirror of the condemning granny passing judgment on him for not keeping his libido in check.

The granny?

Reason tried to niggle through his passion-stunned brain. Think, damn it, back to when he'd seen the old woman standing in the elevator door. The *abuela* in her sweeping caftan.

Holy crap. Her clothes. Not a housekeeping uniform. Too old to be in the military.

What the hell was she doing on the floor reserved exclusively for the people deployed for this op?

JINGLING HIS KEYS in his hand, Cooper climbed the hidden staircase in back of the seaside café, his senses on high alert. Slipping out of his cover for even an hour and a half was more dangerous than months living in the snake's nest.

The CIA safe house on the third floor of the seaside restaurant overlooking Inca ruins would move again before anyone had a chance to ID the place. He didn't make contact often since brushes with his old world threatened his focus in a deep-cover op. His third op since joining the CIA when he woke up in the hospital after his rescue from el Jedr's minions.

He'd worked counterterrorism since recovering from his injuries and completing training, but this assignment offered his first chance to strike back directly. The Cartinian government had appealed to the U.S. for help in bringing stability to their struggling democracy. They didn't want to become like their Colombian neighbor, hampered by crime from capitalizing on their historic beauty with tourist dollars. Aragon's rumored ties to terrorism would rain hell on their heads it left unchecked.

Reaching the top of the stairs, Cooper paused to ease pressure on his knee before sliding in his key. If anyone watched, he would look like a regular guy heading into the apartment of a woman reputed to enjoy many male visitors.

The lock appeared normal—very important. Some high-tech cipher system would attract undue attention. Thus the hidden fingerprint scanner imbedded in the lock, coded to allow only local CIA operatives.

He opened the door. The windowless attic office/apartment even smelled and sounded like the U.S. Who'd have thought prefab furniture had a scent?

Computers whizzed while multiple screens hummed along the walls, three techie agents monitoring and recording data and satellite feed, keeping watch for an order to act. Or an SOS call from an op gone to hell.

He strode to the back room where a fellow operative reclined on a sofa with his grungy tennis shoes on the armrest and an ice pack to his nose.

"Damn, Coop." Special Agent Chip Rodriquez adjusted his cold pack. "You told me this would be a simple setup. Scared the shit out of me when that babe crawled out of the bushes with my knife. You should have warned me she has a spine."

"I didn't know." Lena hadn't shown even hints of the fire before, just a cool plastic woman hanging on the arm of her high-powered keeper.

He should have looked deeper. Basic training told him that. So why hadn't he?

Because then he might be more tempted. He'd already been fighting the rogue attraction since he'd started this undercover op six months ago. Why couldn't his brain and body work in synch? He'd never had trouble keeping his dick in check on his previous assignments.

But Lena was the key to learning more about Aragon. Which meant following her, pumping her for information, befriending her—without pissing off her amoral bastard of a lover.

Cooper pitched his keys on the corner desk, the thin hemp tie twining around metal, much like Brigid's hair used to tangle in his fingers.

Rodriquez tugged the tissue out of his nostrils and stood. "And speaking of surprises, did you have to go overboard on the authenticity of the fight?"

Cooper spun the chair and slid into place behind the computer. "I couldn't have her thinking I'm a puss."

"Point taken, but couldn't you have faked an upper cut to the gut?" Rodriquez scooped an orange Nerf ball from a bin by the desk and pitched it toward the hoop hanging off the back of the closed door.

"Yeah, well, shit happens, right?" His fingers poised over the keyboard itched to curl into fists. "Like how in spite of orders not to hurt her, you still left bruises on her arm."

"Hey, dude!" Rodriquez's next shot went wide. "I didn't leave a mark on her. I never even touched her arm. Sure I talked some smack to keep her subdued. And I twisted a fistful of her dress so she couldn't run if she decided to play feisty before you arrived, but that's it."

Forcing his muscles to relax, Cooper studied his fellow operative's face, searched deeper—and believed. Which left a more obvious answer for who'd grabbed her arm with such force.

Aragon.

Another glimpse into Lena Banuelos's life. More than he wanted to know about a player in this mess, because damn it all, he didn't need weakening emotions. He'd gone two years focused on one goal.

Revenge. He had to make things right for his men he'd lost. All bets were off. All rules out the window.

He refused to feel guilty about setting up that little mugging attempt on Lena. She may have been rattled, but she hadn't been hurt. Not by him, anyway.

Cooper worked a hand over his aching knee as if to massage away the bruises on Lena's arm. She was fucking the guy. It wasn't like she was Aragon's wife or couldn't leave the country.

Maybe she liked it rough. His mama had taken all sorts of shit off her multiple boyfriends, claimed she enjoyed it. He'd even seen *her* leave marks on some of the guys who'd strolled through their antebellum mansion.

He'd only made the mistake of stepping between her and a guy once. His "loving" mama had called the cops on his ass, while crying all over her lover's broken arm and ruptured spleen. His dream of being a Green Beret would have died that day if it hadn't been for Joe's father, the judge, making his juvie record disappear into a trash can under somebody's lunch.

Cooper couldn't dodge the obvious. He'd let the past with his mother haunt him today with Lena. He'd taken a few extra swings at the other agent playing out the role of mugger.

He needed his edge back. "Sorry about the nose. Next round of drinks is on me when we get back to the States."

"Like we'll ever be working in the same part of the world again after this go-round."

The next assignment? He hadn't thought beyond finding a way to strike back at those who'd slaughtered his men. His eyes fell to his desk, to a beaded hair tie that reminded him of another life. He closed his fist around the keychain and jammed it into his pocket, out of sight. He had to finish here before he could think about anything else.

Cooper clicked through the computer keys on the secured screen, memorizing surveillance data he couldn't afford to commit to paper. There wasn't enough data pumping through about security around Aragon's factory, but hopefully that would change as soon as Special Forces dudes were air-dropped. He refused to let himself even think of the rush of that recon.

"Hey, Rodriquez, I've entered the guest list from our man's little soirée on his yacht." An image of Lena flashed to mind in a blaze of sunshine yellow just before she'd disappeared with Aragon into the bastard's stateroom. "How about run a check on the name I've marked on the guest list, the guy from the New York Port Authority."

"New York?" He tucked the Nerf ball under his arm. "I would have expected them to go through Texas, since it's closer."

"Shorter, sure, but also more obvious. Hell, terrorists even tried to channel opium through a South Carolina port about a year ago using shrimp trawlers and minisubmarines, for God's sake. Nowhere's safe."

"They're creative, I'll give them that."

"And patient." A skill he was learning, but tough to cultivate with a clock ticking. Cooper grabbed the armrests and pushed up from the chair. "I'm heading out. You need any more ice for that nose before I go?"

Rodriquez lifted the pack from the sofa and gave it a test rattle. "Nah, I'm good."

Cooper tapped the ball from the other operative's hand and launched it. *Swish*. Nothing but net. "Take it easy."

Twenty minutes later Cooper parked outside his apartment complex, new by local standards, at least. Aragon's goons were back on his tail. No problem. He was cool again, in control.

Once inside, he locked the door out of formality only. The men sitting in their car could break in anytime they chose.

They thought he was clean since their listening devices stayed hooked up, but he didn't care about those. If they wanted to listen to him sing off-key in the shower, pop the occasional beer and belch, then good on 'em.

As long as there weren't any cameras in the stark steel place where he parked his ass each night.

Dodging the weight set in his dining area, Cooper slid into the bathroom, peeled off his shirt, dropped his pants to his ankles and didn't even bother checking his bruised face in the mirror. He turned to the john, flipped down the lid and sat to massage along his abused knee.

The mugging had definitely been risky, but he'd held his own. He could even run a six-minute mile again.

Hoo uh tasted bitter these days.

Still he'd needed to speed up earning Aragon's trust. Terrorist chatter on cell phones indicated something big would happen in connection with that shipment of Aragon's going out over the weekend. But which cargo?

It could be anything, going anywhere. And still they could walk away dry while Aragon slid the real thing behind their backs while they were busy rooting around in a case full of silk nighties.

Damned if that didn't make him think of Lena and thoughts of what Aragon dressed her up in.

Cooper scrubbed a hand over his face. Shit. He had to shake this obsession. Must be his tastes ran toward more jaded types these days, unlike the idealistic Brigid who wanted to change the world with a roll of negatives.

Brigid. He scratched a hand along his chest to scrub away the phantom memory of her hair teasing over his skin. She was better off without him. She had to be in order for him to live with the choices he'd made—and the choices that had been made for him when he'd woken in the shit hole prison, his body on fire with fever from rusty shrapnel that had shredded his calf.

Slowly he peeled off the sleeve suspension along the scarred remnants of his knee—definitely no cameras allowed—and removed his titanium and graphite prosthetic leg.

BRIGID GAZED OUT from her eighth-floor balcony overlooking Cartina's capital starting a new day.

Adrenaline hummed through her in anticipation of all the stories waiting for her to document. Her fingers curved around wrought iron already warming from the late-morning sun, wind from the ocean stirring through her hair she'd left down after her shower.

Would Joe disapprove of her seating choice out in the open on her hotel room terrace? Maybe. But she felt less vulnerable to ambush up here, where she could watch the world from a bird's-eye view and she had

Sonny with her. Joe was off mission planning, anyhow, so he didn't have to know.

She reached behind to scoop her camera from the small café style table. She snapped some standard panoramas, more for her own keepsakes than any reporting. She twisted the focus on her lens until a jewelry vendor outside one of the *Los Bovedas* cleared, and even as she recorded scrapbook memories for herself, other nuances took shape. Her sleeping journalistic spirit had been resurrected.

For now at least, she could channel that into a work session with Sonny. Then she would move on to how to be a better friend to Joe.

Sonny sat behind her at the table clicking away on his laptop, the aroma of coffee and cinnamon doughnuts drifting on the breeze to mingle with the hint of decay in the air from the ancient city. Coffee and doughnuts. The scent of Sonny. The old guy stayed fit to keep up in the field—and to hide his doughnut habit from his cholesterol-conscious wife.

Brigid lowered her camera and pivoted around, leaning back against the sturdy railing. Sonny, teddy-bear big with hair that needed cutting, usually ducked into a barbershop right before he went home.

He sank his teeth into the fried pastry, cinnamon and sugar dusting his keyboard while words poured from his unbelievably fast one-handed, hunt-and-peck typing. How had he managed to replenish the creative well for so long in a profession with unrelenting harsh realities? How had Sonny managed to stick around for so long without getting to see the sunrises? She almost asked. But then she might have to return for good.

She pilfered one of his doughnuts instead. Crunchy on the outside and cakey sweet on the inside melted over her hungry senses that so wanted to indulge in sensation on a number of levels after two years of drought.

"Ohmigod, Sonny, these things are sinful." And man was she hungry, hungry, horny. Ooops. Freudian brain-slip. She rested the doughnut on a napkin. "Might as well mainline the sugar straight into my veins."

"Don't fret about it," he rumbled in his Old South accent that charmed many an interviewee into spilling his or her guts. "I'll do a soup diet before I head home so the wife doesn't guess. I tried to convince her doughnuts are better than other women or fast cars, but she still won't cut me any slack."

"You poor thing." Brigid slid into the chair across the table from him, shuffling aside the pages of proofs she'd printed of yesterday's flight and outing.

Of course his wife knew about his long hair and pastries on the road. But they continued to play the game in a marriage dance thirty-five years in the making. A dance Brigid would never learn. At least she didn't have to worry about repeating her mother's mistakes. "You're lucky to have each other."

"Don't I know it?" He closed the lid on his laptop computer, softening from reporter to friend. "Wish we could have you back in the area on a permanent basis."

"I miss dinners at your town house." He'd been the closest thing to a father in her life since her own walked out the door. She'd missed Sonny, but she couldn't stay in D.C. without caving to the temptation to return to work. Even now the proofs just under her elbow called to her. She would need to fax over copies of the mugging shots to local police.

He nodded to her hand twisting around her camera strap. "Are you really going to try and convince me you aren't itching to dart around buildings with gunfire dogging your heels while you wrangle closer for that perfect shot? You're all but bouncing out of your seat over a few pictures of a simple mugging."

She eased her camera from her shoulder back onto the table, anchoring the photos. "I'm pathetic."

"No, you're just heartbroken and workin' to put all the pieces together again."

Heartbroken? She didn't like the pitiful image that brought to mind. She wouldn't become that desperate woman in the mugging pictures.

Brigid sagged back in her chair, rush hour morning traffic honking softly below. "I am so tired of people telling me I'm not over Cooper yet."

"People?"

"You." She scrunched her toes in her flip-flops. "Joe."

"Joe…" He traced a finger along the top of his closed computer. "He was Cooper's friend, as well as the pilot on that mission, wasn't he?" The old fart knew full well who Joe was.

"Uh-huh."

"You two seem to have struck up quite a friendship over the past couple of years."

"Please don't say I'm drawn to Joe because of his connection to Cooper." And please don't comment on the fact that today she'd worn a sundress to work in rather than her standard khakis and white shirt she used to wear in the field.

"So you're drawn to the guy?"

"He's hot and single and about the most honorable human being I've ever met. I happen to be single and un-attached, too." She slumped forward on her elbows, closer. "So yeah, great big duh on the sexual draw quo-tient."

"Then why haven't you done anything about it?"

"I did." She toyed with the spoon in the sugar dish, clink, clink, clinking it against the crystal side. Maybe she could just suck down a few scoops. "I offered a no-strings, sex-buddies deal. He turned me down."

"Well ouch, that's gonna leave a mark." He raised a bushy brow. "Are you sure this guy's straight?"

"Totally. And unattached."

"Then what reason did he give for his no?"

"That I'm not really over losing Cooper." Saying his name still hurt, but not as much. She *was* better, damn it. It only felt fresh because she'd taken this job.

"Ah, the tired, for-your-own-good excuse."

Except Joe really did think of others first, even when he was wrong. "Okay, sure, Joe and I have a bond from those hellish months of grieving together right after Cooper...died." God, she could hardly say the word, and wouldn't Joe have a field day with that telling little slip? "But I'm totally clear on who Joe is and what it is about him that attracts me."

Sonny pinned her with that laser look she'd seen a hundred times before he wrapped up a story. "And does he know this?"

Well, hell. She'd never considered Joe might think she was using him as a connection—or substitute—for another man. Not a far reach, actually, since she hadn't been nearly as supportive for his grief. She'd been selfish. Leave it to Sonny to get to the heart of the story.

Heart?

Her eyes strayed back to the shoreline, sand and crumbling Inca ruins calling her to explore with Joe. Of course the heart. There was nothing wrong in admitting she had feelings for Joe. He was her friend, an attractive friend. A special friend, but nothing more that would endanger her hard-won peace.

Except, hadn't she already shaken things up? She couldn't ignore the fact that she may have hurt him as much as he hurt her—by letting him think she needed him because of his connection to Cooper. Maybe, just maybe at first that had been true, but certainly not anymore. She was clear on that much, and totally clear on wanting to be his friend again.

Now she needed to let Joe know, as well, while keeping the persistent need to rip off his clothes firmly tucked away.

CHAPTER SEVEN

TUCKING HIS FLIGHT BAG under his seat, Joe cleared more room for his chart on the lengthy conference table in the U.S. embassy. His crew filled the other chairs, working through their part of the mission planning while he and Postal sketched the route.

Joe scrubbed his hands over his eyes to clear his vision blurred by too little sleep, thanks to all-damn-night-long visions of Brigid sprawled on the bed a couple of layers of sheetrock away. For a high-class hotel, the walls sure had been thin. Throughout the night, Brigid's every sigh stroked over him, the rustle of sheets tormented him.

Hell, he didn't even need the sounds. Just thinking of Brigid had him hard even now. He shifted in his chair and thanked heaven for the camouflaging cover of the table.

Work. Now. Their friendship might be important to him, but nothing could be more important than his job—and this mission in particular.

Their flight would only cover a small section of air space on the outskirts of Cartina's capital, but he needed to map out contingencies in case Aragon's security detected them and put up a fight. He and his crew would have to be on the lookout for anything from shoulder-held, rocket-propelled grenade launchers to small-arms fire.

Joe hunched over the map of mountainous terrain. Drug harvesters exploited the jungle landscape to camouflage their illegal activities. The mountainous jungle also offered more places to hide antiaircraft countermeasures.

He traced a line with a water-soluble Sharpie along the mountain-range route, dipped a Q-tip in bleach and erased the markered path next to it that took them too close to a narrow road.

"We'll start our descent into this pass here, flying down this valley and just keep a particular lookout for electrical lines going across." Joe highlighted elevated terrain on either side of the flight path, noting at every leg the altitude needed to climb out if visibility went to pea soup.

With the changed route, they would cross the back road at a ninety-degree angle to minimize exposure. Too easily, one of Aragon's lookouts could hang around in a parked car and pop a low-flying craft with a machine gun, getaway vehicle ready and running.

"I've got 6900 feet here." Postal recorded for briefing again tomorrow evening before takeoff. "Still can't believe how much more bang for the buck we're getting speedwise."

Vegas pulled out the coffeepot, peered inside, grimaced and replaced the carafe. "That mountain kills you the same whether you're going 150 or 250 knots."

"Good point." Postal pitched the ink-stained Q-tips into the trash. "We won't even have time to get the complete 'holy shit' out."

True enough. They would fly the route in nearly half the time they could have done in the Pave Low, a definite plus overall. But it also gave them less time to eyeball threats and react.

Joe stayed silent and drew another leg of the route while his crewmates joked about death, the only way to deal with the ominous companion flying alongside on every mission. No rhyme or reason, peacetime or war, for death to hit. The best they could do? Laugh and watch each other's backs or, in Joe's case, plan like hell.

And speaking of possible lurking threats, no word yet on the granny wandering the halls. Most likely she'd just stepped off the elevator at the wrong floor. Still, unanswered questions made him itchy, especially with Brigid in the equation. There were CIA operatives crawling all over this country, but even they couldn't cover every inch.

At least they didn't have to worry about leaks on this end, since they'd opted to mission plan at the U.S. embassy, rather than at the Cartina National Air Base. The Pave Low crew would do their planning over there, but their mission involved training locals. Even the Cartinians understood they would only be allowed limited information about the new CV-22—especially today.

Thus their need to meet not only at the embassy, but in the embassy's "clean room." Every American embassy had one, a room that was never left empty. A U.S. Marine stood guard 24/7. No bugs to worry about here. The chamber offered a safe place for everything from CIA briefings to meetings with government leaders.

The space looked benign enough. He could have been inside any generic conference room with a long table, computer in the corner to run an overhead projector.

Except there were subtle differences. The computer didn't connect to the outside. No phones. No windows.

Of course their ever-present Marine guard stood in the back corner, eyes forward, wearing his standard uniform of khaki shirt and blue trousers. His white hat sat perched atop his head even though he was indoors, an automatic pistol strapped to his waist. He was under arms, and therefore wore cover.

Embassy Marines were a whole different breed of men. Hard core. It was their job to protect a little piece of America in the middle of another country. They couldn't even risk a date because of the possible spy element. They weren't married, because then their families could be threatened as leverage.

The job came first. It had to. The call to serve, to protect, came with a heavy personal price to everyone around them.

Relationships were tough in the military even without the added stresses of risky duty assignments—a standard norm for Special Ops. He'd lied to Brigid about where he was today, had in the past as well because of his job. How often had he listened to Vegas feed the same cover stories to his wife over the phone?

Wife? Shit. Where the hell had that thought come from? And why was he thinking about this now? He'd never worried about it before.

He shook off distracting thoughts. He needed to get his head in the game. As in the past, Brigid wouldn't know the level of danger in his job, and he intended to keep it that way with this mission, easier to do with a friendship than a relationship.

Green Berets would load up on the CV-22 before Brigid, Sonny and local reporters arrived. The back hatch would stay up, auxiliary power unit cranking the AC, and no one would be the wiser about their Special Forces cargo.

Hiding in plain sight, the best way to avoid detection.

Because of CIA intel, they knew that Aragon had rudimentary radar and listening posts. His guards would carry small arms, rifles, perhaps even shoulder-held, rocket-propelled grenade launchers. Aragon could easily claim ignorance: a stray shot from a farmer perhaps, even a guerrilla.

Joe stretched his plastic plotter over the chart, his Sharpie extending the path. "There's a bridge over here and a small town. Let's turn short of that."

Postal hooked a finger through his mug handle, crossed to the coffeemaker and poured a cup of complimentary sludge. "If we steer clear of those mountains, I'll be back in time for midnight margarita madness."

Joe peered up. "Free drinks?"

"You know it." Postal toasted with his also free coffee.

A shout sounded outside in the hall.

Before his brain could finish translating the word, alarms pierced the air.

The loudspeaker crackled a second after. "Bomb threat. Evacuate immediately. I repeat, bomb threat…"

Nerves snapped to attention. Joe folded his chart, slid it in his bag to stay at his side until takeoff tomorrow.

If there was a takeoff.

He exited the room, their Marine guard staying behind to keep the area secure even under personal threat. The chamber had bomb shelter reinforcements, not as secure as hauling out of the building though.

People—in uniforms and suits—poured into the corridor at a fast jog, sprinting around corners, no one talking, but plenty of heavy breathing and foot thuds to fill the silence.

He'd dodged death through Afghanistan and Iraq. He wouldn't be taken out by some terrorist bomb, especially not now with so much unsettled with Brigid in the past days.

Days? His boots pounded down the corridor toward the blazing Exit sign.

Who the hell was he trying to kid? He'd wanted her for two years. Longer than that. For the five months prior that she and Cooper had been together. Although he'd never made a move in her direction, not once, when Cooper had been alive.

And it hadn't been fucking easy.

The tug between them—tug?—more like lust, attraction, something else he couldn't name, grew every day with no signs of stopping. What if clearing up their past meant they had no future, no chance to dive into each other even once?

Or twice.

He cleared the embassy side door, sunlight blinding him like a flash from Brigid's camera. He jogged down the stone steps, following the security personnel across the manicured lawn, his head full of Brigid and of time racing past. Hell, he took risks for a living and yet he'd balked when she challenged him to make a change in their relationship.

Sex buddies?

Any normal man's dream, and just the type of relationship he needed now. He planned to retire from the Air Force at twenty years service. Then he would think about getting married. Maybe.

Joe stopped under a draping tree, his flight bag still in hand while his chest pumped for air. Mass pandemonium encircled him, separating him from his crew. Words and gasps and even teary discussions of past terrorist attacks on American embassies swelled around him.

He'd lived in a war zone as a kid, experienced the hell and destruction of having his family blown away. He'd also heard about, even watched kids of his crew members envision their dads and moms in that same horror. Too many times to count, he'd been there when it tore Vegas's heart out to place a call home.

Hell, no. Not for him, thanks all the same. He was a fix-it kind of guy, from replacing flat tires to mending friends' broken hearts. But marriage? If things went south, the fix-it solution could well be turning in his papers and resigning his commission.

Also a "hell, no" for him. So he wouldn't put himself in that position.

Which left two choices. Cut Brigid out of his life. Or become sex buddies with a hot, funny woman he'd wanted until it hurt for over two years.

The choice was an absolute no-brainer.

SCOURING HER BRAIN for a clue about Alessandro's reasoning, Lena stepped from one of his limousines outside the factory where he waited for her to arrive, as ordered. What had she done wrong? Had she given herself away? Or had he somehow perceived her unwise desire for Scott Cooper?

Worst of all, what might her unstable lover do to her?

Her heart pounded twice as fast as her heels clicked along the walkway leading to the double steel doors sealing out the world. There had been too much time for her to question his edict during the five-mile ride beyond the city limits, away from the main offices where she worked.

The factory rested within a hole carved out of the dense jungle and surrounded by electrified fences. Regardless of how many times she drove in along the winding two-lane road, she never lost the sense of being sucked into a place where she could disappear without a trace.

Lush undergrowth crawled up and around the fences, masking the steely cage. The looming warehouse even blended in, as well, built of a brown brick the same color as the bark, strangling vines clinging to the mortar.

Security personnel wore camouflage in spite of the sweltering summer heat, assault rifles jacked over their shoulders. She'd once asked why he kept such heavy security around a sweater factory and a few test tubes for mixing dye shades. His answer?

I guard what's mine.

A shiver chased up her spine in defiance of the hundred-degree temperature, chilling the sweat on her skin to icy shards.

Breaks from routine made her nervous. But she would not squander the chance to learn more about Alessandro's business. Even the smallest sliver of knowledge could help her escape this place of choking vines and danger.

Lifting the security pass dangling from her neck, she nodded to the guard stationed at the double doors, mentally recording security placement and coded devices.

Inside the small reception area, a second guard/receptionist waited behind thick plate glass. "May I help you?"

"Lena Banuelos to see Señor Aragon." She dug her heels into the plush carpet and resisted the urge to fidget with the low neckline of her silk dress. Alessandro preferred classic fabrics and cuts, but with a hint of skin. Who would have thought she would ever yearn for a pair of sweatpants and a nappy T-shirt there hadn't been time to wash?

The guard hung up the phone. "He is waiting in his conference room."

Her stomach clenched. She knew that room well from another visit here.

Seconds later the guard buzzed her through, around two corners and at the end of a long corridor. The door swooshed open to his conference area, nothing as elaborate as Alessandro's ornate main offices in the downtown historic district. Simple decor reigned, red leather on a black metal sofa and an array of steel chairs around a large round table.

Walls were covered with fabrics stretched over wooden frames creating splashes of crimson and ebony until she felt swallowed by hellish flames. Not an unrealistic thought when she remembered the things Alessandro had once forced her to do in this room.

She inched away from the couch and the degrading memories it held of the horrible hours spent here, of stumbling to the connecting bathroom afterward to shower and yet never feeling clean enough. Her teeth threatened to chatter, forcing her to clamp her jaws shut. He couldn't have chosen this particular space by accident. He must want to rattle her, but she refused to give him the satisfaction.

The hall door opened again to admit Alessandro—and Scott Cooper.

Her breath slammed to a stop against the knot in her

throat. The air conditioner shushed in the silence, shooting sickeningly familiar floral-scented gusts. She schooled her face to stay blasé rather than risk making things worse.

She should walk over to Alessandro, but she couldn't will her feet to move. "Good afternoon." She nodded, impassive mask still plastered in place. She hoped. "I did not expect to see Señor Cooper here."

Cooper strode deeper into the room, his sway to the side a somehow graceful part of his walk. His muscled strength and healthy tan contrasted with the sallow tinge under Alessandro's olive complexion. Her lover's tailor-made black suit hung from him, cocaine slowly diminishing his good looks.

Her mind filled with memories of unmistakably vital Cooper throwing himself between her and her attacker, in charge, unhesitating. *Dios Mio,* what a balm for her soul to have someone slay dragons for her again. And he hadn't asked for payment, not even a bandage or glass of water—much less the use of her body.

This golden god was far more dangerous than she'd realized.

Alessandro shut the door behind her with an ominous click. "Thank you for joining us out here, my dear. We just finished a walk around the factory. Señor Cooper has some innovative ideas for upping our output."

Lena looked from one man to the other. Innovative ideas? Legal or illegal? Only a few knew the inner workings of Alessandro's dealings. Even she had been privy to very little. How much did this man know?

As much as she wanted him to be the honorable rescuer who'd risked his life for her, a crook would be far easier to resist. "Did you want me to take notes then?"

"No. We're finished." Twitching his head to flick his overlong hair from his forehead, Alessandro stopped beside her, close, too close to be interpreted as anything but intimate even if they did not touch. "Why don't we sit down?"

Her skin crawled, and she couldn't stop a glance to the bathroom door, the need building for a scouring shower.

Alessandro blocked her path to a conference chair, leaving her no choice but to sink to the sofa. Once Cooper claimed a seat across from her, Alessandro took his place beside her.

Black leather clung to her bare arms, perspiration bonding her and reminding her of the horror of another time with too much skin, sweat, pain against that leather sofa. She blinked back dizziness.

She couldn't stand the uncertainty any longer. "If I am not to take notes, then why am I here?"

Alessandro draped his arm along the back of the sofa. "Actually, I called you in because I wanted you here when I thank him for saving you yesterday."

Cooper's eyes lingered on the small fingerprint bruises makeup could not camouflage His jaw flexed. "I'm glad no one was hurt."

Did he know what Alessandro did to her?

Alessandro slid his arm from the sofa back to encircle her shoulders in a rare display of affection at the workplace. Even though everyone knew of their relationship, he kept his touches fairly benign in public.

His hold on her shoulders stayed loose, but implacable. "It's no secret that Lena is a valued friend as well as employee."

Cooper stayed blessedly silent.

She struggled not to wince or angle away. She had endured far more intimate touches from Alessandro than this in private, in this very locale, for that matter. Why, then, did she suddenly feel stripped naked?

She had nothing to be ashamed of. She was saving her child. Soon she would have him safe for good.

Alessandro continued, "There are greedy people out there who would hurt those dear to me for financial gain."

Cooper kept both hands on his knees with a poised tiger aura. "It must be difficult not knowing who you can trust."

So many layers of meaning. She wanted to shout at Scott Cooper to escape while he could, run far away from Alessandro, not just because his world would soon explode, but because Alessandro tainted everything he touched.

"Very difficult." His fingers stroked a slight but unmistakably intimate message along the top of her arm. "I will be quite busy over the next few days with business. I would appreciate knowing that Lena is safely occupied."

And she would appreciate people not talking about her as if she didn't exist.

Alessandro's grip tightened, even though he kept his attention on Cooper. "I need someone I trust to watch out for her."

Cooper didn't even wince, just a simple fast blink to show the comment registered—and mattered. "Wouldn't you be better served hiring a bodyguard?"

"Oh, I have already done that."

What? Lena stiffened, mentally replayed her every step and word for the past week. How long had his goons been trailing her? Watching her? Alessandro might as well have stripped her naked and violated her all over again, because he'd most definitely stolen another piece of her privacy.

Alessandro's arm tensed against her, his body thinning from drug use but muscles still evident, strong enough to harm. "But those incompetents did not keep her safe from the attacker's blade yesterday. You did."

She shuddered at the thought of how that knife could have sliced Cooper.

Alessandro increased the pressure on her arm as if to comfort, his high-priced musky cologne leaving her longing for the simple clean scent of soap.

"I was in the right place at the right time." Cooper shrugged off his role in stopping one of the most horrifying moments in her life. "We're lucky you asked me to check on her."

A putrid notion spilled through her mind. Could Alessandro have set the whole thing up to test Scott?

Cooper.

She would continue calling him by his last name

only, far less familiar. Even in her mind she needed the boundaries, especially if she would be seeing more of him at the office.

"I would consider it a personal favor if you escorted Lena to and from work, through lunchtime, too, until my schedule is clearer again."

What? He would be with her all the time.

This went beyond the scope of his executive duties. She hated Alessandro's sick games, seeming thoughtfulness with strings and agendas attached.

"It would be my pleasure," Cooper agreed as if he had even been given a choice. "No man would ever complain about spending time with someone as charming as Señorita Banuelos."

Señorita? She bit her tongue to stop from correcting him.

"You have my personal gratitude." Alessandro stroked her with his eyes, somehow more intimate than his hands or even the heat of his thigh pressed against hers. "Keep her safe, unharmed, *untouched* and whatever you want, I will make happen."

"No favors are necessary. I work for you now in whatever capacity you need."

Good heavens, this sounded like something from that American Godfather movie—which finished in a bloodbath.

Alessandro rose from the sofa, signaling an end to their meeting. "If you'll call for the car, Lena will meet you out front shortly."

"I'll be waiting."

She peeled herself from the hated leather sofa, her eyes locking on Cooper's retreating back as he left without even a glance in her direction. She remembered well the play of muscles along his shoulders beneath his white shirt.

Hands in his pocket jingling his keys, Alessandro studied the door long after it swished closed before finally turning his attention to her once again. His eyes bore into hers, into *her*, until she struggled not to fidget with guilt.

A smile split his face if not the tension coating the room. He strode forward, one step, two and stopped in front of her, the sofa pressing against the back of her legs.

Sliding his hand from his pocket, he fingered the security pass dangling around her neck. "Do you like him, my dear?"

What was she supposed to say? A piece of honesty would serve. "I think he's arrogant, but smart, an asset to your company."

"That's not what I meant." He traced along the plastic square with her picture, his knuckles grazing her breasts one at a time. "Do you enjoy his company?"

"He is respectful." Something amazingly enticing at a time when she found it difficult even to respect herself anymore.

But she was working to fix that.

"Good. I would not want you to spend the next few days with someone who upsets you."

Oh, Cooper upset her, all right, but not in a way she

would ever acknowledge or act upon. "Why are you doing this? You know that I am loyal to you."

The unwise words slipped free, and she struggled not to wince at her own foolishness. Why push him now, when she was so close to escaping forever?

He flipped the plastic card. The long hair from his side part swung forward over his brow while he toyed with the ID between two fingers, then rasped it along the curve of her breast, further, over her nipple with a hint of pressure. "What is it that you think I'm doing?"

She stayed silent until he looked up at her, flicking aside the long hair with a jerk of his head. Lena studied his pupils for signs he had been using, but couldn't tell for certain. "Why are you having me watched?"

There, that seemed safer than questioning why he would throw an attractive man in her path, a man with barely veiled interest in his crystalline-blue eyes.

"You should be grateful that I did. Otherwise who knows what might have happened to you at the hands of that mugger?" He glided the card up from her breast, to her collarbone.

To her neck, drawing the edge across her throat, the sofa pressing into calves reminding her of options worse than death. "You need me to look out for you."

Suspicion whispered again that he could have staged the mugging to make her feel more vulnerable. He seemed to thrive on times she needed him. She didn't know what to believe other than that Alessandro was capable of anything.

He dropped the card back between her breasts, and

she could not stop her exhale of relief. He slid an arm around her waist, the other caressing her face while that damned sofa waited behind her. "I know I have been neglecting you lately."

This was a problem, why? Much more of his *attention* in addition to the tension and fear, and she would snap.

He palmed her, harder, closer until their hips met. Her nostrils flared at the nauseating blend of his expensive spice and the rose air freshener.

Not here, please. Not now, with Cooper waiting outside and only a handful of days until she could be free.

She willed herself lax in his grip. "I know you're a busy man with many responsibilities."

He liked it when she played to his power. Being a successful mistress involved stroking his ego far more than other parts of him.

"I have business to tie up here this week, but then we will go away for a weekend. Out on the yacht where we can be alone." He trailed gentle fingers along the bruises on her arm, still tender, fresh and a reminder of how quickly this man could turn dangerous. "I want to make things up to you for last weekend, for the past weeks. A woman as beautiful as you deserves to be pampered."

She didn't feel beautiful. She felt ugly and marked and in desperate need of endless showers. For years growing up she had longed to look like the perfect, popular girls, well put together, confident, with all the accessories their moneyed parents could buy. What a fool.

A fool who needed to listen to Alessandro's words. She could not afford to miss a syllable of what he said.

"But I realize I've been selfish in not thinking about your needs. After a couple of days alone, perhaps we could pick up your son to join us."

She bit back a gasp of horror, outrage, denial, and then his lowering face cut off the possibility of answering. Shuttering out sensation, she went through the motions of kissing him goodbye. Just a kiss, thank heavens, nothing more today.

Her mind raced through what he'd said, protectiveness surging through her in elemental maternal waves as old as time. Alessandro had never expressed interest in Miguel before beyond ensuring enough notice for her to arrange for a babysitter.

Even if she would be leaving this life behind soon, she still could not stomach the thought of her little boy even floating through Alessandro's thoughts, much less sharing the same air. Nothing could be as horrible as that.

She had to eliminate Alessandro. And if she died in the process? So be it, as long as she ensured her son's safe passage from Cartina. She'd made her deal to free her child and she would not falter.

First she had to hold herself together during more time with Scott Cooper.

CHAPTER EIGHT

PEERING THROUGH her camera at guns jutting from the side doors of the CV-22 parked on the jungle-encircled runway, Brigid worked to hold herself together. Hopefully, viewing through the lens would provide some much-needed emotional distance so she wouldn't fall apart during her conversation with Joe.

Her research on the six-barrel Gatling gun provided all-too-vivid images of the danger this craft could encounter in the future. Of course, she'd also seen some of that gunfire action firsthand flying with Joe and his crew in Iraq, the gun barrel rotating. Big cans on the flight deck feeding bands of ammo into the guns, brass flying everywhere.

She snapped her photos, refusing to let the job absorb her again. Objectivity would carry her through.

The contrast to another seaside runway in the States didn't escape her. Her photo spread for this piece would make for a mesmerizing comparison. The decay here versus the immaculate starkness of the runway in Florida.

Tropical trees lined the stretch of crumbling cement. Bursts of blooms broke the green monotony with splashes of red and orange, swaying with the salty breeze. A burned-out skeleton of a rusty old plane leaned on its side with vines twining their way through the gaping holes.

She swung the camera back around to the CV-22 a few yards away, waiting with its crew running a pre-flight walk around. Each mission carried the possibility of turning this cutting-edge machine into a burned-out hulk.

Taking Joe with it.

No. She refused to think like that, selfish thoughts of her own fears. Time for her to reassure Joe as soon as they had a solitary moment to talk.

Must be lack of sleep bringing her down. She'd tossed most of the night, finally giving up and kicking aside the fluffy comforter that offered a poor substitute for what she really wanted covering her.

A man.

Joe.

The camera turned heavy in her hands, slowly lowering back to rest against her chest while she studied the man without a glass filter.

She hadn't been alone with him since the day they'd checked in. She'd eaten a room service sandwich with Sonny while they put together an article and photo spread about the bomb threat at the U.S. embassy, based on what little info they'd been able to gather about the false alarm.

By the time she'd arrived at the embassy to take photos, most of the crowd had dispersed. But she'd still snagged some shots. Joe would probably have a cow if he learned she'd hung around to catch the bomb squad, but he'd been safely off mission planning until late in the evening.

Still made for a helluva story. Thank heavens she'd brought along her satellite phone and portable dish. She'd linked her computer right up to her Inmarsat Began, and they'd scooped the rest of the news community.

Wind tore strands of hair free, streaking them across her face and blocking her view of Joe. Brigid tugged off her scrunchie hairband and twisted it around her fingers. The brown fabric reminded her of her old favorite hemp tie, the one she'd given Cooper the last time they'd been together before his final mission— for luck. Fat lot of good it did him.

She swung her Canon back up and pointed the lens toward the joint security forces. She snapped a photo of a South American cop beside the U.S. security police, easy enough to tell them apart even aside from the mismatched uniforms. For so wealthy a country, very little trickled down. Their guns looked like rusty crap, the soldiers ill-trained kids undisciplined in handling their weapons.

And Joe would be flying from this substandard facility.

At the end of the flight line, the trees rustled. She backed a step—only to laugh at herself when a pig trotted along the cracked concrete. Postal broke away and shooed the beastie back toward the jungle with stomping boots and some outlandish permutation of a Polish polka. Brigid welcomed the lighthearted photo after the stressful return to her old job.

The pig scampered back into its nearby natural habitat, startling a squawking macaw from the trees. Nearby habitat? She studied the lush tree line again with a new perspective. The U.S. kept the surrounding areas cleared. She'd always thought of it as aesthetics, but now saw the potential danger of shielded threats lurking close.

Postal knelt to snap off a couple of branches from the bush encroaching on the flight line. He started to fling the limbs into the jungle and paused, tugging off a blossom.

He strutted toward her, a walking contradiction in that uniform, looking more like an escaped convict than a military officer. Definitely a picture. *Click. Click. Click.* Even his buzz-cut short hair with his sunglasses gave off a dangerous, angling-to-make-a-deal air.

"Just say the word." Postal tucked the flower behind her ear. "I'll sweep you off your feet and show you the time of your life."

Vegas snorted a laugh and pulled up alongside Postal. "With a stolen flower and maybe some free samples at a grocery-store grand opening? No disrespect, sir, but you're a cheap-ass. Anybody ever accuse you of throwing around nickels like they're manhole covers?"

"Who me?" Postal laughed, not in the least offended. "I'm merely thrifty."

"We've all seen your car."

"Nothing wrong with an old set of wheels. Just ask the dudes around here." He jabbed a thumb toward the Pave Low parked to the side along with a line of three UH-1s—Vietnam-era Hueys.

Her eyes gravitated to Joe standing with a pilot in Cartina's air force. The past twenty-four hours hadn't given her any brilliant ideas on how to address what would be a touchy subject of reassuring him her feelings for him had nothing to do with Cooper. But the words needed to be said. She owed him that and so much more.

Still, holy guacamole, it would be tough to stay close without touching.

Joe turned toward her, his mouth curving up in a slow smile that smoked through her veins. What the hell was up with that?

Sure she found him hot—make that hott, with double *ts*—but this threatened to singe her skin. How could she be so attracted to two such totally different men?

People had "types," right? Preferences, even for basic attraction, not to mention emotions. Cooper had been a sarcastic, funny extrovert. A lot of bluster and plenty of charm. Whereas Joe was more intense and quiet with his one-liners.

Even physically they differed. Joe tall and lean, with a runner or basketball player's build. Plenty of stark angles to his face, attesting to that Eastern European heritage he didn't talk of often.

Cooper had been shorter, right at six feet tall and with a body-builder's muscles, partly for his Green Beret training and also because he enjoyed the exertion, even pain, of a good workout. Joe got his work-outs on a basketball court or running along the beach with a pack of buddies.

Without looking away from her, Joe angled to say something to one of the South American pilots before starting in her direction. Her mind slipped into a time warp of two and a half years ago. The jungle behind faded.

Trees, desert, it didn't matter. All she saw was Joe—now and then.

She'd met Cooper the day before, and he'd promised her an interview with a combat helicopter pilot if she would agree to a dinner date at the chow hall. He'd been trying to impress her, win her over, and she'd been so interested in being won by the charming Green Beret. She would have had dinner with him, anyway. But what self-respecting magazine photographer turned down the chance for an insider photo op?

She'd waited on a flight line then too, Cooper be-side her, her chemical warfare mask on her other side in case of an attack, danger adding an edge to life.

And there was Joe, striding toward her, dark eyes intense, his helmet hanging from his grip. The whole man so stark and mesmerizing her camera had damn near levitated to her face.

Her mind had already started juxtaposing photos of the two men in action. Cooper with his loose-hipped saunter as if he would get to you when he did and, oh, my, he would make the wait worth it.

Joe, however, walked with steady but purposeful

strides, right toward her until she could have sworn she felt the reverberation of his combat boots through the flight line declaring, *I'm heading for you, only you.* And nothing could stop him.

A heady notion. An all-consuming, somewhat scary tug then—and maybe even now.

So much. Too much. She'd taken a step away—

Right against Cooper Scott's chest. Fun, light-hearted Cooper, and so what she'd wanted in a relationship. She'd been thinking about marriage and kids in those days. Life with a man like Cooper would be uncomplicated, romantic—not like her parents' self-destructive intensity.

Brigid blinked back into the present, only half aware of Postal and Vegas exchanging pointed looks while easing off to the side. She wouldn't let old fears force her to back away again. She knew Joe better now. He certainly wasn't anything like her father, and she refused to be like her dependent mother.

Besides, she wasn't looking for white-picket-fence forever anymore.

Joe stopped in front of her, the pounding of the pavement ceasing, the world going oddly quiet, as well. "Hey, I land late tonight, but how about we grab breakfast together tomorrow?"

Brigid blinked, once, twice. Huh? Breakfast? Breakfast in bed sounded nice, but not conducive to conversation.

She'd seen Joe sleep before, sitting up in the passenger seat when they'd taken a road trip to Arlington

National Cemetery on Cooper's twenty-ninth birthday—the one and only time she'd seen Joe cry for his
friend.

Oh, God, would they ever be able to separate Cooper
from their friendship when so much had been built on
mourning him? "You don't need to wake up early on
my account. If you're worried about me, I promise to
either order room service or take Sonny along."

"Now there's a fearsome protector." He dipped his
head closer to hers, bringing the scent of shaving cream
and soap, which too easily translated to standing naked
in a shower together. "Maybe he could barter your release from an attacker with his doughnuts."

Doughnuts? Oh, yeah, they were talking about
Sonny. "He may look like a teddy bear, but he's spent
some serious time out in the field on assignments."

"I know. Just razzing." Joe tucked a strand of hair
behind her ear. He'd done it a thousand times in the
past, but for some reason the touch seemed more intimate now. "If it's okay with you, I'd rather you knock
on my door and wake me if I'm not up when you are."

Their door. One little flimsy connecting panel between them. "Sure, no problem. I just didn't want you
to feel obligated to look out for me."

"Trust me, you're anything but an obligation."

Warmth spread from her belly upward to her heart—
and lower, too, in a way that made standing still tough.

"Face!" Postal shouted from across the flight line.
"Dude, we need to get rolling."

She glanced at his plane, then back at him. She

would have to ask someday how he'd gotten the call sign "Face." Lord willing, they would have time to discuss it. It was just a demo flight. Still… "Be safe."

"Always."

"Of course." Except she knew that wasn't true. She'd been there with him during the shoot down. His flight engineer blinded. His copilot knocked out. Joe with a broken collarbone protruding through the skin.

And Cooper dead.

This flight line might be in the middle of a jungle rather than some stark desert, but the parallel-universe feeling hit her again all the same. Ohmigod, ohmigod, ohmigod, she so refused to puke on the flight line.

Gulping in deep breaths, she backed toward the observation bleachers cordoned off by security, where the press could wait while the aircraft prepped for takeoff.

Rotors began to spin, stirring the air and noise until she could only feel and hear the vortex created by Joe's plane and her own fears. The spinning propellers swept away the debris and rocks into the surrounding jungle.

The CV-22 rose like a massive helicopter, casting a shadow over her while she stood watching. She couldn't forget how new the plane was in the military inventory. What bugs might still lurk?

To think she'd been so relieved when he told her he was cross-training from the Pave Low to another craft. He'd sworn this plane was safer and could haul his butt out of any situation. But she couldn't get past thinking about "the situation" he would have to haul out of in the first place.

"Brigid?" Sonny's voice broke the fog of fears and nausea.

"Yeah?"

"Pictures."

She glanced down at her camera dangling unused from her neck. "Oh, right."

Pictures. Document the moment, a simple fly around to show off their new toy to Cartinian officials. Nothing spooky or dangerous.

This time.

TIME TO OFF-LOAD their human cargo.

Joe scanned the dense jungle outside his windscreen, his night-vision goggles painting the terrain green and two dimensional. His hands flew over the pristine new control panel and stick, decreasing speed and beginning the rotor rotation process. The heavy jerk never ceased to surprise him, a more violent jolt than in a helicopter that slowed gradually.

The mammoth metal beast hovered at fifty feet over the small clearing while Joe picked his landing spot. Instincts went into high gear as Joe focused on the moment, tuning out the growl of engines until he could only hear the interphone updates from his crew. The weight of his helmet and night-vision goggles anchored him to his seat and in the present far more than the harness strapping him in.

Calls ricocheted from the front and back, load ramp lowering, troops moving toward the door. Once in place, the Special Forces would recon the area for information for the final shakedown when Delta and CIA would seize the factory. If only it could be as simple as arresting Aragon, but they needed to trace his connection to el Jedr first or the fanatical terrorist would simply cultivate a hundred more Aragons.

Joe braced his boots on the rudders, training and instincts working overtime, with an edge since he'd been flying the craft less than a year. As he approached the ground, he drew in even, measured breaths laden with the familiar scent of hydraulic fluid. He needed to keep sharp and well clear of distracting thoughts scratching at his concentration with images of Brigid on the flight line.

Hot.

Sweet.

And doing a poor job at hiding her displeasure at even the sight of a military craft. A fact that didn't bode well for his plan to take her up on the sex-buddies offer.

But first he had to get through the night.

His headset crackled. "Team's clear," Stones, the senior gunner in back, called, with his typical unshakable calm that had garnered his cajones-style call sign.

Joe thumbed his mike button. "Here we go, boys. Time to throttle up and get the hell out of here."

He blinked to adjust his sight through the NVGs, ever ready for a rogue glow to momentarily blind him—the moon, a lone car tooling down a dirt road with headlights—wreaking moments of angst until the blast of blinding white faded and his world returned to ghoulish green.

His hands maneuvered along the controls and stick

as they rose. The CV-22 rotors shifted forward more smoothly, slower, than they rotated up, the overlarge propellers having to chew up a lot of air to get it going.

As the plane roared forward, he allowed himself a small sigh of relief, although their mission was far from complete. They would fly to ten more specified locales in the region, hover, lower the hatch, go through the motions of unloading troops. They'd already stopped at nine random locales prior to the real drop. All a part of their cover of squeezing some extra training out of a demo flight—and masking where they had actually off-loaded the troops in case there had a been a security leak.

Just as he'd done during Cooper's drop, and still things had gone to shit. He would make it right this time—for Cooper, for Brigid and, yeah, maybe even for himself as well.

Joe switched to autopilot for tight terrain-following that would keep them low and well out of any enemy radar. A hard, teeth-jarring ride, since the autopilot adjusted for every hitch and hill, rather than smoothing. But it could fly closer to the ground on a sustained level, with less error overall.

Every time he flew this plane he thought about the difference it would have made in saving Cooper. Being the pilot on that last mission had been some sick trick of fate that stole not only his friend, but diverted Joe's focus in his job.

The mission shouldn't be about avenging Cooper. It should be about defenseless kids and helpless victims who didn't have anyone else to fight for them. Somewhere along the way he'd lost that focus.

They were here to land a blow to terrorism, protect people in the future. How did that synch up with avenging those already hurt? He owed Brigid better than thoughts of Cooper every time he was with her, just as he owed the Air Force his full attention.

Shit. He had to get his head into this mission. This moment.

His hands guarded the controls to take over in case the system failed, his feet poised over the rudders. Vegas reported all engine systems at optimum performance.

Postal studied their chart and the sensors in front of him. With his map in his lap, the copilot cross-referenced data, NVGs strapped to his head, as well. Except, Postal peered underneath to check displays to ensure the craft climbed when it should.

"Terrain at your twelve o'clock," Postal updated. "Three miles out, 6400 feet high."

"Copy," Joe answered, "6400 feet."

"Sixty seconds out from a turn. Gonna be coming right, twenty degrees. Terrain will be falling away."

The plane angled into the turn, nose dipping to lose altitude.

"Road coming, left to right, in one mile."

"Copy, Postal. Can you give me—" A burst of light cut him short. "What the hell?"

The headset filled with Padre's shout from back. "Incoming! Small arms fire at your two o'clock. Break left! Break left!"

On a mission already reminding him too much of the past, the sudden eruption of activity slammed memories one on top of the other faster than the explosive bursts of gunfire spitting from the ground. No time to think. Only react. Joe grabbed the stick and yanked, hauling the plane left and away from the threat.

Gunfire popped from below, sparks of white that blazed across his screen and threatened to bring them down. No choice but to return fire. He was more concerned with not being shot down, than not being noticed.

He called the order to the back to return fire—seconds later *brrrrppppp, brrrrppppp, brrrrppppp* sounding from the back as the gunners engaged the targets.

He thumbed the mike, contacting their joint-task-force command through SATCOM—satellite communications. "Taking fire at point Oscar."

"Roger that. When you have time, report back with an update."

"Copy."

He banked the airplane, tighter, faster, while Sandman returned fire from the door as they swept past and away. From the tail, calm as ever, Stones reported a mini explosion in the background, likely a small vehicle blowing up that wouldn't continue shooting at them.

His heart thundered in his ears. No emergency calls had come over the headset, so he assumed his entire crew was unharmed, but a little affirmation would sure be nice right about now. His head still reverberated with memories of that last mission in Iraq—his flight engineer screaming and blinded, Cooper's voice fading away in a roar of explosions.

Joe swallowed hard. "Anybody other than me piss themselves?"

His headset filled with everyone checking up—Vegas, Stones, Padre, Sandman. Finally Postal piped in with his A-okay, and no follow-up quip.

They would have to hope their previous hovers provided enough cover for the troops on the ground to fade into the landscape. And just because the bad guys had spotted the plane didn't mean they had a clue about the specifics of the mission. "We'll scratch the final hovers and haul butt back to base."

Back to Brigid. His head hammered with that goal.

Adrenaline was no doubt screwing with his mind, but when mortality made a near miss with biting a man on the ass, priorities lined up nice and neat. Being with Brigid ranked number one in line. To hell with all the rest, they'd work through that later.

He intended to make her morning a breakfast feast to remember.

MORNING SUNLIGHT pierced Cooper's sunglasses, even with the max UV protection. Coastal rays blazed, glinting off the geyser spraying from the stone fountain outside Lena's apartment building.

He was all for gas conservation through carpooling, but this was ridiculous.

Sure he wanted to cultivate Lena Banuelos for information, but even he hadn't expected Aragon to make it this easy. Why didn't the man simply send a car for her along with a few extra thugs? Who was being tested? Him or her?

He would have to dance a careful two-step between fulfilling Alessandro's orders to stay close to her, and dodging the urge to get a helluva lot closer. Sadly, dancing wasn't exactly a one-legged man's forte.

Cooper walked up the side stairs leading to her second floor apartment over the export rug shop. His knee rubbing against the fitted prosthetic hurt like a son of a bitch after the way he'd twisted it in the street fight with Rodriguez.

Amputees could lead active lives, even athletic lives. A few servicemen had even made it back onto active duty. He'd actually considered that route, but the CIA recruiter had convinced him since the world already thought he was dead, he had a rare opportunity to do more good for his country by going undercover.

Greater chance to avenge his dead comrades? Easy choice. He'd been fitted with a computerized titanium and graphite prosthetic leg that had helped other war vets return to athletic lives. The microprocessor sensors built in monitored strain to the leg fifty times per second to make rapid adjustments for speed and balance.

He knew damn well he was luckier than most of his

wounded comrades. And he would *not* jeopardize this operation because he had a hard-on for some woman, a woman he didn't even particularly respect. What was it about her that drew him?

Even if he decided to work his way past the awkwardness of explaining, "Hey before we get naked together I should tell you I'm missing half a leg," he went for women opposite of Lena Banuelos. Opposite of his overprivileged, loose-moraled mother who'd damn near trashed his life, would have succeeded if it hadn't been for Joe's judge daddy pulling Cooper's butt out of the legal fire.

He might be balancing on one foot these days, but he refused to allow anything to shake up this op. He wouldn't let personal feelings interfere with bringing justice for his men.

His hands fisted at his sides, and rather than force himself to relax, he simply rapped the knuckles of one clenched hand on her wooden door.

And waited. She probably liked keeping men hanging around at her beck and call.

Finally, the door swung open to reveal a breathless Lena, shiny black hair swirling around her shoulders in a way that made her more approachable. Sexy-mussed and natural, silk shirt untucked from her pencil-thin silky skirt, feet bare of standard high heels. No plastic princess facade in sight today, and holy crap did the image ever catch him right in the solar plexus with a visceral heat.

Just a woman. Not anyone special, he reminded

himself. Even if he had been panting after her for six hellish months.

"You're early," she snapped without even a simple *buenos días*.

So much for saving the woman's life—even if it had been a setup. "To be early is to be on time."

A small laugh filtered through her frazzled frustration. "That sounds like something a military general would say."

Crap. He'd said that very thing to his men a hundred times.

Scott Cooper and Cooper Scott were two different men, and he needed to remember that. "Just a guy with a full plate at work and not enough hours to accomplish it all."

"Spoken like a true workaholic. Give me a moment to finish up and find my shoes." She glanced behind her and back out again. "Uh, perhaps you would like to wait in the car?"

"For the safety of my intestines."

She smiled, and he realized he'd never seen her smile. Not really. She'd curled her lips before, gone through the motions, and he hadn't even known what he was missing until she unleashed the real, full-wattage deal.

He didn't own shades strong enough to protect him from the blinding rays.

Cooper shifted his weight off his bad leg, the knee joint almost as raw as his desire for this woman. He couldn't actually say her smile made her prettier, because that wasn't necessarily the case. She actually looked a little awkward when she smiled, her nose crinkling up while she looked down at her feet as if embarrassed to be caught grinning.

Her veneer peeled away to reveal a woman who appeared—ordinary. Normal. And somehow all the more beautiful in a way he couldn't pinpoint other than she seemed…good, even innocent. Traits he'd once been drawn to and now knew he was long past.

Cooper fished his keys from his pocket again. "I'll be right outside."

He started to turn when a flash of movement from behind Lena snagged his attention. Someone was inside with her. Muscles bunched with tension.

Another man? By her invitation—or as a threat? He couldn't tell which seared his brain more and that royally pissed him off.

Regardless, he had to assume for now that it could be a threat, because of his job and because Aragon had requested he look out for Lena. The mugging had been a setup, but that didn't negate the reality of her lover's dangerous connections to underworld figures and terrorists. A woman alone made too easy a target in this country, particularly in this unsecured building. Why the hell didn't Aragon set her up someplace safer?

Cooper reached inside his jacket for his 9 mm tucked in a shoulder harness, easy enough to explain away now, given Aragon's order to protect her. His heart slugged a slow, hard, ready beat. His eyes scanned for the flash of action, homed…

Down.

Knee level. Where sure as shit, a male stood peering around Lena's legs.

"Buenos dias, señor," a boy of around four or five whispered, a sturdy kid with chocolate on his face and wide dark eyes to match. Eyes just like the woman standing with him.

Well, hell. Cooper's hand eased away from his gun. So much for keeping the world steady, because right now it felt like someone had kicked his computerized titanium and graphite prosthetic leg clear to Canada.

CHAPTER NINE

"MORNIN', BEAUTIFUL."

Brigid slumped against the connecting doorway between her room and Joe's, staring through bleary eyes at him all freshly shaven, wearing dark pants and a black silk T-shirt. *Hello.* Not wearing his preppy-blah clothes today at all. But then, she'd bought these for his thirtieth birthday, and *damn* but he looked hot.

Make that a two-*t* hott again.

And very awake, unlike her. "No fair you look so good and I still haven't even brushed my teeth."

"You look amazing in the morning." He gave her a leisurely once-over—and smiled. Oh, baby. "As a matter of fact, you should probably pull back all that incredible wild hair so I don't have to beat the other men off with a stick."

What was with the Romeo act? She'd seen him romance other women, but the flirting had never come her way.

She eyed him suspiciously. He *had* flown yesterday, and he usually had an extra edge after a mission. He loved the sky, no question. Maybe that accounted for his smoky mood. "How can you be this chipper after getting in so late last night?"

"You know when I got back?"

"I was working on an article with Sonny."

"Until three?"

Busted. "You're noisy."

She clutched the gaping front of her chenille robe over a ratty cotton sleep shirt, kicking herself for not wearing something a little more attractive. Except, she was supposed to be taking a step back, renewing her friendship with Joe and tending to his needs now.

Needs?

Hmmm… Poor word choice.

Feelings. She wanted to be more considerate of his feelings, as he'd been of hers. "I couldn't sleep until I knew you'd made it back okay."

"You were worried."

"Of course I was."

Brigid chewed on her bottom lip and yearned for a cup of coffee—and a hairbrush. She'd spent a lot of restless hours checking the clock, kicking aside covers, listening at the connecting door, afraid to knock, but more afraid of what could happen to him during a flight in a foreign country.

Yes, their friendship went deeper than she'd thought. She couldn't imagine her life without Joe— as a friend, someday lover, perhaps.

She released the neck of her robe and rested her hand on his wrist, hot skin sprinkled with bristly hair tingling a wake-up jolt more effective than a double-shot espresso. "After what happened two years ago…" She drew in a bracing breath. "It's too easy for me to envision what can go wrong."

He cupped the back of her head, typical Joe offering comfort. "Hopefully we'll walk away from this with some answers as to why Cooper died that day."

"I wasn't talking about Cooper's ambush. I was talking about when—" her fingers gripped tighter around his wrist "—your helicopter got shot up."

His head tipped to the side, almost as if he might kiss her, then he frowned. "Let's take this talk inside."

Joe stepped forward, the bulk of his body invading her space. His eyes homed on hers, he continued to walk, backing her in a tandem tango of intimacy. His heat radiated over her until she tingled all over, her breasts drawing tight and hard against the silkiness of her nightshirt under her robe. She squeezed her legs together against the ache pooling low, begging to be eased and opened and released.

Why had she never realized how tall he was? Towering over her in a way that didn't intimidate. This was Joe. They'd been alone together a ka-billion times. She knew him.

Or did she? The sexy-eyed stranger staring at her mouth had her struggling to remember her resolve to have a meaningful conversation with him.

She really, really needed to find her toothbrush.

"Hold on a second. I just need to, um…" Her butt bumped the desk with her laptop and color printer.

She spun away from him to the sink for... Jeez, her brain had gone on stun. "Need to freshen up."

Brigid skirted past him to the vanity. Spitting and rinsing might not be glamorous, but it sure beat morning skunk breath. Just in case.

And wow, even the thought stirred up visions of slow and easy early-morning sex that lasted into intense midmorning sex. She swallowed down a glass of water, leaned to replace the cup and toothbrush.

Her eyes collided with Joe's reflected in the vanity mirror.

He stood a good two feet away, but she couldn't suppress the fantasy image of him stepping closer, closer still and covering her body with his, taking her while their eyes stayed locked in the mirror.

She wasn't so innocent that she couldn't see he was thinking the same fantasy. She hadn't been mistaken about his deliberate touches on the runway.

For some reason he'd changed his mind about them sleeping together.

Part of her argued to jump at the reprieve from conversation. Hell, jump him. Then they wouldn't have to discuss squat, much less about how his job scared her and how she was a real wimp for not being as good a friend to him as he'd been to her.

No. No more wimp. No more hiding.

She straightened, tearing her eyes away from his, her flaming body shrieking in protest.

With shaky hands, she scooped a brush and green

hair scrunchie from her travel bag. She scraped her hair back from her face with brutal swipes.

Joe stepped nearer and she brushed faster. He reached, gripped her wrist and took the brush from her. Her hands fell to her sides, her hair slithering down her back. Static electricity lifted wisps to cling to his shirt as if reaching for him since she didn't dare.

Leaning, he replaced the brush, his hard body grazing hers for a lightning second before he straightened to rest his hands on her shoulders. "I wouldn't have let anything happen to you that day."

What? Her brain scrambled for reason through the fog of passion, struggled to think of what they'd been talking about. That day. When his helicopter had been blasted in midair.

And he thought she was talking about losing Cooper or dying?

Brigid turned to face him, her hand falling on his chest—whoa, wait, she hadn't meant to do that, but oh, baby, silk warmed from his body urged her fingers to curl in time with her toes.

She had to clear her mind and let him know how she felt about him, separate from Cooper. "I'm not talking about me, and I'm not talking about Cooper. I'm talking about *you.*"

"I'm not following."

"*You* almost died that day, too." And no matter how much she'd loved Cooper, she been very aware of Joe's injuries, how close she'd come to losing a friend who'd already started to become special to her, as well. "I may have been a mess, but I saw what was going on around me. I heard."

Her hand glided up his chest to cup the side of his face, tears burning the corners of her eyes and memories. "When the blast hit, I thought I'd lost you."

Her words blindsided him. Joe worked to sort through them when the room was so thick with the scent of her he could get drunk on just the aroma of Brigid and a hint of minty toothpaste.

He wanted her and intended to have her, but slowly. Good sex had a lot to do with the buildup. Okay, so he'd been building up for over two years, but he needed to think about her, and she was trying to talk to him about something important.

"Joe?" Her voice pulled him back. "I unstrapped."

"What?"

"During that flight, when you shouted—"

"Shouted?" He'd shouted a lot of things that flight, commands, curses.

"When you were hurt."

That, he didn't remember. Other than being pissed because he couldn't use his arm, his body failing him when he had men on the ground to save, people in the air counting on him. "You unstrapped?"

"I didn't think. I just unbuckled. One of the gunners shoved me back in my seat, told me I'd get us all killed if they couldn't do their jobs because they were worried about me, and then it would be a cold day in hell before anyone ever let another journalist onboard a military flight ever again. Like I cared about my job at that moment."

He could see it all in his mind. He owed that gunner a thanks.

She fidgeted with her robe, her emerald eyes clouding. "No question, I was scared for Cooper, but I really didn't think he'd died then. Ridiculous optimism, I guess, or maybe my subconscious's way of giving me time to adjust to the shock. But it didn't seem right or real until his coffin came back."

He understood that well, but figured this probably wasn't the best time to tell her he still expected to see Cooper around the next corner.

"Anyhow, I guess I have a point here somewhere. I was worried about Cooper. But I was also worried for you. We all knew in back of the helicopter that things were bad, but your voice was so rock solid. So confident. You may have been injured, but you had control."

He wanted to tell her he hadn't been in control of jack that day. But even more he wanted to hear the rest of what she had to say.

"Then we emergency landed at Baghdad International. I wanted to go up front to you right away, but they wouldn't let me. The gunner pretty much pitched me out onto the flight line."

"We were evacuating a damaged aircraft in case it blew."

"I didn't give a damn about any of that."

Her hand fell flat against his chest, her fingers rubbing along his heart. Her robe slid open, and he couldn't decide whether or not to hope she slept in the nude.

"Then you came out last, Joe, hauling unconscious Postal in a half-dragging kind of way. Military firemen rushed up to take him. And then do you remember what happened next?"

He sure as shit did. Embarrassing as hell.

"You passed out."

His mouth twitched. "Thanks for the reminder."

She gave him a wobbly smile in return. "I remember the flight surgeon shaking his head over you, saying it was amazing you could fly at all with your shattered collarbone. But it made me realize how far you'll go to save other people. So, yeah, I worry about you out there. And, yeah, I waited up until you got back last night to make sure you'd landed safely because…" She hesitated, this verbose woman suddenly looking at a loss for the first time he could remember. "Because…well…you're you."

Her words shifted in his brain, challenging perceptions he'd held for over two years. Sure he'd known she cared about him. They'd been friends even then. He'd kept his own interest hidden for those five months they'd all been together in Kuwait. There hadn't been a choice since Cooper was his bud and had seen her first. One fucking day earlier.

Back on topic, pal.

They had all been friends, but she'd loved Cooper. He accepted that, another reason he'd kept his distance all this time. She'd had wedding dreams in her eyes then. He couldn't promise her anything long-term, so he wasn't going to wreck her chance with a man she seemed gone on, so totally gone she couldn't see anything else around her. Or so he'd thought.

And just like that, ka-ping, it hit him.

She may have been Cooper's once, but at this moment she was totally clear on who stood in front of her, and that mattered more than he'd expected. Joe stepped toward her, no turning back and to hell with the rest.

Because finally he was about to become sex buddies with the hottest woman he'd ever met.

LENA CLENCHED her son's hand. She bit back her frustration at the late babysitter who'd left her unable to scurry her little boy out of the way before Cooper arrived to escort her to the office.

"It's my birthday," Miguel whispered from behind her leg, his sturdy little arms holding strong with a precious familiarity. "We eat cake for breakfast on my birthday. *Mama* says if we have milk, too, it is okay."

Scooting around, Miguel smiled up with a trust that squeezed her heart. She would do anything to preserve that innocence, even sell her soul ten times over again.

Cooper braced a hand on the door frame for balance as he knelt with only a slight compensation for his right leg. Had he wrenched his knee fighting for her release?

Eye level with Miguel, Cooper directed his full attention on the child.

"How old are you, big guy?" Cooper asked in Spanish.

Her son held up five baby-soft fingers. *"Cinco."*

She looped an arm around Miguel's shoulders and tucked him closer to her side. "I'm still waiting for his sitter. Señora de Guerra lives on the third floor and comes down to watch him. She needs the money. I need the help."

"Aragon Industries doesn't have an on-site day care? Those are becoming quite common in the States."

"I would not want him there with me." She struggled to keep her voice steady, pleasant, so as not to upset Miguel. "He is more comfortable with his own toys, in his own home, even if it is not extravagant."

Lena looked over Cooper's broad shoulder, praying she would see Juanita de Guerra fluttering down the stairs. When Lena had called to check, her neighbor had sworn she would arrive shortly.

Miguel tugged the hem of her dress. "May I show him my presents?"

Cooper glanced up at Lena. "I'm guessing Aragon won't worry about my stepping inside, after all, with your little chaperone underfoot."

Uh-oh. He was too quick. She'd used the convenient excuse to keep Cooper at bay last time. No such luck today. But to turn him away would be more telling than inviting him inside.

She smoothed a hand over her son's tousled curls. "Of course you may show Señor Cooper your gifts."

Miguel dashed away, his cheer sailing behind him. He had so little time with adult males, a void she promised herself she would rectify once she made her fresh start. Alessandro truly would have gutted any man lingering around her or her child.

Cooper shoved to his feet. "So Aragon does not provide for him then?"

His assumption sunk into her soul with a thud. She hadn't even considered he would think… "Miguel is not Alessandro's child. We have not—" she struggled for the right word in English, wondered if there was any kind word in any language for her relationship with Alessandro "—been together for that long."

Although the past months certainly felt like forever.

"I didn't mean to pry."

"Yes, you did."

He grinned without answering. Miguel thundered back into the room, two shiny new trucks with over-large wheels clutched in his hands. "Watch this."

Her son raced the vehicles along the curved sofa back. Cooper strode nearer to Miguel, confusion marring her god-protector's confident brow.

Words bubbled inside her to fill the awkward silence. "He loves his trucks, lines them all up along his wall every night and won't go to sleep until they're just right, largest to smallest. Which seems a very smart thing to do, but then I guess all mothers think their children are the brightest."

She chewed on her bottom to lip to shut herself up, but having him in her apartment left her somehow breathless. Surely only because she had so few visitors. None, actually, except for Señora de Guerra.

And, heavens, but her manners were becoming rusty.

"Would you like some coffee while we wait for the

sitter?" He didn't answer, just moved closer to her couch. "Señor Cooper? Coffee?"

He glanced back over his shoulder, studying her as if meeting her for the first time. "Sure. Two sugars. No cream."

"Two sugars." She inched away, then pivoted into the small kitchen nook.

Seeing her with a child should not have affected him that much unless he had given her much thought. And if she trespassed into his thoughts—his dreams—as often as he invaded hers, then heaven help them both.

She looked around her tiny flat, viewing it anew through his eyes. A few pieces of furniture remained from her old home. She'd sold off the hardwood antiques, but kept a sofa set, although they both slept on mattresses now, instead of towering four-posters.

However, the less she had, the more room Miguel had to run in their tiny new home. She spent her money on toys these days rather than overpriced lampshades.

Still she'd kept one of the Limoges teacups from her wedding set. The bone china reminded her how fragile life and security could be. She pulled the sturdy old ceramic coffeepot from the hot plate and filled the delicate cup. Every time she drank from it, she remembered to keep her priorities in order.

They had been well-off. Before. Or rather Miguel had been well-off. Then he'd died in a plane crash. He'd left no insurance and she had no training to support herself, no money remaining because he had been in the middle of a major buyout of another corporation.

Once he died, the stock confidence fell, leaving her with a pile of shares worth a fraction of Miguel's buying price. She'd pawned all she could while waiting for a visa out of the country. There hadn't been enough time or connections.

Now she would make her own connections. She just prayed she had chosen her allegiances well.

She spooned two heaping scoops of sugar into Cooper's coffee, trying not to think about the intimacy of knowing he had a sweet tooth. She would not, would *not* offer him a piece of her son's birthday cake.

Where was Señora de Guerra?

Cradling the warm china in her hand, Lena returned to the living room to find…chaos.

Cooper had pulled the cushions from her sofa and formed two into a vee tunnel for her son's truck. A winding roadway of white paper stretched across the rug, with throw pillows creating mountainous swells.

One leg crooked up, his other extended, Cooper's godlike beauty became enhanced all the more by this peek at his humanity.

He looked up at her, the god and human mixing into something worthy of a Greek myth she'd once read in school, Dionysus, perhaps. The god of wine, a man of mystery. Hair burnished by sun and grace, Cooper only needed brass-plate armor and a sword, which her fertile imagination too readily supplied.

She blinked to moisten her contacts, dry from staring. How silly that she would still hold to such youthful dreams, because an adult view showed her well the other side to those myths—of gods who took on false forms to seduce unsuspecting mortals while promising rescue. But oh, how this mere mortal was tempted by the lure of crystalline blue eyes, muscled arms and a face full of beauty and strength that only promised to grow more appealing with age.

She desired him. Simple passion, of course. And so very wrong, yet she could not shake free of this attraction she had only felt once before in her life.

No, no, no, echoed through her. She didn't want this. Refused to accept it as anything more than her raw nerves short-circuiting because she knew too well how easily promises were broken by mortals and fate.

Even one kiss from this man could lure her straight into the flames of hell.

HOLY GUACAMOLE, Joe sure was a helluva kisser.

Brigid gripped his shoulders and held on for dear life because her knees went unhinged right about the time he made the first swirl, swipe…oh, yeah, do that again, pretty please.

Ahhh, but this man had a special talent. She should have clued in the first time they'd gone to a local beach hangout, and he'd tied a cherry stem into a knot with his tongue. Quite a nifty bar trick, especially when coupled with one of Joe's sleepy-lidded sexy smiles afterward.

And ohmigod, now the image of him working the cherry stem into a twist launched thoughts of other things he could accomplish with all that oral dexterity. She should have suggested the sex-buddies notion a long time ago.

A long time ago?

Chilly reality trickled down her spine. Okay, so she hadn't been ready until recently. But still. They could have already been weeks into exploring this incredible sensation of hot, moist need.

With a heat this strong, weeks could become months. She couldn't think in terms of years, as that required a level of commitment she didn't want to consider. But hadn't they already been friends for over two years? So what would happen after the passion faded?

Except she could only think about what was happening to her right this very moment, with her nerves crackling back to life. She dug her fingers deeper into the broad stretch of his shoulders. He leaned her back, and no way did she intend to protest. His knee braced on the edge of the mattress as he lowered her further still until she felt the giving softness of the comforter beneath her.

Bed. They were finally on a bed together. She may have dreamed of stars and a beach for their first coming together, but she wasn't in the mood to be picky. No way, no how.

And, uh, no stopping please, which meant no thinking, just feeling and savoring the raspy glide of his hands parting her robe, then tunneling up her cotton nightshirt. He gathered threadbare fabric, bunching until he reached her hip, cupping in a firm hand while the other stroked over her breast. The weight of him anchored her into the giving plushness of the comforter and the moment. The hard strength of his thigh rested between her legs, pressing ever so slightly.

Deliberately?

He nudged against her with gentle friction. Yep, definitely deliberate, especially with his erection branding an undeniable heat against her stomach.

She arched against him, closer, wanting, craving to be nearer as his body rocked a slow roll of hips against hips, a tantalizing hint of things to come. So much feeling, so fast, her head spun in a dizzying swell that left her gasping when she longed to respond, give back.

Her heart knocked against her ribs, begging to be set free before it exploded. Louder, harder, the need all but rattling inside her, filling even her ears.

Wait.

The doorknob rattled, twisted.

She shoved against Joe's shoulders. "I think someone's trying to come in."

His whole body tensed over her a second before Joe rolled to his feet, gun in hand, when she hadn't even seen him draw it.

CHAPTER TEN

JOE GRIPPED his military-issue 9 mm in both hands, mentally kicking himself for getting so wrapped up in the feel of Brigid's skin that he'd forgotten where they were. Hell, right now he wasn't sure he could spell his own name.

Thank God for training-honed instincts.

He blocked her body with his as the door swung open. A wide-eyed maid froze. Then screamed. Sprinted behind her cart amid a stream of babbled Spanish exclamations. Brigid yanked her robe back together in a mad scramble for the edge of the bed to escape the prying eyes of the guards and flyboys gathering in the hall to check out the commotion.

Postal led the pack. "Well, shit, dude." The copilot scooped up a small bar of complimentary soap from the maid's cart and pitched it into his other hand, lounging against the door frame. "If you want to be alone, no need to shoot anybody. We'll leave without the threat of firepower."

"Feel free to move along anytime." Joe parked himself between Postal and Brigid.

Vegas almost managed to hide his gosh-golly grin

by swiping a hand across his mouth. "We're just heading down to find some breakfast."

"That reporter buddy of yours recommended a doughnut shop a couple of blocks down." Postal pocketed the miniature soap in his jeans pocket. "What do they call them here instead of doughnuts? Pastries?"

Vegas shrugged linebacker shoulders under his Chicago Bears jersey. "Pastries sounds more Frenchie."

Postal and Vegas's inane banter faded in his head as he assessed everyone in the hall. Sandman poked his head out the door, lipstick smeared on his face, living up to his call sign reputation of always being in a woman's bed—like the sandman.

So why weren't the guards screening this floor better?

And why had the guards been down the corridor, rather than right outside? And how in the hell had he missed the maid's knock? Was there even a knock, or could she have another agenda foiled by so many people pouring out? At least the guards were now questioning her, which cut down on the number of people seeing Brigid in her bathrobe.

"Dough and frosting, it's all the same." Postal plucked a couple of minibottles of shampoo and tucked them into his other pocket.

Vegas nodded to Postal's pilfering hands. "Do you think you can fit a roll of toilet paper in those pockets, as well?"

Postal studied the cart, a veritable smorgasbord of freebie toiletries for their penny-pinching pal, then shook his head. "Nah. That would look obscene, don't you think?"

Enough. Joe stared down his copilot. "Postal? Bobby!"

Postal turned, his hand hovering over a tiny bottle of mouthwash. "Yeah, dude?"

"How about take this cooking class outside? And shut the door behind you."

"Sure. No problem." He pivoted back, thunking his forehead. "Uh, Face?"

"What?" Joe snapped.

"Don't forget we have debrief." He pitched the bottle of mouthwash at Joe before tapping the door shut with his tennis shoes.

Debrief. Damn. Joe slumped back against the closed door and shut his eyes to keep from looking at the temptation of Brigid sitting on the edge of a rumpled bed. He needed a second to will away his hard-on and figure out how things had gotten out of control so fast.

"Sorry about those clowns out there. I promised you breakfast, and I should keep one of my meal promises in a timely fashion. Except, I can't think about anything but getting you naked." When she didn't answer, he pried his eyes open to find tempting, mussed— wary—Brigid on the edge of the bed. "What's wrong?"

Her bare feet too pretty and pink and bare, she gathered her hair back from her face. "I know I'm the one who suggested the whole sex-buddies idea."

Ah, Christ Almighty. Here it came. The pullback. His head hurt. His balls hurt. Hell, his whole body ached to finish what they'd started. So he kept his sorry butt right by the door, a safe distance away, until he could figure why she was frowning and why his hands were shaking. "You've changed your mind."

"No!" She hesitated. "Not really."

A hoarse laugh slid free as he crossed his arms over his chest. "A rousing endorsement."

She twisted the loose robe tie around her fingers. "I do want you." She tugged her hands free and shrugged the chenille robe from her shoulders, faded green cotton sleep shirt seductive as hell with her full breasts peaking an invitation. "Maybe you should just start kissing me again, because it was easier to follow through when you were working that cherry-stem-tying magic on me—"

Huh? "You're losing me here, Red."

Keeping up with this woman's logic was tough enough when he had a full supply of blood to his brain, but a hefty portion of his O positive was currently in demand further south.

"With you and your kisses way across the room, questions start piling up in my head. Like how did we go from zero to sixty—"

He was thinking more along the lines of the number sixty-nine, but now didn't seem a prudent time to mention the possibility.

"—and why does the intensity of that one kiss scare me when I know, really know, what I want."

"Scare?" Whoa. The blood flooded back up to his brain in a painful gush. "*Scare* is not a good word in the bedroom or relationship department."

"Maybe that word's a little harsh. I just want to be sure we don't lose the buddies part." She scrambled off the bed and over to stand between his feet, close enough for him to feel her heat even if they didn't touch. "I know it's totally uncool to be discussing this so analytically, and believe me, it's about killing me not to jump your bones right now."

A smile twitched. "We'd be all the talk down in housekeeping if they'd come in a few seconds later."

"I imagine there would be a rush on shamrock tattoos in South America." She started to touch his chest as she'd done hundreds of times before without thinking, but hesitated.

Screw that. He clasped her hand and pressed it against his chest. "Feel it?" His heart hammered against his ribs so hard she had to know. "That's how much I want you, but nothing, and I mean nothing, happens until we're both on the same page at the same time. Got that, Red?"

"Got it, Captain." The spark returned to her green eyes, thank God. "I love how you make me smile without even trying."

There she was wrong. He was trying his ass off right now. "Your smile's important to me."

"And I appreciate that more than you could know." She peered up at him, her hair tumbling down her back just begging him to gather it in his hands. "What if we have sex and it screws everything up?"

"So to speak."

"I'm being serious." She thumped his chest with her fists. "Are you torqued off at me?"

"*Disappointed* might be a better word choice."

"Much nicer than *torqued*." She toyed with the neckline of his black T-shirt, a shirt she'd given him and he'd been enough of a sap to wear for her. "I wasn't checking out on the idea, only looking for some reassurance we're not risking everything."

He covered her hand with his, thumb stroking the inside of her wrist right at her fluttering pulse point. "Oh, there's plenty at stake here, but we both know there's no turning back."

Sealing his promise with a kiss, Joe grazed her mouth once, twice, until she started to open—

He pulled away before he did a dumb-ass thing like topple her onto the bed. "I have to go to work in a couple of hours and no way do I want to rush being with you—when the time *is* right."

"Two hours, huh? You're a big talker."

He wasn't touching that statement, no way, no how. "I heard what you said and I understand. You need a chance to get used to this new phase of the Joe and Brigid show. I can deal with that. You know the old saying about anything worth having is worth waiting for." God he wanted to kiss her again, but he'd waiting for years, he could hold out a little longer. "*You*'re worth it."

"You can be so sweet sometimes." Her bottom lip trembled, inviting comfort. "But I'm the one who started all of this with my out-of-the-blue sex-buddies proposition on my birthday."

He skimmed his knuckles over her cheek. "That's where you're wrong. This—" his touch traced lower from her face along the curve of her mouth "—started long before your thirtieth birthday."

ALESSANDRO LEANED to kiss his mother's papery dry cheek, the scent of her lilac perfume mixing with the tropical garden off the lanai.

Lilac, not the rosy scent she preferred. A tic tugged at the corner of his eye.

He would speak to the staff before he left. She might not appear to know the difference in smells, given her late stage of Alzheimer's. But on the off chance she perceived more than she showed, he demanded things be just the way she would want.

Including insisting that everyone talk to her as if she could hear and understand. "Time for me to leave, Mama. How about I wheel you back to your room before I return to work?"

As always, he asked questions even though he'd long ago given up expecting answers from his now silent mother.

Her nurse rose from her stony seat by the looming statue. "I can take her now, Señor Aragon."

"*Gracias,* but I have her. I will meet you inside for a brief conference before I leave." He wheeled her chair up the ramp, through the French doors while continuing his one-sided conversation with his mother about…Lena? When had he decided to bring his lover into this part of his life?

Most likely around the same time he'd decided he

wanted to meet her son. "You would like her. She has a child, a boy. I know how you enjoy children."

His sisters did not bring their sons and daughters anymore. An old woman deserved to have grandchildren playing at her feet. Lena would see the logic in that, ever-poised and reasonable Lena.

Her coolness offered relief from the searing tension in his life. She calmed him, and he needed her peace more than ever to make it through the week, perhaps even longer since he had now cemented his path for the future in dealing with these people.

His guards at the factory had reported a suspicious flyover. They had sprayed small-arms fire, taken a hit in return, but the craft had been too quick for them to deploy an RPG.

They labeled the flight coincidental, probably just a local drug runner. Or even if it had been a military airplane, the United States Air Force was in the area on some sort of goodwill mission, teaching flights and practicing for an elaborate donation ceremony this weekend.

Another coincidental timing that made his skin crawl with suspicion, but he had his own "in" with the Cartinian military. Carryovers from the old government understood the need to keep outside influences away from their business. He would look into these flights, had already bugged the hotel housing the deployed aviators.

He'd increased his guards at the compound, too, mercenaries actually, ex-military who fought without the fetters of ridiculous rules of engagement that led men to lose their lives out of some misguided sense of honor. Protecting what was his, winning for his family constituted his sole code of honor.

That mantra had carried him through grueling athletic training as a youth. Track, swimming, baseball, anything to push his endurance had offered an escape from home. His performance had also pleased his father—something Alessandro didn't give a shit about. But he had welcomed the momentary peace and normalcy during the few hours when his family came together to watch him compete.

His mother kept each of his ribbons, medals and trophies here. He had even been training for the Olympic baseball team.

Then his father had died of a heart attack from too much…everything. His father had been a man of vices and excess.

However, once the old man was gone, the family didn't need diversions any longer, and Alessandro hadn't needed the escape. He controlled his world for the first time. And what a vast and lucrative empire it was.

He wheeled his mother across the library floor toward the window overlooking the gardens. Portraits of his sisters filled the walls while framed family snapshots cluttered the top of the grand piano. There were no photos of his father, that far Alessandro could not go, even for his mother.

Adjusting the volume on her stereo piping Beethoven classics through the room, he checked the stacker and timer programmed to ensure all her symphony favorites played throughout the day.

His sisters took their turns checking on their mother, but he did not trust their attention to detail or their level of devotion. They struggled with their own burdens and ghosts thanks to their father, and blamed their mother.

Not that he faulted them. Women could not defend themselves. He understood that and accepted it was up to him to keep them all safe. They needed him, just as Lena did.

Adjusting the afghan over his mother's legs, Alessandro checked her face for signs he had the lap quilt situated correctly. "How is that? Better? I'll speak to the help about your perfume."

Pilar Aragon did not even meet his eyes, just stared out at the yard, her fingers tapping her legs as if performing once again.

He wondered why the songs broke through her apparent ennui when he could not. All his life, he had carried the responsibility for her happiness. A young boy slipping into his mother's room with a cool cloth for her split lip. Or offering a pilfered lily from the hall arrangement to help her forget for a moment that her husband slept with every woman, man and heaven only knew what else that crossed his path with enough of a breeze to stir his ever-horny cock.

Alessandro prided himself on his monogamy and restraint. No excesses. Nothing ruled him, not since his father's death. Lena would never bear the humiliation of seeking treatment for a disease brought home to rot her beautiful body.

Sometimes he worried about his blackouts from the

cocaine and grieved over her occasional bruises. But he had never broken her bones as his father had done to Pilar.

He was not violent. Just somewhat rough at times until he could control his passions again.

After the shipment he would stop the drugs—even his moderate usage—and pamper his Lena. He cherished her, after all.

Standing in his childhood home staring at all of the photos around him, he realized he needed to add new ones. His mother should hear the sounds of happiness, life, children. And who better to trust to oversee the ongoing care of his mother than Lena?

His cell phone vibrated in his pocket. He slid the phone out and checked the caller identification number.

The factory.

Everyone in his business knew not to bother him at this time each week, since he always blocked the hours to visit his mother. They understood the importance of following his orders.

What the hell could have gone wrong?

BREAKFAST with a table packed with flyboys wasn't quite what Brigid had envisioned when Joe showed up at their connecting door. But she had to admit, the chaperones provided a buffer while she found her balance again after what *had* happened when Joe arrived.

Brigid jabbed her fork in a deep-fried apple turnover at the cramped downtown café, guitar pluckings from a street side musician adding more flavor to the morning than the dish in front of her. Food no longer satisfied her real hunger. She and Joe weren't sex buddies yet, but they were well on their way with that first kiss.

She'd expected good—okay, *great*—chemistry. She hadn't been prepared for *the best.*

Now she needed time to think, not retreat, just regroup. Luckily, Joe would go to his debrief, which would give her a whole afternoon. Not much time to repair her shattered self-control before they had supper, but she'd take the extra hours.

They'd eaten together countless times over the past two years—alone and with groups. Except they both knew this time would be different. They would be going out as a couple, on a date, as a prelude to something more. After two years of hanging out in a holding pattern, suddenly her life was hurtling forward at warp speed.

Or zero-to-sixty, as she'd said to Joe earlier.

At least the weight of her camera on her shoulder offered familiarity on an upside-down day. While Joe and his crewdog buddies talked to Sonny, she slid behind her camera, snapping a sweeping montage of Sonny interviewing the aviators against the foreign backdrop of vendors, beggars and a limousine. The Air Force flyboys wore civilian clothes, but there was no mistaking their military bearing, matching aviator sunglasses and sharp haircuts.

How strange that Joe, Postal and Vegas all wore the same shades, yet each man shifted "the look." Postal, with his streetwise air. Vegas, athletic stud with an Irish wholesomeness.

And Joe, intense, mysterious, and then he peered over the tops of those glasses... Whoa, baby.

Back to work.

Sonny pushed his plate aside to make room for his portable keyboard. "Dry data sent to the magazine says the CV-22 is responsible for troop insertion, troop extraction, search and rescue. But I need to make this real for our readership."

"It's all about the speed." Postal rocked back his chair, tipping a little farther each time until she wanted to nudge his seat upright before he cracked his head open on the cobblestones. "This plane kicks ass at low level and at night, really cutting-edge stuff right off the assembly line."

"So you've all only been flying this plane for a short time?" Sonny nodded to include everyone at the table.

"Pretty much," Joe added, refilling his coffee cup. "It only completed testing a few months ago. We finished CV-22 specialty training at Kirtland Air Force Base in New Mexico this spring."

"If you both finished at the same time, why are you the aircraft commander and he's still a copilot?"

"He's senior in hours, had already made AC in the Pave Low." Postal righted the chair to reach for the bread basket. "Anybody gonna eat this last roll?"

Sonny nudged it across the table. "It's all yours. If the plane's so new, then how are the instructors trained?"

Postal started to answer, then looked to Joe who waved for him to go ahead in typical Joe fashion, not needing center stage, which somehow claimed a spotlight in her eyes even more.

The copilot tore into his roll and his explanation. "The instructors are mostly dudes from the testing phase, but even so, it's often the blind leading the blind because they don't know much more about this craft than the student." His smile went a little crazy. "Quite a bit sportier than instructors who have thousands of hours in a craft."

"How so?"

Brigid leaned forward on her elbows, more interested in how this related to Joe than to a news story. And wasn't that a lightbulb moment she didn't want to ponder overlong? Shifting in her seat, she bumped someone's foot under the table by accident. She tucked her legs under the table and tried to focus on Sonny and Postal.

"When you start flying, you have two bags. One holds luck. The other one holds wisdom. The first is full, the second is empty. You hope to fill up your wisdom bag before your luck bag runs out. In a new plane, everybody's wisdom bag is empty."

For the first time, Brigid saw the intelligent aviator behind the nutso veneer. She'd always wondered why Joe chose to fly with someone so out of control. Part of her feared he had put his own butt on the line in a savior-Joe fashion to protect Postal. Listening to him now gave her a new—even reassuring—perspective on how they worked together.

"This beast is quite a handful, a lot of airplane with complicated computer systems," Postal explained while slathering jam on his roll, crumbs spraying the table with each gesture. "There are so many screens with so many options that until your wisdom bag gets full and you're operating on instinct, it's easy to lose sight of your navigation system."

"Give me an example."

A tickly brush started along her ankle. She inched her foot aside and glanced down to make sure she'd hadn't placed her camera bag in the way of—

Joe's foot? Sans shoe, he teased his sock-clad toes along her ankle. A shiver skittered up her spine and forward to pull her nipples tight against her cotton tank top.

Joe kept staring over his sunglasses, his foot stroking low, sensual without pressing too far while Postal rambled on.

"No shit, there I was—" Postal paused, winked for the camera and continued, "That's how all our stories start. So, no shit, there I was. We're on terrain following radar for the first time. That's when the airplane uses a radar signal to fly on autopilot, but you guard the controls, hover your hands over in case the terrain-following system malfunctions and decides to fly you into a mountain."

Joe's grazing touch against her skin became bittersweet. She stifled a wince that might well shut Postal up before Sonny had his story. And might also make Joe pull away when she desperately needed the reassuring warmth of his vitality.

Postal's hand soared plane-style over a ceramic crock of jam. "We're zooming along. Next thing you know, because the screens are spinning info faster than we can keep up, somebody hits a button wrong and puts us into hard ride—"

Joe leaned forward, his arm dropping along the back of her chair, his knee brushing hers under the table, staying. "Hard ride autopilot follows the contour of the terrain precisely," he filled in details Postal missed in his enthusiasm of the telling. "No smoothing things out."

"So I'm choking down my peanut butter and jelly sandwich—"

Joe grinned. "Because he was too much of a cheap ass to buy the in-flight lunch—"

"We've climbed up the hill and we get to this cliff." His flying hand angled off the table. "The airplane just drops its nose and dives off the side, trying as hard as it can to follow the contour. Both of us grabbed the stick and yanked back."

Her breakfast jolted up to her throat, the scent of frying meat, dust and dread overwhelming her. And she couldn't stop listening. Like picking at a scab, she continued to soak in details of Joe's near miss, during a simple training exercise, no less.

"Our instructor," Joe joined in the telling, "who was not strapped in as tightly as he should have been—"

"Because," Postal interrupted, "he was enjoying his in-flight lunch he'd blown three bucks on—"

"—bounces first off the ceiling as it dives. Then as

we pull the nose back, he crashed to the floor." Joe's knee started bouncing against hers, his feet itching to get in the action. "There's fried chicken everywhere. And we have less than no wisdom now because our instructor is unconscious."

Joe lived for this. No one could miss the molten tint to his dark eyes when he peered over the top of his sunglasses, the energy in his rumbling voice. The edge, the risk, fueled him. She remembered the adrenaline high well from snapping photos in danger zones, inching so close to death and somehow slipping away just in time. And sure, you were doing it to be a part of something bigger, something lasting.

But God, it was fun and addictive. And deadly.

Her hand fell to rest on Joe's knee and held. She didn't care who saw her. She needed to touch him, maybe ground him just a little as well.

Postal picked up where the story left off. "We've over-G'd this multikabillion-dollar, cutting-edge aircraft. And now to add to our joy, the generator kicks off-line and all our screens go black. So now even if I was smart enough to have radar up, I couldn't look at it. Nothing but us and our bags of luck—which I may have already overtaxed on previous missions."

His arm still around her, Joe stroked her shoulder even while he talked to Sonny. "It's pitch-black outside, and we're right in the middle of some big-ass mountains in New Mexico. We get our wits about us enough to climb away from the ground, but now we have no clue where we are. Then we spot a glow on

the horizon and we aim for the light. As we get a little closer to the light, we see a baseball field."

Postal flew his hand over his plate. "We circle a couple of times looking for a street sign or lit water tower
with the town's name. Nothing. So, in the spirit of all
great helicopter pilots, we hover, share a laugh and land
in a baseball field as they're singing the national an-
them."

Joe turned to grin at Brigid. "Now, that would have
made for a helluva photo op."

She tried to smile. She really did. But her efforts
must have come across as brittle as she felt inside.
Joe's bouncing knee stopped. A frown pinched his
forehead in time with a muttered "damn" under his
breath.

Sonny cleared his throat and closed up his keyboard.

Postal shrugged, quick, apologetic. "I guess it's
time for me to zip my soup cooler. Sorry, Brigid."

"Nothing to apologize for. I've got a stronger stomach than that when it comes to doing my job." Not totally true at the moment, but at least his story reminded
her of something too important to forget.

Time was precious. She hefted her camera to hide
her expression until she could regain control. She
swept over the table again and beyond, to stores buzzing with business, above-store residents shaking out
laundry or lounging with a cigarette. Living their lives.

How could she have been such an idiot to push Joe
away earlier? She knew better. She'd gotten her wish—

that Joe want her, too—and now she'd gone all scared and soft insisting he romance her, when romance, promises and love were the last thing she wanted. She couldn't avoid the obvious. She'd made up excuses to cover the fact that she was scared of "the best."

Joe's dangerous job, the embassy bomb threat, even that poor woman being mugged in this very neighborhood—all of it served as a reminder that she could never be sure what waited around the next corner.

She wanted Joe Greco and intended to take him before fate had a chance to leap from behind the next corner.

CHAPTER ELEVEN

"AH, SHIT." Cooper stared at the Air Force aviators seated in civvies around the streetside café table and executed an instant one-eighty in the other direction. Not his smoothest pivot ever, but he stayed upright and pointed in a new direction. He wasn't in the military anymore.

And speaking of military.

No way. No way in hell could this be happening. Joe. Here. Now, while he waited at the base of Lena's steps for her to finish settling her son in Mrs. de Guerra's care.

Gripping the banister, Cooper kept his back to the table and reorganized his head while the sounds of conversation and guitar music reminded him of how close he stood to that restaurant—and a blown cover. He shouldn't be recognizable from the back, especially given his different hair color and the longer length brushing his collar.

His brain stayed on stun, locked on one fact—his old pal, best friend, Joe Greco, was sitting about a hundred yards away. Cooper couldn't even wrap his mind around the possibility that the redheaded woman he'd seen in profile might be Brigid. Fate couldn't be that pissed off with him.

He'd known Green Berets would be reconning the area around Aragon's factory, with Delta clearing the factory if other agents in place couldn't stop the shipment. And the Air Force flew nearly all troop insertions for missions like this. The Special Ops community was small, so he'd kept an eye on his cover.

Nowhere on any of the rosters had he seen Joe's name listed—and he *had* looked, unwilling to leave the least detail to chance. He hadn't bothered to check on the media coverage, since Brigid had hung up her press pass two years ago.

But the military rosters for this mission—he'd definitely checked those. Too many damn government walls between agencies sometimes stopped the free flow of information.

He'd just smacked one of those walls head-on.

His best bet? Take Lena to work via an alternate route, concoct an excuse to leave the office and check in at the safe house. Then when he returned to work, he would pray his cover hadn't been compromised. "Fuck."

Lena hesitated on the top step leading from her apartment. "You truly do have a foul mouth."

A holdover from so many years in the Army trenches. She should hear some of his old colonels talk. But she wouldn't. And neither would he. He had new trenches now and needed to play by their rules, which currently called for more finesse in communicating.

"Forgive me." Cooper smiled up at her as she descended the stairs with grace and a tempting length of leg peeking from the slit in her skirt. "I shouldn't have used such language in front of a lady. I twisted my knee the wrong way and then must have slept on it funny, so it's not working quite right."

Under-frigging-statement of the century.

As much as it galled him to mention his injury, the excuse offered the fastest out. "Would you mind if we walked rather than took a cab?"

Since a car would drive them right by that restaurant, whereas he could detour with a walk.

"But your knee—"

"Benefits most from being exercised. It'll loosen the kinks." Tough to work out phantom-pain kinks, but he was giving it a go, one day at a time. "I've got an eye on things, and Aragon's goons are tailing us."

He could also talk to her without being overheard in the bustle of people, unlike in a bugged limo, a fact that shouldn't excite him so much. Just because of the information he could extract. Right.

Loser.

He sent the limousine off, and Lena fell in step alongside him as they left the restaurant behind for the pedestrian-packed shopping district. "I thought you said you hurt your *ankle* in a bad jogging accident, not your knee."

Busted. Women always did screw with a man's head. He needed to remember that. "Both."

"I am sorry for prying."

Did she have to look like he might hit her for mentioning his injury? He guided her around a vendor selling touristy blankets outside a T-shirt shop. The spicy scents from open-air grills steamed the air along with exhaust, a combination smell that would always remind him of this place.

Hell, he'd lived here for a half a year, a damn long time. The crumbling stucco so full of history called to him, a man who'd never even connected to his own family, much less a place. But the crime behind all those walls threatened the infrastructure of the whole country. Veneer masking corruption and lies. Much like Aragon. Maybe even a little like himself.

Cooper glanced at Lena's arms. She'd covered them today with long sleeves, whisper-thin fabric gathered at her wrists, the rest of her blouse and skirt a darker version of the same red. She caught him checking out her arms and winced.

A flinch from this haughty woman twisted something inside him, making him want to land a couple of extra blows on an overprivileged bully like Aragon. "Don't worry. It's not like this limp of mine is a big secret."

"Secrets can be a good thing."

What secrets did she hold inside that pretty head of hers? How many of them could he uncover while plucking pins from her gathered hair until it tumbled down her back?

And why was he thinking about that when his cover was in jeopardy? "You're a unique woman. In my experience, women want to know everything about a guy."

"And has your experience been that vast?"

Not recently, and not many since Brigid, who he very much did *not* want to think about at the moment. One woman in his head at a time offered enough distraction. "So you do want to know everything about me, after all."

"Nice dodge of my question about your past. How reassuring to know that there are still men in the world who do not—how do you say it?—do not 'kiss and tell.'"

"Telling brings a third party into the picture, and I'm not one for a *ménage a trois* or voyeurism. I don't share well."

Her pretty red mouth went tight and prim. "Definitely more information than I needed to know about you, Señor Cooper."

"You can drop the *señor.*"

Her heels clicked along the cobbled sidewalk for a good ten steps before she relented. "All right. Cooper, then."

Why hadn't she called him Scott, his first name for this mission? Instincts jangled an alarm, not that he could do anything more than stay on alert and try not to notice the sexy way her accent wrapped around the last syllable of his name. "Much better…Lena."

Good Lord, her name tasted good on his tongue. He bet she tasted even better.

She paused in front of a street beggar playing his guitar, which reminded Cooper of the restaurant and guitarist he'd left behind a few blocks ago. He needed to think about that instead of Lena's smoky dark eyes.

"I am sorry, Cooper, if your knee or ankle or anything else was further aggravated by helping me the other day."

Oh, a part of him was aggravated all right, but his scarred knee, missing calf and foot were the least of his concerns. He needed to find another topic for discussion, one that didn't involve sexual undertones. "So you have a kid."

"Is that so difficult to believe?" Definitely smoky and very irritated.

She was thirty-five—five years older than him—so he should have considered it. Not that her age mattered in the least to a man who'd aged so much in the past two years.

He palmed her back and guided her forward again before Aragon's goons could catch up and listen. "I've been with the company for months. Seems strange nobody mentioned your kid. Miguel, right?"

"Why is my private life any of your concern?"

"Most women keep pictures of their children on their desk."

Not his mom, but then, she didn't work or have a desk. Well, other than the one in the library at their house. She hadn't used the room for reading, though, as he'd discovered after an early dismissal from high school—okay, he'd cut his last two classes—and got an eyeful of his mom banging the pool guy on the antique mahogany desk.

Voyeurism definitely made him nauseous.

He'd beat the crap out of the pool guy—his mom had

been engaged to another man at the time and everyone, including the pool guy, knew that. The pool guy left. The fiancé, too. Good riddance on both counts, Cooper figured.

His mother wasn't quite so happy. She sentenced him to pool-cleaning duties as punishment for disrupting her life. He figured he'd done that the day he was born.

Did Lena feel the same way about her kid, in spite of chocolate birthday cakes and misty-eyed hugs for breakfast?

"I prefer to keep my life with Aragon Industries and my life at home separate."

"You mean Aragon doesn't know about your son?"

Her face paled. "Of course he knows."

He could see that bothered her, and well it should. Aragon wouldn't hesitate to use the kid against her. "Cake for breakfast, huh?"

"He's a healthy little boy. Cake with a glass of milk in the morning will not hurt him just this once." She tossed her head back. "I have to work late tonight and did not want to miss celebrating with him."

Work late? Screwing Aragon on his desk.

And why the hell did that bother him? She worked for the guy and slept with him. Plenty of men and women enjoyed the same setup throughout the world. B. F. D.

But for some reason it was a big fucking deal to him, and that worried him.

"I have to record shipment data for Alessandro. One of the girls in the typing pool took sick and I offered to help out."

On her son's birthday? Odd. And why did she feel the need to reassure him she wasn't meeting up with Aragon?

Could she be playing him with this new innocent act? He didn't know her well enough to gauge. Something he intended to fix, starting now. "What sorts of things does a five-year-old boy want for his birthday these days besides trucks?"

"Probably the same things you wanted as a little boy."

How about a living father, instead of a picture of an old geezer three times his mother's age who'd conveniently croaked so she could spend all his money?

Or he would have settled for a mother who didn't bring home a different man every night. A mother who gave a crap about her kid beyond the fact that without him, she couldn't be the executor of a hefty estate, and thus collect her monthly fee. "When I was five, I believe I asked for a sack of Army men and a couple of Tonka trucks for my sandbox."

True enough, and a piece of his past that wouldn't hurt to relay. Covers worked best when he stuck as close to the truth as possible.

"We do not have a sandbox, but yes, he likes trucks, as you know." Her eyes went soft, less smoky dark and more of a milk-chocolate brown. "And blocks, many blocks to build bridges to drive those trucks across."

"And blow up?"

Her smile filled her lips to plump and kissable proportions. "So you *were* a little boy once."

Forever ago, with Joe. "I even dug tunnels under my

mother's house, collapsed her landscaped terrace once and, man, was she pissed."

"I will watch my potted ferns carefully."

"You're a wise woman." Cooper guided her around the corner of a stucco church, tension easing in his neck with every step of distance he put between himself and that table of flyers. "He seems to be a happy kid, smart, too."

"This surprises you?"

He stopped, waited for her to turn back to him. "How about you quit being defensive for, say, ten minutes at a stretch? Or at least until we get to the office. I didn't mean a damn thing other than to compliment your son and the way you're bringing him up."

Her stiff stance softened, just a hint, but enough for him to see the woman who'd answered the door earlier. "Thank you. And I am sorry."

The church bell in the steeple overhead swung, bonged, the echo vibrating through the ground, and again, continuing through the nine o'clock pronouncement. They should walk.

Instead he stared down into her dark eyes—more of a melting chocolate now—surprised at how small she was, even with her high heels. The top of her head barely reached eye level on him. Except he wasn't looking at the top of her head, but at her face, open and smiling and, shit, he wanted to kiss her. Right here out in the open, even with Aragon's goons lurking, even with his past dogging his cover a few blocks away.

He. Wanted. Her. With a gripping ache much like

the phantom pains that stabbed through where his leg should have been. He *knew* it wasn't real.

But that didn't stop him from feeling and wanting, anyway. "You're welcome, and it's okay."

Cooper couldn't tear his gaze off Lena's lips curving with a smile meant for him. And he also couldn't dodge the certainty that this woman posed a greater threat to his op than any blast from the past waiting around the next corner.

JOE ROUNDED THE CORNER to his hotel room after the world's longest debrief.

The increased security around Aragon's plant had them all on edge—and made extraction plans to pull out the Green Berets all the more complicated. Only a few more days and he could put this behind him. He would be free to romance Brigid the way she deserved rather than half-assed attempts at dinner out when he was running three hours late.

He'd called Brigid to tell her he would be delayed; great way to start their first official date and a real pain-in-the-butt reminder that this wouldn't be the last time his job screwed up plans in his personal life. At least she'd laughed, since he was always late.

He unlocked his door and crossed straightaway to their connecting door without wasting time to change. He knocked twice and the door creaked open.

The lights were off, the room dark too early for bed, and Brigid had sworn she would be waiting for him. Survival instincts prickled to life. His fingers closed around the grip of his gun as he prepped to ease into the room.

"Hey, Brigid?"

"In here." Her voice sounded all right, if a little breathy.

"Everything okay in there, Red?"

"Everything's more than okay and about to get better," she answered softly from across the room.

Now that sounded less like a woman who might have a knife at her throat. Stepping deeper inside, he scanned over the empty bed and chair to the rustling curtains swept to the sides of the open balcony doors.

With Brigid silhouetted in the archway.

The skyline backlit her, the faint rush of ocean waters in the distance. Both hands pressed to opposite sides, she stood wrapped in her fluffy bathrobe—and apparently nothing else. Her bent knee thrust through the front part, baring a length of creamy skin dusted with freckles he burned to trace with his mouth until he swept open the robe.

Joe jerked his gaze upward. The neck of the robe gaped loosely and his mouth went dry. He couldn't miss her intent, and it shocked him still. He'd been certain Postal's flight story would send her running in the other direction. But then Brigid was anything but predictable.

Still, after her hesitancy earlier and her obvious shakes at the hair-raising training tale, he wondered what she really needed. A tough thought to hold on to when he could already taste her.

Her green eyes glinted in a slow glide down his body. Just past his waist, her gaze hitched and her eyes went wide. "Jesus, Joe, since that's definitely not your gun in your pocket, I guess you're *really* glad to see me."

CHAPTER TWELVE

BRIGID BRACED her hands against the open doorway more for balance than seductive effect. She didn't doubt her decision to sleep with Joe, but big decisions launched big nerves. And speaking of big…

Hello, Joe.

She wished she had more control over the situation, setting—and, yeah, her emotions, maybe. Suggesting they get horizontal had seemed far easier back in familiar Ft. Walton Beach. Still, she'd done her best to recreate her original vision for their first time together. She'd spread the fluffy comforter from the bed out on the balcony, draped a sheet over the ornate railing for privacy, creating a haven for the star-gazing sex she'd dreamed of nearly a week ago.

Well, without a 9 mm pointed in her direction.

"Uh, Joe, do you think you could stow that weapon somewhere before you come over here to join me? And I do hope you intend to join me."

Although he didn't move forward, he eased the gun upward so it pointed at the ceiling. "Sorry about that. I was worried with your room being dark this early in the evening."

"It's called mood setting. There weren't any candles handy, so I settled for stars and moonlight."

He took a wary step forward. "I thought you needed more time to get used to us changing things."

"I was wrong. I don't need more time. I need more you." Her gaze dropped down again. "And it seems there's plenty of you for me to have." She couldn't be any clearer than that.

His tensed shoulders lowered, and he placed his gun on the small corner table where she'd spread her photo proofs. "What about your freaked-out reaction to Postal's flight story?"

"What about it?" Her hand slid from the solid wood frame. She could and would stand steady. Not even her fears managed to cool the heat of anticipation firing in her belly, lower still until the robe itched along her skin yearning for a real touch. "Your job scares the crap out of me. I can't lie about that. But it's not like I'll stop worrying if I move to Timbuktu and never speak to you again."

Heaven forbid.

She took in the image of the whole man—her friend, the intense stranger she'd run from, both filling a military uniform that fit him so well he would never leave it behind. And he shouldn't. To discard it for good would peel away a part of him as effectively as stripping away a layer of skin. She would be woman enough to embrace the whole larger-than-life man.

Brigid inched into the room until she stopped face-to-face with Joe. "Regardless of whether we're friends for life or say goodbye tomorrow, I would always regret never having been with you."

He still didn't touch her, but at least he'd finally moved away from the gun. Soon, for the moment at least, he would be hers, every hard-muscled inch of him. "You're okay with things going from zero to sixty in a day."

"To paraphrase my very wise friend, *this*—" she stroked a hand down his face to rest on his chest, tracing along the Velcro-attached name tag "—started long before a day ago."

His heart picked up speed under her fingers, pounding a resounding answer to her pulse. She tugged at her robe belt, untied the ends, letting the bulky chenille fall apart to reveal her bare skin beneath.

Joe's jaw flexed in a way she recognized well. He was struggling for control and that was the last thing she wanted. If she had to launch into this off balance, then by God, he would be toppling right along with her. She took his wrist and brought his hand up under her open robe to palm her breast.

Timber. Look out below. She didn't think her wobbly knees would hold her much longer.

His hand flexed against her, firmer, while his thumb grazed along the inside curve. "I wish I was a strong enough man to tell you we should talk more, that you were right about safeguarding friendship. I can't think of anything right now except burying myself so deep inside of you neither one of us ever wants to think again."

"Count me in on that for a great big ditto," she whispered before stretching into his hand and up to his kiss, his head already descending toward her, fast, hard, a little rough but fine by her.

Her reawakening senses wanted a feast, not parsimonious hors d'oeuvres. She wanted to lick, taste, even sink her teeth into him, and he didn't seem to mind in the least when she nipped his lip, sucked on his tongue, drew her nails down his back.

The whole zero-to-sixty concept became a mind-blowing reality. Restraints sheered away in the speed and torrent of how fast she fell into savoring the sensation of him touching her, tasting her back, teasing her senses to life with his talented tongue in her mouth. Already her body tingled in anticipation of the all-over exploration yet to come.

And speaking of coming—*not yet, pretty please*, she warned her overrevving body. No way would she finish so soon. She would have the rest of her fantasy time with Joe.

Her hands gripping his taut ass still wearing too many clothes, she whispered against his mouth, steering them both toward the balcony. "Out here, please, under the stars. I so want to see that tattoo of yours in the moon-light."

"On the balcony, huh? I gotta confess I'm not into sharing even a glimpse of you with the whole city."

"We're eight stories up and I draped a sheet over the railing so no one can see us." She rocked her hips against his. "I have an outdoor fantasy to fulfill with you."

"More than happy to comply."

Without breaking apart, they walked, her backward, him ambling in synch with his purposeful strides that left her damp, ready, hungry for more. His boots thudded in time with their steps, sending tingling reverberations up through her bare toes, every part of her hyperaware.

Gusts of night breeze swirled around them in humid bands, rustling the privacy sheet with a slight flap and snap, hair clamps securing the corners.

The distant call of crashing waves roared in her ears in time with the rush of blood through her veins. Sounds of traffic and the late dinner crowd below their high-rise haven faded. His hands tunneled under her robe, inching the fabric over her shoulders, his mouth roving over each patch of revealed skin until the world began to shift out of focus.

Easing a hint of space between them, Brigid shoved him to sit in a patio chair. This was her feast, too, damn it, and she wanted more time to sample. She knelt in front of him, unlacing his black leather combat boots, one, then the other, enjoying the masculine mystery of clothing so different from her own.

His boots and socks gone, he started to stand, but she shoved him back in the chair again, sliding her hands up the legs of his flight suit to stroke his muscled calves. "My turn for a minute."

His breathing went ragged. "A minute's about all I'll have left if you keep this up."

"I have faith in you, my friend." How silly to get turned on by the rasp of hair and skin and legs. But she couldn't get enough of touching him after so long of only looking.

Although she wouldn't be averse to seeing more of him.

Slipping her hands free, she crawled her fingers up to his chest. Brigid inched down the zipper on his flight suit, spreading wide the green fabric to reveal the stark black T-shirt stretched along his muscled pecs. She stroked down, abs clenching under her touch until she reached lower and found, oh, yeah, plenty of Joe. Her hand shaped over him to learn the size and feel of him in prelude to learning more intimately.

Encircling with her fingers, she glided down, slowly back up, rolling her thumb over the glistening drop to moisten her downward slide again and again. She rocked on her knees to take him in her mouth, and his moan turned into a growl.

"We'll definitely get to that later, Red, when I've got some staying power. For now, your minute's just about up."

Before she could unscramble her brain to answer, he angled forward off the chair and tipped her back onto the giving softness of the plump comforter from her bed.

His flight suit, T-shirt, boxers disappeared from his body and somehow landed in a pile off to the side. She wasn't sure how and didn't want to take her mind off the hot pleasure of his mouth on her neck, his hands stroking the bathrobe off her shoulder until the salty night air kissed the heated peaks of her breasts seconds before his mouth covered her instead. Moist, tugging, his mouth drew on her while his tongue circled. He palmed her other breast, then plucked until the dual pleasure sent her arching up for more, harder.

She explored the cut of his muscles with her fingers, her lips, her hands stroking his firm buttocks while she tasted the rippling tendons along his shoulders. She slowed her kisses along his faded scar from his injury in Iraq. "It kills me inside that you didn't know how worried I was about you. You wouldn't let them call your parents to fly overseas. You should have had someone looking out for you."

Joe lifted his head to stare down at her, his eyes as dark and deep as the night sky. "I wasn't so drugged up that I couldn't notice you sitting there when I woke up from surgery."

He'd known that? They'd both been so numb then, him from medications, as well as grief, she'd never been certain what he remembered. "I wasn't much of a comfort though, crying my eyes out."

"We were both pretty fucked up."

"Not the words I would have chosen, but they fit." She'd needed to be near him for such a mishmash of reasons. Because he was a connection to Cooper. Because Joe made everyone feel stronger.

Because she'd been terrified of losing him, too. She still was.

She pulled his head back down for a kiss, full, unending in a need to connect. They'd worked so long and hard for this, she feared if she loosened her grip on the moment, it would slip away.

Hooking her leg over his hip in an outward anchor mirroring her inner need, she writhed against the rigid length of him pressed to her until they both grew damp from sweat and desire. The salty taste of his skin echoed the salty breeze stroking over her bare skin. Would she ever be able to walk along a shoreline again without remembering this night?

His hand skimmed over her stomach, lower, fingers parting, dipping, teasing damp flesh and drawing tingling nerves tighter. He slid from her and she must have whimpered because he shushed her with a brief kiss before trailed his mouth in a nipping path down her stomach, further still until he nuzzled then caressed. No wonder he could tie a cherry stem into a knot, and holy cow he was tying her insides into knots with his deft stroking, circling, flicking, pressing and releasing at just the right moment to increase pleasure, higher, higher still.

She tried to keep her eyes open to savor the stars above in this incredibly elemental moment, but her lids grew heavier until she could only close her eyes and feel. This whole sense of *best* must be from years of abstinence and a body thirsty for touch, connection; and Joe did have such an amazing way of touching her.

Sparks showered behind her lids like an overbright camera flash that blinds even as it illuminates, stinging her inside and out with an almost painful completion that built into another imploding release. She screamed, couldn't contain it, didn't want to hold back anything anymore.

Slowly the tension dispersed inside her and she sagged back into the comforter. Joe pressed a kiss to her hip, so sweet tears stung behind her lids, no surprise, her emotions raw, her defenses blown away.

"Birth control." His voice rumbled his chest against hers as he glided up her body to cover her. "In my wallet."

"You packed for this trip?"

"I may have been planning to keep my distance but I'm not a total idiot."

"And neither am I." She slid a hand under the comforter and pulled free a small packet she'd tucked there earlier when setting their starlit stage.

He slid the condom from her hand and sheathed himself while she watched with hungry eyes. Nerves tightened inside her stomach. Things were about to change between them forever. She already knew sex with Joe would be amazing, but what about after? Did she have enough savvy in this department to avoid what promised to be awkward?

She hadn't done this often, and she didn't take the moment lightly, even if they were in agreement on staying friends. She'd only been with two men—a guy in college she'd thought about marrying, only to realize she didn't know a thing about love. And Cooper—whom she'd also thought she would marry, have his babies and laugh through the years together.

Damn it all, she didn't want to think about Cooper now, and she most definitely didn't want to think about marriage. Plenty of heartbroken women vowed friendship and companionship were the way to go, easier, no complicated messy emotions. And if there was some toe-curling passion to go along with it? Then lucky her, lucky Joe.

Lucky *them,* and please, could Joe speed up his tor-turously thorough foreplay so she wouldn't have so much time to think? Then his erection nudged between her legs and she couldn't think at all, just anticipate the thick, full, pressure of…*yesss*…having Joe inside her. Finally.

The moment went as still as their bodies. She opened her eyes she hadn't even realized she'd closed again and found him staring back down at her. The déjà vu sensa-tion slammed through her anew, reminding her of the first time she'd seen him, intense, so much, almost too much.

But still he held her, too mesmerized to run, with just the power of his darkening eyes probing her soul as deeply as he thrust into her. He held, waited, giving her time to stretch, adjust, somehow become accus-tomed to a man who filled so much of her life and body, more than she'd expected on any level.

Then he moved, withdrawing and pressing home again with a firm rock of his hips that rubbed the perfect friction inside and out. She clamped internal muscles around him, her orgasm having left her passion-swollen flesh oversensitive, each thrust sparking fresh showers of light that increased as he pounded faster. And faster still as she gasped for more, even though she was certain there couldn't be a second orgasm in her future so soon after the all-encompassing release minutes before.

No problem, because just being with Joe, him inside her, her all around him, felt so toe-curling good. She locked her arms around his shoulders, her legs around his hips, and let her body find a matching rhythm to his, much easier than she'd expected. No awkward mismatches or bumped noses.

"Want this," he hissed between his clenched teeth, "to last longer."

"We'll have longer later." And they would. Problem was, right now she couldn't imagine how much of something this good could ever be enough.

"Damn...straight. And next time I won't be coming off two years of waiting."

Two years? Of waiting for her?

His words tore through her, leaving her open and vulnerable, totally blindsided by the explosion inside her, completion catching her so by surprise her arms flung wide. She grappled, clutched the railing, iron latticework cutting into her tight grip, even covered by a sheet. Aftershocks gripped her, spurred to stronger heights again by Joe's body tensing over her, his shout hot against her skin before he fell to rest on top of her.

Somehow she managed to flop her arms around his shoulders, perspiration sealing their skin while he continued to throb inside her. He turned his head to brush a kiss across her mouth. She smiled up at him, finding eyes so dark she could fall into an abyss no flash could illuminate. A sadness swirled in with all the heat and throbbing nerves, a need to lighten the darkness inside him.

She'd gotten her starlight night of amazing sex with

her best friend. Simple, uncomplicated, right? As if. She'd been fooling herself.

Nothing with Joe would ever be simple again.

JOE RECLINED on his side beside Brigid on the blanket and watched her sleep, bathed by moonlight.

He stroked aside strands of long auburn hair clinging to the perspiration on her chest, taking his time to learn more about this new lover who also happened to be his friend. A freckled friend. Gathering up a lock of her hair like the tip of a brush, he painted the freckles along her shoulder, lower, tracing the tip across her breast. Even in her sleep she responded, her breasts tightening as if reaching toward him, her back arching a hint with her sigh.

Primal possessiveness pounded through him, and he didn't even bother stemming the tide. No one was around to see the way he looked at her or held her—thank heaven, since he was lying around bare-ass naked with a shamrock tattoo on his left cheek.

After their first time together, she'd traced the tattoo and asked what made him decide to burn his butt with the imprint of a green clover. The story involved too much Cooper at a time he really needed his friend to stay away from his thoughts. So he'd rolled her on top of him, which stopped any further discussion about tattoos.

He'd waited a long time for this woman and compromised a couple of his own principles to have her. Joe flipped to his back and stared up at the sky, searching for some kind of heavenly absolution from his long dead friend. Silence echoed back from Cooper, the stars, God.

His conscience.

Regardless, he didn't have an answer. Just a sure knowledge that even with the guilt dogging his shamrock-tattooed butt, he could not bring himself to turn away from Brigid.

He thought about waking her, his body already hard and totally awake even though they'd already been together twice in the past two hours. He burned to cup her hips, maybe slide his hand forward and lower to tangle his fingers in soft red curls—but the dark circles under her eyes stopped him. The past days had been hell for her.

Kneeling, he scooped her into his arms. She stirred, then settled against his chest, eyes still closed. Flinging an arm over his shoulder, she nuzzled his neck with a sleepy sigh. The soft fullness of her breasts pressed again his chest, so damn perfect.

Move, feet. He carried her back into the room.

He lowered her to the bed, her bed, when he really wanted her in his. But only an idiot would have missed her wariness. She'd sworn she wanted this. He believed she did. That didn't mean she wasn't scared. Hell, being with Brigid had knocked him back on his heels more than a little. He just had to hope she didn't run anytime soon, because he sure as shit couldn't let her go.

Retrieving the bedspread from his room, he draped the comforter over Brigid, allowing himself an uncensored moment to watch the way she flipped to her back, splaying red hair across her pillow. His erection twitched, urging him to crawl in alongside her.

He needed a few minutes more to get himself under control and she needed sleep. He didn't regret being with her, but still couldn't avoid the need to look over his shoulder for his bud's fist to come flying.

Damn. And he ragged her for not being over Cooper.

Joe looked away from snoozing Brigid, scanning the room for something to distract himself. He didn't want to leave her just yet, and a shower would probably wake her. They would get to the shower—together—soon enough.

Padding across the bare wood floor, onto the wool rug, he made his way to the corner table, a pile of photo proofs scattered along the marble top. He leafed through one page after another packed with rows of miniature proofs, calling up that new perspective she'd challenged him to use.

Joe dropped into a chair, coarse fabric against his bare legs making him wish for a second he'd put on his boxers. He shuffled aside the photo sheets on top of the Cartina National Air Base—a piece-of-shit place that almost cost him an engine when they'd barely avoided ramming a cow at landing.

Cows and crappy runways were the least of his worries.

Except, right now with Brigid's scent clinging to him, the taste and feel of her still with him, he didn't want to think about the danger of their upcoming flight extracting the Green Berets. He definitely didn't want to think about all the things he'd hidden from Brigid, things she would never know about this mission.

Next in the stack—the brunch photos from the morning of his crew around the table, the *Los Bovedas* shopping district behind them. He studied his fellow crewdogs as Brigid had seen them through her camera, her perspective always offering something he hadn't seen before.

Crazy Postal flying his hands through the air.

Vegas half listening as he pulled out his cell phone to take a call from his wife.

For the first time, he wondered about the rest of the picture rather than the overall impression, curious about her work and the way she was seeing much more than ghost crabs now that she was freelancing with Sonny again. He slid Brigid's square magnifier over a couple of shots to isolate close-up details beyond their table. The way an old lady pinched her cigarette between her thumb and pointer. How a middle-aged tourist held his wife's hand but peered behind her at another woman a few yards away.

A man in a gray business suit waiting outside in the heat, with his hand gripping the end of a metal banister.

Joe slid the magnifier away—then inched it back again. He cocked his head to the side, frowned, something niggling that he couldn't quite pinpoint. He shifted the glass to the next photo in the series, and still the man stood in profile, even further turned away. But this time he'd tipped his head to look up the stairs—perhaps at someone descending.

An image blazed through his mind from years ago, of senior prom, Cooper in a gray tuxedo, the nontraditional color chosen to piss off his mother. He and Joe were double dating, and damned if Cooper hadn't stood just like that at the foot of his date's staircase.

No way.

Joe shook his head to clear his vision and shake free of the past. He couldn't be seeing what he thought. His brain must be playing cruel tricks on him, like when he'd sensed Cooper around every corner. His friend was on his mind because of this op, all the talk of capturing el Jedr, of flying a mission with Green Berets.

Of finally giving in to the temptation to make Brigid his.

The man in the photo didn't even have the right hair color, too blond and shaggy rather than Cooper's regular red buzz cut. Still, long-ago images flashed to mind, of summer days when the sun bleached out some of the red in Cooper's hair, giving him more of a strawberry blond look. And of course hair could be colored, grown. Changed.

Behind him, bedsheets rustled, and Joe slapped his hand down over the photos, twisting toward Brigid. She tossed to her other side, mumbled groggy nonsense, and nestled back to sleep again. Peaceful sleep after two hellish years. And he wouldn't let anything fuck that up, certainly not some hallucination from his guilty conscience.

Joe returned to the photos, ready to clear away this bizarre crap once and for all. Sure the guy's height was right, the build slimmer than before but still in keeping with Cooper as he'd looked in his college years before he'd bulked up in the Army. So what? The two men shared a body type.

Joe ran the magnifier over the remaining pictures, praying for a full face shot that showed a guy with a great big honker nose and a mouthful of crooked teeth that couldn't possibly belong to Cooper.

He never got the full face shot. Instead, he found a succession of images of the man pivoting a military turn away from the camera. Not a perfect pivot. Not completely precise.

But unmistakably his old friend, Captain Cooper Scott.

CHAPTER THIRTEEN

LENA WANTED COOPER GONE, out of the cubicle, out of the office building. And, most important, out of her thoughts.

He showed no signs of departing from anywhere, anytime soon.

Swallowing frustration with a sip of her lukewarm coffee, she scrolled the computer page down to find her place again so she could pretend to input data she had completed over an hour ago. After dealing with a security emergency at the factory, Alessandro had planned to stay with her—a prospect that hovered like a toxic cloud all afternoon. But he'd been called out on an emergency for his mother at the last minute.

Leaving Cooper to stay with her, without even one of Alessandro's standard goon guards to act as a chaperone. Having Cooper with her instead made for an upsetting alternative, for a totally different reason altogether. She was fast losing her battle to keep her distance around this man.

She had tried to persuade him to leave, insisting she could call for Alessandro's car to see her safely home. No luck. So she concocted errands for him in hopes of buying time alone in the office, but he always evaded. If she wanted coffee, he offered his own cup. When she asked for food, he called for delivery. The man was unshakable.

Blast him for staying and ruining one of her few chances to peruse Alessandro's files without interruption. Certainly she ran risks in checking his transactions and data logs. But peeking in unwise places could be explained away on those rare occasions he left her alone with information to input. Tonight the security system was suffering from some sort of computer failure that did not affect the office network, which made her evening here all the more important—no need to dodge cameras or fear listening devices.

Now thanks to the ever-present Scott Cooper, she had lost a valuable opportunity when she needed it most. Her contact at the local police department was growing impatient with her minuscule offerings of late, but when local authorities had approached her three months ago, they had only needed her to track Alessandro's whereabouts. Now they wanted more sensitive data, which put her at greater risk.

But they paid for every scrap she passed along. When he left on trips. His favorite restaurants. Who joined him for meals. Every ounce of information added to her pitiful stash of money. Yet for some reason they were offering a larger prize, the ultimate prize, for detailed shipping information about the cargo leaving this weekend.

They could not be so cruel as to take back their offer

of safe haven in another country. If she stayed here after betraying Alessandro, his friends who remained would kill her.

To steady her nerves, she flipped through pages already read beside her computer, pretending interest when in fact her eyes were far more interested in the reflected image of Cooper on her screen.

Arms on the rests, he lounged in an office chair, feet planted far apart as if ready to spring into action. The weight of his heavy-lidded stare tingled awareness through her veins like a showering of sheeting cold rain, painful and invigorating all at once.

For six months she'd felt his eyes on her, but with icy-blue disdain. Now he looked at her with heat, even a little confusion. He wanted her and he didn't like it.

Well, welcome to the club, *señor*, because she understood the feeling.

Unable to stand the tension any longer, Lena spun in her chair to face him. "Would you like a magazine? Or a book or a pillow to rest your head? Because I could be here for a very long time now."

"What're you working on?"

Working on getting through this evening without betraying her better judgment. "Requisition orders for crates and packing materials like those tiny silica antimoisture packets and bubble wrap."

"Hmm. Sounds fascinating."

"It is."

"If you like typing lists at midnight."

Nerves stretched too far today snapped. "I like eating. Better yet, I like feeding my child."

"Admirable, doing whatever it takes to feed your kid."

Her abused nerves went hot just under her skin. Could he know the truth behind her "relationship" with Alessandro? It should not matter to her that he saw through to her real reasons, and perhaps even understood just a little. But it did matter—very much.

She swiveled her chair back toward the computer screen full of now-blurry listings of shipment dates and quantities. She should admit defeat and go home, should have done hours ago, which hinted at wanting to stay with Cooper.

The leather seat behind her creaked as he stood, his footfall soft and slow as he made his way toward her. Her heart tripped, then restarted to match pace with his uneven gait.

He stopped beside her and swung his briefcase onto her desk. Could he finally be leaving after all? She waited, resenting the flash of regret over lost time with him when she should be thrilled at free rein to walk through Alessandro's office—a thought that scared her almost as much as her attraction to the man beside her.

She needed a spine transplant to make it through the next few days with her sanity intact. "Are you going now?"

"Nope." He snapped open the briefcase, the lid blocking her view inside. He rustled inside and lifted...

A mesh sack full of plastic army men. No doubt for Miguel.

Ohhh, this man was good. Maybe too good. "I can not be bought."

A corner of his mouth tipped in what could be humor or insult. "Really?"

"Really," she snapped back. Her *affection* couldn't be purchased, even if her body could, and that fine delineation was all that kept her self-respect. So much for her thoughts that he understood anything about her.

"Good." He dropped the sack on her keyboard, launching a typo line of *yhjkidm* across her screen. "I didn't buy this for you. I picked it up for your kid on my lunch hour."

Either he really was that nice a man or he was worse than Alessandro. She didn't know which posed a bigger threat.

"Thank you." Lena pinched the top of the mesh sack and steeled herself against softer emotions for a man who thought to buy her son a birthday gift, a toy he'd enjoyed as a child. "I think I am too tired to work any longer after all. I should go home now."

He tugged the dangling sack from her hand and pitched it aside, leaning over the desk toward her, palms flat on the padded calendar. "You know, I really don't deserve this ice-princess shit you're giving me. What have I ever done to you?"

Looked at her? Touched her with his eyes? That sounded silly even in her mind, much less spoken aloud. "You are—how do you say it in your country?—crowding my face."

"My space."

"What?"

"The phrase is 'crowding my space.'"

"Yes. That. You are doing it, and it makes me uncomfortable."

"News bulletin for you. You make me uncomfortable too." He did not have to angle closer. The breadth of his shoulders filled her space, face, eyes with all that gorgeous tousled blond hair that lacked the styled perfection of Alessandro. "Yes, I'm attracted to you. Doesn't mean I plan to do anything about it."

"Good, because that would be unwise." Why hadn't she simply said she didn't want him? She'd left a door open and from his narrowing eyes she could tell he knew it.

Shutting off her computer with a lightning click of keys, she rolled her chair away from the desk, away from him and gathered her purse. He could follow her or not. She needed to leave the office, the building.

And how about the whole country?

Right now she would settle for clearing the front door of Aragon Industries to breathe air untainted by Alessandro's favorite rose-scented air freshener piped through all his buildings.

She stepped out into the night, her heels clicking along the cement. Wordlessly he opened the Mercedes passenger door.

Lena slid inside, warm butter-soft leather reminding her of her other life, before her husband died, before she realized how precarious security could be. Cooper settled behind the wheel, bringing her back to the present—a starlit night, in a car alone with a hot man.

He pitched the sack of army men onto her lap.

She picked at the mesh netting and managed to stay quiet through four turns down the silent night streets. Tinted car windows cast an even-darker intimacy inside the vehicle, tempered only by the neon glow of the instrument panel. What an inconvenient time for Alessandro to decide he trusted her alone with another man. The smothering watch of his guards could actually be helpful for once.

How could Cooper just pretend they hadn't discussed a mutual attraction? If anything, the ache in her belly, lower, increased. At this rate they would not be able to sit in the same room together without visible sparks crackling along the air. "It is just science, you know."

"Chemistry. We call it chemistry."

She called it inescapable insanity. But whatever.

Still, the word *chemistry* brought to mind visions of the torch she had used to boil substances in school. Yes, *chemistry* fit. "Why should I trust what you are saying?"

He brought the car to a stop in the alley behind her apartment. Hooking an arm along the back of the seat, Cooper faced her, dead-on and dead serious. "If I planned to act on the chemistry, it wouldn't be through buying your kid presents. Children shouldn't be used. I bought the boy a gift because it sucks that he has to be with a sitter on his birthday night."

She heard the honesty in his voice, perhaps even detected a hint of a young boy who'd once played with army men because he had no one else. She longed to comb her fingers through his tousled hair and sidle close enough to learn if his aftershave smelled as good up close as it did from a distance, subtle, tempting without overpowering.

Like the man. "Why are you so nice to me, even when I am snippy?"

"Uh, did you forget I have to stay with you?" His teasing smile put a blazing South American sun to shame.

How could she resist smiling in return? "And now you are not so nice."

"You would be wise to remember that." His smile tightened, but she still couldn't pull her eyes away from something in his pale-blue eyes that drew her far more than his godlike glow.

He did not lean far. Neither did she. But somehow the subtle give from both of them brought their faces inches apart. "I'm going to kiss you if you don't move back."

"I hope so."

Where had that come from? Not from the timid klutz she had once been. But maybe for a few moments she could be the savvy woman she pretended to be in Alessandro's world.

Cooper cupped her face in the palm of his hand, thumb stroking her cheek while his clear blue eyes telegraphed his desire to kiss her, desire for more. A thousand reasons insisted she should break away. Instead she languished in the near-innocent touch of his hand on her face and the not-so-innocent stroke of his sensual gaze.

A dangerous thought smoked through her, the notion that Alessandro could be in jail this time next week. She would be free for the first time since she'd walked into Aragon Textiles ten months ago. Truly, since Miguel died a year and a half ago.

But she and little Miguel would be leaving as soon as authorities arrested Alessandro.

All the more reason to steal this kiss now.

She swayed forward, not much, in reality, but so much more for a woman terrified. What if he didn't come to—

He did.

Cooper slanted his mouth over hers and *Dios Mio*... just *Dios*. She'd forgotten anything could feel this sweet and sinful all at once. Warm lips and even hotter man pressed to her, a man who understood that true strength could also be shown in restraint. And heaven help her, restraint had her shaking right now. Or perhaps he caused her trembling with the simple first sweep of his tongue. Not so simple at all. She sighed into his mouth, opening further to invite more.

A distant church bell tolled once. So late at night, a time for lovers. Kissing in a car outside her side door called to mind innocent days, teenage kisses and fresh new sensations—shared only with her husband. She wanted to cry.

But she wanted even more to keep kissing Scott Cooper and pretend this could be normal.

He angled around to press her deeper into the comfort of the supple leather seat. She would have liked to shift positions, crawl onto his lap and take control, but then things could well spiral *out* of control.

As if they weren't close enough at the moment?

And how strange was that, when their hands stayed well away from more intimate areas? She clutched at his shoulders and enjoyed the hard play of muscles under her fingertips, his still stroking through her hair. Nothing overtly sexual from him, but so wonderfully sensuous and gentlemanly when he had every indication to expect a different sort of woman. She'd fielded too many sly innuendos from Alessandro's "friends" to take for granted being treated with respect. The honesty of the moment aroused her as much as his kiss.

With a growl-groan, he dragged his mouth from hers and buried his face in her neck. "Damn it."

Her hand stroked along the back of his head, unwilling to lose this moment just yet, and yes, his spicy aftershave smelled every bit as amazing up close. "I thought you didn't plan to do anything about your attraction to me."

"Believe me, lady," his hot breath caressed her throat, "I didn't plan that."

Of course he had not. Only a fool would *want* to be with her. She eased from his arms with more than a little regret. "I should go now."

He sagged back in his seat with a ragged sigh, his hair all the more mussed and enticing. "A wise move, because it's all I can do not to beg you to crawl into the back seat with me."

"I can not see you ever begging for anything."

"You would be surprised how easy it is to bring a man to his knees."

He looked away—she could not decide whether to be relieved or disappointed—and reached onto the floor. His hand came back out with the present for her child that must have fallen unnoticed during that out-of-control kiss.

Cooper dropped the sack of soldiers in her lap again. "Don't forget this. And tell your son—"

"Miguel."

"Tell Miguel happy birthday from me."

"I will." Her fingers twisted in the mesh bagging. She could not stop images of Cooper sprawled on the ground with her child, building tunnels from pillows. "Thank you."

For the toy, the kiss, a moment to enjoy normal dreams and hope that maybe someday she could make them come true again. This time she would cherish them.

His hand draped over the steering wheel, he studied the street so intently she almost wondered if he remembered she sat next to him.

He drummed his fingertips along the dash. "Maybe tomorrow I could have another cup of coffee in your pretty teacup and show him how to build fortresses out of kitchen pots and cookie sheets."

"Maybe you could." The words fell out in a breathless tumble reminiscent of her awkward days when boys made her stutter.

This man was very much not a boy.

What was she thinking? Dreams were one thing, but that was all they could be for now. She was too close to freedom to risk playing with that chemistry flame.

Still, a voice inside insisted there wouldn't be time for Alessandro to grow angry. No harm in sharing coffee. She wouldn't let anything more happen.

Waiting, watching, *wanting* while Cooper circled the hood of the car to open her door, she clutched the bag of army men and dream images hard against her heart.

BRIGID CLUTCHED THE PILLOW to her chest and inhaled the lingering scent of Joe, a hint of bay rum and a masculine sort of soap.

Mixed with the unmistakable perfume of awesome sex. Which also left her absolutely starving. She crawled her hands along the bed, searching until she finally opened her eyes. Empty.

"Joe?" She flipped onto her other side and directed her voice toward the connecting door to his room. Maybe he was in the bathroom.

"Hey, Joe, do you think we can find a cantina open anywhere this late? I wonder if they even have vending machines in a place like this. God, what I wouldn't give for a bag of Cool Ranch Doritos."

She rolled onto her back again. "Or would it be a sacrilege to eat Mexican-style junk food in a country that makes tortilla chips from scratch?"

Kicking aside the comforter, she swung her bare feet to the floor, the bare *rest* of her sliding free of the rumpled sheets. "Hmmm. Too deep a thought for me right now. Maybe you could just feed this other hunger I have going so I forget about my growling stomach."

A definite plan for passing time until a restaurant opened. Later over deep-fried doughnuts she would indulge in an *I told you so* or two. Her sex-buddies idea had been golden. Even the roots of her hair still tingled from the afterglow of a near-pass-out orgasm. Joe's fabulously vocal response assured her.

And speaking of Joe… She rolled to her feet and headed across the rug. "Are you in the shower or something?"

Still no answer or sound of water. She'd been talking to herself. What an idiot. She plucked his discarded black T-shirt from the floor and tugged it over her head. Shoving her arms through, she padded across into his room and checked his balcony.

Nothing, just the distant rush of waves and a handful of late-night traffic.

Where would he go at—she checked the bedside clock—one-thirty in the morning? Postal's junk heap was safely back in Florida, so Joe couldn't be doing an emergency tire-change run. But then, given his always-late, helper complex, who knew what someone else may have needed.

Regardless, it better have been damn good for him to leave her alone in bed without a word. She didn't consider herself the needy type, but sheesh, a bit of post-coital cuddling after their first time wasn't too much to ask, even from buddy sex.

Maybe he'd left a note in her room. Not the coolest thing to do, but acceptable if he wrote something kinda sweet.

Scanning her room, she came up empty at the bed-side table. She even shook out the covers like a total idiot. How juvenile could she get? She would not, would not, *absolutely* would not be clingy. She'd watched her mama wait by the phone for even a call too many times.

Joe was *not* like her father. He wasn't sporting some hidden agenda and he wouldn't fade away without an-other word to her. And she needed to quit paying hom-age to past baggage that wasn't her fault or his. She would check the table for a message from Joe and re-gardless of what she found—or didn't find—she would crawl back into bed and go to sleep. He would no doubt come wake her soon enough, and if their earlier encounters were any indication, she should rest up.

Brigid reached to straighten the proofs fanning along the table, covering every spare space, and possi-bly shielding a note that was fast becoming too impor-tant. Her hand hovered to a standstill over the photos.

Why were they scattered this way? She always made a point of stacking them neatly, in order. Sure she had everything on digital, but still, holding the hard copy images sometimes stirred creative thoughts be-yond the screen.

Joe must have been looking at them while she slept. She sunk down to the chair, spreading the pictures across the table. Aside from any expectations of morn-ing-after cuddling, what could he have seen that would make him leave when he'd been emphatic about stay-ing close whenever possible for her safety?

COOPER SLUMPED against the quarter panel of his Mercedes, staring at the lights flickering on in Lena's apartment, and wondered what the hell possessed him to kiss her.

He knew better, and still he hadn't been able to stop. He'd been seconds away from begging her in earnest to recline the seat and let him find his way up her skirt for a closer exploration of her subtle curves. And even though he'd managed to pull himself off, he hadn't established clear distance. Nah. Instead he'd talked about future cups of coffee.

Hell, yeah, he would damn near beg for a chance to share a drink with her, much less share body fluids, and didn't that just beat all? He'd only begged once before, and the memory wasn't pretty.

Cooper pounded his fist back against the Mercedes. Dazed from the fever and infection, he'd fucking pleaded with the doctor at the Army hospital in Ramstein not to saw off his leg. But the doc had sworn it was too late, gangrene had set into his wound because of crap conditions in the prison. If he had received decent medical care right away, maybe his leg could have been saved.

No. He didn't want to be in a position to beg ever again. Except he couldn't mistake her responsiveness. Any begging would be mutual. So why not have coffee with her? Coffee and more.

He'd told himself he was sticking close to her for possible information. Time to be honest with himself. She hadn't shown a sign of knowing squat. He could be with her without worrying about compromising his objectivity. Her place wasn't bugged—a fact that had surprised the shit out of him when he'd scanned the apartment before playing with her son. She'd been too preoccupied with making coffee to notice.

Either Aragon trusted her—or found her beyond concern securitywise. She didn't seem to be looking for a relationship by any means, which let him off the hook since he would be gone in less than a week.

But if he took things further he would have to mention one pertinent fact. *Oh, yeah, just so you don't freak when I drop my pants, maybe I should tell you...*

No-strings sex had been much easier in the old days.

He'd been with women since his recovery, a couple of quickies where neither of them had fully undressed so the issue of his injury never arose. And there had been a one-month-long semirelationship with another agent who already knew about his amputation and, God love her, didn't seem to care. She'd just gotten a divorce and said she needed a bridge lover. Sex, friendship, no attachment, so she could move on secure in knowing she wouldn't fall into a rebound relationship.

Given the way he'd screwed up with Brigid, he'd figured he was due a bridge lover himself before he ever got back around to the real thing.

Would that make Lena another bridge lover...or the something more which he wasn't in a position to give? Either way, she was not the kind of woman he could sleep with and forget. Shit. He should leave while he could.

He reached for the car door handle. He didn't need this distraction at a critical time in his op any more than she needed him fucking up her already-screwed-up life. He would go back to his apartment and indulge in some serious alone time with his hand—a thought that fell short when Lena waited with those kissed-full lips a flight of stairs away.

Hang tough. Get in the car. He swung open the door. A rustle sounded behind him, a rustle he should have heard a half second earlier if his instincts hadn't been dulled by a woman. Damn. Damn. Damn it all.

He reached inside his jacket for his 9 mm just as a forearm rammed across his throat.

CHAPTER FOURTEEN

JOE JACKED HIS ARM UP tighter across Cooper's neck, still stunned numb by the reality that he had his dead friend in front of him fighting against the throat lock. And no question about it now, this was his best bud back from the grave, and he wasn't giving Cooper a chance to slip away without offering up some fucking explanations.

After seeing those pictures, he'd worked his way back to the location in the photos, near where they'd had brunch. Then he'd waited. It hadn't taken long for Cooper to show up, and after the way he'd salivated all over the woman he'd brought home, apparently he had gotten over Brigid just fine. Thinking of all her tears and grief, Joe sure as hell hoped Cooper had a convenient case of amnesia.

Anger warred with relief and confusion and a crapload of other emotions until he almost missed the blur out of the corner of his eye. Cooper reached for a gun.

Joe blocked the swinging arm. "You may be the baddest dude in the jungle when it comes to a street fight, but you always did need to practice your draw."

"Yeah, yeah, whatever." Cooper tensed without

turning. "Think you could loosen the hold on my Adam's apple, Face?"

The last hope of a simple explanation died with Cooper's open acknowledgment of who had him in a choke hold. No bullshit pretense of having amnesia. Not even surprise at finding Joe hanging out in the same damn town on another continent.

He should be pissed, but instead he worked his throat through two long swallows to keep from choking up. Cooper was alive. The rest could wait.

Joe willed his arm to let go, even as he struggled with the urge to keep Cooper pinned, half certain his resurrected friend would fade or run if released.

Cooper pivoted with that military turn from the photos. Not as tight a turn, but with the same defiant snap.

Joe nodded to Cooper's hand still resting on the shoulder harness. "You gonna shoot me or say hello?"

"You're lucky I didn't." Cooper's hand fell away, and next thing Joe knew they were back-slap hugging in a dark alley, not giving a shit who might walk past. Joe's throat worked hard again to ward off the tightening constriction in his chest trying to push up.

Finally he pulled away and stared at Cooper's face in the dim street light. Just as he'd seen in the photo, thinner, not as bulked up as in his Green Beret days, actually more resembling his teenage build. The blond hair—no buzz cut, instead brushing the top of his collar—differed but not radically so. With those changes and a three-thousand-dollar suit instead of BDU pants and a torn brown T-shirt, his own mother might not have recognized him.

Of course, Cooper's mother was a bitch with fewer maternal instincts than her canine namesake.

But anybody who knew him well couldn't miss the eyes, still the same color of blue even if they were harder, almost blank. What the hell had happened over the past two years? "I can't believe I'm looking at you. We all thought—"

Joe pinched the bridge of his nose with his thumb and forefinger before he did something lame-ass like tear up, but God, this was…too much.

"I know." Cooper stared at the ground, his face pulling tight before he looked up again.

Now that the numb was wearing off, questions piled up. "We buried you, for God's sake, dropped a coffin in the ground with the wrong guy's remains."

Cooper shoveled a hand through his longer hair, then stepped deeper into the alley, farther away from the windows open for a cool breeze on a warm night. "Nobody's remains," he kept his voice low. "The people I work for arranged it."

The people. "Where the hell have you been?"

"Taking care of business."

Business. Only two reasons a guy would play dead and have connections strong enough to cover it—going underground on the wrong side of the law or going undercover *for* the law. "For the good guys?"

"You know you don't even have to ask. I'm Agency."

"Fair enough." He might be confused about a lot of things, but he knew Cooper would never betray his country. He could see where a guy with their Special Ops training could shuffle over to the CIA or some other covert organization. The things they did served a higher purpose than self.

But where did a man draw the line when it came to hurting the people he loved? Sure he understood about the job, but in choosing to be with someone like Brigid... She was the line Cooper shouldn't have crossed. If Cooper had loved her the way she'd loved him, he would have found a way to let her know.

Brigid. Sleeping back in that hotel room—soft, warm and so strong again after two years of agony for nothing, for a man who didn't love her the way she deserved.

Anger kinked inside him, along with a raging need to dodge thinking about how much being with Brigid tonight had meant. His hands fisted at his side. "I do need to ask one thing."

"What's that, pal?"

"Well, *pal*, why the hell did you have to break her fucking heart?"

Joe's fist hammered into Cooper's gut.

SHIT, THAT HURT.

Cooper gasped for breath. He deserved the punch. Absolutely. He'd hurt two good people, the best people, a helluva lot better than him. But he'd forgotten how much punch Joe could pack.

His old pal clipped another off his jaw. Sparks lit behind Cooper's eyes in the dark alley. He shook to clear his head. "I can let one punch pass, maybe two, but I'm not gonna stand here and let you—"

Damn! He hadn't even seen that one coming.

And damned if he would take a beating. He could use a workout tonight to burn off frustrated tension from kissing Lena and then having his past clock him in the face. Nobody ever put up a fight worth a crap except Joe.

Cooper ducked his shoulder and rammed. *Oof.*

They slammed against the crumbling stucco wall at the rear entrance to the carpet shop. He jabbed, took a hit in return and parried. He might not be Special Forces anymore, but could hold his own.

Cooper rammed his forearm across Joe's throat. Joe kicked out, caught him in the gut and broke free. Cooper bit down a curse. If he had two good feet steady under him, he could probably take Joe down, since his friend was pissed enough to make a mistake. Damn it all, amputees skied, for God's sake. Some even managed to stay in the military. Doubts could take him out faster than anything else.

Concentrate. They circled, half on the cobblestone road, half in the dusty garden. The present mirrored the past, going back to elementary days fighting over baseball cards all the way up to the time Joe had walked off with the woman Cooper had been dating in college.

A memory flashed through of Joe sitting beside Brigid at the street-side restaurant…

Joe swiped with his foot, connected with Cooper's prosthetic leg with a thunk, rather than the give of flesh. Cooper stumbled, but stayed on his feet.

Frowning, Joe hesitated, stared down, blinking faster as shock slid over his face. Joe extended his foot and tapped again. Horror, grief, all the pity emotions Cooper had dreaded seeing for two years blazed on empathetic Joe's face.

No. Hell, no. Cooper charged, landing them both on the ground, off their feet, which he figured offered a more level playing field.

He pinned an arm across Joe's throat again and pressed. "Fight back, damn it. No quarter, remember? Rule number one."

Joe's larynx bobbed with emotion. "Coop, dude, I—"

"No fucking quarter." Cooper arced his hand back again.

Joe's knee ratcheted up into Cooper's gut and they rolled, scattering potted plants and trash cans in the deserted street. No one so much as peeked outside. Not a surprise. Hell, help had been in short supply for Lena in broad daylight. The chances of anyone around here getting involved in a dark-of-night fight were slim to none.

He ducked a fist flying toward his face and landed a gut punch, doubling Joe over. Adrenaline fired through his veins. Shit, yeah, he could hold his own.

Then Joe went still against a metal railing. Burning adrenaline turned icy. God, he couldn't have actually knocked him out. They knew how to fight hard without maiming each other. Joe flipped him, jammed his knee in Cooper's back. Oldest trick in the book and one a friend would fall for out of lame-ass concern.

Unsmiling, Joe stared down. "Rule number one. Did you forget it in the past thirty seconds? Don't cut each other slack because slack leads to weakness that could get you killed."

A hoarse chuckle seared up and out as he gasped for air. "Apparently, I'm tougher to kill than everyone thought."

"Bad joke. Not laughing." Joe kept his knee planted firm.

Cooper welcomed the bite of cobblestones against his face. "You never did have much of a sense of humor."

"And you never asked for help when you needed it, just left us poor humorless fools to figure it out on our own." He eased off, allowing Cooper to sit upright— and then knocked on the prosthetic leg. "Now tell me what the hell's going on with this?"

Only Joe would have dared do that. And Joe was the only one who could get away with it.

Cooper kept his eyes steady on Joe. He wouldn't flinch or look away. He'd reconciled himself to the loss, made a helluva comeback in building a career for himself. He wouldn't apologize for his decisions. He'd done his best.

"It's exactly what you think it is. Shit happens, you know. I lost a piece of me in battle, but I'm okay now."

Don't make a big deal out of this, dude. Still Joe

looked full of more questions. Nope. Not now, with his insides scraped raw. Time for a diversion. "What about rule number two? I saw you with Brigid."

He thought for sure another swing was coming his way, and he deserved it. He'd given up rights to Brigid the day he decided to stay dead. Did he regret the decision? Who the hell knew now? Still he couldn't help but think he could have handled this better if she'd chosen someone else.

Joe pulled a tight smile. "She isn't yours. You're dead, remember?"

"Oh, yeah. Fair enough, then." God he'd missed the way Joe could cut through the crap with a one-liner, proving he actually did have a sense of humor after all. Albeit buried damn deep sometimes. "How did you find me?"

God help him if he'd blown his whole cover.

"Dumb luck. We were on the same street at the same time."

If only the channel of information had given him a better list of the military personnel on this op…. But it hadn't. Deal with it and salvage what he could. Over the past two years he'd become an expert at salvaging what he could from a crappy situation.

He'd only bought himself a brief reprieve from questions about his leg, but he would take every second to get his head together. Side by side, they sat on the ground, elbows on knees, until breathing went back to normal. Cooper waited for Joe to look at him again, something that didn't happen as soon as he expected.

"You broke her fucking heart," Joe repeated.

"She seems to have gotten over me just fine from what I saw of you two hanging out at breakfast." He had no right to feel jealous and he knew it.

"You didn't give her much of a choice."

"She's better off. I may have been the baddest dude in the jungle, but you were always the best."

"Don't make me shove your magnanimous teeth down your throat."

"You're welcome to try."

Joe looked up, unwavering, dark eyes pinning him. No more dodging. "You can't convince me you stepped aside because of—" he pointed to Cooper's foot "—because of an injury that wouldn't mean jack to Brigid."

"Maybe it meant something to me." Understatement. The missing limb reminded him every day that he'd only lost his leg. His men had lost their lives. He never once lost sight of the difference or forgot their faces.

Reisner who carried Tootsie Pop suckers in his BDUs.

McIntyre with a family Disney photo in his wallet.

Jefferson sketching everything he saw in hopes of publishing his impressions after the war.

Cooper brought every soldier to mind, easy enough since each of them marched across his nightmares, still alive with plans and dreams. How could he just take up his life where it left off? Settle down with a picket fence and grill some burgers like nothing changed.

Joe slumped against the wall beside him. "Did it happen…then? That last mission in Iraq?"

He nodded.

Joe's eyes slid closed, his face pained more than when Cooper had landed a fist to his face. "I'm so damned sorry. I should have gotten there."

No fucking pity. "The mighty Joe, responsible for everyone else. Good God, it was a terrorist's grenade that tore my leg up, not you."

He glared. "Don't be an ass. I'm already pissed at you."

Anger felt much safer than pity or guilt. Old, familiar ribbing felt even better. "Then go ahead and swing again. Nobody's stopping you."

"Would serve you right."

"Think you can take me, Air Force puke? You barely held your own against a one-legged Green Beret."

Barking out a laugh, Joe sagged against the brick wall, laughs echoing, fading, down the alley. Silence echoed back, broken only by a distant cat shriek.

Joe studied his hands clasped between his bent knees. "You'll have to tell her about this soon."

His gut pitched. "There's a lot going on here securitywise. I'm not sure when I'll be out from under it."

A cop-out and he knew it since one way or the other, Aragon would be in jail within a week.

Joe worked his jaw where Cooper had racked it. "These sorts of occupations don't leave us much in the way of choices sometimes."

How could anyone build a relationship in this kind of job? What woman would put up with this sort of life and why was he thinking about that anyway when he'd said goodbye to Brigid in his mind long ago? "I'll come clean when I can."

"You need to know, I can't promise to keep this from her for long. You have to get your shit in a pile soon and figure out a way to resurrect yourself. There are plenty of people who do your job and manage to stay alive to the rest of the world."

"Once I settle this score, I'll become one of those people again. I promise." He held out his fist for Joe to pound his against it as they'd done hundreds of times in the past.

Joe wasn't playing, serious and intense as ever. "Meanwhile, I'm just supposed to walk away and wait for you to show up again? I don't think so. How about pony up a way to contact you if I need to?"

"Hmm. Some kind of code, huh? That's work-able." He leaned close, lowering his voice to a near-whisper. "Okay, you know that old vendor outside the *Los Bovedas,* the one that sells those *panchos*—hot dog looking things—over there. The one-eyed dude with that psychedelic patch?"

"Yeah."

"If you approach him on the third Tuesday of the month—" he paused for effect "—he'll still be selling *panchos.*"

A beat of silence followed before Joe laughed again, easier this time. "What? No chalk marks on mailboxes or dead drops under a table in a bodega?"

"Dude, the Cold War's dead. We've simplified things. Pagers are untraceable. Memorize this number." Cooper rattled off ten digits, then repeated. "You got it?"

"What's that? Some bank's time and temperature? I have to confess the trust element's low here right now."

"And I'm sorry. A man's gotta do what he thinks is right." The closest he could come to admitting maybe he'd hidden away to lick his wounds. "The number's valid. You will see me again. Hey, I know I'm busted."

"I wouldn't talk."

"To anyone except Brigid. Yeah, I realize that. But once the dominoes start falling, it's all over soon. I only have to get through a few more days. After this assignment, I'll…"

"Come back to life?"

"Sure." Cooper reached to massage his aching knee and stopped himself short. "Just don't tell her yet. Give me a chance to figure out a way to make it right."

A selfish request and he knew it. He'd seen them together, saw the connection—hell, he'd seen it two and half years ago when Joe met her for the first time. Cooper gave up and massaged his knee. He'd been a selfish bastard in hanging on to her then, too.

Joe shoved to his feet and offered his hand. Cooper bristled, his palm sliding from his knee. He wasn't an invalid and didn't want to be treated like one. Except, this was Joe, hurting like hell and undoubtedly blaming himself. Didn't the guy assume responsibility for everything? Smacking aside his hand would only make Joe feel worse. Besides, hadn't they offered each other a hand up on the playground, basketball court, gym? Wins going fifty-fifty.

He'd hurt people and still didn't know what he would do differently. Cooper clapped his hand into

Joe's and stood, testing his weight on his prosthesis, finding it stable.

Joe pulled away and tucked both hands in his back pockets. "All job security issues aside, I'm not sure I'm going to be able to forgive you for this, you fucker."

"I know." Guilt bit the big one.

Joe's throat worked. "But I'm damned glad you're around for me to kick the shit out of while I try."

Cooper watched his best friend since childhood disappear into the dark and knew he didn't deserve Joe's forgiveness. He understood that as surely as he knew ever-honorable Joe would forgive him, anyway, and probably offer to give up Brigid while he was at it.

Could he have screwed things up any worse in one night? He'd blown a serious hole in his cover. Made a move on a crime lord's mistress, a crime lord with terrorist connections who just happened to hold a key to landing some serious revenge. Things couldn't get much worse.

So why not go for broke? He looked away, back across the street and up the side stairs leading to an apartment with a china cup and dangerous woman.

Fitting, since he was in a helluva dangerous mood.

JOE COULDN'T SHAKE the dark mood fogging through him as his tennis shoes pounded cobblestones on his way back to the hotel.

He should be happy. Cooper was alive. Two years of black-hole grief had come to an end.

And wasn't that a kick-in-the-ass notion since he'd

thought he was over Cooper's death and Brigid was the one who needed help? Must be the shock of it all distorting things in his head. Sure the pictures had shown him Cooper, but seeing his friend in the flesh, hearing his voice, even feeling the familiar jolt of his fist… It was all too much on a night with Brigid that had already knocked him off balance.

Brigid. He definitely couldn't think about her yet.

Back to Cooper, who was apparently hooked up with the CIA. He'd chosen another path for his life after a grenade in Iraq took away his job, stole his leg. Leave it to Cooper to figure out how to turn a life-altering loss into another way to kick more ass. But why was he here? Now?

In a crime-riddled area like this, Cooper could be operating for the CIA in any number of capacities. Joe sidestepped the closed and covered *panchos* stand Cooper had joked about.

Cooper could have any number of tasks here with all the arms and drug running. But he couldn't ignore the close proximity of his own op bringing down Aragon Industries. Then there was the whole ol Jedr connection that had drawn Joe here in the first place to avenge Cooper. Made sense that same connection could have drawn Cooper here.

Hands in his pockets, he paused a corner short of his hotel. He needed to have a serious sit-down with Air Force intel first thing tomorrow about protecting Cooper's cover—and gathering more information on this mess for himself. Which left a few short hours to get his head together enough to lie to Brigid. He'd lied for his job in the past.

But he hadn't been sleeping with her before.

He arced his hand back to slam the stucco wall—and hesitated. His knuckles were already red and raw. If he broke his hand he couldn't fly, couldn't finish this mission, a reminder that he needed to get his head and priorities together. Safety came first.

Brigid's safety most of all.

He'd known getting closer to her would mess with his mind and he'd been right. He couldn't tell her a thing, for Cooper's safety as well as her own. Security dictated that he—as Postal would say—keep his soup cooler shut.

Or was he justifying keeping her to himself for a while longer? His feet propelled him forward. She'd loved the guy, tough enough to reconcile when he'd thought Cooper was dead. Not so easy now, because one way or the other, she would find out eventually.

He didn't want jealousy. He wanted to bang back a beer with his friend and celebrate. He wanted Brigid there at his side, against his side. His. But tonight more than ever reminded him of all the problems inherent in a lasting relationship.

Lasting? They'd only had sex. Mind-blowing, earth-shattering sex that he couldn't imagine never experiencing again.

He stopped outside the Cartina Royal, stared up to the eighth-floor balcony, thick curtains drawn over the double doors.

Walk. He would just walk a while longer. She was

sleeping, anyway, so he could afford to wait and pretend he couldn't still smell the scent of her clinging to his skin.

LENA POURED a steaming Colombian roast into her china cup, decaffeinated, even though she doubted she could sleep, anyway, after that reckless kiss with Scott Cooper. Just a kiss. Nothing more. Never anything more, a thought that left her sipping to heat her chilly insides.

But she had invited him back. Such a dangerous move, letting loneliness and longing get the better of her. Silence never used to bother her before, in fact soothed her, because she never needed to worry about Alessandro coming to her apartment.

Quiet coated the room in a suffocating blanket as she blew into the cup. Not even the sweet whisper of little Miguel dreaming sounded in the empty next room since he'd fallen asleep at Señora de Guerra's right after supper. Exhausted from his birthday celebrations and all the attention, his sitter had said. What a relief that his day was special, complete with singing alongside Señora de Guerra while she played birthday tunes on her piano. But still it stung not to have been there for every little smile.

Her telephone jangled from across the room. A call this late? Her heart lurched. Miguel?

She set her cup on the cracked kitchen counter and sprinted for the receiver. *"Sí?"*

"Lena, baby, it's me," Alessandro's slurred voice echoed through the receiver. "I'm lonely here without you. It's too long until we can get away. I need you now."

She shuddered at the thought of going to him with the taste of Cooper still on her lips. Dangerous enough to hide her feelings when he was reasonable, but no way could she reason with a stoned Alessandro. "You know I have to look out for Miguel." There. Not technically a lie, but if he knew her son slept upstairs at Señora de Guerra's, Alessandro would expect her to come to him.

"Then I can come to you there, in your home that you never let me see. We will be quiet, slow, together."

Gooseflesh crawled over her in a rash of revulsion. "I am a mother. You have always known my son's welfare must be my top priority."

Had she pushed too far? But he must realize her child came first, had in fact exploited that on more than one occasion to keep her under his thumb.

Under him.

Please, please, please, she only needed to stay out of his bed for a few more days. Usually he accepted her edict that they not sleep together at her home, but his drug-slurred tones did not inspire confidence at the moment.

"You are a good mother. A good mother is important. You're right that a son should not see his mother shown anything but respect."

Even as she trembled with relief, his ramblings set her on edge. "I am glad you understand."

"I want to understand more about you. Do you know how much I need you?"

Sadly, she did. "You can show me next week, once this important shipment is past and you're not so preoccupied. You mentioned going away together. We'll have time then."

Saints willing, he would be in jail.

"I meant it when I said I need you. You are the only thing that keeps me going. Your calm, it's like a drug to me. I will not lose you."

A shiver iced up her spine at the intensity in his tones, a possessiveness that couldn't be totally explained away by the cocaine no doubt flowing through his system. Her ribs ached with the memory of blows less than a week ago. His obsession was growing.

How far would he go to keep her? "I hear Miguel stirring. I should check on him."

"Soon," he slurred into the phone. "We will be together soon—"

The line went dead. Replacing the receiver, she drew in a shuddering breath, hating Alessandro's power, resenting the power she let him have through his ability to frighten her, and not knowing how to shake the fear. The revulsion.

A knock sounded at the door. She gasped, gripping the table behind her for support. Panic tightened her chest until she struggled to breathe. It could not be him. They had only just hung up.

He could have used his cellular phone. He could have been right outside the whole time she'd said goodnight to Cooper—kissed Cooper.

If Alessandro entered her apartment he would realize she had lied about Miguel. But Alessandro also knew she was inside.

She had no choice but to answer. Unless she saved Cartina's corrupt government the trouble of a trial and just killed him. Her eyes skated to the kitchen. A knife? A cast-iron pan? She actually considered it rather than let him in—let him *into* her. Considered, and tossed aside the tempting notion as quickly.

For her son, she had to hold on for a few more days. She could claim her time of the month. She might still have to service him, but at least she could avoid anything more.

Why did she feel like curling up to cry? She'd survived worse, and she could survive this. Maybe luck would smile on her and her late-night guest was simply Señora de Guerra.

Sí. Perhaps Miguel woke and needed her. Blinking hard against her tears, she gripped the doorknob, twisted to find…a man.

Scott Cooper instead of Alessandro.

Relief flooded through her until she grasped the molding for support. She'd deluded herself that she could survive Alessandro's touch any longer. For some reason *this* man had changed everything.

Her eyes adjusted to the dark, giving her a clearer view of the man on her doorstep who had somehow changed everything with one kiss and a sack of plastic army soldiers. Cooper's normally immaculate white shirt was stained with dirt and leaf stains. His hair disheveled, blood trickling from a nick in his eyebrow.

He pulled a smile and winced at the crease to his bruise. An irresistible smile from an irresistible man. "Is that 'maybe' offer for a cup of coffee in your pretty teacup still a possibility?"

CHAPTER FIFTEEN

TEARS? CRAP.

Already Cooper regretted his half-baked decision to climb back up the stairs to Lena's apartment. Thinking that he might have brought the glint to her sad brown eyes gut punched him far harder than Joe ever could.

Cooper resisted the urge to offer her his shoulder, a confusing urge given he'd never been a sucker for a crying woman. So why was he falling victim to eyes that were a little misty? And scared. And vulnerable.

Holy hell, he was in a shit-load of trouble.

He'd seen his mother pump out fake tears too often to fall for the leaky faucet act. But somehow he found himself wanting to believe Lena wasn't acting. Which was stupid because that meant he wanted their kiss to have stuck around in her thoughts after she closed her door. Joe must have hit him harder than he'd thought.

All the same, his vision was totally clear even with the dim ambient light from her apartment cutting the night. She still wore that silky blouse cut a little too low, her pert nose too high in a haughty act blown all to hell by her watery eyes. How many times in the past had he misread her cool exterior and missed the vulnerability?

She pulled her chin tight to stop the quiver. "Are you all right?" Her hand gravitated toward his battered face. "What happened? Were you mugged? All because you brought me home."

"Lots of question there, lady. I'm fine—" other than feeling like a dickhead for hurting two of the best people in the world "—just walked into a wall."

"A wall that left knuckle prints on your face." She traced a featherlight touch along his brow.

He didn't want to think about the fight with Joe for at least a few more hours, and the arousing glide of Lena's touch provided the perfect distraction.

Cooper trapped her hand still on his face and linked his fingers with hers. "Coffee?"

They both knew he was asking for more than a drink. Indecision stained her eyes, fear too, along with temptation. And finally resignation. They couldn't fight this anymore.

She smiled, seeming to find some kind of peace simply in having made the choice. God, what he wouldn't give for a taste of that peace. He would settle for a taste of her, a fine way to escape from an ache inside him that far outstripped any pain on the outside.

Lena swung the door wide. "Come in and I will find you a bandage to go with that cup of coffee."

She kept her fingers linked with his, walking ahead as she led him through her sparsely decorated apartment toward the cubicle bathroom with outdated fixtures. Hell. Eyes off the big tub. What a waste of energy to fantasize when he still needed to figure out how to get past explaining about his leg. What the hell had he been thinking walking up here?

Look instead at the yellow towel with childish ducks marching along the hem. Which brought to mind a whole 'nother problem. "Where's Miguel?"

She flicked down the lid on the toilet and motioned for him to sit. "He fell asleep upstairs at Señora de Guerra's so she said to leave him for the night rather than wake him."

They were alone. He must have done something good in his life after all.

Her hair swishing in a curtain as she looked down, she cranked on the faucet, wet a washcloth, twisted the excess water free. Shaking her hair back over her shoulder, she smoothed the cool rag along his brow, his sore cheekbone, dabbing at the corner of his mouth. "Do you want to tell me what is wrong?"

"I can't talk about it."

"But it obviously upset you."

"Let me rephrase. I don't *want* to talk about it." He plucked the rag from her hand. "That okay with you?"

She nodded once, quickly. Enough.

Flinging the damp cloth back into the sink with a slap against porcelain, he palmed her back, guided her toward him, waited for her to stop him. Hoping she wouldn't.

Lena inched forward between his knees, swayed until her breasts grazed his chest. A growl rumbled a second before he surged up to stand, and took her mouth. They slammed against the wall, just missing the towel rack. She opened to him, gripped his shoulders, crawled her hands up until her arms locked tight around his shoulders with an urgency echoed inside him.

Months of wanting her crashed through him. Unwise, thinking about that now, but then, he'd already blown his world to hell and back tonight.

Lena tunneled her fingers through his hair, her hands trembling. Trembling? With desire or fear? Reservations? Crap.

He trailed his mouth off her lips, over her cheek up to her ear. "I need for you to tell me how far you want this to go."

Her hands fluttered up to cup his face as she angled to meet his eyes, whisper against his mouth. "Why is that so important when we can both see the heat in each others' eyes?"

"Because I have to *hear* from you this is what you want."

She tensed in his arms. "I just told you what I see in your eyes and know you must see in mine. Are you trying to make me beg? Because if you are, then leave." Haughtiness slid across the delicate face in a shield that didn't fool him anymore. "I will not demean myself for—"

"Whoa. Hold on a second." He raised his hands in surrender. "You're throwing some whole other agenda in here because that is not what I meant." He slumped against the sink. "Shit. Let me try this again."

Her back still to the wall, she crossed her arms over her chest, her snooty posture muted her by the subtle plumping of her breasts. "That would be wise."

"God, you're cute when you get prim like that."

"I am not *cute*."

"Whatever." He reached for her arm and tugged her toward him. "I do see in your eyes a draw as strong as the one I'm feeling for you. But I also understand you're in a helluva tough position. What you want here—" he tapped her temple "—and what you want here." He slid his hand down to cup her breast. Oh, yeah. Perfect, and thank heaven for the support of the sink against his ass or he would be on his knees. "Those wants aren't always the same."

"Does this have to be so complicated?"

Yeah, it did. And it would get a lot more complicated when time came to ditch their clothes. "Because our situation is beyond complicated and I don't want you to regret this later."

"If you are honest with yourself, I do not believe you totally want me here—" she tapped his temple as he'd done to her "—nearly as much as you want me here."

She traced her fingernail past his belt buckle, down his zipper, strained tight against his erection.

Cooper stifled a groan. The woman had a point, and if she kept this up much longer, he would have a permanent zipper imprint on his erection.

Now he had to figure out how the hell to bring up the fact that he was sporting a wooden leg—and he didn't mean his hard-on. Okay, technically prostheses had come a long way since the wooden days, but that was beside the point.

Time to talk. But she kissed him. Whoa, did she ever kiss him, with an enthusiasm that almost made him miss a sweet innocence that set off warning bells in his head. Not possible. She had a kid and had been Aragon's lover. He was simply misreading.

Although her hand pressed to his fly left no room for misunderstanding.

Their feet tangled as they shuffled toward the wall, pausing every couple of steps. He flattened her to the cool plaster, bracing his arms to hold his weight off her. Her writhing body against his suit hitched her silky skirt up higher. He slid his hands down to her thigh— the band of her hose and garter hooks—holy crap, he didn't stand a chance now.

Heat seared through her silken panties, through his pants, through him. Her deft fingers worked free his belt and zipper.

Time was running out, but shit, her hand slid into his shorts and he couldn't form thoughts, much less words.

"Cooper," she breathed his name against his mouth, again along his neck, over his chest. "I want you now, no waiting."

With their clothes on? Yeah, he could work with the pants staying put. And if she was game for against a wall, no problem. Apparently, she needed this as much as he did.

She shimmied out of her panties, kicking them free

with a flick of her high-heeled shoe. Thank goodness for the practicality of a woman who knew to wear her underwear over the garters. The pool of white satin on dark wood fogged his brain.

"Lady, you sure do know how to make your point. To hell with our brains and better judgment, then."

He took her mouth, his entire body on fire with the knowledge that soon he would take her.

Lena wanted this. She knew that with a certainty as strong as the desire surging through her veins, but couldn't stop the twinge of remorse over what Cooper must think of her—sleeping with one man while still mistress to another.

She could not tell him she never planned to be with Alessandro again, and that grieved her more than it should have. Of course she'd never planned to be with her coke-snorting lover in the first place. She certainly didn't feel she owed him any loyalty.

How much could she say to Cooper without putting her life at risk? And how could she even think of willingly making love with a man she did not trust with the truth?

Yet the time for talking had passed. No more words, just the hot escape of their bodies touching, tingling, fitting together in a way that was frighteningly right. But after so long with a man horrifyingly wrong, perhaps anyone would feel amazing in comparison.

How could she not soak up the glorious sensation of enjoying a man's touch? Like an allover massage to her soul. She melted into the pleasure, the odd sense of safety after so long in fear. She writhed closer, welcoming the wash of sensations that helped cleanse away the horror of Alessandro's call, the nightmare of what could happen to her if she did not escape.

She had lost and given up nearly everything. Surely she could have this—have Cooper, for just a moment.

Not that he showed signs of finishing in a mere moment. Their tangled bodies bumped the sink, knocking a drinking glass and toothbrush to the ground in a shatter of glass around their feet.

He traced her ear with his tongue. "Don't want you to cut your feet." He cupped her bottom and lifted until she followed his lead and wrapped her legs around his waist. "Need to shuffle this party somewhere else. Pick. Preferably soon."

So where would they go next? Stay against the wall like some backstreet whore? No.

To her room—in her bed, or rather her mattress on the floor, but still *her* space. Which only left her rickety dining room table or the sofa.

She shoved away memories of Alessandro weighing her down on the leather couch at the factory, taking her during one of those times he'd consumed enough drugs to be rough, but not enough to steal his erection.

Maybe she needed a new sofa memory to banish old ghosts.

"The couch, behind you. Definitely soon."

"Heading that way." His shoes crunched against

broken glass, his limp creating a mismatched cadence. Still his secure hold left her with no doubt of his ability to carry her much farther if she so chose.

Stopping by her brocade sofa, he slid her down the length of his body in a sensuous glide. He dropped to sit on the overstuffed cushions and hauled Lena right along with him, his face going tight, serious. "If we're planning to get naked anytime soon, then we need to talk about one thing. And it may be a serious mood breaker."

"Then let's do not talk or 'get naked,' as you say." Less intimate, anyway, keeping some clothes and boundaries. "I want this to be uncomplicated. Spontaneous. No thinking."

"What we're doing here is definitely something two thinking people wouldn't even consider."

"But you have been watching me."

"I would like to watch more of you, but we just instituted this no-naked-rule which suddenly seems damn dumb."

"Not naked, does not mean totally covered."

A masculine growl rumbled in his chest, against hers in a primal sound of want that stirred an answer in her. "I like the way you think, lady."

He slid the blouse over her shoulders until the silk pooled around her waist in a sensual glide against her awakening senses, leaving her only in her satiny lace push-up bra—with her bruised ribs.

His eyes locked on the purplish stain on her skin, and his breathing went ragged in a way she knew had nothing to do with desire. She prayed he wouldn't speak and spoil the mood. She wasn't even sure she could bear if he looked up at her.

He bent his head to graze a kiss so soft along her side as her eyes went misty at the tenderness.

"Lena," he whispered, his hot breath a healing balm to her sore skin and soul. "Let me know if I hurt you."

If only she could tell him everything. "I'll hurt more if you stop."

"Then I won't stop." He reached for the back clasp.

In spite of her wish to continue, a tremor of insecurity rippled through her. How silly to care about her small breasts. He obviously found her attractive, but she so did not want to be found lacking when already her morals must be in doubt.

No apologies. She would hold her head high and brazen this out. "Just a warning, there is less than advertised beneath this undergarment."

"Somehow I don't think that's going to be a problem." He popped free the hooks, and eased her bra straps down her arms. His eyes heated to blue flames. "Not a problem at all. There's definitely something to that old saying about less being more."

He dipped his head to take a taut peak in his mouth. Sighing, she arched into the moist heat of his light suction followed by the flick of his tongue.

A simple touch, artful in its complete devotion to one task, no hopscotching from body part to body part in a mad dash that never left time to enjoy anything.

Although even if Alessandro had been the most devoted, artful lover in the world, she still would have been left cold. In the early months he had tried to woo her response with bedroom tricks and toys, never seeming to realize arousal depended on an elemental attraction.

An elemental attraction very much in play with Cooper.

Her fingers tugged at his tie, plucked down his buttons until his shirt flapped free and she could tunnel up under his white T-shirt. "You must work out in a gym."

"Weights. Burns tension."

"I would like to watch someday." She could dream, couldn't she?

"I get sweaty."

"Hmm. I like sweaty sometimes."

She rejoiced in the simple feel of Cooper's chest under her palms, bristly hair tickling her skin. He massaged down her back, twisting in the silk of her skirt bunched around her waist, arching her closer to his mouth. His grip traveled lower to her hips, his already rocking a subtle precursor.

With impatient fingers, she tugged the open fly of his pants wider, to reveal his straining arousal. The coarse sofa fabric abraded her knees, her skin suddenly hypersensitive to the least sensation. Her knees wriggled closer around his hips until she pressed against him, nothing between them but the cotton of his pin-striped boxers.

She had enjoyed sex with her husband, but never had time to miss it, first overrun by grief, then by Alessandro. Now her body flamed back to life demanding to be fulfilled. Her soul hungered for tender touches and the simple pleasure of giving and taking and giving back again, and, oh, but she was letting her thoughts grow too romantic when this was about escape and need.

Lena freed him from his boxers. He stopped her with a hand around her wrist. "In my pants pocket. Wallet. Condom."

"I like a responsible man." She slipped her fingers into his back pocket, enjoying the taut curve of his buttocks as she searched deeper.

"Temptress."

She wasn't, but perhaps she could fool him a while longer. Tugging his wallet free, she sank back to sit on his knees.

He winced.

Through the thin barrier of fabric, she felt some sort of bandage, like an elastic brace. She angled up to kneel. "Your bad knee, ankle, or whatever it was you hurt. I am sorry. Maybe we should go to my bed."

His grip tightened on her hips. "I'm cool with here, unless you want to swap out positions."

"I like this." Being on top, in control.

"Good. And I predict we're both going to like it a helluva lot more very soon." He reached to take the packet from her.

She closed her fist. "Let me."

"Whatever the lady wants."

And she *did* want, so very much.

Once she finished sheathing him, he gripped her hips and guided her down, her hands braced on his shoulders. She took him inside her, her *choice* to have a man, her first *choice* in over a year, and the power of it filled and pleasured her as fully as he did.

How could she have forgotten this wonderful sense of freedom? A freedom all the more precious after losing it. And still she wondered if she'd ever felt so free or had she merely not appreciated the wonder of it before now?

Thrusting his hips up, he cradled her face in his hands and kissed her, somehow even more intimate than just the coming together of bodies rocking against each other. But she couldn't pull away, couldn't stop moving and riding this swell of pleasure building, higher, harder until completion poured through her. Like filling her cup that had been empty for far too long. She let the sensations soothe over her, warm, rich, heady and overflowing far too soon until…

She sagged against his chest. Aftersurges washed over her while she listened to the hammering thud of his heart, slowly grounding her in the present, where too many questions waited. Such as what was the mood breaker they had dodged discussing?

And what had sent him running back to her tonight after he'd kissed her in his car?

BRIGID HEARD THE CLICK of Joe's hotel room door as he finally came back to her.

Wrapped in a comforter, tucked into the wingback chair, she waited for him in the darkened room, sunrise nowhere near ready to pierce the curtains. Light had already shown her more than she could absorb in one night when she'd seen Cooper in those photos.

Scrubbing the tattered and damp tissue under her nose, she burrowed deeper into the blanket, chilled to the bone in spite of the lackluster air-conditioning that barely dented the tropical summer heat. Ghosts from the past had a way of icing a person's soul. The printouts stayed scattered on the table where she'd left them after studying them with her magnifying glass. She should be happy to see Cooper alive. Instead the shock of it all left her teeth chattering, with tears trekking down her face and clogging her nose.

She couldn't let herself believe fully until she saw him in the flesh. Of course, Joe would have felt the same shock, probably the reason he'd run from her bed and stayed away for most of the night. Right? Nothing more.

Now that he'd returned, he would talk to her, tell her what he'd seen so they could check it out together. Like partners. Like friends. Like lovers—who'd just found out her past lover, a man she'd vowed she loved, had come back from the dead.

What a mess.

She listened to him bump around in his room, the bed creak as he must have sat on the edge, his shoes hitting the floor. He couldn't actually plan to go to sleep in there without coming back to her? Ever-thoughtful Joe wouldn't do that, no matter how much he was hurting.

The bed creaked again, followed by the slow tread of determined feet. Joe. Her tummy tightened.

As much as she wanted Cooper to be alive, she wished they could have discovered it a few hours later, after they had woken together, talked, made love one more time before she had to think about whatever feelings she might still have for Cooper.

Joe filled the connecting doorway, night shadows masking his face. She thought about clicking on the lamp, but then he would see her face and puffy eyes. Dark was better.

He started toward the bed, paused midtread and pivoted, searching the room until he faced her.

"Hey." He crouched in front of her, taking one of her cold hands in his and pressing a kiss to her wrist that made her want more, his arms, his shoulders. Him. "Sorry I wasn't here when you woke. I got up early for a run."

Before two in the morning, for hours? Sure, he wore basketball shorts and a T-shirt with the sleeves hacked off-running clothes, but also clothes a man would grab in a fast dash out the door.

She thought about confronting him straightaway, but damn it all, she wanted him to talk to her. In a world fracturing faster than if she'd shattered her favorite lens, she needed something to hold on to. She needed Joe…to be Joe. "I missed you."

"Would you like to find breakfast together or go back to sleep?"

He didn't suggest making love. Why? "How about we talk."

Joe looked as though he'd rather eat his gun. "Sure, whatever you want."

She wanted him to tell her about the pictures. She wanted them to share this. Could he be protecting her? Possible, but not good enough. After her father's awful deception and her mother's little lies as she held his secret, who wouldn't have a real problem with being left in the dark? As a matter of fact, lies attacked her stomach like an overdose of developing chemicals eating away at a photo.

In a night already chock-full of rocking changes, she needed for Joe to be his ever-honorable self now more than ever.

"How come you're called Face?" A story he'd never shared because he said it reminded him of Cooper and they were better off not discussing him. *Discuss him now, please. Talk to me.*

"My handsome mug of course." He stroked her wrist but still didn't come closer, much less kiss her, or better yet, scoop her into his lap to warm away the chill.

Come on, Joe. "I learned long ago from hanging out with you flyers that you don't give each other call signs to be nice. You use them to pick on each other. Like Vegas's pasties."

His teasing smile didn't come close to reaching his stormy eyes. "Wanna hear how Postal got his? It's a helluva story."

"I want to hear about you." And she really wanted to know what he'd been doing for the past few hours and how he'd gotten a bruise on his cheekbone.

"Sure, okay." He sank back on his haunches. "Truth is, I got drunk at the Officer's Club. I tripped on a step leading out of the bar, fell on my face. Thus the call sign 'Face.'"

But Joe didn't get drunk. He drank a beer or two with his friends, but she'd never seen him falling-down drunk. There was more to this story, and since he didn't seem in a hurry to discuss his late-night jog, she would have to dig on her own. "You were drunk because...?"

"You really want to talk about this?"

"I really do."

Dropping her hand onto her lap, he stood, backing away, which poured extra acid on her stomach. He strode to the open balcony doors and snatched his flight suit draped over a wrought-iron chair. "Woman troubles. What else drives a man to drown his sorrows in a bottle?" Backlit by the city lights, he grabbed his boots he'd discarded earlier before making love to her. "Her name was Victoria. I chose poorly, paid the price."

"How so?"

He stopped in the open doorway, his face in total shadow again, his shoulders blocking out the city skylight. "She was Cooper's, which should have meant hands-off. But I couldn't stay away from her."

She *so* didn't like where this was going and she *so* couldn't stop herself from digging for more. "Victoria was Cooper's?"

"Yeah, I met her when I went to visit him on vacation, nearly ruined my friendship with Cooper. And then she went and dumped me a year later because I was too much of a workaholic. So I guess it was actually a lucky break that we found out before we did something stupid like get married."

"Which would have really put a crimp in your friendship with Cooper, since she was *his* first, after all."

"Hey, wait, I just said—"

"I heard what you said." Her soul went as cold as her toes. She tucked her feet snugger into the folds of the blanket still carrying the scent of sex. Their sex. Sex that she'd enjoyed and wanted far more than sex with Cooper, which confused the hell out of her. She'd wanted to marry Cooper, but she and Joe weren't even looking at forever.

And she certainly didn't want forever with a man who lied to her, even if he justified it as being for her own good, which she was certain Joe had somehow managed to do.

He stepped deeper into the room, the slight light from the clock casting a red glow over his frown. "What's wrong?"

"Is that how you see me?"

"I'm not following."

"Did I *belong* to Cooper first?"

He stopped, went silent.

She rose from the chair, the comforter pooling around her ankles, leaving her wearing only his overlong T-shirt. "Do I now *belong* to you?"

"They're just words, and sometimes I don't express myself well. Maybe it has something to do with the fact I learned another language first."

"What would the word be, then, in your native language?"

Joe dropped to the corner of the bed. "I think I just fucked up."

"Damn straight you did. I don't 'belong' to anyone, pal." Anger driving her closer, she jabbed a finger in the middle of his chest. "I've been telling you all week that our friendship is separate from Cooper. If there had been no Cooper Scott, you and I would still have ended up in bed together someday. But not because I 'belong' to you, either. And if that's the way you see me—as some sort of possession to be taken care of—then you can just march your fine ass right out that door."

"Fine ass?" He smiled, stroking her cheek.

Too little, too late. She'd needed that smile when he walked into the room. More important, she'd needed his honesty. For whatever reason, he chose to stay silent about the truth imprinted in those photos. And her journalistic instincts left her with no doubts. He, too, had seen Cooper in those shots.

As much as she might wish to wait longer for Joe to come clean, those same pictures proved time had run out. "Don't try to distract me. I'm not done with you yet."

He stopped midcaress. "What is it you want to know?"

"Just one thing. What if Cooper was still alive?

Would you just step aside since I was 'his' before I was 'yours'? Or do the childish games between the two of you go more toward 'finders keepers'?"

CHAPTER SIXTEEN

COOPER WOKE in degrees of awareness.

Warm woman draped over him.

Dark blanketing the room.

The sweet smell of Lena almost erasing the nightmare scent of that final battle and the Iraqi prison.

He worked his head from side to side along the back of her sofa to ease the kinks in his neck while keeping the rest of him still so as not to disturb her. They'd both fallen asleep sitting up on the couch, with her straddling his lap. Way to go impressing the woman. One big finish and then pass out.

His leg ached from the awkward position. He needed to go back to his place soon for more practical reasons than gaining distance to clear his head.

While an amputee could lead an active life—hell, he even had a hospital roommate who could paratroop again—he still had very real and practical care concerns. His computerized titanium and graphite prosthetic leg brought more mobility, but the sucker needed recharging. Then there was the matter of stump care, keeping the scarred skin dry. And of course the longer he stayed like this, the more likely he would have to explain to her.

Lena's breathy sigh caressed his neck and blew away practical thoughts. "Is it morning yet?"

"Not yet. We only just drifted off."

"Good." She started to wriggle from his lap to the floor, then winced.

"Is something wrong?" Had she noticed?

"My feet have fallen into slumber."

"Fallen asleep."

"Whatever. It hurts."

"Try this." He lifted her by her waist and plopped her onto the sofa beside him so her legs draped over his lap. He glided his hands along her calves and massaged. "How's that?"

"Hmm." She sagged forward against his shoulder while he rubbed.

He studied the room over her shoulder, his eyes focusing in the dark. The wall seemed to crawl with shadows. His instincts burned...then relaxed as the spidery images took shape and shook free a laugh.

"What is so funny?" Lena stayed limp and sated against him

"Your son colors on the walls."

Her light laugh joined his. "Yes, he does."

"You're not upset?" Good thing since he hadn't thought when blurting out the observation. He just hadn't expected to see a kiddie mountain range behind her straight-back chair. "My mother would have blistered my butt if I marked her walls."

"You mentioned digging up your mother's gardens

once for your trucks. Did you get your—how did you say it—behind blistered very often?"

Lena kissed his neck. *Hello, morning wood.* Okay, technically not morning yet, but apparently his body was already anticipating "Reveille."

"Cooper?"

"Oh, uh, blistering and my mother. Not too often, actually." He so didn't want to talk about his mama, but if he quit talking, Lena might stop blowing in his ear. "She traveled a lot so I mostly stayed under the radar when it came to pissing her off."

"Her job took her away from you?"

Why all the questions?

Duh, because they'd enjoyed mind-blowing sex and now she deserved some intimacy. He pressed a kiss to her temple and stroked aside her sleep-tangled hair. "My mother traveled because she enjoyed it and had boatloads of money to spend, thanks to my father's convenient demise."

"I'm sorry." She angled back to look in his face. "What happened to him?"

"Natural causes. Old age." He had few memories beyond the photos and his mother's stories. Nice ones, actually, as if she might have actually liked the old coot. Why hadn't he noticed that before? "He lived a full life, died having sex with his trophy wife, which made him the envy of all his friends."

He watched for tearful compassion and found instead a hint of a smile.

"I believe you have what they would call in your country—issues with your mother, no?"

Well, damn. She wasn't crying. He could get to like this woman who already turned his libido inside out. "Yep, I'm a textbook classic."

"Who is justifiably angry but does not let it rule him." She nodded her approval, which for some reason meant a lot to him.

You're losing it here, pal. Shift the focus. "What about *your* parents?"

"Good people who let me draw on walls and explore the world. They encouraged me in my education, even though I wasn't much of a student. They treasured love—" she looked away "—and honesty. They died in a car accident shortly after I turned thirty."

"No siblings?"

She shook her head, silken hair gliding back over her shoulder to reveal the red scrape from his beard along her tender skin.

Come to think of it, he hadn't seen her with anyone at work—other than Aragon, and he would rather not think about that bastard at the moment. "So you're alone?"

"I have my son."

He sketched his knuckles down her cheek. "A son who also draws on walls."

"He has too few toys, and we made an agreement that he would keep the artwork behind the furniture. I will simply repaint when we leave."

"And when will that be?"

She stared at him without answering, then made a

fluttery wave gesture with her hand as if brushing aside his question. "We never got ice or a bandage for your face."

"I'm fine."

"Oh, well, we only have a couple more hours until I need to retrieve my son. Do you want to sleep? Or eat?"

He wanted to have sex again. Wanted to have sex with *her.* There couldn't be anything long-term—a thought that bothered him more than it should—but if he went for even once more tonight, he wouldn't be able to dodge getting naked, which meant a few explanations.

Did he want to be with her again enough to step onto that ledge? During his adult years, he'd jumped from planes, faced death in the form of a gun barrel shoved between his eyes, defeated death threatening with putrid wounds in a POW camp.

But his gut clenched tight now at the thought of taking one simple step with this woman.

His gut twisted tighter at the prospect of walking away. "I would rather go to bed with you. No sleeping."

She purred in his ear and started to slide off him.

He palmed her waist to stop her. "But first, I should probably clue you in some more about the accident involving my leg."

"Are you worried I'll become squeamish over a few scars? I can assure you, while I have my flaws, I am not that shallow."

"This is about more than scars—" although he had his fair share of those, too, inside and out "—and no hard feelings if you decide this is more than you can handle."

"Try me, and soon, please, because I suspect the hints are more upsetting than reality." She caressed his cheek. "Tell me. Show me."

"All right, then." He took her hand from his face and placed it on his thigh, then moved it to his knee.

A frown flickered across her features, confusion, not disgust. So far, so good. He released her hand and let her find her way lower to the hard shell casing of his prosthesis that couldn't be confused with the give of flesh and muscle.

Then her expression blanked while she explored with a featherlight touch and absorbed the truth. He waited, wondering which would be worse. Her disgust or pity.

Please not pity. He could hate a person for disgust, which would easily fire him out the door. God knows, he refused to feel sorry for himself. During his stint at Walter Reed Hospital, he had seen too many patients missing two and even three limbs. Others blind or brain damaged. He was one of the lucky ones in comparison. And the computerized prosthesis offered him a life and hope beyond what had been offered to WWII vets who had strapped on wooden legs.

He was more than a missing limb. He'd built himself a fucking full life, was coping. Hanging tough.

But God, no pity.

An odd rogue thought trickled through the barrage zipping through his head while Lena explored his leg—and yeah, he'd noticed how she didn't shy away.

But back to that rogue thought to keep him distracted while he waited for Lena's verdict. Had he submerged himself in the CIA undercover so he wouldn't have to face moments like this with people close to him? Had he hidden from his mother's pity? Brigid's tears he remembered every time he touched that hemp tie? Even Joe's intense ways that would make Cooper think about losses too often?

He forced his fists to relax against the brocade sofa. He'd made the best decision he could. He'd wanted to avenge his men. And since he'd known Joe had a thing for Brigid, and since Joe was the best man on the planet, Joe would take care of Brigid.

Except, he didn't want to think about Joe and Brigid right now. A woman, Lena, deserved all of his attention.

Skimming her hand back up to his knee, she squeezed, a whimsical smile flickering. "I guess we were both advertising more than we actually had beneath our clothes."

Her smile teased along with her words referencing her own concern about wearing a Wonderbra. Not really a valid analogy as he considered her pert breasts perfect, but he still appreciated like hell her light approach. No pity. No tears or heavy discussions. Just smiling acceptance and undiminished desire.

An answering drive blazed through him.

Without speaking—God, how had he been lucky enough to find a woman who knew when to stay silent?—she stood and held out her hand in a follow-me gesture rather than any offer of help. Lena linked her fingers with his and led him back to her surprisingly sparse room.

An overlarge armoire dominated from a corner, looming even more as the only real piece of furniture in a room with nothing else but a squat end table and a mattress neatly made, the sheets and tightly tucked blankets, cream colored, plain but painstakingly clean.

What was she doing with her paycheck?

Then her hands slid inside the open waistband of his pants to cup his butt, and finances became the last thing he wanted to think about.

Bare from the waist up, she shimmied out of her skirt until it slithered down around her ankles, leaving her in nothing more than her garter belt and stockings. Her glossy hair tumbled in a dark cloud over her shoulders to tease along the tips of her definitely perfect breasts.

She knelt at the edge of the mattress and lounged back waiting, watching, intuitively leaving herself vulnerable and bare before she asked the same of him.

He shrugged out of his shirt, bent to slide one shoe then the other free. His pants went next in a quick sweep that took his boxers with them.

Propped on her elbows, dusky skin gleaming in the moonlight, she lay unmoving and studied him. All of him, his shoulders, chest, lingering on his straining erection with a sultry smile that made him twitch in response. Her gaze sketched lower and up again as thoroughly.

"Does all this mean I get the pleasure of being on top again?"

This woman was definitely heavensent. He appreciated her sensitivity that didn't insult him by dodging the situation, but still offered him a face-saving out if he needed it.

Cooper knelt on the edge of the mattress and worked his way up her body, starting with a nibble along her stomach. "Only if you want to be on top. I'm cool either way."

"Hmm." She eased from her elbows to her back, her neck arching as he licked the underside of her breast. "In that case, perhaps it is your turn to take control."

He stretched over her, skin to overheated skin, the scent and feel of her too familiar for someone he'd only known once before. "Lady, somehow I don't think I've been in control of a damn thing around you for a long time now."

FINDERS KEEPERS?

Joe studied Brigid through narrowed eyes as she stood too still in front of her chair wearing his T-shirt and no smile. Something was off here, but the dark room and shadows hid nuances in her expression he might otherwise have seen. Could she possibly know about Cooper? But if so, logic indicated she would have said something right away.

On a better day, he could follow her train of thought. But he felt as if life was blindsiding him from every direction.

First the mind-blowing moment finding Brigid waiting for him in nothing but a robe. He couldn't even let himself think about the best-ever sex they'd shared.

Then stumbling on photos of Cooper, followed by Cooper for real… No freaking wonder he couldn't take his brain off stun long enough to decipher Brigid's cryptic words.

Her pissed-off tone, however, couldn't be missed.

Tread warily. "Are you upset with me for not being here when you woke up?" He shouldn't have taken that selfish walk afterward. No matter what happened between them because of Cooper, Brigid deserved better than to wake up alone. "I didn't expect you to wake up that early. I am so damn sorry, Red."

He reached for her arm.

She dodged his hand, walked past and to the small table, keeping her back to him. "You didn't answer my question." She toyed with the edge of one of the photos, bent the corner and straightened, bent and straightened. "Would you pass me back to Cooper if he suddenly walked through that door?"

His brain went off stun with a startling blast of understanding. She knew, must have found out the same way he did.

Why couldn't they have looked at the photos together in the morning? Or after this week? Cooper would have still been alive and they wouldn't be having this conversation.

He refused to regret being with her. That far he couldn't go, even for his friendship with Cooper. "I should have gotten rid of those pictures when I left."

Spinning back, she faced him, eyes accusing. "Yes, you should have, but I would have gone looking for them and figured it out anyway." She blinked hard against tears, glinting in the dark room. "Do you really think he's alive?"

"Apparently so."

She sank back to the chair, her hands twisted in her lap pressing his shirt taut against her breasts.

Fuck this. He wasn't keeping his distance when she needed him. He dropped to a knee in front of her again. "Are you okay?"

"No."

"It's a shock."

"Hell, yes, it's a shock. How could you lie to me?"

Huh? "What are you talking about?"

She thumped his arm which happened to still be sore from slugging it out with Cooper. "You knew and didn't say anything when I gave you an opening."

Cooper was the one who'd hidden for the past two years and she was pissed off at *him?* Well, he was torqued at Cooper and then felt like shit for being angry when his friend had lost a leg, for crying out loud. Even though he knew it wasn't his fault, he couldn't shake the feeling that he should have done something.

Worse yet, resentment and guilt went into afterburners over the timing of it all. But this probably wasn't the right moment to tell Brigid that, damn straight she was *his* now. Cooper had given up any rights with his two-year-long possum act. "I only just found out myself."

"Still, you walked right in here and didn't say one word." Her brows pleated together. "Where were you?"

He couldn't answer.

She went pale and dropped her head between her knees. "Ohmigod, ohmigod, ohmigod." She straightened, sweeping her hair from her face. "You already saw him? You found him somehow?"

He nodded.

"How?" She gasped. "He's okay?"

"Appears so. I just tracked the location in the picture and hung out there until he showed up."

"No amnesia or something that would explain why he's been lying for two years?"

"I wondered the same thing. But he's…basically okay. Answers may be slow in coming."

She blinked hard and fast, but the tears pooled faster, slipping over to trail down her face. "I can't believe this is real." She gasped for air, pressed the heel of her hand to her forehead until her breathing slowed, if not the tears. "I have to see him."

Shit. He resented this convoluted mess that left him in the position of having to cover for Cooper, when more than anything he wanted to waltz Brigid right back out onto that balcony where they could lose themselves in each other and forget about everything else.

But how could he sleep with her when he wasn't sure about her feelings for Cooper? "Give it time. There are things he can't explain just yet—"

"Don't you dare." She held up a hand. "*Don't* you dare tell me no. I mean it. If you won't make it happen, I'll just take out a front-page ad in the local paper."

Looking at her right now, full of fire and pain, he

believed her. God, this woman made him crazy and turned him inside out all at once. No wonder she kicked ass at her job. She didn't take no for an answer. "I'll set something up."

"Thank you." She angled forward in her chair to rest against his chest, her arms looping around his neck. "I can't believe all of this is happening and I can't decide whether to cheer or cry or both. Where has he been? Why didn't he contact us?"

As she continued her rambling outpouring of questions without giving him time to answer, her face fit so perfectly against his neck he ground his teeth against the urge to haul her up into his arms and take her back to bed.

This wasn't the time or place, not with so much mess between them and Cooper. His arms hung at his sides.

Brigid inched back. "You still see me as his."

"Aren't you?"

She hesitated a second too long before saying, "No. No, damn it. I don't belong to anyone."

"That's not what I meant and you know it. You can't pretend this doesn't change things." Christ Almighty, his hopes for deepening their friendship, taking it to another level while keeping things uncomplicated, were spiraling downward faster than a plane in a death stall.

"Why can't we both just celebrate that he's still alive?"

"How would you suggest we celebrate? I gotta tell

you I don't feel much like naked Jell-O wrestling right now."

She offered him a wobbly smile. "Wow, a one-liner you didn't even have to look up on your PalmPilot."

He wanted to touch her, to comfort her, but couldn't take that step without then peeling that T-shirt off her supple body so they could both escape the questions piling up faster than anyone could answer. "We can't do this, not until you see him again and know for sure."

She rubbed her hands along her arms, even though the air conditioner sucked as always. "Then figure out a way for me to see him."

CHAPTER SEVENTEEN

LENA RECLINED into her pillows propped against the wall, her mattress on the floor a far more sensual haven than she ever would have expected. Early-morning rays slashed through the slim part in her drapes, offering just enough light as she blinked to moisten her contact lenses for a better view. She watched Cooper button his shirt, his pants fly unzipped, belt hanging loose.

The intimacy of the moment permeated her dehydrated heart after so long without the simple pleasures of normalcy. Sure she had seen Alessandro dress, but there was nothing normal about their encounters.

Her world would be flipped soon enough regardless of what happened in the coming days. She didn't want to think about any of that just yet, when she could hold on to normalcy for a few precious seconds longer.

Her eyes drifted down Cooper's body, honed, muscular, yet not a perfect golden god, after all, but rather very mortal. Of course his imperfection was merely physical, therefore nothing that diminished his appeal, nothing to do with the core person.

Unlike the marks on her soul. No matter how many

times she told herself there were no other choices she could have made, the shame still shadowed her. The subjugation, a rape of her soul. The wounds reopened, raw and painful again, as Cooper reawakened her senses and emotions.

So much for not thinking of Alessandro.

Cooper zipped his pants, the rasp of metal echoing in the quiet room. He extended his hand to her. "Walk with me to the door?"

She suspected if she wasn't careful she would walk just about anywhere with this man.

Tucking the sheet around her, she rose from her baseboard-level bed, her feet tangling in the covers and sending her crashing against his chest. She caught her breath, which now happened to be full of the shower-clean scent of him, the toothpaste on his breath.

Mixed with the aroma of *them* still clinging to the sheet.

He kissed her once, twice, slow and simple kisses of goodbye. "I wish I could stay longer."

"You can't, and I shouldn't." She breezed her hand over the roughened rasp of his unshaven face, careful of the bruise he wouldn't discuss or let her tend. "I have responsibilities to my son. I need to gather myself and my thoughts, which won't be as easy as I would have expected."

As much as she could share of her chaotic emotions without falling to pieces—or betraying herself. She wasn't one for weepy displays that gained nothing.

His forehead dropped to rest against hers. "You're a good woman. Your son is lucky to have you."

"You do not have to pacify me or pretend you do not know who I have spent my time with over the past months. Tonight was just…"

"Was what?"

"Inevitable."

"Excellent word choice." His hands roved her back, the strength and sensation unmuted even by the sheet. "But it shouldn't happen again."

She already knew, but hearing him confirm it poured alcohol on those open wounds. What did she expect? That he would demand she walk away from Alessandro for him?

How ridiculous based on one night of sex. And six months of longing.

Time ticked away fast. Soon she would be leaving this place, a dream of over a year. He lived and worked here. Although, who knew what he would do once Alessandro's business folded. He was from the States after all.

Dangerous thoughts, thinking beyond tonight with him, especially when she didn't have a clue whether or not she could trust this man. She had already risked too much.

"Of course it cannot happen again."

"Because you're with Aragon." His emotionless voice, warm and peppermint scented against her face, betrayed little, but she could not ground the butterflies in her stomach at the notion he might be jealous.

Very unwise for both of them. "Just because we shared each other's bodies for one night does not give you the right to question me about my life."

"Understood," he conceded with a single word, but still held her, his forehead against hers and pale blue gaze piercing her thoughts.

She squeezed her eyes shut to block out temptation. She had to stay strong for her son, but couldn't escape more tender feelings for this man. Feelings and concerns.

His injury did not upset her in the way he had seemed to fear initially—other than regret for the pain and loss he'd suffered. But it did serve as a reminder of even an oh-so-strong man's mortality.

"Be careful," the words fell out of her mouth without warning. He went so tense in her arms her eyes opened of their own volition. "You have to know what Alessandro is capable of. Be careful."

His blue eyes lightened to a cooler shade, the piercing probe more like an icicle now.

"I can look out for myself." His voice stayed level, even if his eyes went sharp. "And it's not like I plan to go into his office and announce what happened here tonight, any more than you would."

A frightening scenario. "There are…layers to his business. I would hate for something to happen to you if things went badly someday."

"Layers."

She wanted to trust him, but could not risk her son. She looked at the floor, at their feet, which again reminded her of how easily life could be taken away.

He tipped her chin up. "Maybe you need to listen to your own words, then. If you know so much about what he is doing and don't approve, then get the hell out. Now, before it's too late for you and your son."

She bit the insides of her mouth to stay silent when she wanted to shout back in his condemning face that she had tried to leave this country, more than once, and knew how impossible it could be for a woman alone. In the beginning she had pursued conventional methods with no luck. Then her neighbor had disappeared, a young college girl with no family. Everyone knew she had been bartered into prostitution, what happened to too many defenseless women in her country.

As a last resort she had sold what little remained to purchase a forged visa out of the country, only to be stopped at the border, her train tickets taken without any refund, leaving her with no money. No hope. And all because a corrupt border patrol agent decided she would have to sleep her way out of the country.

She'd been so naive then, spitting in his face and vowing to find another way. *Any* other way.

Panic chewed inside her stomach. At least her contacts with local authorities had paid her for bits and pieces of information on Alessandro. Their money, doled out along the way, reassured her somewhat that hopefully they could be trusted to secure her safe passage.

What did she know about Cooper except he worked for a corrupt boss and touched her soul with his love-making?

And bought toy soldiers for her son because he had enjoyed them as a child. Heaven help her, she wanted to trust again.

"Lena, why don't you leave, for your son at least?" Cooper gripped her shoulders in hands not quite gentle anymore. "Unless you know what kind of man Aragon is and simply don't care."

Dios Mio, his condemning words hurt so much worse than she would have expected. But then, hadn't he already stripped away her numb defenses over the past weeks?

She wrenched away before she weakened. "Who the hell do you think you are to judge me?" She hitched her sheet higher with as much dignity as she could muster. "What do you know of me? My life? My choices? You have your own secrets and I have mine. Just because we shared a bed does not give you the right to all of me."

He backed, hands raised in surrender, *his* defenses apparently in full working order. "That's the way you want it then? Fine. But I was willing to offer more."

No. No, no, no, she would not listen to this, words that were most likely only after-sex platitudes, or just a hollow offer to appease his conscience because he knew she would turn him down. Why couldn't this be as simple as she had planned?

She spun away to school her face, kicking the tangle of sheet from her feet as she made her way toward the bathroom. "Men and their 'more.' I am so tired of men and their offers of more, which demand even more of me than they give."

He stood unmoving while she raged, which further angered her for some perverse reason. She snatched her robe off a hook on the bathroom door.

The sheet slithered to the bed as she slid her arms into the robe and yanked the tie closed. "You assume much about me and my son and how I live my life. You refer to me as *señorita*." Her voice rose in time with her steps closer. "Did you ever once think perhaps I once had a husband and all his *more?*"

Her throat closed on the last word, but she didn't break. And at least she had stunned him silent.

"You see what you want to see, not the real me." Why had she said that? Something that would make him look deeper when it was far safer he did not see her heart. "Go home. Just get the hell out of my apartment and my life. I will take care of myself and my son."

He blinked once, exhaled slow and long, his face going tight. With anger or hurt? "Is that what was going on here tonight with us? Keeping yourself safe?"

She couldn't decide whether to slap him for the insult or scream with frustration over his denseness. Men and their egos that kept them from seeing the obvious. Sleeping with him could have in no way helped her. But if she clued him in on that little fact, then she would make herself vulnerable at a time when she trusted him less than ever.

A buzz cut the thick silence. Still they stared at each other without moving—until the buzz sounded again. And again, until Cooper snatched his pager from his belt, studied the panel.

His fist went white-knuckled. "Shit. Looks like you're going to get your wish after all. I have to go."

ALESSANDRO DISCONNECTED the phone and pitched it to the foot of his bed where it landed with a thud in the tangle of covers from a restless night. He'd hoped a night of pure pleasure in the safe room under his factory would give him a release from the pressure of terrorist bastards breathing down his neck for a smooth delivery.

His eyes drifted to the wet bar across the room where the anthrax bacteria were stored, the pseudo silica packages had already been prepared in a lab with the laced cocaine.

Scratching his hands through his hair, raking it from his face, he resisted the urge to grab for the half-empty packet of his untainted coke stashed just a reach away in a drawer. Disappointment, pain—rage—sliced through the foggy hangover from his midnight line.

Lena had lied to him.

A call to Señora de Guerra confirmed suspicions he'd actually hoped were cocaine-induced paranoia. But no. The hesitation and guilt he'd heard in Lena's voice were all too real.

Her son had not been in the next room as she'd insisted to keep him away. The little boy had spent the night at Señora de Guerra's. Lena had denied him her presence when he'd needed her. His hand slid back and forth over the cool—empty—stretch of satin beside him.

He slumped back on the pile of pillows and tried to soak in the sounds of classical music piping through the sound system along with rose-scented air freshener. If he closed his eyes, perhaps he could pretend his mother played instead of some CD. He could imagine a time when he could talk to her, be her favored child and ask the question pounding through his aching head.

Was it so wrong to expect the people he cared for to be there when he needed them? He understood Lena did not overly enjoy sex, but he had needed her. He had begged her, demeaned himself, and after all he had done for her, she'd lied to him.

Flinging aside the satin sheet, he swung his feet to the carpeted floor. She deserved to die for betraying him. Anyone else who betrayed him would die or be sold into a hellish life of degrading pain.

His throbbing head fell into his hands. Except he couldn't live without her. He loved her, adored her. Worshipped her.

Always.

Which left him with a serious problem—how to subdue her, how to tie her to him more effectively. His gaze fell to the bedside table with its open drawer holding the plastic bag dusted with remnants of white powder.

Perhaps she would benefit from some relaxation, as well. The options were endless for slipping any number of drugs into her drink, increase slowly over the next few days to keep her with him when he needed her, then more in the future until she couldn't live without him either.

The phone jangled him from his plans. He snagged the receiver. "Aragon."

"Sir, Sanchez here," his head of security said with fast intensity. "I am sorry to disturb you so early, but we have discovered something interesting in the listening devices at the hotel. You'll want to hear a conversation between the American photographer and her pilot boyfriend."

TAKING A LOVER to see her old boyfriend ranked number one on Joe's "Things That Suck" list.

Waiting at his table in the packed cantina, Joe peered over his aviator sunglasses while Brigid make her way to the bathroom to find tissues since she was having trouble reining in tears. Cooper had insisted on a crowded, noisy locale. Easier to explain away than sneaking off.

And safer to be out in the open, given Cooper's current dealings.

A mariachi band played too loudly in the corner, but would overpower conversation if anyone tried to eavesdrop. He'd already ordered plates of enchiladas for everyone so they wouldn't draw attention by sitting without food, then instructed the waitress to stay away until they were ready for the check.

Shadows, low lighting and the lunchtime crowd offered plenty of camouflage even at high noon. No one would notice Brigid's tears.

Except for him.

She needed this as much as she wanted it. This was the right thing to do, even if it hurt like hell.

After the confrontation with Brigid, he'd paged Cooper and set up this meeting. Joe wore civilian clothes, the dark pants and shirt Brigid gave him seemed best, inconspicuous and less touristy than shorts and a polo. Or God forbid, his flight suit.

He hadn't mentioned the reason for the meeting— not trusting phone lines to be secure. And not trusting Cooper to show, if he knew.

Joe had, however, told Brigid as much as he could about Cooper. That Cooper had been an unreported POW, the reason they hadn't heard from him. That after his rescue, he'd gone undercover for a govern- ment-endorsed agency to catch some of the bastards responsible for the death of his team. And yes, he'd even told her about the amputation, because knowing might make Cooper's need to fade away for a while easier to understand. She might hurt less.

Peering through the smoke-stained window, Joe studied the crowds flowing in cross-currents stream on both sides of the street in an indistinguishable mass. A man peeled off from the crush and strode through the open doorway of the cantina.

Cooper.

It still blew him away seeing his friend alive, even in a double-breasted suit and hair brushing his collar.

Cooper dropped into the chair across from him. "What's up? I assume it's important for you to risk contacting me so soon."

Joe tipped back his bottled water. Slowly he centered it back on the damp ring in the tablecloth. "She knows."

He wouldn't have to say who.

"Damn." Cooper leaned on his elbows, hunching closer so they could keep their voices low. "How?"

Joe angled closer, too, over the plate of cooling food. "I saw you in the background of photos, and she got to them before I could dispose of them."

Cooper exhaled long, picked up a fork and see-sawed it between two fingers, tapping the table. "Her knowing changes things."

"No shit, Sherlock." He should warn Cooper that Brigid would be showing up any second now, but some perverse part of him was still pissed off.

Or maybe he needed to line up this meeting with no warning to get a look at Cooper's unguarded reaction to seeing her again.

The fork tapped faster. "We're going to need to talk more than we can here. I've got a place."

A safe house? Of course. "Not a bad idea. Later."

"Why not now?"

"Cooper?" Brigid's voice drifted over his shoulder.

His friend's eyes went wide and jerked to look at her. Joe watched for a reaction— emotion—and found only wariness. Relief damn near knocked him over.

"Cooper? Is it really you?"

"Yeah," he pushed from the table to stand, "it's me."

Brigid's hitched breath sent Joe's hands fisting on the white linen cloth.

She skirted around the table to Cooper, stopping, swaying. The sun steamed through the smoky glass, creating some kind of sappy silhouette effect, a time-lessness. This could have been two years ago.

Shit.

Her shaky hand gravitated up, landed on his cheek

lightly, as if she was afraid he would disappear if she touched too hard. Her fingers trembled up to skim over his blond-streaked hair.

Tears filled her eyes, pooled over and beaded down her face. Joy and pain radiated from her in waves that threatened to rock the water bottles on the table.

Cooper hauled her in for a hug. She rested her head against his chest—comforting or concealing her tears? She cried while he stroked her hair gathered in the overlong lens cloth. Patted her back the way Joe knew he should have done for her the night before.

Of course she was crying. He'd been damn near in tears seeing Cooper the night before. Wasn't feeling too steady right now.

Finally she eased apart from him with a laughing sniffle. "We should probably sit before we draw some kind of crowd."

"You always did have more sense than me." Cooper guided her to a chair, his hand benignly touching her arm—not even her shoulder or waist—but still he glanced at Joe quickly. Then looked away.

"Awkward as hell" didn't begin to cover it.

Brigid swept her hand behind her to clear her flowing skirt as she sat. Any other day he would have taken macho pride out of the fact she wore one of his T-shirts with that skirt, but he knew she'd been in such a rush to see Cooper, she'd grabbed the first thing her hands found before she'd jammed her feet in flip-flops.

Joe passed her a napkin. Yeah, he was really Captain Sensitivity offering up the comfort in the form of grease-stained linen. She took it with a quivery smile of gratitude, their fingers brushing, sparking memories of tangling naked on her balcony under the stars.

To hell with gratitude. Seeing the emotion ripping through her over this reunion, he wondered how Cooper could throw that away. Didn't he realize how much he'd put her through?

Being the survivor hurt like hell. He'd learned that early on as a kid. That Cooper would do that to her on purpose… Joe opened his fists, flattening his palms to the table as he fought the urge to pummel Cooper all over again.

Hell, yeah, he was jealous, the main reason he and Cooper had agreed never to go after the same woman.

But hadn't the jealousy been there anyway, back when Brigid and Cooper dated?

Cooper passed her a second napkin since she'd soaked the first. "I told you I would come back alive."

She tugged the napkin from Cooper without so much as casual contact, a fact that meant too much. "You're a little late."

"Sorry about that." His face creased with the Cooper-style grin that had charmed their tenth-grade teacher when she questioned what had happened to the ice chest full of frogs for dissection.

When Brigid's weak attempt to smile back failed, Cooper continued, "I don't have a perfect excuse to offer you, and I don't deserve to be forgiven. I did what I felt I had to do at the time."

She tipped back a drink of water but looked in need of something stronger. "How long were you a POW?"

His gaze shot to Joe.

Joe spread his hands. "I had to tell her something. The truth seemed to work."

"Oh, yeah, the truth." Cooper winced, then turned back to Brigid. "Honest to God, I've never been sure. A few weeks. I was pretty much out of it."

"Your leg—"

Cooper's jaw flexed. "So you told her about that, too? Maybe I should get you a megaphone for Christmas?"

"Maybe you could get me a pair to make up for the past two Christmases you blew off."

Cooper sagged back in his chair, grinning. He never could stay mad long. *"Touché."*

"She deserved to know."

She would have found out eventually even if he hadn't told her, and he figured it would make this first meeting easier on her if she understood at least a part of Cooper's need to hide from life.

Brigid straightened and tossed aside her tear-soaked napkin. "We can talk about all of that later. The important thing is that you're still alive to discuss everything."

"Thanks." Cooper rested his hand on top of hers. "I know I owe you more. I swear when I wrap up some loose ends I'm going to try and explain things better."

Hang tough; Joe resisted the urge to drape his arm along the back of Brigid's chair in a proprietary stake that would only pitch a match on a situation already fueled to blow.

She inched her hand from under his and folded it in her lap. "You don't owe me a thing. We never made any promises."

Watching her dodge Cooper's touch, Joe figured he should be relieved, but he kept thinking she would only be this reserved if she was hurt. And she would only be hurt if she still had feelings. He was finding he didn't forgive as easily, even when he understood the reasons.

So take a swing at Cooper, his conscious prodded.

Except Brigid would cry again.

Shit, being fair sucked about as much as bringing his lover to meet her old boyfriend. But he didn't want her to be hurt anymore. He would do anything to keep her happy. Even if giving her up ripped his heart out.

His heart? Joe went still in his seat, mariachi music and diners, even the smoke and Cooper fading until nothing remained but Brigid. Her hair twisted up in a lens cloth. Her face so open. Her toes scrunching in her flip-flops like she did when she was nervous. He *knew* Brigid.

What a helluva time to realize he loved her.

CHAPTER EIGHTEEN

THREE HOURS LATER Cooper shut the safe house's back room door behind Joe. Thank God for equitable security clearances which made briefing his military bud all the easier.

Brigid knowing about his return from the dead, on the other hand, posed a problem. A problem they would get around to discussing as soon as he finished catching Joe up on details. Then they could better decide what to do, now that someone without a top security clearance had learned sensitive information about his undercover op.

The surprise reunion with Brigid had gone much the same as he had envisioned when he dared let himself think of living long enough to see her again. She'd cried tears almost as immense as his guilt. Overall, he should count himself lucky, since his darkest nightmares included her screaming well-deserved accusations at him.

Now he would add some new nightmares to the mix where Joe beat the crap out of him all over again for breaking her heart even if she didn't have romantic feelings for him anymore. Only an idiot would miss the jealousy, possessiveness, anger pulsing from Joe earlier. That reunion just about killed his friend. And hurting Joe cut right through him, too.

It was probably for the best he wouldn't be seeing Brigid again until they all got back to the States.

Joe tapped the basketball hoop on the closed door with a slow dunk. "You brought a Nerf basketball hoop with you to South America?"

"It relaxes me." And he couldn't let himself remember a much better way to relax—with Lena. "Basketball always did help."

Cooper strode over to the bin by the lone desk, peered inside and found…nothing. Three steps across the hardwood floor and he yanked the door open again to shout into the outer office space. "Rodriquez, where the hell are my Nerf balls?"

Ratty tennis shoes propped on a desk, Rodriquez smirked, tugging the bottom drawer. "It's a piss-poor-pitiful man who can't keep up with his own balls."

The first orange foam basketball whizzed across the room.

"And it's a piss-poor-pitiful man who steals them." Cooper snagged one, then two more as they sailed toward him. "Thanks."

"Anytime."

Cooper shut the door again and lobbed one to Joe. "I checked the military rosters for that big dedication ceremony Sunday and didn't see your name."

Joe aimed, then flicked his wrist for a cross room shot, *swish*, nothing but net. "The Pave Low roster was the only one posted. The CV-22 was a variable right to the last minute, with finishing training in time and testing out the craft for these early operational runs."

"Makes sense." He launched a three pointer, shooting hoops preferable to looking each other in the eyes.

And there was something oddly comforting about sliding into an old routine with Joe.

"Once I heard el Jedr was sniffing around here, I couldn't pass up the chance to take a swipe at him after what happened in Iraq. Same reason I assume you're here…"

"Pretty much." *Aim. Shoot. Swish. Keep it simple.* "So here we are."

"Word is he's planning something big."

"With the help of a local small businessman— Alessandro Aragon. Aragon was already a well-known drug trafficker, so he'd already crossed a line. Which made him the perfect patsy for el Jedr's network. Aragon's next shipments of clothing into the U.S. will carry his standard cocaine haul—laced with a hybrid form of anthrax that's more resilient when airborne."

"Holy crap." Joe's shot smacked the door above the net and rebounded back wild against the gray plaster wall.

Cooper chunked his two extra Nerf balls in the storage bin and faced Joe for a real bout of one-on-one. He stared Joe down, silently daring him to hold back.

Joe's eyes narrowed a flash before he charged toward the basket, the bare lightbulb above the lone illumination in a room with the only window blackened and secured.

Yes. Cooper boxed out, thanking God for the computerized sensors that read any strain to his leg and made speedy adjustments. "I've located the anthrax stash in his factory. Problem is, we have to find who's the supplier. That's our direct link to el Jedr. With those two players still in the field, they'll just find replacements for Aragon."

"You've been busy the past couple of years." He faked left then right.

"Yeah, well, when the CIA showed up at my bedside and asked if I wanted to stay dead and do some work for them in their counterterrorism division, I couldn't say no."

Joe tucked the ball under his arm, no dodging his intense stare full of remorse. "I wish I could have helped you then. You have to know you would have felt the same if the positions were reversed."

Valid point that stung. "And you have to know this is something I had to do for myself. Something I owe my men who didn't get out alive."

"Understood." Joe scrubbed a hand over his face as if shifting gears. "So back to this Aragon dude."

"I'm still working conventional angles," Cooper said, snagging the ball from Joe while his defenses were down, "trying to get the information from his files, even straight from him or one of his people."

"Your branch plans?"

Practical Joe always reminded him to have backups.

Something of his friend he'd carried with him these past months without even realizing it until now. "If we can't trace the anthrax conventionally, I'll lift a sample of the anthrax and have it analyzed to trace its genetic makeup back to that strain's country of origin."

"Dangerous."

"That's all relative in this job. Up to now I've been more concerned with them noticing the sample's gone. It's not like they have buckets of this crap lying around so a sprinkle isn't missed. Mere ounces of this stuff spread out in different packets of cocaine could wipe out entire cities."

"What if he moves it before you find what you're looking for?"

"We'll call for an immediate air strike that will incinerate the whole factory. We'll pray none of the anthrax manages to survive and disperse. We've got a B-2 Stealth Bomber standing by to drop a thermobaric bomb."

"A BLU-118/B?" Rebound, shoot.

Rebound shoot. "Yeah."

Joe nodded as they alternated sinking shots. "Good choice, payload with a high-energy temperature burst. The fireball has a powerful shock wave that should incinerate everything around it."

"Of course, then we can't trace the anthrax, so while sure we save the day, we delay plowing through this investigative bullshit all over again, with el Jedr even more on guard."

"How close are you?"

"Aragon trusts me as much as he trusts anyone. I need more time—and can't have it. No surprise. I've got an in with his, uh, girlfriend who works at the place. I've been hoping to cross-reference information in her computer with info in mine to make a link. But no luck."

Swish. And stop. The ball stuck in the net, much like their conversation stalled as they ran out of diversionary conversation.

He couldn't avoid the obvious any longer. "Is Brigid okay?"

Joe moved to the net to smack free the ball, his back to Cooper. "Shell-shocked. Pissed. Hurt. But functioning. She and Sonny Fielding—"

"With *World Weekly?*"

"Right." Joe slumped against the door with the ball stowed under his arm and out of play. "I left the two of them talking about his article on the upcoming Pave Low dedication ceremony."

"We have a problem there." Cooper sat on a wide ledge, the window behind him covered with reinforced glass and steel shutters. "I was confident in riding this out when you were the only one who knew about me, but Brigid gums up the works here. Her being in the news business…damn, could it be any worse?"

"Actually, she hung up her news camera two years ago and has been working as a portrait photographer."

"I know."

"Kept tabs on her, have you?" Joe's fingers dug deep into the Nerf ball, even as he kept his face expressionless.

"Wouldn't you?" If he had been in the same position, which of course honorable Joe never would have been. "But then you wouldn't have left her high and dry like that. Question of the moment, though, is Brigid mad enough to turn me in for the scoop of the century?"

"No." Joe shook his head without hesitation. "She thinks you're a rat bastard—but she'll keep quiet. She may want you dead, but only by her own hand."

"You're sure?"

"Yeah, I'm sure. She kicks ass at her job, but she would never knowingly put anyone in danger. It's that humanity in her that actually makes her photos so damned incredible."

"Sounds like you understand her better than I ever did."

Joe looked away, closing off his thoughts. Fat lot of good, since they'd always known each other too well. Joe loved Brigid. Always had, and that caused a breach between them he wasn't sure how to step over now any more than then.

Joe faced him again, expression impenetrable. "Getting back to whether or not to worry about your cover being blown," he continued, obviously bent on ignoring the subject of any feelings for Brigid. "It's your ass on the line out there. You're the one who'll take a bullet if the shit hits the fan. And suddenly that makes me want to threaten to out you myself so you'll have to pack up and go home."

"But you won't."

"You need to go with your gut."

"Which tells me I need to see it through." Like in the old days, talking with Joe helped him see things clearer, faster.

Time had run out, so move on to plan B ASAP. He would have to slip into the factory and steal a sample of the anthrax to send off for analysis. Dangerous as hell, but the stakes were higher. The clock was ticking anyway until the dedication ceremony they intended to use as a cover. He needed to move on this.

With the intel gathered by the Special Forces on the ground, Delta had more than enough information to blast inside and rope in the whole operation—Aragon included.

Lena would be free. With no job, in a country not renowned for its enlightened treatment of the female sex. Their argument earlier hammered through his head. He believed more than ever, now, that she'd turned to Aragon as a way to provide for her son, probably not too long after her husband had died. And why hadn't the man looked out for his wife and son?

But if she was willing to go so far to keep her son safe, then why not ask him for help? Because she had no reason to trust him, given who she thought he was. And if she knew the reality, his chances probably wouldn't be much better.

Still, whether or not she asked, he would make sure she was safe. "If something happens to me—"

Joe's fist hit the crumbling plaster beside a sprawling map of Cartina. "Shut the hell up."

God, this would have been so much simpler if he

could have stayed dead. "Can't, dude, sorry. I need to know you'll take care of something for me. Or rather, some*body*."

"This somebody wouldn't happen to be female?"

He slid a piece of paper from his pocket, a note card with Lena's name and address. "Memorize this and destroy it. She's someone I met while working for Aragon."

Joe thumped himself on the forehead. "You have got to be baggin' me. I assume this is the woman you've been working with at Aragon's. Well, I've had about all I can take of looking out for your grieving girlfriends."

"Yeah, well, hands off this one even if I'm blown to bits. You never know when I'll come back to hold your ass accountable."

"Then stick around long enough to hang on to her."

Cooper couldn't stop a self-deprecating snort. "As if that would matter. They may go for me first initially, but they always fall for the steady, noble guys like you."

A guy who had the freaking decency to use his own name when he kissed her. Between his half a leg, false ID and past failures with women, he had an uphill road with Lena even if he got out of all of this alive.

With Lena?

Afterward?

What the hell? Hadn't he told her earlier he had been willing to offer more? Wasn't he trying to look after her now?

During their fight, he'd meant he would pick up the tab for two plane tickets out for her and her son. Now he wasn't so sure that was all he'd meant, and it scared the spit right out of his mouth,

"Dude?" Joe's voice snapped Cooper back to the present.

"Huh?" At this rate he would be ambushed by sundown.

"It's not that they dump you to go for me. You're the one who pushes them away when they get too close."

No need to question if Joe was right or wrong. Joe never spoke until he was certain.

Which meant Cooper had yet another thing to blame himself for—shoving away perfectly good women. "Will you look out for her or not if the need arises?"

The smirk, laugh, gloating all fell away to pure serious Joe. "You don't even have to ask."

"Thank you." His friend deserved some groveling for what he'd been put through. "I really am sorry for all I put you through. I told myself you would understand because of your job, but I was so screwed up back then—now too, probably—who the hell knows what's right and wrong?"

Joe studied the ball as if looking for answers, taking the question seriously rather than just blowing it off as most would have done. "For what it's worth, I'm not sure what I would have done if I had been in your shoes. I very well might have considered it the honorable thing to do, staying dead and fighting for my men who didn't have the option of fighting for themselves. I just don't know for sure. I do know there's no one on the fucking planet I would trust more than you to watch my back in a battle."

Cooper swallowed down a lump of emotions he couldn't handle right now much less express. "Thanks."

"No problem." Joe pitched the ball at Cooper's head. "You're still not totally off the hook."

He deflected and smiled. "I know." But they were closer. Joe's opinion meant a helluva lot to him, always had.

Cooper chest-passed the ball back. He might be the baddest dude in the jungle, but Joe was the absolute best. And damned if shooting hoops and the breeze with Joe hadn't clarified more than one thing in his head.

His path was clear again. Bring down Aragon, el Jedr, anyone in between, and only death could stop him. And Lena? He had to talk to her one more time to make sure she was safe before he went to the factory and took the anthrax sample.

This time he would shelve his insecurities about crap he'd sworn didn't matter. He owed her better than he'd given her this morning. Lena had done and said exactly what he'd needed when he'd bared more than his ass in dropping his pants.

Yet, when she'd opened up to him, he'd shown his ass in a more figurative sense. Because the feelings this woman stirred scared him more than the business end of an assault rifle.

Hadn't he done the same in running from Brigid? And to complicate the whole thing more, he had to be honest that Lena reached him in a way no woman had before.

Suddenly the thought of digging around for a pouch of deadly anthrax seemed a lot less daunting than talking to one wisp of a woman.

IN HER HOTEL ROOM, Brigid clicked keys on her Macintosh, cord leading to her portable satellite dish, photos transmitting online back home since the phone connections had failed again. She wanted to lose herself in work so she could forget about the emotional reunion with Cooper, the ache of having suffered for two years over a lie. So much pain at the table, both men sporting hints of bruises on their faces that attested to a fight when they'd once been like brothers.

Except work reminded her too much of her desert days when she'd used the satellite transmission for other reasons—security. Army personnel would give them sensitive data as long as she and Sonny signed an agreement promising to send sensitive stories using 256-bit encryption. Cracking that code would involve trillions of different permutations that would take even computers millions of years to break.

She'd never considered that her job included national security secrets, much as Joe's did. Being trusted. Like now. She had the scoop of the century and couldn't tell Sonny a thing without endangering lives. Because she didn't trust him?

Joe always insisted someone had leaked the location of Cooper's team. Could Sonny have somehow been culpable? And if so, how dangerous was it to have him here now?

The weight of Sonny's stare pulled her attention from the computer screen up to his teddy-bear face, a teddy bear with a balding head and gray ponytail. "Yes?"

He dusted powdered sugar off his fingers, indulging in doughnuts even at dinnertime. "Is something wrong?"

Was there? She didn't know anymore. She'd always thought of Sonny as a mentor, even a surrogate father figure. But then, even her own father had played fast and loose with the truth. "I'm just tired."

"Joe kept you awake that late?"

She worked up a half a smile.

"You don't look happy."

"Things are complicated." Big-time understatement. Aside from having her faith in men seriously rocked, Joe, her best friend as well as lover, had shut her out.

"That's life, darlin'. If it was always easy we would just turn into complacent slugs."

"Then I guess I'm not in danger of turning into a slug."

"Are you sure there's nothing else going on here?"

She shook her head, not trusting her voice. Only two more days until the dedication ceremony and final demo. What would happen when they returned to the States?

Joe's lie of a few hours seemed small in comparison to Cooper's deception of two years, but somehow Joe's omission—his distance—hurt her so much more.

Her computer pinged with transmission complete and the perfect excuse. "Sonny, do you mind if we call it a day? I'll treat to doughnuts early. But I really need to get some sleep."

Please, no more jokes about Joe.

"Sure, darlin', we've done enough." He shuffled papers into his leather portfolio and closed up his computer.

"Thanks. You really are a great friend as well as one helluva journalist."

He reached across the table and patted her hand, just as Cooper had earlier, except the old journalist left behind a little powdered sugar. "You know I feel the same way." Standing, he shrugged the laptop strap onto his shoulder. "As much as I enjoy working with you again—and you are as damn good as ever—you may have been right after all about stepping away from this line of work two years ago."

His praise didn't take away the sting of hearing her mentor say she might not be cut out for this profession. Could this day stink any more?

He backed toward the door. "I've said my piece. Have a good rest."

The door clicked closed behind him, leaving her in a lonely room with nothing but her memories of being with Joe, seeing Cooper again, hearing Sonny's doubts—and even doubting Sonny.

She needed to escape from it all, even if only for an

hour. But with Cooper on some superspy CIA mission that made her question all the U.S. military presence, she knew better than to leave her room.

Which only left her the bathroom for escape. She eyed the overlarge clawfoot tub perfect for a much-needed bubblebath haven. Before she could change her mind and do something silly like quit this job, she took the phone off the hook and charged back into the bathroom. She twisted on the faucets, pouring a hefty dose of her kiwi shower gel in until bubbles frothed and the scent wafted upward.

"Hmm." Better. She piled her hair on top of her head, securing it with a banana clip and started peeling off her clothes. She hooked her thumbs in her thong—just as a sound from the next room stopped her. Her stomach flipped. She grabbed for the cottony robe on the back of the door and cranked off the bathwater.

Stepping into her room, she shrugged on the robe and tugged the tie tighter around her waist. "Joe?"

He swung open the connecting door, filling the doorway, his broad shoulders and dark clothes creating a powerful image she itched to catch on camera almost as much as she yearned to touch. "I got back as fast as I could. Are you okay?"

Propping her shoulder against the bathroom door frame, she shrugged. "As much as anyone can be when the bottom falls out."

"Helluva day."

For him as well as her. Joe took the world and responsibilities so seriously. She could reassure him on one front at least. "I didn't say anything to Sonny."

"I never thought you would."

"Thank you." God, her heart was heavy and tired, and yet, looking at Joe, she sensed his burdens must weigh double hers. If he wouldn't hug her, then maybe she should just hug him. "Why are you standing all the way over there?"

"I'm trying to be fair to you, to give you time to figure out what you're feeling."

He wanted reassurance? She scavenged for words, tough to do on a day when her emotions twisted and tangled like a whipped-free roll of negatives, showing shadowy reverse images all the tougher to decipher. "I can forgive him for what he did, but I can't trust him again, which means I can't love him." Just saying the words helped solidify things in her mind. "I'm glad he's alive, more than I can express, but whatever we felt for each other died, even if he didn't."

Joe still didn't move. "Things are fresh now. You may feel different later."

Frustration bubbled faster and fuller than the suds in her tub. She was so damn tired of people turning away from her. Who cared about their litany of reasons? Couldn't they at least tell her to her face before they disappeared? If Joe wanted her out of his life, then he could be honest about why.

Brigid stepped from the bathroom door and met Joe nose to nose, truth for truth. "Right from the start you've said this was about me getting my thoughts and feelings in line. But instead you were the one not over Cooper's death. You say you're keeping your distance now until I can sort out my feelings. Except I can't help wondering. Is it *you* who can't get past the fact that I slept with your best friend?"

CHAPTER NINETEEN

JEALOUSY WAS AN UGLY EMOTION that tore through Joe like one of those incineration bombs. But the only thing worse than that jealousy was the thought of never being with Brigid again.

Brigid's bald statement about having slept with Cooper wasn't news. So why did hearing her voice it mess with his head more now than before?

Because he hadn't loved her before.

Joe fought the urge to charge out of her room—which would just verify what she'd said. And while it was true, he needed to tread warily. He'd screwed up enough earlier when they'd discussed the subject of her dating Cooper. Palms raised in surrender, he backed away to give himself space to resist her.

"Call me a Neanderthal. I'm jealous. I admit you're that damn special to me, being with you was that incredible. So yeah, I've got this—" he struggled for the word while churning the air with his hands "—weight in my gut wondering what's going to happen now that Cooper's back in the picture. I saw you grieve, Red, I know what you went through."

Her shoulders braced in fighter mode under her robe as she opened her mouth—

"Hold on." He raised a hand. "Let me finish."

And, Good Lord, please let him get it right this time. He'd shot himself in the foot so often with this woman, the next blast could be lethal. "I also know that if I don't get past this jealousy now, you're going to walk."

She eyed him warily, her piled hair slipping to the side. "That's it then? *Poof.*" She snapped her fingers. "Jealousy gone?"

"Honestly? More like, *poof,* I've realized I have to trust that you'll always be honest with me. One day at a time, we work our way through a situation neither of us could have ever imagined facing. We've been through worse together—" he gave her a slow grin "—and didn't even have the amazing sex to ease the tension."

Steam wafted from the bathroom, saturating the air with her kiwi scent and heat while he waited and hoped he'd said the right thing.

Finally her lips twitched. "Damn it, Joe, do you save those one-liners to pull your butt out of the fire with unexpected humor?"

"Did it work?"

"Yes, my sexy friend, it most certainly did."

Thank God.

Seeing her standing framed in the bathroom entryway, bare legs stretching from her robe, hair twisted up on her head, with the clawfoot tub behind her gave him the perfect idea for how to spend what could be their last chance together if he didn't figure out some way to sort out the mess in his head. One slow step at a time, he closed the distance between them, giving her time to say no, instead seeing her *yes* in the way she didn't take her eyes off him.

He stopped in front of her, so close he could feel her heat he'd felt far more intimately when he'd been buried heart-deep inside her. "I want you."

Brigid draped her arms over his shoulders. "Well that's very convenient since I want you, too."

He speared his fingers through her hair, cupped her head and lowered his. She sighed into his kiss with a melt of her body against him. "Your bed or mine?"

"How about your tub?"

"I like the way you think." She nipped his bottom lip.

"Tough call topping your balcony idea." He needed her free spirit in his life to balance him out, couldn't imagine giving her up.

"A bed with you would still be an adventure."

He totally agreed. Joe backed her toward the bathroom. Her kiwi scent grew stronger in the steam rising from the tub.

He peeled her robe from her shoulders, a growl of appreciation rolling free as he eyed her thong, then stroked it away. Brushing his hands aside, she tore away his clothes, as well, until they both stood bare against each other. Skin to skin, his throbbing erection pressed to the soft cradle of her stomach.

Scooping her in his arms, he secured her against his chest for a lingering kiss, exploring the damp recesses of her mouth before he lowered her into the fragrant bath. Water enveloped her long legs, lapping around her waist just below the curves of her breasts. Bubbles foamed and popped, revealing her nipples. Damn, but he could stand here all night long just looking at her, with her arms extended along the sides of the tub as if in open welcome for him.

Her hair piled up on top of her head gave her a timeless quality to match her ageless beauty. In this moment, he could see forever with her, this woman he loved. But taking that step would call for tough decisions on his part that he wasn't sure he was in any shape to make.

"Are you going to join me or not?"

"I wish I had your talent with a camera so I could capture you like this on film."

She quirked a delicately arched brow. "You want risqué shots of me to carry around?"

As sexy as he found her right now, he'd been thinking more about her earthy beauty than the sexuality of her pose. "I think you're imprinted in my brain enough that I wouldn't need the picture."

"You can be so sweet sometimes."

"I'll show you sweet."

"Promise?" Her legs parted ever so slightly in an unmistakable invitation.

Ooh-rah. He climbed into the tub, knees straddling either side of her hips, water sloshing over the rim to slap the floor. Suds dispersed with the press of his chest to hers as he sealed his mouth to hers again.

Brigid's hands glided along his back, cool and wet

against his flaming skin. The slick friction of her writhing body against his hard-on threatened to send him over the edge. Legs and bodies tangling, they shifted, rolled, reversing positions until he lay in the tub on his back with her over him. Her topknot slid sideways from the movement and humidity, locks sneaking loose. Steam stuck a stray strand to her cheek.

Perspiration dotted along the tops of her breasts and up her neck, her body flushing with heat and unmistakable arousal. He soaped his hands—why dilute the sensation of her skin with a washcloth?—and slicked the suds over her shoulders, lower to circle her breasts. Her moan encouraged him to linger and thumb the tightening peaks until she arched for firmer contact.

She writhed against him, so teasingly close to penetration his hands started to shake.

"Condom. In my pants pocket." All the way across the bathroom which freaking felt like miles.

"I'm on the pill," she panted, "for health reasons, involving regularity and that's *so* not the sort of thing I want to get into discussing at the moment. I haven't been with anyone but you for a long time."

"Me, neither."

"But Phoebe, five months ago—"

"I told you before I've wanted you for two years and I meant it. No one could compare to you."

Her eyes going misty, she palmed his face and kissed him with full lips and attention.

He drew her down onto him, eased inside, the giving softness of her a silken fist around him. His eyes slid closed, his head falling back against the rim of the tub, unable to process anything more than the feel of *her.* He gritted his teeth to restrain the urge to thrust and launch them both that much closer to finishing.

Her muscles tensed around him, clenching him, and he knew he could well finish without moving so he might as well go for broke. He filled her deeper, in, back out, just as she rolled her hips against him in matching rhythm. Faster, until water flowed over the sides, sloshing the bare tile floor.

"More, Joe, more—"

"As much as you want—"

"Need you, please, want…" Her words hitched on a groaning whimper.

"Yeah, Red, talk to me, I wanna make it happen for you—"

Her fingers bit into his shoulders. "Let me…something, for you—"

"For us." He thrust up, harder, faster.

"Yes, yes," she gasped, back arching, her head falling back, bundled hair tumbling free and down. "Love you, so much, Joe, more…"

What the hell?

Her words rocketed into his brain, blasted through his restraints, sending him into a freefalling release until he couldn't think, just feel and soar as her rambling revelation tapered off into a sweet cry of her own. A second cry, followed by dwindling moans.

She sagged against his chest, damp, flushed and her heart hammering so hard he could feel it through her skin, maybe even hear it echo in his head along with her whispering chant, "Love you, Joe."

He should be shouting a great big *ooh-rah*. He loved her, too. Except, for some reason, the tub went ice cube cold and he could only grunt out, "Uh, yeah…me, too."

ALESSANDRO'S HANDS SHOOK as he poured himself a cup of coffee from the silver carafe in his office.

He needed another hit a lot more than caffeine, but there wasn't time. He had things to do, and increasingly little time to accomplish them since he'd been forced to move up the shipment. The anthrax bacteria had to leave the country before all hell broke loose with the law and U.S. military on his tail.

The surveillance audio tapes from the Cartina Royal had been sparse. Those men and women were careful about what they said outside the security of their base or an embassy.

Except for one small slip about a man named Cooper Scott who everyone had apparently thought was dead. A man resurrected here. Even if the name hadn't been so coincidentally close to the Scott Cooper who worked for him, Alessandro would have wondered about a miraculous resurrection that screamed of secret agencies and plots.

He still had not been able to crack the man's official cover. Whoever had sponsored him—CIA, DIA or some other fucking shadow government agency—had done their work well. But he knew in his gut. Scott Cooper had betrayed him.

On more than one level. Censorious Señora de Guerra was all too willing to tell how long Cooper stayed at Lena's, all about the sounds that drifted through the floorboards.

If Cooper had just been guilty of spying, then his death could have been painless. After all, it was only business. He, too, made business choices that would harm others. How could he judge Cooper for doing the same?

But trying to steal Lena?

For that transgression, Cooper would suffer immense pain before dying. And he knew well how to inflict the worst pain possible—torture those Cooper loved. Like that pilot and the woman journalist.

And Lena? He couldn't give her up, but he would have to keep her in line until he could deal with her. The best way? Accelerate his plan to expose her to the benefits of the ultimate relaxation found in drugs.

He set aside his china cup on the coffee table in front of the sofa, then reached inside his jacket to pull a small plastic bag from the inner pocket. Unsealing the tiny pouch, he tapped the powder into the carafe—crushed Rohypnol tablets, the date-rape drug. They would take effect in under a half hour, increased doses would lead to addiction. But he wasn't certain yet which drug of choice he wanted to share with her long-term.

Lena would have to pay for her indiscretion, but eventually he would forgive her. She was a weak woman, in need of his strength and protection. He took care of his mother and his sisters, didn't he? He'd protected them from a terrorist threat, making him a hero, even if they would never know. He was nothing like his father who abdicated responsibilities and thought only of himself.

He perched on the corner of his desk. Now he only had to wait for her to...walk through the door.

"Good afternoon, my dear." He kept his voice steady in spite of the rage roiling inside him. "Did you sleep well last night after I called?"

Lena hovered near the door, her slim body rigid in a green silk dress he fantasized about stripping off her and inspecting her naked skin for evidence of her night with another man.

"I slept fine, thank you."

She lied so poorly sometimes. Dark circles stained her pale complexion. Weariness strained her face. She did need him, and he wouldn't let her down. He knew what was best for her, not this man who slipped into her bed under false pretenses.

"And your son?" Shoving away from the desk, he twitched his head to flick his hair from his face. "I hope his restlessness settled so you weren't up too late."

"Miguel is well." She smoothed a hand over her already immaculate twist of hair.

He gestured toward the sitting area and silver tray of food and coffee. "Have a seat."

Edging past him, she sank into the wingback chair. Unwilling to sit next to him on the sofa? He would let her have her little victory for now. Her last.

"Eat with me."

"What?"

"Did you miss breakfast this morning, perhaps catch only a light lunch, if any?"

She stared stunned at him.

"As I thought. You rushed to feed your son and forgot about yourself." He filled her cup from the tainted silver carafe and passed it to her. "Is there something wrong with us eating together and talking?"

He watched her sip the coffee and wince. At the bitterness? Couldn't be helped. But she wouldn't complain or argue with him, not when she walked such a tightrope with her guilt. He offered her a plate of sandwiches.

She shook her head and drank from her cup again, as if eager to finish all the faster and be on her way.

How sad that he wouldn't have time to enjoy her placid body beneath him once the knockout amnesia drug took effect, but he had to check on the shipment at the factory, because heaven help them all if he failed the demands of el Jedr's network.

Afterward he would be free to shower Lena with his undivided attention. In fact, he already had another packet of Rohypnol squirreled away for later, once he had el Jedr's network off his back. He had an extensive list of ways he planned to enjoy her once she was totally and completely his.

He reached for the carafe. "More coffee, Lena-mine?"

She was his, make no mistake. And he looked forward to reminding Cooper of that very fact as he put a bullet between the eyes of the traitorous bastard's two friends.

CHAPTER TWENTY

OHMIGOD.

Pressing her face into the strong column of Joe's neck, Brigid wondered how long she could pretend to be drifting off to sleep so they could pretend she hadn't just said the "L" word during sex. Well, technically, *after* sex. But still. They *were* naked and tangled up in a tub of cooling bathwater.

She couldn't believe she'd actually said it. Hadn't even known she felt it. Well, other than the sense of loving your best friend. Affection, emotion, with lust spicing up the mix.

But *in* love?

Now the words were out there—and being ignored other than an obligatory sounding, *Uh, yeah...me, too.*

Just what every woman dreamed of hearing after she'd vowed her love. And if Joe wasn't talking, then she'd either upset him or scared him. He'd always told her he planned to wait until he got out of the service to commit to a woman.

Why couldn't he have just said *I love you, too, Red?* Real easy and laid-back-like. No big deal. He'd already said he had feelings for her.

Except, Joe didn't do easy and laid-back. Cooper had, and ultimately it hadn't been what either of them needed. Joe was all about intensity and brooding seriousness. If he used the "L" word, he would mean it with every fiber of his deep and honorable soul. And didn't that just give her amazing chills?

Okay, think. So she loved Joe. For real, beyond the sex-buddies deal. Of course she did. How could she not love this generous sexy man?

But with the feeling still new and scary—and unanswered by the big lug under her—she wasn't ready to talk about it yet. Maybe his silence was for the best.

He toed the hot water faucet on, refilling and reheating their bath. While she couldn't avoid talking forever, she could take the time to explore him, enjoying the rasp of hair against her fingertips. Searching further, she dug her fingers into the taut muscles of his butt she'd so admired more than once.

And thinking about his nice butt offered the perfect lighthearted topic to break this awkward silence and possibly help her understand him better, along with her shifting feelings. "You never did tell me how you got the shamrock tattoo."

He stayed quiet until she began to think maybe he was asleep in spite of his stroking hands. Or worse yet, he would bring up her blurted admission before she had a chance to settle her fizzy stomach.

Then he exhaled and said, "Christmas break our senior year at Notre Dame—"

"Ah, I should have guessed the connection."

"Go, Irish," he chanted in her ear.

"Was it some fraternity party initiation?"

His stroking hands slowed and he wrapped his arms around her. "Cooper came up with this idea that we should both get a shamrock tattoo to commemorate our friendship before we went our separate ways in the Air Force and Army. I thought he was nuts."

Way to go choosing a benign subject. But since he seemed cool with forging ahead, she would, too. "Then why did you do it?"

"He double-dog-dared me."

A much-needed snort of laughter burst free, blowing a spray of water by his shoulder. "Oh, of course. That explains everything."

Joe pressed kisses along the sensitive curve of her neck. "Gee, Red, you sure are mouthy after a few orgasms."

Hmm...and she wouldn't mind one or two more now that they were past that awkward moment earlier. This time she would keep her mouth shut, and think about that shamrock tattoo on his taut buttocks and how cute it must have been watching somber Joe hauled by Cooper into that tattoo parlor to get matching—

Wait. Matching?

She bit her lip to keep from asking something sure to upset a man who'd already admitted being jealous.

"Yeah, right," Joe voiced her thoughts in a steady voice like nothing was wrong. "Cooper doesn't have a shamrock tattoo. I went first, and he passed out at the sight of the needle. I considered paying the guy extra to ink a little kitty cat on Cooper instead…but then I passed out too."

Deep breath. Smile along. He was being cool with this. Maybe he'd meant it when he said he would work past the jealousy.

Brigid rocked back to sit up and grin down at him. "I'm assuming there were libations involved in this expedition."

"A fair guess."

She traced the faded scar along his shoulder, popping bubbles in her path, unable to escape thinking about how that scar came about from a shattered shoulder blade in Iraq. The horrible day scrolled through her mind like a stretched-out roll of negatives.

She'd made a mistake with Cooper in not learning more about him and his past. Maybe she could have saved them all a lot of heartache if she'd been deeper, thought deeper, dug deeper back then. She refused to make the same mistake with Joe, especially with the stakes rising by the second with her runaway mouth and emotions. "Tell me about when you were a kid."

"Geez, you can't really want stories about the time the judge's golf cart accidentally ended up in the pool?"

"While that sounds potentially fascinating, I was thinking more of stories before that, before you came to the United States."

He shrugged, stirring ripples in the water. "I came over when I was six, so I don't really have that many memories."

"You still have a little bit of an accent, you know."

A half smile kicked a dimple in one side of his face. "No shit?"

"Just sometimes, when you're really emotional."

"Excuse me, ma'am, but I have a penis. I do *not* get 'really emotional.'"

She smacked his rock-solid six-pack. "Okay, macho-man, perhaps what I really meant is your accent sneaks back in when you're trying valiantly to hold in emotions."

He captured her hand and kissed her palm. "Holding in my emotions? You make me sound like a greeting-card commercial."

Her hand curved to the side of his face. "It's actually very attractive, makes you all the more exotic."

His ears turned red. "All right. Enough."

"It's this hint of a guttural sound, your consonants get harder."

"I'll show you harder." He gripped her hips.

"Not yet." The urge to writhe almost broke through, but this sudden rush of love made her hungry for more of Joe on so many levels.

"Ten more minutes?"

"After you tell me something important about yourself. I'm a woman—"

"I noticed—"

"And we just had sex. I need—"

"For me to bare my soul as well as my ass."

She couldn't resist Joe and his surprise one-liners. "True, and so eloquently expressed."

"Okay, you win your soul baring." His hands slid

to palm her back and nudge her forward to rest her head against his shoulder again—as if he didn't want her looking into his eyes, windows to the soul. "I have scattered memories of my childhood overseas, tough to know which are real. Mom—my adoptive mother— was really great about showing me photos of the area where I'd lived. There weren't any personal pictures because our house was bombed out, but she wanted me to have a sense of where I came from. Mom's a generous woman when she could have erased all of that time from my head and made me totally 'theirs.'"

"She sounds like a wonderful mother." She'd only met Mrs. Greco twice, briefly, but right now wanted to get to know this woman better who'd embraced and loved the young wounded boy. Brigid well knew parental love wasn't a given.

"I always thought they should have had more kids. But they adopted me when they were forty and said I kept them plenty busy."

"You were a handful?"

"Just a normally active boy." He cleared his throat once, then again. "I, uh, actually tried to keep out of their way as much as I could so they would let me stay."

She could see the little boy Joe, a child with a mop of dark hair, angular features too hard for cuteness on a child, but already hinting at the strong man he would become. She could also see those dark eyes too wide, scared, confused on a child who couldn't speak English. A child who had already seen the worst war had to offer so reassurances meant nothing.

Brigid slid her arm over his bare chest and held as tightly as he would allow, the steaming water from the faucet lapping higher and over her back. "Do you remember your other parents?"

"Bits and pieces. And a brother whose name I can't even recall. I was told he died, but I never got to see his body." He stretched his leg to turn off the water. "But my strongest memory? The day the soldiers came to the orphanage to evacuate us before the civil war spread closer. I remember watching them carry kid after kid into an airplane that seemed so huge I thought it must be a flying house."

She smiled against his shoulder even as her heart squeezed at the thought of Joe losing so much, even the comfort of knowing his brother's name.

"Then rebels started shooting from the trees. I knew to take cover when gunfire came. This soldier, he was probably all of twenty, found me. He already had a baby in his arms, but he gestured for me to climb on his back and hold on to his neck."

His voice going gruff, he scraped a hand over his face, the steady beat in his chest hammering louder and louder in her ears. "Some kids want to be a football player or cowboy or a policeman when they grow up. I always knew—I wanted to be that soldier. I opted for the Air Force, and here I am, still living in my flying house."

Her tight heart expanded to hold more love for Joe. He'd been through so much more than she had as a kid, and yet he always focused on helping other people.

Perpetually late Joe who didn't have enough hours in the day to take on everyone's problems.

His heart pounded harder and she held tighter. Abruptly, he hefted her off him, sloshing water onto the floor in a tidal wave that would seriously torque off housekeeping if she didn't toss down a couple towels soon.

"Joe?"

"There's someone at the door." He snagged his shorts from the bedroom floor, leaving damp footprints behind him.

Huh? She cleared her head enough to hear…thumping from the hall.

Snatching her robe from the hook, she jammed her arms through on her way toward the door. "Yes?"

The knocking stopped. "Hey, Bridge? It's me, Postal. I hate to bother you, but uh, Face wouldn't happen to be in there, would he?"

"Oh, uh, hold on a second." She knotted the tie, the cottony fabric sticking to her damp skin.

Joe stepped in front of her, buttoning his pants. He jerked the door open. "This better be good."

"Dude, I hate to bother you." The normally flip pilot radiated tension, wearing his flight suit when they were supposed to have the day off. "But you weren't answering the phone in your room, and the one in here was off the hook. A call just came in. We need to be airborne, ASAP."

LENA FORCED HERSELF to stay unmoving while Alessandro opened a file drawer. Keeping still proved far easier than fighting the urge to drift off to sleep.

How much of Alessandro's drug had infiltrated her system? Halfway into her second cup of bitter coffee she had realized something was wrong. Alessandro accepted nothing less than the best. In no world would he have tolerated such hideous coffee.

At first she doubted her instincts since he was drinking, too—but soon remembered his cup had already been poured when she entered the room. Then the dizziness started and she'd known for certain. Alessandro had drugged her. The only question was, lethal or not?

His footsteps thudded through the carpet as he stood guard over her. Either he knew about her snooping into his files over the past months. Or he knew about her night with Cooper. Either way, he would kill her. And heaven help her poor son.

Lethargy weighted her limbs to the sofa. A sofa? No. Not again, with Alessandro.

Why, why hadn't she asked for Cooper's help while she had the chance? Or at least gained some sort of promise from him that he would ensure her son was taken care of if something happened to her? She'd been so insistent on solving her own problems and now her child would pay the deadly price if she didn't find a way out.

She had almost lost her mind waiting for an opportunity, and then finally Alesandro had stepped out of the room to speak with his receptionist. She'd stumbled to the bathroom and thrown up, hoping to rid herself of enough of the drug to keep her wits.

She'd returned to the room and collapsed on the sofa, feigning sleep with mere seconds to spare before Alessandro had returned. If only he would leave so she could slip away completely. She couldn't afford to wait much longer. There were only two choices—go to local authorities and explain that she needed their assistance now.

Or appeal to Cooper for his help.

Her brain fogged in and out, sleep luring her. Could she even call for help, much less walk out of here? She just wanted to drift off, curl up on the sofa in her own place while her son crawled around the floor, racing his truck over a mountainous pile of pillows, a collection of Army men clustered in the foothills.

Army men. A gift from a handsome man with a tempting smile and touch.

She wanted a simple life. She would have that, after one more trip to the factory. And if she did not find what she needed then...what? Alessandro would likely go to jail soon one way or another, and if she didn't secure safe passage out of here she would be in exactly the same position all over again. No money. A little more job training, but a tainted reputation.

What to do? Trust Cooper's offer of no-strings help?

Squinting her eyelids tight, she tried to clear the dry gritty sensation building behind her lids. She started to ask Cooper for a glass of water— Cooper?

No, wait. He wasn't here. She had sent him away out of silly pride which made her blink harder to hold back tears that would betray her as still being awake. But his words had cut so deeply.

Still, it was for the best that he stay away. If Alessandro found out about their night together…

Dios Mio, she had been reckless to indulge. Again she was helpless, dependent on men for rescue. To keep her son safe, she would swallow her pride and go to Cooper.

The office chair across the room squeaked, long and slow with the weight of a body tipping it back. Then clicks, like a phone being dialed.

"*Sí,* it is me," Alessandro said.

Who was he speaking to?

"Things have changed. The shipment has been accelerated. All is already taken care of for tonight." Silence. More. "I had no choice. We have a mole in our business, someone working with authorities who must be neutralized."

Fear iced through her drugged veins. She peeked through her lashes.

Phone to his ear, Alessandro rocked in the office chair. "The shipment is being readied to move from the factory."

She squeezed her eyes shut, then forced them to rest lightly. Relaxed. Even breaths.

"I know, I know, but the risk of waiting is greater since the United States has already sent troops to the area. Our bugs indicate they're actively working to stop us. We can't afford to wait."

What? She'd known her government was after him, but could the investigation be that widespread? All the way to another country? What in the world had Alessandro done?

"They are already being taken care of. My men are on the way over. And my men should already have Scott Cooper in their custody."

She bit back her cry of denial, struggled not to let burning tears slide from beneath her eyelids. She couldn't bear images of her wounded golden god in the hands of Alessandro's minions.

"We will turn him over to our Middle-Eastern *friends* eventually. They will relish the chance to interrogate a CIA operative. Or DIA. I'm not certain exactly which, but full of information either way."

CIA? Cooper? Her tears evaporated inward, bathing over her bruised soul. He'd lied to her, maybe even used her, all for his higher good. An honorable government servant who'd never been hers at all, not even for one night. How silly she'd been to dream of more.

Anger stirred. Enough. She'd lost her husband, her independence, her body, her confidence and damn near her soul.

She would not lose her life, most especially not at Alessandro's hand, and she would protect her son. And Cooper? She would never wish Alessandro's revenge on any man, but right now the need for a small dose of her own burned through her. Cooper would be all right—had to be—because she wasn't close to finished with him yet.

Lena forced herself to stay awake, listen. Plan.

"I am going to fax over two photos of a man and woman I want picked up immediately. They are staying in the Cartina Royal. A U.S. military pilot, Captain Joe Greco and his photojournalist girlfriend, Brigid Wheeler."

NIGHT VISION GOGGLES strapped onto his helmet, Joe kept his eyes trained on the jungle terrain below.

Nobody knew what to expect from this flight. Recon data from the Green Berets scoping the area showed a sudden burst of activity and increased security. For some heretofore unknown reason, massive activity had erupted at Aragon's factory. All signs indicated Aragon was about to send out an unscheduled shipment.

The smaller Army Delta Force team in back of the CV-22 would secure the compound. The larger Green Beret/Special Forces team already in place farther out in the surrounding jungle would serve as backup if things went to shit and an all-out battle erupted.

Joe's hands guarded the controls as the CV-22 crested a ridge, pushed over on the downhill side in response to the terrain following radar's guidance to keep the aircraft pegged to three hundred feet above the ground. Dangerous on a good day. Potentially deadly when his head kept pounding an echo of Brigid's breathy cry during sex.

She loved him? She said she did, and he had no reason to doubt her. Be happy, grab the brass ring—or rather a diamond ring. So why was he choking when it came to answering back?

He'd waited for two and half years for this woman.

Been there for her. Damn near lost his mind wanting her. He couldn't even delude himself he was staying away for Cooper any longer. Great. He was a freaking mess right in the middle of a mission.

To steady his thoughts, he reviewed the target landing zone in his head while he monitored the aircraft's path, scanning ahead for wires and obstructions. He'd run through the route so many times since the emergency mission planning, it took on a songlike chant in his thoughts.

Sixty seconds past the access road.

Left to heading two-three-zero. Slow to 120.

Open area near the stream, come to a hover at 50 feet.

Set her down in the clearing. Kick out the boys.

Clean up.

Transition back to forward flight, heading of two-one-five.

Piece of cake. He could do this in his sleep.

He hoped.

"Face," Postal called through the headset. "Got a road coming up in one mile."

"Roger, one mile." Joe took a visual on the road, a hazy emerald-looking snake of a path through the NVGs. "Negative traffic, anything on the warning receivers?"

"Nope, clean and green cause we are just that good."

"Roger." Joe shifted his attention to the back of the craft. "Chief, get them up and ready in the back. Five minutes out."

"Copy, sir," Stones answered, acting as crew chief to off-load the troops, "all the Delta boys are up and ready to go."

Postal cross-referenced with the chart in his lap. "You should see the access road now."

"Got it. Slowing." Joe eased back on the throttle.

"Copy, looking for 120 knots, and standby turn to heading two-three-zero. Turn heading two-three-zero… *now.*"

"Coming left to two-three-zero, and I have a visual on the landing zone. Standby in the back, thirty seconds out."

Rotors shifting, *thunk,* Joe brought the aircraft to a hover, dropped fifty feet of altitude. Checked his radar altimeter—exactly fifty feet. "Heads up in back, fifty feet, get ready."

The aircraft settled quickly on the ground with a bounce. Stones's calm echo of *go, go, go* reverberated through the headset. Delta boys in back were sprinting down the open load ramp. Through his NVGs, he watched them melt into the jungle.

"All clear, sir," Stones reported up. "Let's haul out."

Joe thumbed his mike. "Copy. Clearing out."

He climbed rapidly to fifty feet again. Lowering the wings and rotors, he transitioned to forward flight again. He kept at fifty feet, just over the jungle canopy until the wings were fully in aircraft mode and forward speed was back to cruise. "Postal, how about set me back to terrain following."

"Terrain following engaged, all green."

Finally he allowed himself a sigh of relief, a few muscles unkinking along his shoulders for the first time since Postal had shown up at Brigid's door with the emergency message to report in.

Brigid. He would have to get his head together before he landed. He couldn't keep tossing away clothes to avoid talking. Although the idea had its merits at the moment.

Okay, so he didn't have a clue how they would blend their lives. Who said he had to have all the answers? Before he landed, he would damn well find his *cajones* and tell her he loved her, too—no bullshit, "Uh, yeah…me, too" grunts this time.

But first, he had to get this mission out of the way. "Well that was fun."

"Can o' corn my friend, can o' corn. When you're the best you *are* the best."

"It's not over yet so don't be getting complacent on me." They still had to hang around until the all-clear came that the compound had been secured and their air support was no longer needed. "And what in the hell does 'can o' corn' mean?"

"It's an old baseball term for an easy catch—oh, shit, break left."

A bloom of light in his NVGs blinded him, leaving him to momentarily fly by instinct. Joe racked the aircraft into a steep left turn, kicked off the terrain following and dove for the jungle canopy. "Postal? Talk to me."

"I got small-arms fire at two o'clock," answered his

insane copilot who always managed to sound cool in a crisis, "Right gunner, you got it in sight?"

"I got it, I got it," Padre answered. "Fire is clear of us now, behind us. Looks like they were shooting at the sound."

Just a coincidence? Like the one Gomer shooting at them in their earlier flight? Joe's instincts itched with premonition—

The jungle on either side of the aircraft exploded in gunfire. Tracers reached out toward the aircraft.

Ambush.

Can o'corn, my ass. Somebody knew they were here. Somebody with the arms, resources and intent to take them down.

Time to put the CV-22 to the battle test. "Heads up in back. That first guy drove us right into an ambush. Gunners, cleared to fire."

COOPER TOOK COVER in an archway in the narrow shaft connecting to Aragon's safe room below the factory—the place where he'd hidden the anthrax.

He'd tried to find Lena all afternoon before his planned sneak trip into the factory to slip out with an anthrax sample, but Aragon's secretary had said Lena went home. And Señora de Guerra said Lena was at work. Then the emergency notice had come through from the Green Berets indicating Aragon might be moving the deadly shipment early. Leaving Cooper with minimal time to snag that sample in case things went to hell when Delta moved in to secure the place.

Seemed that hell had certainly come to pass.

The basement bomb shelter might protect him from the explosions above ground raining plaster on his head. But his ass would be toast if anyone else found him here, or if some wayward shot blasted open the crate of deadly bacteria stored in the freaking wet bar, for God's sake, among cases of bourbon and tequila.

One guard already lay dead at his feet—a man currently forfeiting his uniform so Cooper stood a chance of getting out of here alive. Gunfire stuttered, closer. Followed by a blast. More plaster shaking loose.

Hey, Joe? This would sure be a great time for you to fly in a rescue.

Cooper zipped the jungle-green cammo pants and shrugged into the jacket damp and reeking of sweat. He buckled his waist holster, securing his Glock, then emptied the pockets from his discarded pants to scoop up his wallet, cell phone, pager, keys. Slipping into the factory had been normal-hairy, all the way to Aragon's panic room.

He'd considered taking the whole stash of anthrax. The box wasn't all that heavy. But then the world had started blowing up outside, and he couldn't risk someone exploding—or God forbid, stealing—the larger target.

Taking the one small presealed silica package was dangerous enough, even stored in a small bulletproof and blast-reinforced Kevlar box. But less obvious now that the place was crawling with guards. Sweat popping on his forehead, but his hands steady, he slid the small silver case made to resemble a cigar holder from his other clothes and tucked it inside the cammo jacket. Jamming his feet in the boots was tougher, but doable.

A boom reverberated from above, vibrating the floor beneath him. Had he tripped an alarm without realizing it? Damn, but he'd been careful, gone over this place a hundred times the past months. Even made dry runs.

He couldn't die now. He still had apologies to make to Joe, Brigid.

Lena. And where the hell was she, anyway?

As long as she was safely away from the factory. He would just have to talk to her afterward. He *would* make it out of here alive. For the first time in two years he wanted to live more than he wanted revenge.

Hooking the guard's MP-5 over his shoulder, Cooper reached to grab a rung of the mounted ladder and hoped there wasn't a welcoming party at the top waiting to eliminate him.

CHAPTER TWENTY-ONE

DELETE.

Brigid clicked through the photos stored on her hard drive, ridding her Cartina file of any pictures that contained the least hint of Cooper. She thought through the images she'd already sent via satellite. Sure, that was a secure transmission with the encryption, and even top officials in the military okayed the procedure.

Still, her instincts and imagination niggled at her with what-ifs…

She let the possibilities suck her in until the screen in front of her blurred. She welcomed the distraction from thinking about Joe flying tonight, and there was no denying something must be afoot since Postal had skidded to their hotel door to announce the surprise mission. Something dangerous. With Joe soaring into the line of fire.

The photo in front of her jelled back into focus. His plane. The guns. The crew. All the best, but would it be enough?

A shout from the hall startled her from her daze. Shout? An argument. Masculine voices and a woman, all speaking in Spanish and so fast she only caught stray words like *help, military, trouble.*

Enough to power Brigid out of her seat.

Knotting her robe tighter, she peered through the peephole. A younger and older guard blocked the path of a woman, apparently a local based on her muffled accent. Her long dark hair rose with static as if her frantic energy electrified her beyond her delicate frame.

Something about her seemed familiar, but she couldn't place just what. Brigid creaked the door open for a better view just as the Army guard swapped their discussion to English.

"Señorita," the older Army guard in cammo braced his feet, hand on his side arm, "this is a restricted area. You have to leave or we're going to escort you from the premises."

"I am not crazy or dangerous, I swear. I only need someone to listen."

Something about the woman's desperation resonated.

"You can walk out or we can carry you, but you must go."

"No! Help me, *por favor.*"

Help me. The woman's eyes pleaded with wide desperation.

Brigid stepped through the door, drawn by the need to remember where she'd seen... The woman from the photos. The woman who'd been mugged. What was she doing here?

Voice rising, the woman continued to shout as the guard's bulk backed her toward the elevator. "I have to talk to a man named Greco about another man, Cooper."

Brigid froze in the open doorway. "What did you say?"

The woman stretched up onto her toes to peer over the guard's shoulder. "Do you know Cooper?"

Cooper? Not Mr. Scott, or even Cooper Scott. This woman knew him—well. "Hello," Brigid stepped forward, wishing she could snag a private conversation in her room with this woman without the looming guards between them, "I'm Brigid—"

"Wheeler?" The woman dodged past in a frenzy of flowing hair and fear, then staggered when the guard grabbed her arm. "*Dios Mio,* you're in danger, too. My name is Lena Banuelos, I work with Cooper at Aragon Textiles, which is a front for moving drugs. They are doing something tonight, something big."

Aragon Textiles? A reputed front for a drug lord? Her research on the area before leaving the States indicated the same. But what did all of that have to do with Joc and Cooper and the threat of terrorism here?

And he was flying tonight.

A shiver chased up her spine as she stopped by the guard. "What will it hurt to let her talk?"

"She's a crazy druggie. Can't you see she's high on something?"

The woman visibly pulled her tattered nerves together. "He, Alessandro, tried to drug me to keep me out of the way. While he was out of the room I—" she swayed "—I threw up the drugged drink. Some still made it into my system, but I am all right. I know what I heard him talking about. We don't have much time."

The guard kept his weapon steady on the woman—Lena—directing his words to Brigid. "With all due respect, ma'am, she could be here to blow us up. It's more disturbing that she knows the names than if she didn't."

Lena laughed, high, with a hysterical edge. "I do not want to lead you anywhere, and if you want to search me, then fine." She splayed her arms wide, legs spread.

The younger local guard looked to the older Air Force master sergeant—who finally nodded for him to go ahead. She stood rigidly still during the efficient pat-down over her silky dress. He nodded the all clear.

The Army sergeant holstered his weapon. "Okay, we need to move this to the security officer at the embassy. I'll wake the night shift guard to take my shift while I escort you over."

Brigid backed toward her door, almost afraid to step out of sight for fear the woman would disappear. "I'll get dressed and be right back out."

Lena sagged with relief. "Thank you."

The Army sergeant glanced up from his phone. "You have to realize, ma'am, that once you step into the embassy, they're not going to let you back out until they've completely checked your story."

"Of course, so long as they listen to me." She pressed a hand to her head, sucking in deep breaths that did little to bring life to her drug-pale face. Good God, this woman needed a doctor. "But I have to get my son. *Dios,* I am not thinking well. I will get him and then come back or meet you at the embassy. Whichever is best for you."

The guard blustered forward. "I'm afraid I can't let you just walk away now."

"But I can't just leave him."

"Then I'll accompany you there."

Swaying with relief, Lena seemed to stay on her feet by pure grit. "*Gracias*. But please, let's hurry."

Brigid rested a steadying hand on the woman's shoulder. "I'm going, as well, just give me two minutes, tops."

The guard wouldn't argue since her press privileges gave her access. He would likely think she was pursuing a story, which was fine by her as long as she got to climb in the car.

Brigid sprinted into her room, tearing clothes out of the drawers, each second ticking too loud in her head, too much time passing with Joe in the air and heaven only knew what kind of hell exploding on the ground. Jamming her hands through a T-shirt, she wondered why she hadn't found her backbone earlier and shouted from the rooftops how much she loved Joe Greco.

She stepped into her favorite skirt, the one she'd worn for her birthday dinner with Joe that never happened. Her feet got tangled and she stumbled. Damn. Damn. Damn it!

Hand slapped to the wall, she righted, untangled and grabbed for a pair of flip-flops, keeping an ear peeled for sounds from the hall.

Deep breaths. One. Two. Three. She wouldn't be any good to Joe if she passed out, thunk, on the floor.

She hooked her camera bag over her shoulder. Funny how she hadn't realized until now how much she'd depended on Joe for strength. How could she have expected him to see her as a partner when she'd let him carry all the burdens?

She would be stronger than that, had to be, for him, because she refused to let the past play out again by losing a man she loved. *The* man she loved. Joe.

Only Joe.

SWEAT STINGING HIS PORES, his hair soaked under his helmet, Joe squinted against the latest blast to blind him through his NVGs.

These mothers were overarmed and overeager. But the same sparks from every gun firing at them glowed in the goggles, making easy pickings for the high-rate miniguns in the doors and on the back ramp. *Brrrrppp. Brrrrppp.*

The sound of gunfire and acrid stench of gunpowder filled the cockpit. A light flashed on his panel, the DIRCM—directed infrared counter measure—activated. Saving them just in time by sending a deadly missile arcing away.

He only had to hang tough a few minutes more, pick up the Delta squad and Green Berets who had neutralized most of the opposition, disabling the shipment long enough to buy them time for the B-2 to fly over and incinerate the place. He swallowed down frustration over not locating the link to el Jedr, but at least they'd kept the anthrax virus from crossing into the U.S. They'd accomplished something.

As the factory came into view, muzzle flashes of small arms fire sparked from the roof and in the landing zone. Joe slowed the aircraft, allowing Stones, Padre and Sandman time to clear the patch where they needed to put down. *Brrrrpppp. Brrrrrpppp. Brrrrrppp.*

He spotted a guard on the ground at the corner of the building fumbling to hoist a weapon on his shoulder.

"Shit! Postal! Heads up! Portable missile, two o' clock, right at the corner of the building."

Postal engaged the helmet-mounted controller on the chin gun and lined up the sight on the corner of the building. "I don't see him, switching to infrared. Ahhh. There. Got him. Firing."

The chin turret mounted minigun added its *brrpppp* to the already earsplitting din and smoke mushrooming in front of the windscreen, obscuring the threat. The haze cleared, revealing the guard blasted off onto the grass, dead. His shattered missile smoked beside him.

"Time to cowboy up and end this." Joe worked the stick and rudder in synch. "I'm going to set it down. There'll be friendlies out there in a second, so watch your fire. They should pop red smoke before they come into the open."

"Roger."

"Roger."

Affirmations from his crew marched through his headset.

Joe brought the aircraft to a hover, the roar damn near deafening—or was that the blood rushing in his ears?—and landed in the parking lot in front of the factory.

"Heads up," called Stones from the tail, voice steady, earning his large *cajones* call sign tonight. "Red smoke to the rear. Here they come. Anyone in front or to the sides is a bad guy."

Crimson fog rolled from an outbuilding just before men streamed, sprinting toward the aircraft and safety. Miniguns continued to burp off and on as the Delta and Special Forces troopers rushed up the rear ramp and into the aircraft.

Stones radioed again. "Looks like we got 'em all on. Pilot cleared to get out of here."

"Roger. Buckle in tight. We're ready to blow this Popsicle stand."

Upping the throttle, he fed power to the engines to begin liftoff.

"Hold, hold!" Stones shouted, such a rarity Joe's blood iced. "The Green Beret commander says we're missing one."

"Copy. But where the hell is he? I thought you counted all the D-boys and Greenie Beanies."

"A CIA guy."

CIA? No. Fate couldn't be this twisted. It couldn't be Cooper.

"The operative should be coming from the factory."

Damn. It *had* to be Cooper.

"Hold fire in the forward quadrant, crew." Joe regulated his breathing, refusing to even think of burying his friend—again. "We've got a friendly in the factory."

Postal swung the chin turret back and forth looking with the infrared cameras through the smoke and carnage at the factory. "I don't see anything, and we can't stay much longer. We're a sitting duck here."

Come on, come on, Coop.

Dread churned as hard as the rotors chewing at the air and stirring a steady storm pushing back the jungle foliage. No fucking way could this be happening again like two years ago.

Postal angled forward, peering harder. "I got movement in the door, Face—"

His gut fisted.

"—but it looks like a guard."

Denial roared through him. He forced his voice to stay steady as he scanned the landscape. "Make sure, Postal. We've got a friendly in there."

"Sorry, Face, but it's a Gomer. Look at the uniform. I've gotta pop him."

Joe peered through the smoke and saw the guard coming toward them, sure enough wearing the same uniform as the dead security goon from the rooftop, the black cording on the cammo different from U.S. uniforms.

Cammo.

And the man was limping, which could mean anything. There'd been a gun battle in there, for crying out loud. But still, as Joe studied the guy charging toward them, there was something about the way that uniform looked on the man. The way it seemed…right.

Familiar.

Joe shouted, "Hold fire! Hold fire! It's our guy."

Relief stole all the oxygen out of the cockpit, but that was freaking fine since he couldn't breathe, anyway. Joe winged a silent thanks to Brigid for showing him how to look for the nuances in the image. Cooper neared—and no doubt about it now as his face came into focus.

Joe cranked around to look behind him into the hold as Stones reached out to clap forearms in a locking grip to haul Cooper inside. His friend dropped onto the floor, gasping but alive.

Throttles up, Joe lifted off, transitioned forward and left the factory behind to give Brigid that thanks in person.

SITTING BESIDE the lady photographer, Lena willed their military escort to drive faster.

Streetlights blazed overhead, Cartina's nightlife in full swing, the glow taking on a kaleidoscope aura in the aftereffects of the drugs Alessandro had fed her. She watched, semimesmerized by so many people with few worries. She'd been one of them once. Having dinner out with her husband, holding hands across the table without realizing the gift of that simple moment. A gift she almost dared dream of sharing with Cooper.

Soon she would be at the American embassy, with her child, a place she'd turned to for help before, only to be swallowed by the "proper channels" her government insisted on. For Miguel and Cooper she had to fight to keep her head clear and make them listen.

"Breathe," Brigid instructed softly. "Deep and slow. We'll be out of here before you know it."

Pulling her attention from the hypnotic mix of

lights, Lena turned to the woman beside her—tall, with a casual elegance and some kind of tie to Scott Cooper, or rather Cooper Scott. A CIA operative for the United States. A man Lena apparently did not know at all.

Yet now that her head wasn't quite as fuzzy as in Alessandro's office, she realized that Cooper had bared himself for her, made himself vulnerable in letting her see his injury. Surely that meant something since his job placed him in such danger.

Or was she merely grasping for hope?

Lena shifted, the cracked leather seat scraping the back of her legs through silk. "Thank you for taking me seriously when I arrived at your hotel."

"I assume from what you said earlier that you know Cooper?" she asked as if seeing into Lena's thoughts.

"You know him, as well?"

"I met him a couple of years ago, and Joe Greco has known him even longer, since they were children." Flinging her loose red hair over her shoulder, she tugged her camera bag from the floorboards of the vehicle. "I keep a few of my favorite photos with me when I travel, like a sense of home, family and friends away from home." She tugged a wallet-size stack of plastic-covered pictures. "Here's one of the three of us together."

A trio stood together on a desert flight line, Cooper in tan camouflage, hair shorter and with a reddish cast. Thicker muscled then, and lighter hearted. Her attention shifted to his buff-colored boots and the cocky stance. She knew without question now how he had lost his leg. What a steely-strong man he must be to have rebuilt his life so fully. She envied him that strength.

His brightness in the picture was almost more than she could bear to view, knowing what pain waited for him sometime after the picture was taken.

She studied the other two figures, a dark and brooding man in a flight suit. And Brigid Wheeler—in the crook of Cooper's arm.

"I think you were more than Cooper's friend." She didn't like the jealousy stabbing her heart.

"We were more, once. But not anymore." Nostalgia shaded her voice but not regret. Her pointer finger shifted to the brooding aviator. "Joe and I are together now."

Brigid's smile faltered. Apparently, other people's love lives were a mess as well.

Love life?

"Could I see another photograph?" Her soul suddenly yearned for more about Cooper's past in hopes of seeing what parts of him were real.

Brigid flipped the stack through group shots and individual close-ups, finally ending with one of the two men together, an arm hooked over each other's shoulder.

Lena traced the edges of the photo, careful to keep her touch clear of smudging the image. "They are brothers with different last names? Half brothers, perhaps?"

Brigid's eyes went wide with surprise. "No, just really good friends."

"Oh, of course they do look very different. I just thought there is a—what do you call it?—band?"

"Bond." Her gaze went back to the photo, brow furrowing.

"Yes, a bond between them. Like brothers." Lena nodded. "You are lucky to have had the affection of two such honorable men."

"But you've never met Joe. How do you know they're both honorable?"

Lena pointed to the flight-suit-clad man. "I do not have to meet him. This picture lives. There is so much here in his eyes. He is a man to trust." She couldn't miss it after so long in the company of a corrupt spirit.

She couldn't miss it?

Her eyes tracked back to Cooper, beyond his shorter hair with a reddish tinge, to his deep-blue eyes and saw what she'd feared believing before. A man of honor who said he'd been prepared to offer *more* and meant that vow.

Before she could savor the realization, the car pulled to stop outside her home, ending conversation and placing her that much closer to her son and thus to protecting Cooper from Alessandro's horrific plans. She couldn't let anything happen to that honorable spirit still lurking beneath the darker shadows in Cooper's older and wiser eyes.

Once their Army guard stepped around to the walkway, she swung open the car door. Muffled music—a piano concerto—echoed from Señora de Guerra's apartment. Guard at their side, Lena climbed the stairs with Brigid, feet drumming fast.

Knocking, she called, "Señora de Guerra? *Señora?* I need to pick up my son."

The music stopped seconds before the door creaked open. "*Sí?* Come in, come in. I was just playing a lullaby for little Miguel."

Their guard slid an arm in front of Lena. "Hold on."

Lena smiled an apology to the older *abuela* waiting inside. "He is along for protection. I am a lucky woman, no?"

He stepped ahead and into the apartment, then gestured the women to follow.

Once inside, Brigid swung from behind the guard, tipped her head, frowned, then gasped. "You!" She pointed to Señora de Guerra. "I know you from that first day at the Cartina Royal, in the elevator."

Juanita de Guerra smiled, her eyes cold and calculating, no signs of the gentle grandmotherly sort in sight. "You do?" She pivoted to address the back corner of the room. "That is unfortunate."

The roots of Lena's hair tingled, rising with a horrible premonition exacerbated by the unmistakable slide click of a readied gun from across the room. The guard jacked his weapon up in response.

From the shadows, Alessandro stepped free, sleeping Miguel cradled against his shoulder as a frighteningly fragile shield, a heavy silver gun in his other hand. "My mother's old friend from the conservatory has been quite loyal—a trait I value. Señora de Guerra is wonderfully adept at surveillance both at the hotel and in keeping me informed of the comings and goings of my precious Lena."

Nausea overwhelmed her, even though she'd already emptied her stomach earlier in an attempt to rid herself of Alessandro's damned drugs. In spite of everything she'd done to keep Miguel safe, her baby rested in a monster's arms. Desperation sent her stumbling across the room, jerking free of the guard's hand reaching to halt her.

But the shift of the gun to her child's head stopped her cold.

"Alessandro, please, please." Her voice quavered as she pleaded. "Put my son down. He's just a child. I'll do whatever you wish. It's me you want to hurt, not him."

She would beg, do anything for her child, but as she peered deeper into Alessandro's eyes, hoping to reach him, she recognized the drugged and soulless gleam well.

"All I wanted was for us to be a family." Alessandro raised his gun. Toward her?

No! Her heart screamed for her baby, horrified that Miguel might see his mother die, grieving that she would never have a chance to build a family for him with someone like Cooper.

Alessandro's finger twitched. *Hiss.*

The Army guard crumbled to the floor with a thud.

The thud rumbled. Harder? Until the windows rattled with the force of an—

Explosion.

CHAPTER TWENTY-TWO

LEANING ON THE DECK RAIL of his yacht, Alessandro watched plumes of smoke billow from the lush jungle shoreline.

Nothing left to lose. The words thundered through Alessandro's head for hours like secondary explosions from the blast that had taken out his factory. Destroyed the tainted cocaine and any chance of completing his shipment.

Even from across town at Lena's apartment, the source of the explosion had been unmistakable, confirmed by a phone call from his associates near the smoking ruins outside the city limits. He didn't even want to think about the repercussions if the bombs hadn't obliterated the anthrax.

Waves slapped the hull of his remaining haven. Salty wind carried sounds across the crystal-smooth surface, disturbed only by the distant plop of a leaping fish. He shifted his focus to the other side of the harbor, with city lights still glowing—no smoke. Temporary peace.

He wouldn't be able to hide on his yacht for long, probably not even through the night. Only one question remained. Who would find him first? The authorities or el Jedr's men?

Either way, he was prepared. Kneeling, he opened the small hatch on the stowing compartment under the padded bench beneath the rail. Stars and a full globe moon overhead offered enough light to illuminate the simple plastique explosives. Once he started the timer, their fate would be irreversibly sealed—and he would die on his terms.

Because he knew without question that, one way or another, he was a dead man. If he ran, el Jedr would find and kill him. Even if he turned himself in to the police in hope of exchanging information for leniency, el Jedr's network had people on the inside who would murder him. And more important, either way, run or stay, they would kill his sisters. His mother.

The glint of the SIG-Sauer resting a reach away on the padded bench reassured him. He was in control of his final moments. He had a plan.

He would release the women and child from their cabin below soon. Lena was still too dazed to put up much of a struggle. How she'd gotten away in the first place, he couldn't imagine, and he couldn't think about her betrayal long or he would snap. He wished there was time to seclude himself with her, to imprint himself on her one last time, make her understand what she'd thrown away in turning from him. But, damn it all, he'd taken too much coke to help him get through the week, and that had robbed him of the final pleasure.

There was nothing left for him now but to orches-trate his own death in order to save his family and escape the painful torture el Jedr would inflict before ending it all.

Nothing left…except the satisfaction of extracting revenge on that traitorous bastard Cooper Scott in the process.

COOPER SWIPED A HAND over his face as he thundered down the load ramp out the back of the CV-22, the Cartina Air Base runway sprawling a welcome. Halogen lights created a stadium dome over the pocked cement packed with U.S. troops heading to debrief after the successful mission. Only a couple more hours and he could go to Lena, and hopefully figure out a way to persuade her to leave this country and come to the U.S. with him.

First he had to finish up with debrief and turn over the anthrax sample tucked safely inside his jacket. He searched for Joe in the crowd, trucks filling and pulling away in a trail of fading taillights until one pickup remained—with his old bud waiting on the bench seat in back.

Cooper stepped onto the tailgate and boosted up. He dropped onto the seat across, reached into his pocket to reactivate his cell phone and restart his life. "Dude, I owe you a beer."

"Hell, yeah, you do." Joe lounged back on his elbows, studying Cooper through narrowed eyes while the truck ground into first gear. "Someday we're going to need to talk about what happened to you over there."

"I guess we will. Over that beer, after we clean up here and get back to the States."

"I can wait on that conversation as long as I know you're doing okay. So, are you?"

Question of the hour that resonated with a hollow thud inside him rather than the victory swell he'd expected. Damn. He should be celebrating. He'd sprinted out of that compound alive and carrying a key piece of evidence to track a major player in the terrorist network.

But...nothing. Just the need to find Lena and sleep with her in his arms. "I always thought putting a hole in el Jedr's network would make everything magically okay again. And, sure, it helps. But I'm realizing this... healing...will be ongoing." He stared down into the floor of the truck bed, his hand falling on his throbbing knee. "I don't have all the answers, probably because I'm still working on the questions."

"I'm here for you, dude." Joe tapped his combat boot against Cooper's muddy boots from his pilfered uniform.

"I know." Cooper looked up and met his friend's concerned gaze dead-on. "It's something I won't forget again."

The truck bounced along the pocked and rutted cement, bringing them closer to the end of this trip and a return to everyday life.

Joe folded his hands over his chest. "So we're okay about me and Brigid? Because I'm not going to be able to walk away from her, even if you ask me."

"Then it's a good thing I don't intend to ask. That whole rule about women was a dumb-ass college thing, anyway. I'm sorry that held you back these past couple of years." He owed Joe more than a beer-apology.

"I'm sorry for putting you two through hell. If there's something I can do beyond picking up the tab on a six-pack, just name it."

"Anything?" Joe angled forward to lean on his knees, his bud at his most intense, serious, and holy crap what was going on in that brooding head of his?

"Anything." He just hoped the ass kicking could wait until he'd logged in a good night's sleep along with a couple of Motrin. The bruises from their alley fight hadn't even faded.

Joe stayed unwavering through a teeth-rattling jostle in a pothole before continuing, "Get that fucking shamrock tattooed on your ass like you promised."

Choking on a surprised laugh, Cooper punched Joe in the arm and ducked to avoid a return slug, damn near falling off the seat when the truck jolted to a stop outside the base ops building. God, it felt good to be back on track again.

A small contingent waited for them, security, military officials, and an older burly guy wearing a press pass.

"Hey, Sonny," Joe called, vaulting from the truck bed. "Where's Brigid?"

"I'm not sure." Notepad in hand, the man ambled forward. "The guards said she went off with a local woman and another guard. No one has heard from her since."

Visible tension kinked along Joe's back, setting off alarms in Cooper's already adrenaline burned instincts. Alarms?

Buzzing. His cell phone.

He tugged the phone from his pocket and saw… Aragon's private number. There was no real reason to expect this was anything more than a business call about the explosion at the factory. Stay calm. "Yes."

"Ah, Cooper," Aragon said, without bothering to identify himself. "How good to know you survived the difficulties at the factory. Now you can attend the party on my yacht. And please, bring your friend Captain Greco. I have something—or rather someone— here for both of you."

He jerked toward Joe, who was still talking to the reporter about missing Brigid, who'd been hauled away by a panicked local woman.

Instincts blared with certainty that Aragon knew exactly who was responsible for the factory explosion. And his guest list included Lena and Brigid.

A deadly list.

FOLLOWING LENA carrying her sleeping child, Brigid climbed the steps up onto the windswept deck. No plebeian ladder on his luxury yacht for this amoral mogul. She wanted to spit on Alessandro Aragon, but better sense stopped her.

Well, and the fact that the bastard had tied her hands in front of her and gagged her before herding them out of their stateroom below. She'd spent hours down there trying to keep lethargic Lena awake, searching for ideas, a weapon, but the bastard had planned well. Even cleared the room of so much as a nail file.

She'd overheard Aragon's phone call earlier and

shuddered to think of Joe and Cooper walking into a trap set by this coked-up nutcase. Surely Joe and Cooper would bring in reinforcements. And could Aragon actually be stupid enough to believe the two men would come alone to exchange their lives for the women and child?

Likely not. Which meant Aragon must be on a suicide mission. She'd covered a suicide-by-cop story once, a heinous way to die that left so much emotional destruction in its wake for those involved in the horror.

As long as they got through this night, however, she could face anything else. She searched the near-deserted blanket of murky night sea, other dim boat lights too far to be of help. The shoreline gleamed benignly calm in the moonlight, with a smattering of city skyline to one side, and the looming black shadow of Inca ruins on the other.

"Sit, my dear," he ordered Lena with mocking affection, waggling his SIG-Sauer toward the long stretch of bench beneath the railing.

Silently she sagged onto the padded seat, her arms shaking from the strain of carrying her son so long. Brigid had offered to carry Miguel, but even in Lena's semidrugged state, she clung to her maternal instincts. A yearning stirred deep in Brigid's gut to experience that kind of love one day, along with grief that she may have lost the chance by hiding from life for the past two years.

Aragon leaned toward Lena and skimmed a kiss across her lips. "I loved you, you know."

Staying quiet under his caress even as Brigid longed to scream in protest, Lena shivered in the heat of the night, her arms bloodless from clenching her son.

"And in honor of that love, even though you betrayed me—" he raised the bulky gun "—I'm ensuring your death will be painless."

Brigid gasped. Lena shifted her son behind her, her groggy eyes clearing, shining with determination—and resignation.

Screw resignation. Brigid screamed from behind her gag, horrified, her bound hands flailing for any kind of weapon to stop the unthinkable. She grabbed an iron chair and hefted as his hand lowered and he—

Brought the butt of his gun down on the back of Lena's head, once, hard. Lena crumpled onto her side. Little Miguel barely stirred, simply sniffling and tucking his knees under his chin.

Aragon spun, weapon raised, stopping Brigid midcharge. He shrugged his shirt smooth again. "Lena has this nasty habit of overcoming drugs. Sometimes old-fashioned methods work best." He swung her legs up on the long stretch of bench, stroked back a strand of the unconscious woman's hair as she "slept" alongside her child. "Sweet dreams, my dear."

Brigid worked her jaw against her gag, finally spitting it free. He could tie it again if he wanted but at least she would have a second to breathe freely. And breathe she did, gulping in air to clear her head, hunger gnawing along with nerves since she hadn't dared eat anything.

Aragon eyed her dangling gag, smiled, seemingly content to let her defiance slide for now. He plowed a hand through the overlong locks of hair draping along his forehead, a picture-perfect image of the indolent playboy living off inherited wealth. She couldn't help but admire Joe and Cooper all the more. Both men had come from privileged homes and yet both maintained down-to-earth values. Lena was right. Brigid had been blessed to have the affection of two such honorable men.

But what about love? She wanted Joe's full, all-out love and the chance to enjoy a life with each other, make babies and grow old together.

"Over there." Aragon waggled the barrel, urging her toward the deck chairs glowing like white thrones under the luminescent moon.

Edging into a chair, she called on old instincts from her days in the field, honing the edge and letting it sharpen her senses. She spared a quick glance to double-check that—yes—Lena was still breathing, slow, deep. Brigid shifted all her attention back to the man who claimed to know love and then threatened murder. How could she reason with such a depraved monster?

"Do we just sit here and wait?" Her wrists bound together and resting on her knees, she wriggled her tingling fingers, wishing this knot sucked as bad as the bandanna tie.

"Would you rather go for a swim?" He hooked an ankle over one knee as if casually shooting the breeze rather than threatening to shoot *her*. "I didn't think so. Now we wait for your lover and your back-from-the-dead lover to show up."

"How did you—"

"How quickly you forget about Señora de Guerra's presence at the hotel. She's very skilled with placing listening devices."

"But how did you find out so much from a few conversations?" And how revolting to think of him listening to tapes made in her room. Hopefully the balcony and tub where she'd been with Joe were more soundproof. She shuddered to think of what Lena must have experienced at the hands of this man.

"The people I work with have ears in many places. No one is safe from terrorists like el Jedr. Not even you."

Terrorists. Finding links to the ambush in Iraq. The reason they were all here in the first place. Her mind churned with far more horrible ways to die than at the wrong end of a gun. "Why would they be interested in me?"

"You and your news friends are privy to *helpful* information—if your pesky encryption codes can be cracked. So, we find someone at a satellite control facility. A person with a bad drug habit or an indiscretion who is open to 'persuasion.' We claim to want to scoop a news competitor. He or she passes along a media outlet's encryption code…and secrets flow."

A chill iced her skin in spite of the steamy tropical night air. Could the magazine's portable satellite dish—not Sonny—have been responsible for the leak that had led el Jedr's men to Cooper that horrible day two years ago when the Green Beret's were slaughtered, when Joe had almost died, too? She thought of times in Iraq when they'd been privy to sensitive information, given the okay to send it back with the encryption code so the story could be ready for release to the public.

With a deep certainty, she trusted her journalistic instincts that insisted just such a scenario had happened the day of Cooper's ambush, the day Joe had been wounded, as well.

A low drone in the distance, an approaching boat, focused her thoughts and fears on the present. Fear for Joe, Cooper too, both men only seconds way from God only knew what. No doubt both would step into the line of fire in a heartbeat. They might never have a chance to heal the broken bonds and make peace with Cooper's decisions.

She might never have a chance to hold Joe again.

Aragon stood. "I'm sorry, Señorita Wheeler, but we'll need to retie that gag."

She bit back a shout of denial that would only further anger him right before Joe and Cooper arrived in a boat as directed. Her captor leaned, his cloying cologne gagging her as effectively as the bandanna he stuffed in her mouth again, tightening until it bit into the corners of her lips. The chugging engine grew louder, announcing the incoming boat's arrival minutes before the sleek craft parted the mist, two men standing in the boat chopping through the waves. The engine cut back, one of the men stepping out onto the nose as the smaller vessel closed in on the yacht.

From his chair Aragon swung a mounted light on the rail to spotlight Cooper while Joe manned the wheel. Even from a distance and with his face cast in shadows, she knew Joe. The unmovable set of his broad shoulders never let anyone down, never bowing or even acknowledging his own mortality.

Of course Joe was here. He was always there for her. Why did she need a handful of words when she had a wealth of commitment from this man? He'd shown his love for her a hundred different ways through actions, support, laughs and simply being there. The emotion had been there all the time. She'd just been too scared to see it. Joe loved her, loved her so much he'd been willing to hold her while she grieved for another man.

She'd been so emphatic about looking for the layers in photos, but she'd been too afraid to pull the camera away from her face and embrace the layers of life and loving. No wonder he'd doubted her words during the heat of sex, leading him to offer up a befuddled "me, too" response.

Her eyes held on Joe, and she hoped when he looked he would see the fullness of her emotions, just as she now felt his.

Aragon eased up from his chair. Readying for the final showdown? He opened a small door in the hull. She tensed, prepared for anything, her active journalistic imagining churning with possibilities except…

A bomb.

Horror slapped over her. Jerking in a fruitless attempt to free her hands, she screamed against the choking gag, against the very real possibility that this monster could kill Joe, Cooper, Lena and an innocent child, *no!*

Joe! She chewed and struggled to slip the gag.

Unruffled, Aragon simply smiled and tapped the tiny control panel, firing red numbers to life.

10:00.

9:59.

9:58.

CHAPTER TWENTY-THREE

STEERING THE BOAT the last few yards toward the yacht, Joe battled the rage flowing through him at the sight of Brigid bound and gagged, fire spitting from her eyes so fierce it shone as bright as her silky hair in the moonlight.

God, what an incredible woman. And he'd be damned if he would let that bastard Aragon harm even one of her fingernails.

Joe let his eyes linger, settling on her, all the while vowing this would *not* be the last time, not now when there was still so much left to be said.

Or rather one short sentence that said so much more.

Lord willing he would have that chance, with the help of an Army Delta Force sharpshooter in the jungle foliage along the shoreline. It was a risky shot, but they had brought the best.

The past couple of hours had been a blur, working with the CIA, the military and local government to set up an emergency sting that would bring home the hostages alive. They'd blanketed the area with troops, including the sharpshooter in the Inca ruins. The U.S.-donated Pave Low hovered nearby, ready for any water rescue contingencies. Cooper was wired for sound, with an earpiece, listening for instructions on luring Aragon into position to give the sharpshooter a clear shot. So far, it seemed Aragon truly was alone, but they still needed to wrangle close enough to protect Brigid, Lena and the child if goons suddenly starting pouring out through the hatches like roaches.

There was nothing more they could do but press on and pray.

Water rocking beneath Joe's feet, the boat bumped against the side of the yacht. Aragon stood in the shadows, Brigid tucked at his side. So damn close, but maybe if he would move under one of the lights. Where was the other woman and her child? The woman Cooper had asked Joe to look out for if something happened to him. Joe's eyes tracked to his friend's back, cords straining in his neck.

Cooper went up the ladder first, Joe trailing, assessing, watching for his friend's finger twitch that would signal the sharpshooter had a clear shot lined up.

Once on deck, the other woman came into sight, asleep but breathing, along with her son on a padded bench. Cooper's shudder of relief was so damn hard Joe half expected the boat to pitch under his feet.

What a helluva time to realize his old pal really was over Brigid.

Without once taking his eyes off Brigid—damned if he would let her out of his sight again—Joe started to loop the rope around the rail.

"Don't tie it up." Aragon raised the gun to Brigid's temple. "Let the boat drift."

Damn. One less escape option, and he didn't see a life raft anywhere on deck. With a SIG-Sauer kissing Brigid's head, Joe couldn't wrap his head around an option other than to drop the rope on the deck and hope they would be lucky enough for it not to slither into the ocean.

Brigid blinked hard, darting her eyes to the side. What was she trying to tell him? He looked to the other woman for a hint, but Lena still snoozed on.

Cooper stepped around a deck chair, farther from Lena, closer to the glowing light mounted on the side. "Aragon, I'm here. My friend's here, just like you ordered. Now let the women and the kid go. Your problem is with me, not them."

Joe sidestepped, placing himself between Aragon and the child, putting himself that much closer to Brigid, where he had a clear dash to tackle her away once the signal came from Cooper. Just a twitch of his pointer finger. Come on.

Aragon stroked the barrel along Brigid's ear. "You're right, and the best way to get to you is through them. Your old girlfriend, your pal, and the woman who meant enough for you to risk everything. Well, unless you're just that weak and stupid of a man to risk all simply to scratch an itch."

Cooper snapped, launching around a chair. "If you want a chance at me, come get me."

Snarling, Aragon pivoted a half turn toward Cooper—his face mottled with rage, bathed in the full illumination of the overhead light.

Cooper's finger twitched. Joe readied to launch.

Whizz. A silencer bullet hissed past his ear. From the sharpshooter.

Silence hung in the aftermath. Utter stillness reigned. Who? The gun remained nestled against Brigid. He couldn't risk—

Aragon's SIG-Sauer dropped from his hand.

The weapon thudded to the deck a second before blood seeped from the hole in the middle of his forehead. Aragon crumpled, dead.

Relief scorching through his veins, Joe reached for Brigid. A plaintive cry echoed from behind them—a child—Miguel, waking up. Cooper bolted past to gather Lena and the boy. Joe caught Brigid as she fell into his arms. His heart thundering, he locked her tight against him, his face buried in her hair while he breathed in her familiar kiwi scent and whispered a litany of *thank God, thank God, thank God.*

Brigid jerked in his arms.

"Oh, sorry. Too tight, I guess." He loosened his hold and scanned the deck over her shoulder, almost afraid to hope things could have ended this quickly, cleanly. "Are we clear? Is there anyone else on the boat?"

She shook her head against his chest, stomping her foot, flip-flop slapping the deck.

He tugged at the ties around her wrists. "I'll have you loose in a second."

She tried to talk through the gag, louder.

"Hold on. I'm getting to it." He moved his hands up and untied the red bandanna.

Spitting the rag free, she screamed, "Bomb! He's rigged the boat to blow any minute."

Oh, shit. So much for easy and clean. But he wouldn't let that bastard win.

Joe spun toward the boat—now floating at least a hundred yards away, heading out to sea. "Into the water," he shouted.

He didn't even want to consider Aragon could have some of the deadly anthrax onboard. Regardless, he didn't have time to search. All he could do was swim and hope.

The incoming helicopter could pick them up eventually, but they needed to get as far away from the yacht as possible before the blast. "We have to get the hell out of here. Cooper? Can you—"

"Yeah, I'm not a hundred percent in the water, but I can hold my own and then some. Take Miguel. I'll get Lena." Cooper hefted the limp and unconscious woman up into his arms with unmistakable tenderness.

Joe scooped the stirring child against his shoulder, palm firm against the too-small and innocent back. He'd dreamed of being like those soldiers who'd saved him as a kid, but he'd never imagined the past playing out quite so literally.

Racing across the deck, he tucked the child against his chest. Brigid was waiting by the rail, red hair a tangled mess, her resolve shining strong.

Frustration snapped. "Don't wait for me. Jump, damn it."

She smiled. "I love you, too."

Arms stretched, she leaped, diving overboard. God, he adored that amazing woman and wouldn't miss out on the chance to show her over and over again.

Cooper at his side, Joe hurtled over in synch, like hundreds of other jumps during their childhood into pools, teenage years into lakes, adult years from the back of airplanes.

In midair, Joe held tight to the now wide-awake and stunned-silent kid. The ocean swallowed him, brackish salt water surging up his nose, stinging his eyes that he kept open to search for the others in the murky haze. Finally, he found swirling, moving, feet kicking.

Propelling upward, he broke the surface. Counting heads. Brigid swimming. Atta girl. Cooper, arm hooked around Lena, the woman blinking and spluttering awake.

He scooped his hand through the murky water, side stroking while he held the kid with his other arm. "Gotcha, kiddo. Hang on."

How much longer? Would he even have a chance at a future with Brigid if the boat spewed anthrax into the air? A regular bomb wouldn't carry near the incineration power needed to destroy the bacteria. All a moot point if they didn't survive the blast.

He kicked and stroked, harder, hoping the drift would carry them further away from the yacht before it—

Boom.

The explosion split the night sky, the luxury boat erupting into flames, slamming a percussion through the water in a rush of waves.

His grip locked around the kid, sound fading away

in the wake of the deafening explosion. Slowly his senses returned, the little boy chattering in his arms, the sound of Brigid calling his name, Cooper chanting reassurances to Lena crying for her son.

"Over here," Joe called. "I've got him and he's fine."

The most welcome and ever-familiar sound of helicopter blades chopped the air, closer, louder, stirring the air and creating waves. A rope ladder dropped from the Pave Low, a crewman appearing in the open side door, prepping to scale down. The old war hound may not have been fast enough two years ago, but it had served him well tonight.

Little Miguel started whimpering in his arms, his cries gurgling in the sheeting water.

"It's okay, bud, I've gotcha, and your mama is right here. She'll be up with you in the helicopter soon," he gasped out reassurances in English, not even sure if the kid understood but hoping to infuse the calm.

The boy's wide eyes locked with his in the mist, the moment spinning into a timeless second, a slow-time fugue that drowned out the pandemonium of waves, flames, shouts all around. The kid appeared about the same age as the brother he'd lost all those years ago, the brother he'd lost by looking away at a critical moment in the mayhem.

Past and present merged in the face of a little boy with chocolate-dark eyes and curly brown hair. Memories melded and then separated in his head and Joe peeled away the layers of then and now in an image, as Brigid had taught him through the magic of her camera lens. And there in the dark waters of a faraway land, Miguel became…Peter. His brother's name had been Peter.

How odd to take such comfort from just remembering a name. Peace settled over him as he gave the kid a quick hug before passing him up to the helicopter crew.

He'd given up remembering that slice of his past, his family. Another incredible gift from Brigid. He just hoped he could come close to giving her as much as she gave him.

COOPER WAITED OUTSIDE Lena's hospital room at the Cartina Air Base Clinic, sunrise filtering through the slatted blinds.

He jingled his keys hooked on the pager clipped to the surgical scrubs he'd been given in the E.R. Lena had asked Brigid to stay with her, a surprise request, but then, the two women had been through a lot together. He, of all people, should understand the reassurance of having a buddy by your side.

Of course, his bud was still in debrief across the base, and the upcoming discussion with Lena was something Cooper would have to tackle on his own, anyway. At least everyone was alive, healthy, tests proving no one had been exposed to anthrax.

The halls bustled with activity, doctors and nurses in military uniforms, early visitors. The medicinal scent of rubbing alcohol brought memories of his own days in military hospitals. There hadn't been any visitors other than his CIA handlers.

A food cart rattled past, the aroma of powdered eggs and limp bacon unmistakable. He wanted to pace, but he'd pretty much taxed his knee for one day. Before climbing into the speedboat, he'd slid a waterproof sleeve over his leg, but his type of prosthesis wasn't designed for that kind of leap and swimming.

Frustrating. But a part of life he was learning to live with day by day, finally accepting the journey would be ongoing.

He'd met with his CIA contact before leaving to confront Aragon, and had turned over the anthrax sample for analysis. While they'd lost Aragon as a source—damn the twisted bastard to hell—at least they had a solid chance of tracing the supplier, which would give them a link to el Jedr.

Brigid's surprise tip about a possible leak of encryption codes for news stories could prove invaluable. When she'd told him during the questioning after the rescue, her eyes had gleamed as she spun scenarios of how she and some of her news contacts would enjoy working with the CIA to filter misleading disinformation to terrorists. A damn good idea to pursue.

Later.

Now he was finally free to talk to Lena. If the doctor would ever step out. Could there have been something lethal in the crap Aragon pumped into her? He refused to accept that he would lose her after surviving so much.

Remorse stabbed through him. If Brigid and Joe and suffered even half this much two years ago, he owed them so much more than an apology.

The door to Lena's room opened. He stopped breathing—only to find Brigid stepping through. Remorse kicked into overdrive as he clutched the keychain clipped to his pager. Thoughts of her had carried him through hell, and he'd done nothing but hurt her. And he didn't have a clue how to make that right.

Another journey for him to take a day at a time.

Cooper lurched to his feet—his knee locking and forcing him to straighten slower. "How is Lena? And Miguel?"

The kid had driven straight into his heart with a simple roll of his dump truck and a chocolate-covered grin that looked so much like his mother's too-rare smiles. Just thinking about how close the little guy had come to dying, or imagining him in the care of a nanny secretly on Aragon's payroll... Cooper swallowed down bile. At least Juanita de Guerra was now in custody.

Brigid shuffled across the room in borrowed hospital scrubs like the ones he wore. "She's doing well, perking up, ready for the doctor to get out of her face. Miguel is sleeping like a baby...resilient kid."

He hung his head and sucked in air for his starved lungs when he hadn't even realized he'd been holding his breath. "Thank you."

She held up a hand. "Before you thank me, maybe you should know I've offered to help Lena find a job in the States."

"Why would that be a problem?"

"Good man." Brigid nodded, her damp braid bobbing. "She needs her independence. I offered to hook her up with some of my old contacts in D.C. about a translator job in any one of those thousand government departments and underdepartments. I hope that was okay with you."

"Like that would have stopped you." He'd always admired her determination, one of the things that had drawn him to her when they first met. They were alike in that—alike in many ways. Maybe some of those things they shared in common would help them build a stronger friendship.

"I figured you would want her close, but it would be better if the help came from me. Puts you two on a more even footing."

"You're a wise woman."

"And I hope you're a patient man."

"I am." He suffered no delusions. Lena had a lot of nightmares to process before she could move forward. But he hoped she would let him take that walk with her, one day at a time, two wounded warriors finding the answers together.

Brigid raised her hand and cupped his cheek. "I grieved for you, you know."

"I do know, and I'm so damn sorry."

Nodding, she let her hand slide away. "What we had was good."

"Yeah, it sure was." So good that thoughts of her had kept him alive in hell. She may not have been the right one for him—or him for her—but he had great taste in women.

"I don't want to take that away from either of us, but I'm realizing I hung on to you a long time rather than risk falling for Joe. I'd been hurt before, and you were safer."

"Safe? Ouch."

"First time you've been called something like that?"

"Joe's always the honorable guy, the sort who makes women feel safe."

She snorted, inelegant and all natural as always. "I beg to differ. What I feel for Joe is the scariest, most wonderful thing out there. With Joe, it's..." She chewed her lip, struggling for words. "Joe's the—"

"The best."

"He is." She smiled, one of those all-out-emotional Brigid smiles that had drawn him to her before he knew what he really needed. She stepped away from the door. "Lena told me to let you know she's ready to see you."

Cooper considered showing Brigid the hemp tie he'd saved for the past two years to let her know that she'd meant something to him, too—a helluva woman he hadn't been man enough to appreciate then.

"Hey, Brigid?"

"Yes?" She glanced over her shoulder, her feet obviously itching to go to Joe—the right man who should have been with her two years ago.

Cooper closed his fist over the keychain to hide the tie. He should make a clean break with Brigid, no muddying the waters with old baggage. "Thank you again."

With a nose-crinkling smile, she waved him off. "It's only a few phone calls so you can live near your girlfriend. Now go talk to her."

She spun away, red braid flying over her shoulder as she made her way down the hall.

His fist relaxed. Cooper untied the hair band with fumbling fingers, finally twisting it free. Foot on the trash can opener, he flipped up the lid and tossed the braided strand of hemp on top of a pile of bloodied bandages. "G'bye, babe."

Letting the lid clang closed, he turned toward Lena's door. He'd never given a hundred percent to any woman, yet he couldn't imagine giving anything but his all to the woman waiting beyond that door. He'd been so determined to be noble and honorable—like Joe—he'd missed a big picture. He'd never felt stronger than he had since being with Lena.

Being with her recharged him much like he recharged his leg. A real relationship fed him in ways he'd never imagined, made him stronger.

Now that he was able to step back from his cause enough to see the forest for the trees, he realized he could still be a warrior—an even better, badder one than ever—by being human.

For six months he'd wanted her but hadn't been free of the past or enough of a man to fully appreciate her until now.

He suspected she had feelings for him, too. What else could have compelled her to take such a huge risk in sleeping with him? He'd just been too much of a lughead to see the truth, and like a jackass, had walked at the first sign of trouble.

Time to take a risk by stepping out on the limb first.

WATCHING THE DOOR CLOSE behind her doctor, Lena stretched on the hospital bed, her snoozing son cradled at her side. Exhaustion tugged, but only in a normal mellow way that had nothing to do with drugs. She stroked back his feather-soft curls, so dark against the stark white of industrial hospital sheets, and winged a prayer of thanksgiving, for so many things.

That Cooper lived.

That Alessandro couldn't threaten her child anymore.

And she was also thankful for the gift of a newfound friend in Brigid Wheeler. They may have only met yesterday, but they shared a bond from surviving a lifetime of terror in less than twenty-four hours.

And of course they were connected through these two men, brothers in spirit.

How strange it felt to have a friend after so long alone. Brigid had even offered to check with old contacts of hers in Washington, D.C., about a translator's job. She'd warned that sort of job was usually low paying and not nearly as glamorous as it sounded. To Lena, it sounded heaven-sent.

With the possibility of living near Cooper if he worked in the CIA headquarters.

If she dared.

Trust came hard to her after the way her husband had let her down by not looking out for their son and after the way Alessandro had used her. Even Juanita de Guerra had lied for months, putting Miguel in danger.

Lena forced her fingers to relax their grip on the sheet. She'd found she was tougher than she'd thought these past days, tougher than that coke-snorting bastard had given her credit for.

A tap sounded on the door. Her stomach clenched before she could remind herself she didn't need to be afraid. Alessandro couldn't hurt or use her anymore. *"Sí?"*

"Just me." Cooper's voice rumbled through.

Lena's stomach clenched, but in a completely good and wonderful way this time. "Come in."

He stepped inside, hair still wet from a shower, slicked back with drying strands streaking lighter. She'd been mesmerized by him since the first time she'd seen him in a tailored gray suit, and found the baggy surgical scrubs he wore equally as enticing because of the man inside them.

But what about him? How much of his feelings for her had been real? Or was it all an undercover act? She'd found herself to be stronger than she'd ever known these past months, but, *Dios,* the thought that Cooper could have been using her, too—even for some higher good—was more than her battered heart could accept.

He leaned back against the door, favoring his injured leg. "I'm sorry."

"For what?" She pushed the words past her closed throat. Sorry for lying about caring for her? Wanting there to be "more" between them?

"O-kay." He exhaled long and slow, a near whistle.

"You want me to crawl. I can do that." He strode slowly across the room, rolling away the bed table and stopping at the chair beside her. He sat, rested his elbows on his knees and stared her straight in the eyes. "I'm sorry for sleeping with you when I wasn't able to be straight with you about who I am and what I do for a living."

She twisted the sheet in nervous fingers that longed to inch over and grab hold of his strong hands that brought such pleasure and comfort. "It's all right. I understand you had an important job to do."

"Well, that job sure as hell didn't include sleeping with you. I should have—"

"Stayed away?"

He hadn't planned their time together out of some agenda? Her throat relaxed as relief flowered.

"Hell, yes."

She swung her legs over the side of the bed, allowing herself to move closer under the guise of straightening her scrubs and sheet as hope sent warmth flowing through her like a sip from her favorite tea-cup. "We both tried that for six months, since the first time I saw you strut into one of Alessandro's meetings."

"Jesus, woman." His brow trenched with deep furrows. "I lied to you. How can you just shrug that off? Be mad at me. Shout at me, slap me or anything that shows I mean something to you."

She lifted a finger to his lips. "Shhh. You'll wake Miguel." She traced his mouth that had brought her as much pleasure with his kisses as his smiles. "We will get around to the 'or something' later."

"We will?"

"We most certainly will, if you are in agreement."

"Well, damn, I most certainly am." He took her hands and led her over to the window, sunlight streaking through the slats, muting with shadows and then brightening again as a plane roared overhead. "But before you let me off the hook so easily, there were things I did during these months that you need to know about. I bugged Aragon's offices for surveillance."

Her hands turned icy against his warmth at memories of the degradation she'd suffered there. "Did you listen to private…conversations?"

He squeezed her fingers in his grip. "I told you before I'm not into voyeurism."

A truly honorable man to the core. How could she have doubted? "Good. Anything else?"

"I staged that mugging to accelerate gaining Aragon's trust."

"Are you trying to discourage me from wanting you?" He'd staged a rescue? Yet he'd provided a far better authentic rescue last night when the stakes were so much higher.

"God no. I just need to make sure you really want me, that you know me and what kind of man I am."

"I do know, just as I hope you understand what kind of woman I am. Like you, I will do whatever it takes to keep those I love safe. So I understand you did not have any choice."

Shock sent him slack-jawed, an almost comical sight from this superconfident superspy. "That's it? You're cool with the fact that I sent a man to hold you at knife point?"

"Was I ever in danger?"

"Of course not."

She peered down her nose with her best indignant huff. "I'm not such a ninny that I can't see the big picture of what you had to do."

He shook his head, still wearing that stunned stupid expression. "There are guys in my profession who would give anything to hear that from a woman. Lady, you are a treasure."

"I have a more practical nature these days."

"That's one of the things I respect most about you."

Respect? A word she hadn't heard in reference to her—ever. "Excuse me? I do not think I understand what you are saying. Maybe there is a language nuance I am not picking up on."

"You speak English just fine, but I'll say it again in your language if that will help." He swapped to Spanish. "I respect you. You fought for your child and kept him safe like a mother should."

"I appreciate what you are saying, more than you can know, and I'm not going to apologize for what I had to do. But don't you know that I was—"

He squeezed her hands. "I know that you did what you had to do." His blue eyes went stormy, troubled. "I've been a prisoner of war—like you."

"But I wasn't—"

"Yes, you were," he insisted with an understanding she hadn't dreamed of finding. "I understand the scars it leaves on a person's soul to be stripped of dignity and choices. Healing is a slow process. Maybe we could help each other."

She gave up the battle and let her hands shake with the terror she'd held in for months. "Giving information about him to the police was frightening, and it was so hard knowing whom to trust when they approached me—"

"Whoa. Hold on." His stormy eyes shifted back to that confused clear blue. "You were working with the police?"

"Yes. Nothing big or grand like the sorts of things you do, but I kept them apprised of Alessandro's trips in and out of the country, as well as his shipment schedules."

She'd thought he'd been told in his debrief, but there was no mistaking his surprise now that he didn't keep his emotions hidden. He hadn't known and still he'd been all right with the life she'd led and the choices she'd made for her son.

Healing began to seep into her soul. "You didn't know."

"I had no idea. Those governmental walls blocking communication could have made these past months a lot easier on my heart if someone had clued me in."

Her bottom lip trembled. "And you are still all right with me—him—the past months?"

"You did what you had to do." Cooper raised her

hands to press a kiss on each wrist. "You kept your objective in mind, focused on the mission and got your kid through the tough times safely at great personal risk, regardless of whether or not you were working with the police. You're definitely a warrior who's fought a helluva battle for her son."

Tears pooled in her eyes, big fat tears, as if double the size from being restrained for so long. She would never be an all-out weeper, but the trickle down her face eased a constriction in her chest months in the making.

Cooper hauled her into his arms and against his heart, pressing a kiss into her hair. "I realize that even after knowing each other for six months, all of this, us, is still kinda new. We have a lot to learn about each other. But I love you, Lena Banuelos. And I want more than anything to keep telling you I love you every chance I get."

Love. She let the word settle in her heart, savoring and memorizing every perfect detail of this exquisite moment in a stark exam room with both of them wearing baggy surgical scrubs. She'd learned well to look beyond superficial trappings to find the real gem of beauty.

"Uh, Lena, this would be a good time for you to say something. Anything. Although I'd prefer that the anything isn't, 'sorry, not interested.'"

Her arms slid around his waist, her face still buried in his shirt. "Will you be living in the Washington, D.C. area now that you're through with this assignment?"

"Probably. It's open to discussion. Are you saying

you don't want to leave Cartina? That's quite a commute for me, but I could talk to the consulate—"

She covered his mouth. "Stop. Brigid mentioned the possibility of a job for me in the D.C. area."

His smile dented a dimple in his handsome face. "Are you angling for a date, beautiful?"

"I am not angling for anything. *I* am asking *you* out to dinner. Perhaps a simple picnic by the water." She toyed with the neckline of his shirt. "Does your D.C. have water nearby?"

"Plenty of water and parks for picnics where Miguel could spread out his trucks and Army men. And 'not fancy' works well for me since, in spite of the glitz in movies about CIA spies, government operatives really don't rake in that much of a paycheck."

Like she cared about money. There was more than enough sparkle for her in his blue eyes. "It's a date."

"The first of many." He lowered his head to hers, sealing his promise with the heat of his kiss, the stirring stroke of his tongue, the gentle strength of his hands against her skin.

Lena whispered against his mouth, "How could any woman help but fall in love with an amazing man like you?"

"I'm not interested in just any woman."

"And a very good thing that is."

His smile caressed her lips before he gathered her closer. She slid her arms around the broad shoulders of a man to trust, finding it so very easy to hang on, now that she knew she could stand on her own.

CHAPTER TWENTY-FOUR

"WAIT... WAIT FOR IT, baby," Brigid chanted to herself as she stared through the viewfinder at the sun cresting over the Inca ruins. Patience almost always brought the perfect camera shot.

Seated in the sand along the Cartinian shoreline to pass time until Joe arrived from his debrief, she aimed, focused, *click, click, clicked* images of the Inca ruins to accompany Sonny's piece on Cartina and Aragon's tie to terrorism. They would be filing a second story on the Pave Low dedication ceremony as a follow-up.

Couples strolled past, locals and tourists, all unaware of how close such serious danger had lurked. And wasn't that an interestingly layered picture, as well?

She'd learned to blend the mystery of beauty rising from destruction, something that she suspected would sustain her in her job from now on. She'd once thought to change the world with her trusty Canon and wide-eyed ideals.

Instead, the world—and Joe—had changed her for the better.

She'd learned that life didn't have to be extremes. She didn't have to make it an either/or proposition, an emotionally draining full-tilt versus cutting herself off from her photojournalism calling altogether. With Joe's steady focus she'd found the beauty of balance. Freelance work could well be the way for her to go, the chance to follow the adrenaline edge and still get to enjoy sunrises and the innocence of the occasional portrait studio sitting.

Tide sipping at her crossed legs, she savored the salty breeze cooling the sweat pooling in the small of her back where her T-shirt rode up, the gentle abrasion of damp sand against her legs. So what if her favorite silk skirt got soggy? Life was all about experiencing, feeling.

Loving.

She and Joe had been friends, lovers, shared a bond in their grief for Cooper and then in their struggle to survive. Now she hoped they would forge a forever bond that went beyond everything else.

If Joe ever got here.

Not that she was worried. Joe was always late, but he never let her down. She swung her camera around to snap more shots of the city skyline and found battered deck shoes beside her, no socks, strong ankles and luscious sworls of dark hair dusted with sand.

Joe.

She hadn't even heard him arrive. Her heart stuttered with nerves and, oh, so much desire. The width of his chest in a navy polo filled her lens, eyes and senses.

Brigid narrowed the focus past broad shoulders up to his face. Bold cheekbones and stark angles spoke of his Eastern European heritage, adding an elusive air to an otherwise all-American guy. Close-cropped hair glistened in the humidity, dark, the total picture so very different from her sunny and auburn-haired Cooper, which somehow made Joe all the more appealing.

She reassessed him as a potential husband, as well as a friend and lover.

But she didn't need her camera to do that. In fact, found Joe too much man to be contained in the simple scope of a camera lens. She slid her Canon from her eyes and hugged it to her stomach, right over where she hoped to someday carry his children.

He hunkered down beside her. "Sorry I'm late."

"No worries. I knew you'd come."

A surety she would never take for granted again.

LAPPING WAVES filling his deck shoes, Joe wondered how the sheer perfection of one woman's smile could knock him on his butt faster than an exploding boat. But then, he'd given up trying to understand the mystery of Brigid. He simply knew he loved every free-spirited inch of her luscious body, brain and soul.

And that thong of hers forming a T-back just over her skirt line could give a man heart failure.

Joe kicked off his shoes, sending them airborne to land further inland beside her discarded flip-flops. He reached for her braid, testing the weight and softness in his hand, then looping it around to draw her closer to brush his mouth against hers, once, again, and hell he'd better pull back now or he'd never get around to talking.

He extended a hand. "Wanna go for a walk? I promised you a tropical vacation, complete with beach walks."

Hooking her camera around her neck, she tucked her soft hand in his. "You always come through."

"I try." Rising, he tugged her up and into his arms as the tide stole sand from beneath their feet. "And I haven't forgotten I still owe you a real birthday celebration."

"What did you have in mind?"

He looped his arms around her back, enjoying the damp cling of her skirt to her mile-long legs that wrapped so perfectly around him during sex. "I was thinking about taking a couple of weeks off, maybe even go to Europe and visit the place where I was born."

She'd asked him about his past, and he found he was ready to discuss it, tell her about Peter, explore the memories and perhaps unearth some others he'd submerged. He'd been so determined to make sure Brigid needed him, he'd closed her off from giving in return. A mistake he planned to fix.

"Sounds wonderfully romantic, and the perfect chance for us to enjoy being a couple."

A couple. He liked the sound of that. "I want the chance to get it right the next time we climb in a tub together."

"I seem to recall you got it right a couple of times."

She teased featherlight touches along the nape of his neck as soft as the breeze against his skin.

"That's not what I meant and you know it." He wouldn't screw up again. "Hearing you love me… God, Brigid, it was everything, you're everything, and I fell short in answering. I'm not always good at verbalizing, and 'I love you, too' just doesn't seem like enough to say it all."

"Bullshit."

Seabirds overhead squawked and dipped in the silence until he pulled together his thoughts enough to answer. Leave it to Brigid to surprise the hell out of him. "What? I tell you I love you, too, and you say bullshit?"

"You still haven't said it, not really." She pinned him with those perceptive green eyes that cut no slack, challenging him to always give his best. "You're too busy looking for what you think I want to hear or how I should hear it. And *that* is bullshit. I don't want some perfect words picked from your PalmPilot. Just talk to me from your great big heart."

Taking a bullet for her would probably be easier, yet anything worth having was worth working for, and Brigid was worth everything. But, damn, he felt an awful lot like that kid stepping off the plane in the U.S., scared as hell of losing more. "Knowing you has changed me for the better. I see the world through different eyes by hanging out with you. You bring a humor and brightness that I need. I'm just not sure what you need from me."

She went still with surprise in his arms. "Joe, you don't have to win me or win my love. I love you because you're, well…"

"Do you want to borrow my PalmPilot?"

God, he loved her laugh as much as he loved her.

"I love you, Joe, because you're you. Sexy as hell, funny—even if you don't think so—and always, always there for me."

"I'm always late, you mean, for dates and the right words."

She cuffed him gently on the side of the head. "I'm not talking about some clock. I'm talking about here." Her hand trailing from his shoulder, she splayed her fingers over his heart. "I've had a lot of people let me down enough that I know what an amazing gift it is to have the constancy of your full attention and love."

He soaked in her words along with the gentle pressure of her hand against his thundering heart. He dug deep to give his all to this woman who deserved that and more. "From the heart, I loved you since the first time I saw you two and half years ago. I have loved you every minute of every day since then as you became my best friend and finally my lover. And if you'll let me, I want the chance to show you how much I love you every day for the rest of my life."

Her eyes filled with those ever-ready tears from an emotional woman who threw open doors and embraced feelings. "I think you need to put away your PalmPilot more often."

"So, Red, will you marry me?"

Her green eyes went wide with surprise and—ooh-rah—wary happiness. "I thought you didn't want to get married until you were through flying?"

He sifted the reasoning around in his head and saw it for what it was. An excuse to keep his emotions locked up tight. "Right now that sounds an awful lot like a convenient excuse from a commitment-phobic guy."

"Oh, really? Hmm. And that guy's ditched his commitment phobia, has he?"

"Yeah, he most definitely has." He wanted it all with Brigid, no waiting, no half measures. "Are you ready to take that birthday walk on the beach now?"

She trailed her hand down his arm to link fingers, trudging backward through the surf. "How about a birthday run to our hotel instead? Loser has to do whatever the winner says."

"You're on." And how convenient that ever-late Joe planned to make sure he crossed that doorstep a pace behind the ever-imaginative Brigid. Sometimes the smartest guys finished last. "But first you'd better answer my question."

A wicked grin curled her lips, excitement firing her eyes a deeper shade of green that matched the reef waters in the distance. The kind of eyes a guy could get lost in for days. Or a lifetime.

"I already said I was ready for that walk on the beach, Joe."

"Not that question." He pulled her closer, claiming the happiness he hadn't been ready to indulge in the tub earlier. "I need you in my life, Brigid. Not just for a few days or a few years. I need you forever."

She wriggled near, toes sifting through the moist sand until they brushed his. "Yes and yes again, just to make sure you totally heard me. I'll marry you."

Her answer damn near took his breath away, knocking any sort of response clean out of his head as the reality of her love, her willingness to take that forever step with him, bowled him over more than any rogue tidal wave.

To hell with words.

He pulled her, her big heart, her sweet smile and her ever-present camera into his arms for the only kind of answer he could make. He let the knowledge of their future together fill up a longtime-empty part of him. He might spend a few weeks in Europe looking around for his past, but here in her arms, on a beach in Cartina, he'd found his future.

* * * * *

Be sure to look for Catherine Mann's next release
THE CAPTIVE'S RETURN
available this October
from Silhouette Intimate Moments.

HQN™

We *are* romance™

Catch the second SIZZLING read in the HOT ZONE
trilogy from *New York Times* bestselling author

CARLY
PHILLIPS

Win a free makeover!
See inside book for details.

Sports publicist Micki Jordan has always been just one of the
guys. But enter Damian Fuller—professional ballplayer and
major league playboy—and suddenly it's time for Micki to retire
her tomboy ways and reveal the hot number that she really is!

He'll never know what hit him.

Pick up your copy of

Hot Number

**in August for further details on how
YOU can become a hot number, too!**

www.HQNBooks.com

PHCP055

HQN™

We *are* romance™

Under the wide open skies,
even a broken man can find peace....

GENELL DELLIN

Recently released from prison, Blue Bowman has one more
score to settle: to destroy the wealthy father who abandoned
his mother and shattered his family. In his quest, he meets gentle
veterinarian Andie Lee Hart, who will challenge him as no one
has before—and either satisfy the demons within, or open his
heart to the woman who has brought him back to life.

Montana Blue

Available in bookstores this August.

www.HQNBooks.com

PHGD044

From #1 bestselling author

NORA ROBERTS

comes the second installment in the
Night Tales **trilogy, where the pull of**
men in uniform is undeniable....

Lieutenant Althea Grayson and Colt Nightshade team up to
investigate a case, but their unspoken attraction gives rise to
painful memories better left forgotten in NIGHTSHADE. He
was brisk, abrupt and rude but Natalie needed Ryan's help,
and as the sparks fly, danger is hot on their trail in NIGHT SMOKE.

The hours between dusk and dawn are filled with mystery,
danger...and romance.

Available in bookstores this August.

NIGHTSHADE
NIGHT SMOKE

Silhouette®
Where love comes alive™

Visit Silhouette Books at www.eHarlequin.com   PSNR512

If you enjoyed what you just read,
then we've got an offer you can't resist!

Take 2 bestselling novels FREE!
Plus get a FREE surprise gift!

Clip this page and mail it to MIRA®

IN U.S.A.
3010 Walden Ave.
P.O. Box 1867
Buffalo, N.Y. 14240-1867

IN CANADA
P.O. Box 609
Fort Erie, Ontario
L2A 5X3

YES! Please send me 2 free MIRA® novels and my free surprise gift. After receiving them, if I don't wish to receive anymore, I can return the shipping statement marked cancel. If I don't cancel, I will receive 4 brand-new novels every month, before they're available in stores! In the U.S.A., bill me at the bargain price of $4.99 plus 25¢ shipping and handling per book and applicable sales tax, if any*. In Canada, bill me at the bargain price of $5.49 plus 25¢ shipping and handling per book and applicable taxes**. That's the complete price and a savings of over 20% off the cover prices—what a great deal! I understand that accepting the 2 free books and gift places me under no obligation ever to buy any books. I can always return a shipment and cancel at any time. Even if I never buy another The Best of the Best™ book, the 2 free books and gift are mine to keep forever.

185 MDN DZ7J
385 MDN DZ7K

Name	(PLEASE PRINT)
Address	Apt.#
City	State/Prov. Zip/Postal Code

Not valid to current The Best of the Best™, Mira®,
suspense and romance subscribers.

Want to try two free books from another series?
Call 1-800-873-8635 or visit www.morefreebooks.com.

* Terms and prices subject to change without notice. Sales tax applicable in N.Y.
** Canadian residents will be charged applicable provincial taxes and GST.
  All orders subject to approval. Offer limited to one per household.
  ® and ™are registered trademarks owned and used by the trademark owner and or its licensee.

BOB04R   ©2004 Harlequin Enterprises Limited

HARLEQUIN®
Next™

Sometimes…life happens.

When she opened her front door, the last person Mya Donohue
ever expected to see was the daughter she'd given up at birth.
And the second-to-last person…her baby granddaughter!

LIFE HAPPENS

From award-winning author Sandra Steffen

*Don't miss this funny, fulfilling and fabulously emotional novel,
available this September.*

www.TheNextNovel.com

Four new titles available each month wherever Harlequin books are sold.

HNLH

HQN™

We *are* romance™

The Costas sisters return in this perfect-for-the-beach romance by *New York Times* bestselling author

CARLY PHILLIPS

Summer Lovin'

Win a makeover. See book for details.

Available this August wherever hardcover books are sold.

www.HQNBooks.com

PHCP019MMPB